The Heath

Abigail Frith lives in Yorkshire, dividing her spare time between gardening and working in the peace and conservation movements. *The Heath* is her second novel, following *The Water Garden*, which was set in Yorkshire and described by the *Yorkshire Evening Post* as 'a beautifully told story of a 19th century love affair'.

D1329974

Also available in Fontana by the same author

The Water Garden

ABIGAIL FRITH

The Heath

FONTANA/Collins

First published by Fontana Paperbacks 1988
Copyright © Abigail Frith 1988

Printed and bound in Great Britain by
William Collins Sons & Co Ltd, Glasgow

CONDITIONS OF SALE

This book is sold subject to the condition
that it shall not, by way of trade or otherwise,
be lent, re-sold, hired out or otherwise circulated
without the publisher's prior consent in any form of
binding or cover other than that in which it is
published and without a similar condition including
this condition being imposed on the subsequent purchaser.

DEDICATION

In 1980, a local history group published a booklet called 'The Story of Aspley Guise' which traced the history of their rural Bedfordshire parish in the early and mid-nineteenth century. This drew the moving picture of the poverty, courage and enterprise of the labouring families and their often dramatic confrontations with the local gentry, which inspired me to write 'The Heath'. Although the main characters in this novel are fictional, their adventures are often based on actual events and I have allowed some of the minor characters to bear their real names, which I trust will not offend their descendants.

This book must be dedicated to all those who carried out the research and the people whose memories and family records helped them, but I should like to mention particularly Arthur Parker (1892–1984). He was the local estate agent and devoted his twenty-six years of retirement to local historical research which he would discuss with infectious enthusiasm, so his was the original inspiration for both these projects. In a letter accompanying a copy of the 1851 census returns for Aspley Heath he wrote 'I seem to know those old inhabitants as if they are walking about now.'

Map drawn by Paul Chadwick

The Parish of
Aspley Guise
in Bedfordshire

parish
boundary

Hockliffe

Leighton Buzzard

Bow
Brickhill

Wavendon

Ridgemont

Husborne Crawley

Aspley Guise

Weburn

The Heath

Hog St.
End

Water End

Salford

BEDS. GLOS. BUCKS.

THE HEATH

CHAPTER 1

The Select Vestry Committee Meeting

One gusty November evening in 1830, five members of the Select Vestry Committee were taking off wet over-coats and stamping mud from their gaiters and boots on to the ruddy brick floor of the taproom parlour in The Swan at the small South Bedfordshire village of Aspley Guise.

''Tis good to see the fire lively, anyways!' remarked Farmer Green to Harry Vane, the landlord.

'Aye. It took a pretty time to get it going though, what with all the timber soaking,' he said as he pushed on another couple of hissing logs.

The last member of the committee thrust open the door and strode in. He was a tall austere man in his forties with an angular nose and iron grey hair. The clerical collar revealed when he drew off his great-coat proclaimed him to be the Rector of St Botolph's Church.

'Sorry I'm late, gentlemen. Been over to Water End,' he announced curtly.

'Ah! How's poor old Jeffrey Parker?' enquired a portly white-haired man seated by the fire. He was about sixty-five, soberly and neatly dressed in black tunic and old-fashioned knee breeches. His usual expression of cheerful serenity was full of concern as he asked the question.

'He's failing still. No hope, I'm afraid, Mr Hall.' A note of impatience in the rector's voice suggested that he preferred faster failings on windy, wet November nights.

'It's a parson's lot, Devereux. At least the old fellow's not spoiling your hunting, tonight,' chaffed Francis

9

Vaughan, a man of thirty or more, ebullient and lively, the headmaster of the Classical Academy.

'No, a small mercy,' conceded the Rector.

Vane finished trimming the candles and enquired deferentially about drinks.

'Yes. Ale all round, Harry, please, excepting Mr Hall of course. What will you have, sir?' asked Richard Miller, a prosperous young farmer.

'Nothing, Dick my boy, thankee. I've only just left my supper,' smiled Hall.

The Reverend Devereux seated himself at the head of the deal table and the others drew up chairs, grating the legs on the herringbone patterned brick.

'Right-ho. To business, gentlemen. The first letter I have is from my counterpart at Wavendon, the Reverend Jenkins. There is yet another disagreement over that wretched meadow at Water End. As you all know, Miss Bates grazes her two cows and geese there, declaring it's her land because she owns up to the parish boundary which runs along the south-east hedge putting the meadow in our parish. Joseph Locke, on the other hand, declares that the boundary goes through the middle, so the Wavendon half is his.'

The Rector sighed. 'Locke has put one of Hannah Bates's cows in the pound and she won't pay the fine. Jenkins begs us to meet him and sort it out once and for all.'

'That's all fine and sensible, but if it do go across the middle it'll mean a new bit of fencing to save any more trouble, and who's to pay for it?' asked Farmer Green.

'It don't go across the middle. It follows Salford Brook down to Gray's Holler and then along the furthermost hedge which is a real old 'un. You can tell from them hollies and ash in it,' stated Farmer Miller firmly.

'So Hannah Bates is certainly right then, as we have told them many times?' asked Devereux.

'Aye. And Joe Locke knows full well she is. He just can't abide the woman.'

'What am I to write back?' asked the Rector wearily. Francis Vaughan cleared his throat and drew in his chair, well practised in the art of gaining attention. With Dick Miller he was one of the younger men there, a well-preserved thirty-three, even-featured and well-dressed in a high-necked jacket, cravat and embroidered waistcoat.

'Plain facts are rarely serviceable in such a situation, as we know. Write to Jenkins accepting the invitation and suggest that the aggrieved parties and several members of their Vestry be there to see fair play. Then we shall arrive with a good map and Dick here will tell them firmly, on the authority of his great-grandfather, that the county and parish boundaries run together undoubtedly to Miss Bates's advantage. We shall all then retire to the Red Lion and Wavendon Parish shall pay for the ale.'

'Aye. Good!' chuckled Farmer Green. 'If we take along one or two old fellers besides, to back up the map, it will cost them so dear they'll let this nonsense drop.'

Devereux made a note and moved on to the next item.

'Eliza Ruddock wants two shillings and sixpence for the midwife for her lying-in at the end of the month and two shillings for boots for son Thomas so he can go back to school.'

'We keep them Ruddocks,' growled Green.

'Doesn't John Ruddock work for thee?' asked Hall.

'On and off, when he don't dislike what I want him to do,' answered Green irritably.

'Well, you only pay half his wage. The poor rate pays the other half,' pointed out Vaughan.

Green and Miller exchanged wary glances and sat up defensively.

'It's us that makes work for the men. There'd be a sight more trouble if they were idle,' rejoined Miller.

11

'There's been ricks fired at Liddlington last week. Had you heard that?' Green leant forward aggressively.

'Liddlington last week; Aspley or Woburn next week!' Hall shook his head miserably.

'You can't blame 'em too much. How would any of us keep our families on eight shillings a week? The Duke's got that automatic seed-drill and the new cultivator he's been showing off to the Agricultural Society, proud as a peacock, and so he should be – but what if we all got one for our farms? We could drop off ten men each and this is only the beginning. We must stand by them,' pleaded the old man.

Green and Miller glanced darkly at him. What could they say to an educated Quaker like Hall, particularly when he was one of the wealthiest landowners in the parish? What they thought to themselves was that he could better afford to be philanthropic than they could.

'Them machines won't work. Not for long, anyways, and no-one will know how to mend them when they break,' said Green.

'Well the Ruddocks haven't been to church since their last child was christened,' said Devereux. 'The diocesan meeting was in favour of poor relief only being given to regular churchgoers.'

'That will soon fill out the congregation,' smiled Vaughan. Devereux regarded him sharply.

'Church attendance compares well with the rest of the country's rural population.'

'Oh yes. No offence meant, Rector. Just a joke.'

'Perhaps you could take the money round to Mrs Ruddock and mention you would like to see her family in church more often, Devereux?' suggested Hall.

'I'm a busy man you know, Mr Hall. I don't regard delivering poor relief to be among my duties.'

'No, no, perhaps not,' said Hall mildly.

'The first decision to make, gentlemen, is whether we

give Mrs Ruddock the money, before we decide who takes it,' said Devereux impatiently.

Hall opened his mouth and shut it again. The two farmers exchanged words quietly.

'I think we must. The baby will come willy-nilly and they've already four to feed,' said Vaughan.

'I agree entirely, and if you would like me to take it round and put in a word about the churchgoing, I shall be very happy to do so,' said Hall.

'It seems perhaps a little inappropriate for a Friend to be encouraging the family to attend another church, doesn't it?' queried Vaughan.

'Oh, not at all,' chuckled the old man. 'There's only one God above and we are all at liberty to honour him in the way we wish.'

CHAPTER 2

The Ruddocks' Cottage

The street plan of Aspley Guise and the lives of its working people had not changed very much since the Domesday surveyors noted that there was plough land for twelve teams, woodland for fifty pigs and a mill. The wooden church had been rebuilt in handsome brown and ochre sandstone but Church Lane was still connected to the Square by the short High Street and the 'square' was still generous in size but triangular in shape due to the asymmetrical arrangement of the four roads which led off it. Church Lane led to Wavendon; East Street to Husborne Crawley and Ridgemont; Woburn Lane to Woburn and West Street to the Turnpike, 'The Heath' and Bow Brickhill. In 1830 the village boasted no less thàn four inns, all on or near the Square: The Bell, The

Swan, The Anchor and The Steamer. The nautical nature of their names is a mystery, since the village sits on the edge of a sandy escarpment, a hundred feet above the marshy plain which forms the northerly part of the parish.

On the November afternoon that Mr Hall visited the Ruddocks, the farm labourers' wives and children hurried home with their bundles of sticks, grateful for the steep hill-side which protected the High Street from the gusting west wind with its squalls of sleet. Most of them pushed open ill-fitting wooden doors and hurried in to light fires for tea, in the little brick terraces which opened straight on to the pavements of the High Street and Square. In the summer, the soft checkering of the alternating pinky-rust and beige brickwork looked warm and mellow, relieving the absence of gardens but the heaps of muck formed of vegetable, pig and human waste which steamed convenient to the back doors was more apparent to passers-by then, so each season had its merits.

Mr Hall alighted stiffly from his bay cob in the yard of The Anchor and tethered it to a metal ring in the wall. He made his way along the High Street to a tiny wattle and daub cottage built up against the brick wall of a terrace of generous two-storey houses. The cottage was also two-storeyed, as a little window projected through the tattered thatch, although the roof ridge only reached halfway up the first floor of the terrace. Hall looked pityingly at the tiny hovel, his thoughts running to the extravagance of his own Tudor farmhouse which housed his sister, himself and their retinue of servants. He carried a small green canvas bag and a bunch of flowers in one hand and, in the other, his riding cane, which he used to tap gently on the front door. A child of ten untied the string which held the broken latch and opened the door just enough to peer up at him enquiringly. He smiled down into her large tawny eyes framed by a tangle of ill-combed hair. She didn't seem quite as timid as he would have expected. There was even a hint of hostility in the way her small pointed chin challenged his presence on their doorstep.

'Who is it, Sarah?' asked a weary woman's voice.

Her question wasn't answered so she pushed back her stool and came to the door. Eliza Ruddock had probably been quite a beauty in the robust village style, but at thirty-five, with a grubby fat toddler across her hip, an older child peeping round her skirt and heavily pregnant, she looked like a worn-out fifty year old to Mr Hall. Her expression livened with anxious concern as soon as she saw him.

'Oh, Mr Hall, sir! I'se so sorry, I weren't expecting callers.' She stepped back as if to invite him in and then cast a panic-stricken glance over her shoulder.

'Don't worry yourself, Mrs Ruddock. It's all my fault for not letting you know and I've only come to see how you are and bring you a small . . . er . . . "Gift" from the Vestry,' he beamed. 'And a bunch of flowers and jar of honey from my sister.'

''Tis so kind,' she said helplessly. He hesitated a moment and then made up his mind.

'Do you mind me stepping in just a moment. I know you're not prepared but I should have felt dreadful to put you to an extra bit of work when you have the bairns to look after. I don't know how you manage.'

He gently steered her back into the room, careful not to show any hint of the despair he felt as he looked around.

'Look, Sarah. How about you getting some water in a jar for these flowers, eh?'

The guarded expression on the angular little face relaxed as she took the bunch of flowers from him.

'Oh, aren't they bonny!' smiled her mother awkwardly. ''Tis so kind. Please thank Miss Hall very much.'

He took a pot of honey and a small package from the

green bag and placed them on the table. At least that was commendably clean, its worn surface scoured white. There was a heap of ashes in the grate and a board supported on logs which he guessed served as a temporary table for the youngsters. A few logs round it must be their seats and the only other furniture standing on the pounded brick and earth floor was a stool at either end of the rickety deal table, but there was no room for much else. Sarah was pouring water from a container in the tiny lean-to shed at the back of the house which must have served as the scullery.

'Well now, let me think. This must be Elisabeth, mustn't it?' he said, prodding the mobile youngster playfully with his cane.

'Yes. Say hello to the gentleman, Tize.' Tize coyly hid her face in her mother's skirts.

'And who is the little one? Memory fails me. It gets worse by the day. Old age, I fear.'

'Ah, that's our Bobby. He's a cherub, isn't he.' His mother kissed the chubby cheek beside her own pale, drawn one. Sarah stood at the back door with downcast eyes, perhaps a little jealous or just embarrassed, thought Hall.

'And where's your big brother Tom this afternoon?' he asked.

'Playin' marbles,' she answered sulkily.

Her mother looked reproachfully at her. 'You go and get him. Tell him Mr Hall's here.'

'Just a little word before they get back, Mrs Ruddock. This is the money you need.'

She looked up eagerly. 'For the boots as well?'

'Yes. There's five shillings there.'

'Oh, thank the Lord. Times *is* hard, sir.'

'I know, I know. And they don't seem to get any better. It won't be easy with the new baby, but if you could get them all to church it might be helpful.'

'Church?'

16

'Yes – just once on a Sunday morning or afternoon. It doesn't matter. Whatever suits you. You know I don't go because I have my own place of worship, but the Rector's rather a . . .' he hesitated. 'Hard' was the word on his lips, but it sounded less than flattering. '. . . he likes to see the church full, naturally, and it seems as if there's been recommendations about distributing the poor relief only to churchgoers you know. So just a little effort would help.'

Eliza shook her head hopelessly. 'It ain't that I don't hold with church, but getting the bairns smartened up isn't easy and it's so shaming if they look forlorn. You know what I mean?'

'I do indeed, Mrs Ruddock.'

'You see, it ain't so bad for them that has older girls in service. They're always bringing or sending clothes from their mistresses. Only this Tuesday, Mrs Munn got a parcel from their Liza. There were some lovely flannelette petti . . . well, p'raps I shouldn't mention *them* . . . but there were some good stockings and dresses too, and that helps a deal . . . but our Sarah's only ten. And then there's John . . .' she tailed off shaking her head sadly.

'Yes. What about John?' he prompted gently.

'Well, he's so proud – and he don't hold with churchgoing – not that he ain't a good Christian . . . but . . . well . . . you know how the men talk down at The Bell . . . they're allus grumbling, but what is the use of grumbling when there's naught to be done. Burning ricks down don't help nobody – except getting them put away – and that's no help to their families at all.'

'Indeed it isn't. You mustn't let him get mixed up in that – you really mustn't. It's not that I don't see their point of view. I do, and I can tell you I am not the most popular man on the Vestry, because I say what I think about those sort of things – but it can do no good at all.

Just as you say, Mrs Ruddock. You must reason with him.'

'I try. My goodness, I try – but he's so hot-headed is John. He goes and blurts out things he don't really mean and certainly shouldn't say to Master Green, even if it *is* what he thinks.'

'Yes, that's the other thing I was going to mention. But it's hard for leopards to change their spots, isn't it?' Hall shook his head sadly.

Their talk was ended by Sarah appearing at the front door pulling a bashful Tom in after her.

'Ah. Here's the second man of the household. How do you do, Tom!'

He was a tall well-built lad for his twelve years, with a broad face, fresh complexion and fair curly hair. His sturdy good looks contrasted markedly with the mousy-haired angularity of his sister. Small and thin for her age, her only physical asset seemed to be her large tawny eyes, but these were almost too big and their expression usually disturbing. At the moment they were upbraiding Tom for his shyness. She nudged him with her elbow.

'Well enough – thankee,' he muttered inaudibly.

Mr Hall rose laughing and rumpled Tom's hair.

'I must be on my way, but why don't you two come up to see us at the Red House? My sister loves showing off her bees and her garden, Sarah, and I'll show you my cattle and pigs, Tom. How about it?'

Tom smiled and muttered his thanks.

'Thank you. That would be very nice, sir,' replied Sarah. Her assurance again surprised Hall.

'Goodbye, Mrs Ruddock. Look after yourself my dear, won't you.' He waved his cane to the little group standing at the door of their humble home.

CHAPTER 3

The Notice on the Church Door

As soon as he had gone Eliza put Bobby down to play on the floor and opened the packet. She counted out the five silver shillings reverently, replaced them and reached up to pop the packet into the only ornament in the room, a pink lustre decorated sugar basin with a chipped lid which stood on the narrow wooden shelf above the grate.

'Sarah, please get some kindling in for the fire. Tom, can you split a couple of those logs that Mr Kemp gave you? We won't have your father's supper ready in time if we don't buck up.'

Eliza struggled in from the scullery with a sooty three-legged pot and hung it on the hook of the chimney chain.

'It's a good thing I got them vegetables done this morning else we'd be all behind like a donkey's tail.'

When John Ruddock swung through the rickety door an hour later the table was scoured clean and on it were set four deep wooden trenchers with a wooden-handled knife and fork beside each. An appetizing smell of stewed vegetables with a whiff of smoked bacon steamed from the stewpot, and Tom and Sarah squatted on the wooden logs clasping their hollow bellies in a frenzy of anticipation. At last they were sitting at the table and Eliza was carefully dividing the small cube of bacon into five unequal parts with painful slowness. Tize got mainly gravy on some broken pieces of bread and Bobby shared his mother's portion. Tom and Sarah got a slither of bacon each and cast envious eyes at their father's 'lion's share'.

19

'We've had a caller today, John.' Eliza spoke archly and nodded to the children to start eating.

'Ah. Who was that then?'

'Mr Hall.'

'What? From the Red House?'

'Yes.'

'What did he want? Want us to join the Friends, did he?' teased John.

'No, 'course not! He brought the money for the midwife and Tom's boots.'

'Ugh.'

John's bantering manner changed abruptly. 'That will be pinned up on the church door, then,' he said grimly.

'I don't think so. They didn't last time,' said Eliza.

'Nay, but they did for old Nick Wright and Mrs Hill and the Lunds last month, didn't they?'

'I never saw them.'

'No, because they were torn down pretty sharpish. They went up all right. That's about the only thing that Rector Devereux enjoys doing for us.'

'Well there's nothing to be done about it, John. We can't manage without,' rejoined Eliza bitterly.

'We could if they paid a man a living wage for a day's work. We wouldn't need to live in shame then.'

'But they don't and they won't and there's nothing you can do about it.'

'I don't know so much,' said John darkly.

'None of your pot-house talk here, John Ruddock. It just makes matters worse. Tom's going to learn straw-plaiting off Cecil Higgins. I said to him about it yesterday and I think Sarah might start with him, or perhaps Old Betsy Munn will learn her lace-making. She's very nimble with her fingers.'

'Yes. Well I s'pose I can retire then. No-one wants to pay me, so I can live off my children and wife, can't I? We used to have a word for fellers like that and it weren't a pretty one.'

He had half risen from his seat in his anger. His straight black hair falling across his flushed face quivered as he emphasized his words. Although he was only of average height and build, he seemed to fill the little room.

Eliza remained quite calm.

'Oh, sit tha down, do! You're letting your supper go cold. You had your way about them not starting plaiting earlier. Some of the village children have been doing it since they were eight or nine.'

'They deserve a bit of childhood,' he answered sullenly.

''Course they do, but they've had more than most now.'

'Little Sarah's only nine.'

'Ten, Father! I'm ten!' she piped indignantly.

'Yes, you are,' soothed her mother. 'Off you go and play now. Off you go, Tom. You can have your piece of bread and lard later. You know, I think Sarah would be a good little lace-maker. She'd enjoy it. She likes dainty little things.'

'There ain't much in it 'cept blindness.'

'They can earn two or three shillings a week. Old Betty must earn a mint more than that with the rate she works at, and it ain't so rough on the hands as plaiting.'

John shook his head. His fire was spent and it seemed easier to leave decisions like that to his wife. Besides, he was keen to get off to The Bell. The way to put the world right seemed so much easier with a half-pint tankard in one's fist.

As soon as he had gone Eliza got a bowl of water from the bucket in the scullery and warmed it up from the hob kettle. She undressed Tize and Bobby in turn, washed the grubbiest bits and put their little night shifts on, shaking her head over the shortness and tightness of Tize's which barely reached below her chubby pink buttocks.

21

'Sing lullaby,' commanded Tize.

'Just a little one, love. Up the stairs you go. Come on Bobby. Come to Mama.

> Lulla, Lullay, my little tiny child
> Lulla, Lullay, Lullay . . . mmm . . . mmm.'

As soon as they had settled, thumbs in mouths, her humming faded and she crept downstairs and slipped out of the house to look for Sarah. It was almost dark and no-one was about. The oil lamps shone greenly through the curtains of the more prosperous cottages and a smell of woodsmoke scented the chill evening air. She guessed correctly where to find the girls. They were in a small yard at the back of the terraces near the well, playing 'Poor Mary'. Dressed in long cotton skirts with a shawl or a piece of blanket round their shoulders, crossed over their fronts and knotted at the back of their waists, they walked in a circle with ceremonial gravity. The girl in the centre covered her face with her hands.

'Poor Mary is a-weeping, a-weeping, a-weeping,
Poor Mary is a-weeping on a bright summer's day', they sang.
'She's a-weeping for her own true love, her own true love, her own true love,
She's a-weeping for her own true love on a bright summer's day.'

Eliza paused to listen. How well she remembered being one of such a stately circle in this very yard. Supposing she had known what was in store for her then? She wondered what lay ahead of these girls, so absorbed in the ageless ritual of their game that they hadn't even noticed her. Would it be her own poverty, the same hapless battle to find food for one more day; to keep the children decently covered until . . . until what? Nothing ever changed. The only miracle was that they still existed one year later . . . two years . . . one child . . . two . . .

three, four, and soon five children later. But *why* were they still here? What was life's rhyme and reason?

The singers answered mockingly,

'Then let her choose another love, another love, another love,
Then let her choose another love, on a bright summer's day.'

Yes! Existence was a circle in which each generation of girls walked and sang and married and managed and made way for the next. The only rhyme was theirs and the reason was circular.

One of the younger players caught sight of Eliza and nudged Sarah who broke away as the circle closed round a new Mary.

'Sarah, will you do something for me?' whispered Eliza urgently.

Sarah's eyes opened round.

'Don't tell Tom or yer father. Just run up to the church and look on the door and then come back and tell me if there's a notice pinned on it.'

Sarah was soon back at the cottage to report that there *was* a notice pinned on the church door. Eliza couldn't decide what to do. She didn't want to be seen going up there herself, and Sarah couldn't read. The little girl sat on a log in front of the dying fire, hugging her knees and watching her mother with dark worried eyes.

'I'll bring it back to you and you can see then,' she suggested.

'What if it's not what it may be? Might just be a note for the bellringers or something.'

'I'll take it back then. It's nailed on. I can pull it off careful and push it back on the nails.'

'You're an artful little puss, you are.' Sarah was up

and gone in a twinkling saving her mother the problem of deciding what to do.

The notice was headed 'Poor Relief' and read

'At their meeting on Thurs. 30th November 1830 the Select Vestry Committee awarded two shillings and sixpence to John Ruddock for a midwife and two shillings for boots.

signed H. L. O. Devereux,
Rector.'

Eliza's reading wasn't strong but she made out 'John Ruddock' and enough of the rest and pursed her lips bitterly.

Sarah watched her intently, her mouth slightly open.

'Up to bed my girl, quick,' said her mother abruptly. 'Not a word to your father or Tom, mind you.'

As soon as Sarah's light foot sounded overhead, Eliza poked a bit of life into the smouldering ashes and, glancing guiltily towards the open stair, little more than a ladder really, she pushed the paper in and blew on it until it smouldered and burnt.

'Mr Hall must have changed sixpence for a shilling,' she pondered.

CHAPTER 4

The Fine Gentry and The Bell Reformers

The following morning was the meet of the Woburn Foxhounds so it was hardly light when Devereux rode past the church porch on his way to the Abbey. Church notices were not uppermost in his mind so he only saw that the one about the Ruddocks had gone on his return late that afternoon.

The drawing-room of the rectory was large and high,

showing off the elegance of the furnishings, the china tea service and also the Rector's wife, Beatrice, to perfection.

'Your face, Hugh, tells me that the hounds drew a series of blind coverts, then led you across the fields of farmers who don't hunt and leave their beasts out and your horse has gone lame.' She spoke as elegantly as she dressed while she poured out the tea with fastidious grace. She would have been so clearly out of place in one of the village cottages that she saved embarrassment on both sides by never visiting the poor and sick.

'No. You are quite wrong, dear. I have enjoyed a remarkably good day's hunting and Sir Geoffrey has invited us to dine next month. Her Ladyship will let you know the date.'

'That sounds a welcome diversion; but why the long face?'

'Oh, nothing really. It's just these confounded paupers removing church notices again.'

'I suppose they feel ashamed.'

'And so they should. Nobody wants them on the poor rate, particularly when they're not prepared to go to the workhouse. The outside poor relief will stop soon, then they will have to go, and a very good thing too. Just look at Ruddock; there's a strong healthy man in his prime and he won't do a decent day's work if he can help it. All full of fine talk about social revolutions in The Bell each night, of course.'

'Really! How do you know, dear?'

'Oh, I have my informants.'

'I hope *he* had nothing to do with the Liddlington ricks.'

'Wouldn't surprise me, but there weren't any of my parishioners apprehended. It's only the stupid ones who do it, of course. It's the fellows who set them on who ought to feel the sharp edge of the law.'

His wife looked pensive. 'I remember Eliza Ruddock

when she was married. She was a strikingly pretty girl, but just look at her now. They let themselves go so!'

Another member of the village community had just returned from hunting as well and was taking tea in the comfort of his drawing-room. This was Francis Vaughan, whose Classical Academy educated the sons of business-men. The curriculum he offered belied the name of the school, because philosophy took precedence over classical literature and so the boys learnt practical accountancy as well as mathematics and were told of the progress of the French chemists and the experiments of Boyle, Priestley and Davy. This appealed to their fathers who had factories and mills in London and Birmingham and wanted their heirs to know something of the new technologies.

Theresa Vaughan was plump and homely. Her auburn silk afternoon dress was expensive but it didn't flatter her figure nor match her stole and the cap she wore on her head was quite out of date.

Francis was aware of these things but he was a fair man and acknowledged that an assistant master who aspired to marry the head's daughter couldn't expect a fashionable beauty into the bargain. It had been a good bargain because Theresa's father had died conveniently young, leaving them the school.

'How was the hunting today, dear?'

'Quite a reasonable day. We made two kills.'

Theresa winced but only enquired who comprised the field.

'Well, Devereux, of course; he never misses a day. Farmer Miller; he had a new bay gelding that was going remarkably well. Got it off the Osborne estate, he said. Sir Geoffrey was there but not the Duke . . . This tea tastes excellent!'

'Yes. I had it sent down from Jacksons. You remember saying how you liked Mrs Devereux's tea?'

26

'Ah, very good. You had better keep it locked up.'

'Of course, dear. I have the caddy keys here.' She indicated a substantial bunch of keys on her chatelaine.

'I don't know how you struggle around with all those. See you don't fall into Hall's lake when you go visiting Lucy. You'd sink straight to the bottom,' he joked.

Theresa looked hurt.

'Well, it's not that I *like* carrying all these about, but there are the pantry keys and the boys' lockers and we're having to keep the infirmary doors locked after their last escapade, the naughty little monkeys.'

'Of course, dear. You're the perfect wife for a busy teacher, and I must get back to relieve Mr Griffiths now.'

He patted her shoulder affectionately as he rose to go.

After supper that evening, John Ruddock pushed through the door of The Bell and greeted his friends seated at the round table. There was an elderly widower with a pair of brass-rimmed spectacles askew on his long nose. These, combined with his receding hair and stooping posture gave him a rather academic look and George Dunne *was* well-read, although self-educated. He earned a little by book-keeping for several local businesses.

'Halloa John, our good comrade,' he cried in a high cracked voice.

'Good evening to thee George and Dickie and Philip,' replied John boisterously, walking over to the bar to get a pint of beer. 'Where's young Jerry, eh?'

'Jerry Dilks has walked to Ampthill. They've opened an institute for self-improvement in literature and the philosophies,' explained Dicken Phelps gravely. He was a middle-aged man of medium build with hair of an indeterminate sort of colour and curl, and an unremarkable face. His opinions seemed to reflect his general middliness and rarely provoked any of his friends.

However heated a discussion became, each adversary instinctively felt that Dicken was solidly behind him.

'It's open two nights each week, John. That must be a good thing, eh?' said George.

'Oh, aye. If he bain't too tired to listen when he gets there. When do it finish?'

'It don't start till half past seven to give them a chance to get there after work, so it can't finish afore half past nine I reckons.'

'He'll never get risen in time for work tomorrow,' said John.

'He'll manage. He's a good fellow is Jerry. I had to teach myself all *I* know so it should make it a lot easier for him,' said old George.

'I don't suppose they'll learn him much what's important,' said Philip Wooding, a lean man in his thirties, with a sallow complexion. 'I mean, they won't have Cobbett's Register to read and discuss the merits of this 'ere laisser faire policy and what these "swing" riots is all about.'

'What's happened to the two men they caught for the Liddlington ricks?' asked John.

'In gaol, awaiting "Justice".'

'A fat lot of justice they'll get.'

'Yes. It's likely to be swinging, like that mysterious leader of theirs calls himself. He signs all his letters "Swing", don't he?'

'They transported them two young 'uns from Wiltshire,' said George bitterly.

'Aye. New South Wales for life and only lads they was, seventeen and eighteen year old. It's a wicked shame,' said Dicken.

'We ought to start a collection. They were talking about getting some money together for their wives and children at Husborne Crawley and Ridgemont,' suggested Philip. The group shifted uneasily.

George drew some coins from his pocket and sorted

out several which he placed in the middle of the table, keeping his hand over them.

'I'll start it off because I haven't so much call on my pocket as you fellows. There's no need to put down much, you know. The more folks that contribute, the less that's needed from each.'

Dicken and Philip produced a penny or two while John flushed and fidgetted and then rapidly drew four pennies out and slapped them down on the table with a flourish.

'Can thee afford that much, John?' asked George.

'Nay, you mustn't let the children go short,' said Dicken.

''Course I can. It's a just cause, ain't it? I admire their courage,' replied John, a little too loudly.

George Dunne withdrew his hand to reveal twelve pence. The others shook their heads in admiration.

'Who'll keep it?'

'You take it, George, and we'll see if we can't get some more.'

'Yes. Martha Lyle and Betty Munn will find some for us.'

'It's worth tramping up to the Heath to ol' Harry Nursall.'

'Aye, I'll do that,' volunteered George.

CHAPTER 5

Planning for Paradise

Although John Ruddock was spared the humiliation of having his pauperism proclaimed to the village, he was not pleased to find his little home in a turmoil of activity the following Sunday morning.

'What are you getting the bairns dressed up like Aunt Sallys for?' he demanded.

'Just thought we'd go to church, John,' replied Eliza evenly.

'For God's sake why, 'ooman?'

'Yes, that's right, I suppose. That's why one usually goes, ain't it?' said Eliza testily.

'You know what I mean,' growled John.

'Well, we ain't been for a while. Not since our Robert was christened.'

'And none the worse for that. Christians they that act like Christians. No need to be seen in your Sunday best sitting and sizing up the other women's hats. If you want to worship, go to the chapel up Mount Pleasant. You'll find more honest folk there.'

'The church is nearer and it can't do no harm.'

John flounced out slamming the door which swung back and forth creaking violently until Sarah caught it and hooked the string loop over the broken catch.

'You ready, Tom, Sarah? Here Tom, carry Bobby for me, there's a good lad. It's as much as I can do to get me own body up the rise. Sarah, hold Tize's other hand in case she stumbles.'

'Bobby's bin sick, Mam.'

'Oh, lawks-a-mussy. Quick, get the dish cloth, Sarah.'

'It's all over me shoulder,' moaned Tom.

'Oh dear, deary-me. It's your only decent jacket.'

The family eventually got under way and arrived breathless and late at the church door. Eliza was upset to find that the Rector had already gone in to don his cassock. Even if he shook hands with them at the end of the service he would know that they'd arrived late.

'Me new boots is pinching awful, Mam.'

'Hush Tom. You'll be sitting down now.'

That evening, when the two youngest were asleep, John enquired whether they felt better for the churchgoing.

'No worse, anyways,' replied Eliza shortly.

'Who was there then?'

'There were Mr and Mrs Peach with Ellen, and the Crosses. The Lunnons weren't there. I thought they usually went.'

'They've moved on to the Heath,' said John.

'Have they, then!' exclaimed Eliza in surprise.

'Yes. *They*'ve got enough pride not to relish him pinning their poor relief list on the church door.'

'It may be cutting off their nose to spite their face, of course.'

'Nay. It's where we ought to go. I could soon put up a little place if we found some timber and Tom and me could throw up a bank round the outside and plant some fruit and vegetables. We'd be real snug up there.'

'The soil's too light. It's all sand. Father used to say "the Heath's all right for furze and starvation".'

'It's all right with muck on it.'

'And where's that going to come from? Can you see Farmer Green sending you a load or two up to Aspley Heath?'

'There's ways and means. You can't tell 'til you've tried. They say Miller let Jeffrey Lunnon have some timber and two days off work with pay to get a place put up.'

'Farmer Miller is a gentler man than Green, and Lunnon's regular with him; not jobbing as a roundsman with the Vestry making up his wage,' said Eliza derisorily.

John flushed.

'Aye, and look what a slack-twisted fellow he is! If he can make it work, I certainly can.'

Eliza shook her head sadly. A squatter's shack on the Heath was one of John's pipe-dreams but there was no poor relief for a squatter and no security. At the moment the Select Vestry turned a blind eye to the 'common' rights just to save the poor relief but if they had a change of heart it could mean eviction and the workhouse.

'This time of year's no good for a move like that,' she said appeasingly. 'Wait 'til the baby's come and we'll think about it in the spring. Up to bed you two! Now! This very minute,' cried Eliza, countering the wails of protest from Tom and Sarah.

John took himself off to The Bell, Eliza mended socks and Tom and Sarah whispered to each other from their straw mattresses.

'What's the Heath like, Tom?'

'It's just rough. Furze and little trees and paths and bits of grass.'

'What, tall grass – wavy like the fifteen-acre before they cut it?'

'Neow, very short, bright green. The rabbits keep it down.'

'Rabbits!'

'Yes. If we moved up there I'd have a dog and me and you could go rabbiting, Sare.'

'Mam could cook them. R-a-b-b-i-t S-t-e-w,' murmured Sarah ecstatically.

'Stop it! You're making me hungry.'

'Our own garden full of strawberries and rasps and apple trees and some marigolds like Missus Hall's. It *would* be good, Tom, wouldn't it? Me and you could grow them.'

'Yeah. And we could earn a ha'penny a yard for straw plaiting. We wouldn't need the relief any more.'

'Father'd need timber to build the house.'

'I don't know how we'd get that.'

'There's little trees up there!'

'Not allowed to cut them, though. Get taken to court for that. Anyway, they'm only little birches; not big enough to split.'

'You know what Mr Hall said when he came?'

'About going up to the Red House?'

32

'Yes. Let's go. *He*'d help us to get the timber.'

'I'm not going,' stated Tom.

'Cowardy! I'll go!'

'Can't go by yourself.'

'Well, you come with me then.'

As usual, Sarah won and Wednesday morning found her bravely climbing the steps leading to the front door of the Red House. Its name was a mystery because it was covered with cream plaster between age-dark oak. Just a section of the first floor had powdery old herringbone set bricks in the porch gable high above the children's heads.

Tom hung back reluctantly.

'You can't knock on the front door, Sare,' he hissed.

'Where then?' she demanded petulantly, trying to hide her nervousness.

'Well, the back, where the tradesmen go I s'pose.'

The problem was happily resolved by Miss Hall catching sight of them and throwing open the front door. Out tumbled a welter of dogs: two spaniels, three small terriers and a bull terrier, which all rushed down the steps barking and jumping up to lick the children's faces.

'Hey, Rory – down sir! Down! Be quiet Kipper, Pickles, hush! They won't hurt you children. Don't worry, dears.'

Mary Hall looked a bit younger than her brother but she had a similar round plump face with the same air of serenity even as she tried to control her unruly pack. Her brown satin dress with its high cream collar fitted her generous figure with hardly a wrinkle. 'Sort of well-upholstered, like that chair Mr Gibbons was doing for Mrs Wetherall,' confided Sarah to Tom that evening.

Laughing and breathless, the two children found themselves in the kitchen at the back of the house.

'There, I've just been helping Cook to bake these oat cakes. You couldn't have arrived at a better moment.

They've just come out of the oven!' The sight of the two pairs of wide round eyes made her smile.

'The poor mites are ravenous,' she thought.

'We always bake far more than we can eat so you must help us, and here's a glass of milk to see them down.'

The pair sat down on chunkily-made oak stools and ate their cakes off blue and white pot plates. With three cakes stowed away Sarah felt able to consider her surroundings.

The kitchen was low and long and the sunlight from the mullioned windows chequered the stone flags and long oak table with its five-inch thick top. Their tiny hovel of a home would have fitted three times into this room. A massive pine chopping table occupied one corner and several Windsor-back chairs with pretty flower-embroidered cushions stood about. She particularly noted six sides of salted bacon hanging from the wide oak beams near the huge fireplace and the bundles of drying herbs in between them.

If heaven had a smell, it must be this one of freshly baked cakes spiced with smoked bacon and herbs.

If heaven had a taste, it must be the luxurious creaminess of fresh milk, cool from the dairy. Sarah and Tom had hardly tasted milk since they were weaned.

Mary Hall took them out into the garden to look for her brother. Sarah was enchanted by the paved courtyard with its random scattering of troughs and red clay pots. A few late marigolds and cornflowers straggled here and there but most of them were planted up with gilly flowers.

'Will! Will, we have some visitors.'

Mr Hall took Tom off to see the pigs. Sarah gave him a long meaningful look as he left, but Tom seemed too shy to notice.

'He won't ask,' she thought to herself.

Mary Hall interpreted the long look as a reluctance to leave her brother.

'There dear, let them look at the smelly old pigs. We'll go to the greenhouse and see if we can find a few grapes left on the vine. Tom will soon be back for you.'

Sarah's pointed little face wore a slight frown. She seemed preoccupied rather than shy.

'Do you like flowers?' asked Mary.

'Oh yes, a lot,' piped Sarah gravely.

'And grapes?'

'I don't know. I've never had none.'

'Oh well, this will be a treat then. We must save some for Tom.'

'Yes, thank you, Mum.'

'What else do you like? What do you like the very best of all?'

Sarah stopped to consider this, looking up at Mary with her head on one side.

'I like rabbit stew. We don't have it often but Tom says there's lots of rabbits on the Heath.'

'Yes, I should think there are.' Mary wondered where this conversation was leading.

'If we lived on the Heath, me and Tom could catch them. Tom says he'd have a dog.'

'That would be nice. I'm very fond of my dogs. But, might you go to live on the Heath?'

'I don't know.' Sarah shook her head sadly and surveyed her toe sticking out of her worn slipper. 'Father wants to go but we've no timber to build a house. Mam says we should wait till spring.'

'Yes, you should do that. The new baby . . .' Mary's voice trailed off as she recollected that such a subject was not a proper one for children and Sarah tactfully ignored the unfinished sentence.

Soon Tom and Sarah were on their way home, laden with a huge bunch of Michaelmas daisies and some grapes for their mother.

'Did you ask him?' asked Sarah.

'Ask him what?'

''Bout the timber.'

'No, course not, silly. I couldn't have.'

'Ha!'

CHAPTER 6

The Claim Staked

It was about three weeks later that the Heath was
discussed again in the Ruddock home. The last week
had been a harrowing one for Eliza. She sat huddled in
her chair which was standing almost in the grate beside
the little heap of smouldering wood. She had a torn dark
blanket pinned round her shoulders, her thin pale hand
supported her even thinner paler face, and her dull hair
straggled across her forehead. Her other hand clutched
a piece of rag and her eyes were red-rimmed from
crying. Sarah crouched silently on her log and her
mother's eyes stared dully over her.

After a bit Eliza roused herself and rose weakly,
holding on to the chair arm for support. She reached
down a coin off the mantel shelf and it was clear that she
was no longer pregnant.

'Sarah, take the jug and fetch me a ha'pennyworth of
beer from The Anchor, child. And see if you can find
Tom and bring him back.'

While Sarah was away, John came in.

'You're home early. I ain't got supper ready,' said
Eliza.

'Aye. I thought maybe you'd like some company,' he
said gently. 'Where's Sare?'

'I've just sent her off to look for Tom and fetch some
beer.'

'Good!'

'How am I going to pay Martha Lyle?' she asked dully.

'I dunno. How much did she give you?'

'Two shillings.'

'I don't know why you had to have it christened and buried proper.'

'He were your child, too. How can you be so unfeeling?'

'I just meant the living could have used the money better.'

'The poor wee mite hardly lived at all.' There was a warning break in her voice but John didn't heed it.

'Aye. That's just what I meant.'

'Oh-oh.' Eliza broke down into convulsive sobs and John went over and put his arms round her shoulders consolingly.

'There, there. Don't take on so. You can't bring him back. Women feel these things more than men, I suppose. That's all there is to it. I'll get the two shillings.'

'Don't lend it off no-one, John. Martha can wait a bit.'

Sarah and Tom returned with the jug of beer.

'Do you want it warming?' asked John.

'No, it will do,' she said, trying to stifle her sobs in front of the children.

'I went up the Heath this afternoon,' said John. 'There weren't anything to do at the farm.'

'There'll be less money this week then.'

John shifted uncomfortably. 'There's a real good little place we could have. There's a little hollow for the cottage and a bit of a south slope at the back of it.'

'What, where them three young birches is with a little pine on the way up to Leighton Hollow, Father?' asked Tom, his eyes shining.

'Yes. Just hard by and there's already a bit of a bank

around. We'd only need to build it up and put one down the other side.'

'It's winter,' said Eliza.

'Now's the time to start and have the ground ready for the spring.'

Sarah's eyes were shining too.

'Miss Hall visited this morning,' she said.

Eliza glanced uneasily at her.

'What did *she* want?' John asked guardedly, looking towards his wife.

She twisted her handkerchief and pursed her lips, then said slowly: 'She said some'at about some timber if we needed it.'

Sarah looked triumphantly towards her father.

'Oh, she did, did she. How does she know that we may be needing timber?'

'The children must have been chattering.'

John looked at Tom who shrugged his shoulders and blushed.

'I ain't said nothing.'

John turned to Sarah but she just pushed out her chin and put her head on one side. He kept his eyes on her for a moment.

'Well it so happens as we could use it. Where would we get it?'

'We don't want to be beholden to them, John.'

'Why not? If they want to help us, why not?'

'They're good people.'

'Of course. That's why we should let them help us, if they want to. Shall I go up and see William Hall?'

Eliza knew that aggressive tone of mock-confidence well. He could not be trusted to be tactful and she didn't want the Halls' feelings hurt.

'I'll go up and speak to Miss Lucy and say as how we've talked it over and would like a bit, but I won't say what for, John Ruddock. They may guess well enough, but it mustn't get back to the Select Vestry else they'll give us no more help, and Mr Hall mustn't know proper.'

'We can manage all right without the Select Vestry,' said John sullenly.

'Maybe, maybe not, but we certainly can't manage without Farmer Green if he wants rid of you.'

'I can work as well for him from the Heath.'

'Wait till we've got some vegetables growing. I ain't budging an inch till then and none of your pot-house talk, else it will be all round the village in next to no time.'

It may have been the effect of the beer, but more likely the excitement of her vehemence which had made Eliza's eyes come to life again, and with her cheeks slightly flushed she looked twice as well as she had done half an hour earlier.

'Can you walk up to the Red House?' John's fire had subsided as Eliza's rose and he asked the question almost timidly.

'I'll be right enough in a day or so. Sarah can come with me.'

'Eliza Ruddock wants two shillings towards the baby's funeral,' stated Devereux.

'First it's money for the midwife and now it's money for the funeral,' muttered Green.

'It would have cost us more had it lived,' quipped Vaughan.

William Hall averted his eyes sadly but said nothing. Another member of the committee was at this meeting, a young builder called Graham Dudley. He was the most recently elected member of the Select Vestry, in his early thirties and owned a bit of property in the village.

'Is it the Ruddocks that have that little shack near Newsomes' on the High Street?' Dudley asked.

'Yes, that's them,' replied Vaughan.

'It's a wonder how they fit in the children they've got already. Who's their landlord?'

'Alfred Barnstable from Broughton, and they'd be a sight better off on the Heath if you ask me,' said Miller.

'At least they'd be off the Poor Rate there,' said Vaughan.

'It is common land, you know,' said Devereux sharply. 'I think there'll come a time when we've got to make a stand on that. It's the workhouse where those people ought to be. They'll have a right to that land through long tenure if we don't stamp it out soon.'

'Aye, but we could all buy the land off them then,' pointed out Dudley.

Devereux smiled wanly.

Hall opened his mouth as if to speak but then closed it. He felt uncomfortable in his knowledge of Ruddock's intention but the nonchalant heartlessness of his fellows appalled him.

'Surely the Lord must pardon my concealment,' he thought. 'After all, Vaughan has five children of his own and Devereux three, yet they seem to have no compassion for this family they condemn. If they could imagine their own wives looking as fragile and grief-stricken as Eliza Ruddock did this morning when Lucy visited her, might that make them realize the agony of grinding poverty?'

'Well, what about this two shillings, gentlemen?' asked Devereux impatiently.

'I suppose so.'

'Yes.'

'Let's hope we hear no more from the Ruddocks for a bit,' Green muttered.

'How far are these riots going to reach, eh?' asked Miller. 'High Wycombe is uncomfortably close.'

'They ought to make more use of the army. The

Yeomanry stopped their nonsense pretty effectively at Tisbury,' said Devereux.

'Yes, but with one poor fellow killed and several others badly injured . . .' countered Hall.

'They haven't got enough militia to spare, anyway. Peel just can't raise them,' said Vaughan.

Hall's eyes were no longer mild. He had half risen from his seat. Vaughan and Dudley gazed at him in astonishment. It was the first time they had seen him roused to anger.

'Do you really condone meeting these poor wretches with violence? They were harming nobody. They were showing no violence. They were walking from village to village calling for a wage that is less than fair. Nine shillings a week they asked for. How many of you can begin to imagine keeping a family on nine shillings a week, let alone the six or seven shillings these men are earning now?'

'They do some violence to the threshing machines and the ricks, though,' muttered Green.

'Rarely. That is only a small minority that resort to violent actions and it is never against persons . . . I am sorry for my outburst, gentlemen.' The old man sat down, wiping his face with his pocket handkerchief. His hands were shaking with emotion.

Devereux's face showed no trace of that.

'I have arranged for our visit to Wavendon to sort out the Bates versus Locke dispute. How many of us can manage Thursday the 24th? We meet at the rectory at eleven o'clock.'

'When are the Hunt meets that week?' asked Miller.

'Tuesday and Wednesday,' said Devereux promptly.

'Should be fine then.'

On the following Sunday, John and Tom left home before it was light. John had brought two spades back from work, trusting that they would not be missed on a Sunday. Eliza had insisted on the early start so that they should not be seen and she had packed them up 'baviour' for their breakfasts and dinners, exhorting them not to return until after dusk.

The Heath is one and a half miles from Aspley village along the edge of the green sand ridge which separates the chalk hills of the Chilterns from the brick clay of the plain between Oxford and Bedford. The boundaries of the Parish of Aspley have not changed since Saxon times and they encompass both the light dry sand-hills sculpted into miniature mountain scenery and the heavy grey clay of the plain. John Ruddock and Tom left the sandy lane, which runs sunken between high banks up Leighton Hollow, and climbed to the crest of a knoll so that they could gaze down and out across the flatness of the plain to the far horizon. It was not really featureless because the squat square tower of Wavendon Church crowned a small rise about three miles away, and beyond it, the tower of Milton Keynes Church was just visible while, away to the right, Salford too at the diagonally opposite and aptly named 'Water End' corner of the parish. The chequered field patterns were interrupted by masses of dark woods and coppices and scrubby ochrous marshes. Through the water-meadows, the meandering lines of Salford Brook and the Lovent and, out of sight to the east, Crawley Brook, were marked by rows of pollarded willows.

''Tis a clear view today, Tom. More rain to come.'

They turned back to the lane, as impervious to the prettiness of the immediate scenery as most working country folk are. There were no meandering brooks here, only the odd small pond dug out and puddled with clay, fed by an iron red, peaty trickle from a spring or ditch. On the steep hillsides grew the odd oak, ash, birch and holly tree but between them patches of nibbled short turf were surrounded by bracken, bilberry and ling, with furze bushes and blackberries in the dells. Wherever the

42

earth beneath had been exposed by man or an uprooted tree, there were rain-ravaged scars of sand in a great variety of colours. Only a couple of yards might separate auburn red from sunny yellow or the purest silver-white, criss-crossed by sooty black marbling. A few leisured visitors came to wonder at the lovely scenery and fill shapely slim glass vases with undulating layers of sand, a band of silver next to auburn and pale sulphur yellow or warm orange, but John and Tom did not wonder. The impressive contours, the vegetation, the coloured sand and the sunken lane that was old when the Romans rode along it, were just the furniture of their lives. They were barely noticed features which had no bearing on how much money there would be to feed and clothe the family that month. What *was* to affect their lives more than they could guess was the erratic line of the Parish and County Boundary which bit out the narrow sliver of Aspley Heath for Bedfordshire from the middle of Wavendon Heath in Buckinghamshire.

As they trudged on up the lane they met Harry Nursall, a robust sixty year old.

'Ah, hallo John. Be thee thinking of joining us then? There's bin some talk o'evictions but I don't reckon it will come to nothing. The Vestry's only too glad to save on the poor rate.'

'Aye, that's just what I told our Eliza but the women-folk are always timid. They hold back when there ain't nothing to hold back for.'

'Has thee got some timber for building?'

'Aye. I have the promise of some at any rate.'

'Oh! Farmer Green doing his bit, is he?'

'No! Not him. That wouldn't be like him, would it?'

'Nay. He's a tight-fisted one, him!'

Harry couldn't conceal his curiosity but he forebore to question John any further.

'Well, must be getting along,' said John.

'Aye. You start work and if you need a hand with

some'at just let me know. You'll soon talk that 'ooman of yourn round when she sees a little cottage.'

CHAPTER 7

Friends Indeed

Eliza, Sarah and Tom set out for the Red House the following Tuesday. It was a cold windy day with the sun shining fitfully between squalls of sleet. The bare branches of the elms along the edge of the churchyard tossed and sawed. Eliza averted her eyes from them, trying to shut out the thought of the pathetic tiny body that lay beneath them. She had made herself very neat and got Sarah to plait her long hair into a dull brown rope and help her pin it round her head. Even the exertion of raising her hands to her head soon exhausted her but she walked upright through the village with as light a step as she could manage. Once out on the Crawley road her pace slackened and she began to lean on Tom's shoulder. Sarah carried a little basket with a pot of rosemary lard in it covered by a piece of clean linen.

The Red House stood on a rise, and as the road got steeper their progress got slower and slower. Sarah's face puckered and she bit her lip, holding a little tighter to her mother's hand.

'Soon be there, Mam,' said Tom encouragingly.

Lucy Hall greeted them in consternation.

'You shouldn't have walked out here, Mrs Ruddock. You'd only to send up Tom or Sarah and I would have come down straight away.'

'Oh no. I'm not one for flinching. The fresh air will do me good. Give Miss Hall the lard, Sarah. It's only a little thing, I'm afraid.'

44

'Oh, rosemary lard, I do declare! Why, that's one of my brother's favourites on his toast. That's very kind of you, Mrs Ruddock. Now, sit yourself down here, dear, nice and close to the fire, and I'm going to take Tom and Sarah straight out to Ezra Munn, our cowman. My brother's gone all the way to Dunstable today but Ezra will keep them amused and Cook will make us all some nice hot tea.'

Eliza sank gratefully into the cushioned chair and appraised the kitchen, just as Sarah had done the week before. She was even more awe-struck by the huge space, not that she could ever feel comfortable in such a palace, she told herself, but how wonderful to have a little kitchen, so warm and light, as well as a cosy little parlour next to it. How wonderful it would be to have time to sit by the fire and embroider beautiful flowers on cushion covers like these. She shook her head ruefully. There was hardly enough time to darn the stockings and mend the pinafores and breeches . . . *if* one could afford the thread to fill one's needle with, of course.

When Lucy returned, she escorted Eliza into a panelled parlour smelling of pot-pourri and a neat maid brought them a tray of tea and toasted muffins. Eliza enjoyed the tea. It was the first time she had drunk it from new tea leaves. The villagers only had tea discarded from the kitchens of the well-to-do. But she could only manage half a muffin despite Lucy's urgings.

'No, really. It's so kind of you Miss Hall, but I just haven't had the stomach for victuals since . . . since . . .'

'I know, my dear, but you must force yourself to eat just a little more each day until your appetite returns. You have so many depending on you – John, Tom, Sarah and the little ones. Where are Elisabeth and Robert today?'

'Martha Lyle has got them. Hers are at school and so should Tom be, but I don't think I could have managed the hill without him.'

'No, of course not. But do tell me why you've come, Mrs Ruddock. Is it about the timber I mentioned?'

'Aye.' Eliza looked down uncomfortably. 'John and me talked it over and I'm not sure it's right but he's set his heart on it and we're that hard pressed to pay the rent at the moment, I suppose it's the only thing. But there again, I don't want to make any trouble for Mr Hall, I'm sure.' She raised her eyes questioningly to Lucy's face.

'Do you mean because he's on the Select Vestry committee?'

'Yes, that's just it. They shouldn't like him to help us.'

'Well, I really don't see why. After all, Farmer Miller helped Jeffrey Lunnon with wood to put up a cottage.'

Eliza shook her head.

'It ain't the same. They don't like us. It's John. He don't mean no harm but he's so full of ideas about how this and that should be better and he can't hold his tongue when he should. I'm scared to death they'll evict us and then we shall have nothing.' She shook her head and dabbed at her eyes with the corner of her shawl.

'Don't you worry, Mrs Ruddock. No-one will know where you've got that wood from if you don't say. Tell John very firmly not to talk about it and no-one will be any the wiser. And you stay put in your little cottage until you're sure you can manage on your own. Who is your landlord?'

'Mr Barnstable over at Broughton.'

'Would you let me give you a month's rent? It would be such a comfort to me to feel you weren't worrying about that and it is so little to us. We'd never notice it.'

'Oh no! I couldn't. John would never hear of it. He's such a proud man,' said Eliza vehemently.

'Need he know?'

'Oh no! I couldn't neither. It's ever so good of you.

46

The timber's enough and I don't know how we can ever repay your kindness to us . . . but . . . no . . .'

Her words failed, she was so overcome and Lucy regretted making the offer. She had been tactless.

'Now where shall the timber be put?'

Eliza pulled herself together.

'Tom will tell thee.'

'When can Mr Ruddock and Tom see to it?'

'Next Sunday.'

'Right. A heap of boards will mysteriously appear where Tom tells me, late on Saturday and you just forget all about it, dear. Leave it to the menfolk.'

Unfortunately it was raining hard on Sunday as John and Tom trudged up the sandy lane. They had to avoid the rivulet that wore deep furrows in their path and the water plashed down steadily on the sodden sacks which covered their heads and shoulders. It had sculpted fairy castles of a myriad tiny minarets in the high sandy banks of the sunken lane. The normally dark holly bushes that surmounted these gleamed in prickly wetness. John and Tom scrambled up the bank to the hollow and there, lying palely between the dripping birch trees, was a magnificent heap of freshly sawn boards. Beneath them, concealed in a canvas bag, were two heavy hammers, a pair of pincers, a saw and four pounds of nails. There were also eight five-inch-square posts. John flung his arms around Tom and waltzed about whooping like a boy. Tom, laughing and blushing, pushed his father away.

'There be just one thing a-bothering me, lad.'

'Yes, Father?'

'How are we to keep this lot safe? Even if we were able to keep our eye on it all day, which we ain't, some fellows may come along and make off with it in the night.'

'I can stay here.'

'You can't stay on your own all night?'

'I reckon so,' said Tom, sounding much braver than he felt.

'We can make a sort of little shed place to sleep in, today. Some'at to just keep out the rain, p'raps,' said John doubtfully.

'Can't you get more of them sacks from the farm to keep warm under?'

John shook his head. He knew Eliza would never entertain the idea of Tom staying out here on his own all night.

They started digging holes for the corner posts. Tom thought they should make it bigger. He thought of his mother's face aglow with surprised excitement when they took her to see her huge new house. John assured him that houses always seemed much bigger when they were finished than the space pegged out on a bit of ground.

'Besides, the bigger the home, the bigger the fire you need to warm it. We can always add another room or so after, lad. We ought to pitch the bottom of these posts before we set them in. There's some pitch at the farm. I wonder whether I might not get the bailiff to let me have a bit but I'll have to tell him a cock an' bull story about what I wants it for.'

The heavy rain continued right through the afternoon, so at four o'clock they pushed the posts well under the boards, partly to give them a chance to dry out for pitching and partly to deter theft.

'Will we leave the bag with the hammers and nails, Father?'

'No, we'll take that with us. We can hide it upstairs. Best be getting home. No-one will be poking around here on a night like this and it's that dark no-one's likely to see much of us slipping back with the bag.'

'I'll come up as soon as I gets out of school tomorrow,' said Tom.

'Right! Just to see it's not been tampered with, eh?'
Eliza wasn't surprised to see them back early.

'Was the timber there?' she asked eagerly.

'Yes, Mam. It was a real big pile, weren't it, Father?'

'Aye, and look . . .' He opened up the canvas bag.

'Oh, ain't that good of them. Everything you could want. Where shall we put it? Don't want no prying eyes, and Mr Barnstable will probably be here for the rent tomorrow. He never came Friday.'

'Upstairs. It will push into the corner by the window. Sare's feet don't go right down there and we can put her blanket over it.'

CHAPTER 8

Tom and Sarah on the Heath

On Monday evening Tom returned from the Heath in a distraught state.

'Some of them boards has gone!' His father rose from the table grimly.

'Nay, son! How many?'

'About five I reckon, maybe six. Just as many as will go under your arm.'

John's fist hit the table, making the cans and platters dance.

'The bastard. Whoever can it be? Just he watch out when I catches him.'

'Hush, John. That won't do any good. How many is left? Is it enough?'

'It won't be if six goes walking each night,' said John.

'Let me have my supper, Mam, then I'll go back to watch them.'

'You can't stay up there all night, Tom,' said Eliza.

'No. I'd best go,' said John.

'Where can you shelter? Fred Little's got a bit of oilskin. Go round, John, and say as how our roof's been leaking – and that's no lie, I'll have to say some'at to Mr Barnstable – and if they aren't using it we'd be very grateful to lend it for a bit.'

'Good girl! You've got a good little headpiece on th'shoulders.'

John spent a wet cold night crouching by the pile of wood and the next evening Tom insisted on going up, and John took over at half past eleven. He was flushed with ale and two hours later than he had promised.

The following evening Tom was again crouching in the roughly-made shelter with the oilskin over the top. His feet and hands were numb with cold but he might have dozed off for a bit because some sound or feeling seemed suddenly to rouse him and with wide eyes he peeped under the corner of the piece of sacking which served as a door. It had stopped raining and a nearly full moon shone bright and clear between the masses of speeding cloud. There was a faint sound of many hooves thudding and harness clinking as if a large number of horses were passing by some distance away and then much nearer and then faded.

In his terror-struck perplexity Tom had stopped breathing and now his chest began to heave and fall as he gasped for breath. His heart was pounding. He dropped the corner of the sack and cowered back against the boards praying that his father would come soon. It seemed hours later that he heard the familiar voice singing lustily

> Oh, I'm going away from my Nancy Bell,
> Away to a far countree, tree, tree,
> Away to a far countree.

Tom crept forward and peeped out and, as soon as he could distinguish his father's figure, walking with the exaggerated care of intoxication, he ran to him.

'Well, well, well! What's this, son? Has someone been around?'

'No. Yes. I don't know.'

'Did they try to get the timber?'

'No.'

'Well, they certainly affrighted you. Your teeth is chattering. Did you see who it were?'

Tom shook his head vigorously.

'Would you walk back with me a bit, Father?'

'Aye, if that's what you want.'

Tom wouldn't go up to the Heath again until Saturday. He only confided in Sarah, whose eyes opened so wide they seemed to fill her face.

'What do you think they were?'

'I dunno.'

'Ghosts? Were there footmarks from the horses?'

'I didn't go to look. Well, it were night, weren't it?' he said defensively.

'But the moon was shining.'

'*You* wouldn't have gone out looking if you'd been there.'

'I'll come up tomorrow with you.'

'Mam won't let you.'

'I'll get out after I go up to bed, when she goes for her beer.'

Tom and John set up the posts on Saturday afternoon.

'This damn sand don't hold anything steady,' grumbled John. 'We'll have to wedge them in with sandstones. It's a mercy there's plenty of them around.'

They began to nail on the planks they had sawn to size the previous Sunday. They worked until it was too dark to see and then John said he'd go off for a tankard.

'You'd best stay here, lad. Saturday night's always a bad one for strangers being abroad.'

Tom was reluctant.

'Don't be silly, lad. There's Mary and Harry Nursall

within shout. Anyone moving about you just holler. That will send them packing.'

Tom occupied himself with re-arranging the shelter in a corner of the new building. The moon was brilliant but its blue light was eerie and the deep dark shadows seemed to change their shape just perceptively – now larger as if advancing on him, now retreating as he turned fearfully towards them. Each birch thicket and tangle of briar or bramble seemed menacingly alive as if concealing some malignant presence waiting its chance.

He thought he heard a cry. He froze in the centre of a clearing near the four posts and, to his horror, heard crackling bracken and breaking twigs as a small figure broke through the bushes and pelted towards him. He flung out his arms for protection and the thing fell into them, sobbing convulsively.

'Sare!'

'Tom! I thought I heard them horses coming.'

They clung to each other and felt infinitely braver than they had done.

A day or two later, Sarah and Tom came home to find Eliza and the children out. It was hardly any warmer inside than on the street so they huddled together over the smouldering heap of twigs and turf trying to soak up every bit of warmth that escaped.

'I'se that cold, Tom,' said Sarah plaintively.

He unbuttoned his jacket and pulled her inside it, pressed to his side.

'Let's pretend it's summer. Do you remember going up the sandy lane to Leighton Hollow on that real hot day?' asked Sarah.

'Yeah.'

'Do you remember me sliding down the sandy banking over and over and getting me backside and pinny all yeller and you saying Mama would be cross?'

'Yeah, and then ol' Mr Lee chased us off from by his

cottage. He was shouting fit to burst and waving one of them besoms what he makes.'

'Yeah. It were ever so hot. We were all of a sweat when we stopped running,' sighed Sarah, happily.

'And he were still hollering. Just standing and hollering. He must be wrong in the head,' surmised Tom.

'He lives by himself. Perhaps he's murdered someone.' Sarah's eyes dilated in agreeable horror.

'No, silly. That's what you said then. 'Spose he just likes living on his own and not having no-one keep asking him nothing.'

'Would you like to live on your own, Tom?'

'Shouldn't mind.'

'You'd let me live with you, Tom, shouldn't you?'

'I shouldn't be on me own if you were there.'

'No, but you'd like it better, wouldn't you?'

'Girls is always asking things!' said Tom crossly.

Sarah looked hurt and kept quiet for a few seconds.

'Do you remember that den we made when we'd run away from ol' Mr Lee? Do you see, it was exactly where you and Father are building our cottage?' They considered gravely how this made the site peculiarly propitious.

'Remember, we scraped out a really big hole with them sandstones and the sand were so dry it kept falling back in as fast as we put it out until we got down more?'

'Yeah! It kept doing that with them post holes Father and me was digging.'

'And all round was that lovely short grass, as green as green and covered with dry rabbit droppings what look like little marbles and the banks at the edge were full of rabbit holes with great big piles of yeller sand what they'd dug out. How do they do it with them little paws?'

'They just keeps on all night doing it. They never does it in the day.'

'An' remember them tiny little white flowers what grew right against the sand where the grass was thin and

53

them yeller flowers like small dandelions what I put in my pin-a-sight? Remember them, Tom?'

'Yeah.' Tom shook his head in boredom but Sarah's vivid recollections brooked no discouragement.

'That were a good pin-a-sight. I got the bits of glass from that fallen-down cottage up New Town and I got them red smelly flowers what sound like sneezing from Mrs Brown's wall on East Street. I had to tear the petals up because they was too big and I made a little house with them and made the yeller and the white petals like flowers in the garden and Mrs Munn gave me the bit of brown paper to cover it up.'

'You didn't get many pins for looking at it though,' said Tom disparagingly.

'I got seven,' replied Sarah indignantly. 'Mrs Allen looked and gave me one as we was coming back down the lane and then Betty Lunnon and Meggy Jenkins were playing with theirs on Aspley Hill and we took them to that big house at the top and the lady at the back door give us two pins each, and I found one on the Square.'

'An' then you went and dropped it and broke it and came home booing.'

'I gave Mama the pins. P'raps I'll make another one next summer.'

'I shan't have time to go with you next summer, Sare.'

'Why?'

'I'll be working for money like Father.'

'I'll work too.'

'What can you do?' laughed Tom.

'I can make straw plaits.'

'They'd say you was too little.'

'I can help you,' said Sarah triumphantly.

'You're a girl!'

'So what! So what! Clever sticks!' shouted Sarah, disengaging herself and jumping up.

'All you can do is play them silly girls' games.'

'Boys can't remember the words to play them. They're soft-heads and donkeys!'

'Sarah! Stop shouting at Tom this minute! Go out!' cried Eliza. She had been 'wooding' and held a large bundle of sticks under one arm and Bobby's hand in her free one. Bobby's plump red cheeks were puffed out and his rotund little body was tied up in such a large shawl that he resembled nothing so much as a suet pudding clanger ready for the pot, thought Sarah. His podgy pink fingers clasped a few sticks to his front and Tize was embracing an awkward bundle of them in her arms.

'You two could be away doing some'at useful like wooding instead of moping round the hearth,' grumbled Eliza, but this suggestion was lost on Sarah who had already slipped away. She retrieved the frayed piece of rope that Martha Lyle had trimmed off her clothes line, which she kept hidden in a pile of stones at the back, and skipped off down Church Lane in search of her friends. She found them and with two turning the three ropes tied together and one skipping, they withdrew into a secure make-believe world of garbled history which had comforted untold thousands of children for as many centuries as little girls have skipped.

> Queenie, Queenie Caroline
> Dipped her hair in turpentine,
> Turpentine to make it shine.
> Queenie, Queenie Caroline.
> Salt! Mustard! Vinegar! Pepper!
> Salt! Mustard! Vinegar! Pepper!

CHAPTER 9

Sorting Out the Dispute

Just before eleven o'clock on the following Thursday John Shinfield, the groom at Wavendon Rectory, and a stable lad were helping the Visiting Committee to dismount and leading the horses away. The Reverend Jenkins, a plump ebullient man with a very red face, greeted his Aspley colleague jovially.

'Well, well, Hugh. You look flourishing. How's the hunting season going?'

'Not too bad. We had two draws last week, but we've missed you,' replied Devereux.

'Yes. I shall be along in the New Year I hope. It's this wretched gout. The surgeons don't seem to know what to do, drat them. "Stop eating and drinking anything that you enjoy" they say. Now what good is that to a man, I ask you?

'Hallo, Mr Hall. Nice to see you, sir. And Farmer Green and Farmer Miller. Well done.'

He patted them on the shoulder and shook hands.

'You must all come in for a wee noggin before we start. Is this everyone from your parish?'

'Yes. Vaughan and Dudley send their apologies. Trade has to go on, of course,' said Devereux.

After a glass of mulled wine, Jenkins climbed into his pony chaise and the others remounted and set off for the disputed field. The groom and stable lads followed on foot. Once there, Devereux unfolded a copy of the 1761 ordnance map and Miller produced a half-furlong rope. Hannah Bates joined the group standing in the centre of the field. She was a well-built upstanding woman in her early forties with a gleaming plait of dark hair wound round the crown of her head. Her coal-black eyes were

56

steady as she stood with arms folded to see how things would turn out. This seemed to have an unnerving effect on the men, who fumbled and dropped their measures.

'Here is the parish boundary you see, Cecil,' said Devereux, 'and the scale is clear, one inch to two furlongs. This is the southern edge running by the brook, so it's just a matter of measuring out from here to the western boundary which appears to be that hedge on the map.'

Joseph Locke had appeared at Devereux's side. He was a stooping arthritic-looking man, some fifty years old, with a drooping tawny moustache.

'Yer map ain't right then, your Reverence. The boundary ain't so far from the brook.'

Devereux looked down at him with distaste.

'Well we must measure it. The scale is undoubtedly correct, and we can't argue about where the brook is,' interposed Jenkins hurriedly.

'Aye. Git it measured due west from the brook,' said Hannah Bates firmly.

One of the stable lads produced a rod and the Wavendon contingent, supervised by Locke, began to measure across the field. The Aspley group did likewise a few yards away and Hannah Bates watched them disdainfully.

'Yer map's all wrong,' muttered Joseph Locke.

'Oh, no, Mr Locke. My grandfather farmed these fields and I've walked the parish boundary with him many a time as a boy. It's that hedge all right,' said Farmer Miller.

'Aye! It be there right enough,' confirmed a toothless octogenarian who had joined the disputants with a couple of his friends.

'It were there in *my* grandfer's time and that takes you back far enough, don't it, Mr Locke?' he called heartily as Locke stumped off, muttering darkly.

'Well, that should settle this nonsense once and for

all, I hope,' said Hannah Bates loudly. 'And I should like a proper apology for 'pounding my cow, Rector.'

'Well, yes, Miss Bates. All most unfortunate. I am sure you'll get a letter from Mr Dickinson about that.'

'And the fine?' she demanded.

'You clearly won't have to pay that, and you've got your cow back,' reasoned the Rector cajolingly.

'She missed a milking and she's been down by half a gallon ever since. The best milker in the parish she were, too,' scolded Miss Bates.

Rector Jenkins smiled and shook his head in the most conciliatory manner as he withdrew discreetly towards his chaise.

'See you gentlemen at the Red Lion for lunch,' he whispered as he passed Devereux and Hall.

'It's all you can expect from a gypsy!' Locke's voice sounded faintly across the field.

'At least *I* know who my father were,' shouted back Hannah Bates.

CHAPTER 10

The Landlord's Visit

By mid-January, the wooden cottage on the Heath was nearly completed. The evenings were beginning to draw out and Tom was busy as long as there was light to see by. He always hurried home at dusk unless Sarah was with him but they had not heard or seen any sign of the ghostly riders since November. Towards the end of the month a mild spell set in and the children began to plan the garden.

'A long line of raspberries by the bank here, Tom, and apple trees at the top end,' said Sarah.

'Where are you going to get raspberries and apple trees from?' asked Tom smiling.

'Mrs Hall p'raps.'

'Miss Hall,' corrected Tom. 'You can't ask her, Mam wouldn't like it.'

'She don't have to know.'

Tom looked helplessly at her determined sullen little face. He had an uncomfortable feeling that this was not how girls were meant to behave. She ought to let him decide things but she always thought of everything first. She was tiny too, not nearly as strong as him but she never seemed to care and you can't fight girls. He wondered what Jeff Brown would do if his sister behaved like Sare. Jeff was nearly two years older than Tom and a strapping big youth. Tom went on to imagine what Jeff Brown would do if he had Sare for a sister instead of soft little Rosemary; would he put her down and make her behave properly? Just for one moment Tom doubted the prowess of his idol but such conjectures were too imaginative to occupy his mind for long.

'Well, I suppose we can start digging trenches and holes and see what we can find to go in them. We must have some muck. This sand's no good without that.' Tom spoke with the authoritative air of a veteran gardener.

'There's a big heap by Mrs Munn's pigsties.'

'She keeps it for her bit of land. Harry Kilpin does it for her.'

'She'd never notice if we only took a bit each time.'

Tom's mouth dropped open in astonishment.

'What, take it without asking?'

'She's going to learn me lace-making so each time I go I can put a bit over the fence, where it's broken, then we'll bring something along to put it in – like a sack from Farmer Green's and we'll come that way up to the Heath each night.'

Sarah's plan worked pretty well but they had to bury

each consignment of pig manure before their father saw it and Tom's life became a misery of concealment.

'I'll dig a patch over for the 'tatoes this Sunday,' declared John as the three of them stood surveying the plot.

'Which patch, Father?' asked Sarah innocently.

'Well, don't matter too much. Just where Tom's made a start will do, I reckon.'

'We was going to put rasps in there. Why don't you do a new bit over here.'

'Ha, ha! Where are the raspberry canes coming from may I ask, madam?' asked John.

'Someone might be thinning out,' said Sarah.

John turned away chuckling.

Sarah rounded on Tom.

'Why do you have to let your face go all red like that?' she hissed.

'What's in the sack at the back?' asked Eliza at teatime on Thursday.

'A bit of muck,' muttered John defensively.

'Did Farmer Green give it you?'

'Well, not exactly. He's got so much he won't miss that bit.'

'You see you don't get into trouble. If he's got so much he ought to spare you a bit if you asked.'

'He'd want to know what I wanted it for then, wouldn't he?'

Eliza sighed.

'He's got to know sooner or later. We can't just flit with no-one noticing that we've gone.'

'The sooner we flits the sooner it can all be made proper. When shall it be, gal?'

'Not 'till there's some'at to eat up there!'

'Why don't you just come up and look, Liza? The cottage is nearly finished. It's big you know; bigger than here at any rate. We've only got the chimney to do when

60

I can get some bricks. Just think of having your *own* cottage.'

'Yes, yes. It will be fine I'm sure. The thing that's bothering me is if they stop hiring you. There'll be nothing at all to live on then.'

'We won't need rent.'

Eliza sighed. Mr Barnstable would come tomorrow. She had put him off last week, promising him two weeks' rent now and she barely had enough for one. She daren't tell John. He'd say she shouldn't have paid Martha Lyle back, but friends were friends and even though she wasn't pressing, Eliza knew full well she couldn't afford to be without any longer.

'Where are the bricks coming from then, John?'

'Oh, I know some chaps . . . Jim Holton works at the brick kilns down Lower End way.'

'They'll want paying for them won't they?'

'Not much,' John muttered. He knew with bricks fetching a half-penny apiece he shouldn't have much confidence in pub-promises of gifts . . .

'Ah – Johnny – Don't you worry. I'll see you're all right for a few bricks,' bawled Jim, well in his cups. A murmur of beery approbation ran through the tap room at The Bell and Jim glowed . . .

Farmer Green was putting up some new stabling. He'd had a four-ox waggon deliver a load of bricks from Ridgemont only that afternoon. It was a sore temptation for John Ruddock.

About three o'clock the following afternoon there was a tap on the door. Eliza's stomach turned to stone.

'Oh, Mr Barnstable! Do come in, sir.'

'Good afternoon, Mrs Ruddock. I trust I find you well again?'

'Oh yes, sir. Pretty fair.' After an awkward pause she added, 'Would you like a pot of Yarb beer, sir? It's some of Mrs Lyle's and she *do* make it good . . . Our

Sarah's learning to make lace with ol' Mrs Munn and she's getting on ever so well. She has such nimble fingers, does our Sare.'

Eliza prattled on in a gossipy way that was quite unlike her as she fetched the bottle and two small cans.

'In fact, she's already made two sets of edgings, did you ever! Mrs Munn's going to sell them for her next week. She says she's never known a child learn so quick. She's a very sharp little soul, our Sarah, and she's only just ten.'

Barnstable accepted the beer and sighed. He knew these symptoms well. He wasn't a hard man but it did no-one any good to be soft-hearted in his profession, least of all with the poorer tenants. If the rent was not there one week it would be twice as hard to find it the next and if that went on how did he feed his own family? It was a hard profession.

'Tom, that's our eldest, he's just started straw plaiting for the hat factory at Leighton. Mr Cox will be over next week collecting up the lengths. Do you know the factory, Mr Barnstable? They say he has ever so many girls working there.'

'Oh yes, he has about forty, I believe. They don't get much of a wage and to see all the town youths hanging about outside makes me think most of them girls need watching better than they are. It's not a place I'd let *my* daughters go to.'

'Oh dear no!' exclaimed Eliza in a shocked tone. 'Still, there can't be no harm in straw plaiting.'

'That's not everyone's view, Mrs Ruddock,' said Barnstable weightily. Eliza was taken aback by the fervent expression of offended morality on her land-lord's face. She remembered hearing that he was a lay-preacher at Mount Pleasant Methodist Chapel and real-ized that she had probably innocently hit upon an ideal ploy for delay; not that it would do her much good, of course. There would be no more money in the lustre sugar basin unless she could keep him talking there for several days.

'No?' she asked encouragingly.

'No, certainly not! There was an article in the *Chronicle* written by the Vicar of St Mary's, Bedford, only last month. He said how disagreeable it was to see the way young girls as well as youths were taking up straw plaiting and found time to loiter in country lanes *together*. He said how much healthier it was for our youths to work on the land, which resulted in *decent* bodily exhaustion. They can earn too much money, you see, Mrs Ruddock. It is not good for young girls to be independent of their parents before they marry. The female is not a well-regulated creature. It is most essential that she be guided, you see.'

Mr Barnstable had become quite flushed, drawing closer and closer to Eliza to press his points home. He moved his stool back now, looking a trifle embarrassed. He realized that he had been carried away in his condemnation of the moral degeneracy which the hat-trade encouraged in the younger generation. Eliza couldn't help a fleeting thought that such earning capacity might alleviate their mothers' moral indignation a bit.

'Well, that's why I decided to set Sarah on to the lacemaking, though it don't earn nearly so much.' This should make a good impression.

Barnstable cast about in his mind for references to the moral vicissitudes inherent in lacemaking but he couldn't recall any. He also cast a suspicious glance at his Yarb beer can which Eliza had gently refilled twice as he was talking.

'I do hope this is not an intoxicating beverage, Mrs Ruddock?'

'Oh no! Well, not really strong as you'd sort of notice, like,' simpered Eliza most untruthfully. 'Have one more glass, it's such a raw day and they say it's wonderfully

63

good for keeping out the cold.' He acquiesced absent-mindedly as he opened up his rent-book and began to turn the pages. It didn't seem as clearly set out as usual. The figures were tending to slip from one column to another and back again. He peered more closely and took a mouthful or two more of the Yarb beer.

Eliza braced herself for the final confrontation.

'Now this rent, Mrs Ruddock. I believe you are going to pay me two weeks today. That will be four and sixpence, and threepence owing from the week before last makes it four and . . . and . . .' He found it difficult to fix his mind. He wondered if he had caught a chill.

'Well, it's just a little bit ockard because I had to pay Martha Lyle a bit of money I owed her and half pence a day for Sarah to Betty Munn and I had to give Cecil Higgins one and sixpence for learning Tom which is all worthwhile, you see, because they will get it back soon in work, like I said. In fact Mr Higgins said he would be able to sell Tom's first plaits next week when Mr Cox comes but what with all that extra and Tize having some stockings knit because she'd growed out of them and I just ain't been able to do it what with the baby, and . . .' her voice faltered.

'How much have you got, Mrs Ruddock?' he asked testily, but his voice was slightly slurred.

'I've got two shillings and twopence right here ready.' She reached down the sugar basin and counted out the coins with alacrity.

'It won't do, Mrs Ruddock! It won't do! I let you off last week and it's going from bad to worse, isn't it?'

Eliza raised her red-rimmed eyes to him appealingly.

'I'll have the children's earnings next week, sir.'

'How about that husband of yours? If he weren't lifting his elbow down at The Bell each evening you'd have a bit more for me, wouldn't you?'

'John don't spend much, sir. He only has a half pint

of beer each night and he's had some extra expenses just now too.'

Barnstable raised his brow interrogatively but she just turned her head aside.

'I am a foolish soft-hearted man, Eliza Ruddock, and I am bound to suffer for my weakness. If I take this now, I must have four and tenpence and not one halfpenny less a week tomorrow, else I shall have to send the bailiffs round.'

'Oh, thankee so much, sir. I'll have it next week come what may. It's very good of you, sir.' She slipped him a little bob-curtsey by way of gratitude and farewell and as she rose he chucked her under the chin in quite a familiar manner.

'I'm a *very* foolish man,' he said.

Eliza peeped round the doorframe to watch his slightly unsteady progress up the High Street towards his next tenant. Her fingers were touching her chin and there was a look of astonishment on her face.

'Well I never! Fancy being so beholden to Martha's Yarb beer. She'll laugh her head off when I tells her.'

As she was standing there, Sarah slipped in unobtrusively.

'She's bin a-listening to all that by the door,' thought Eliza, but Sarah just sat down on a log by the hearth and hugged her knees, saying nothing.

Eliza desperately needed some flour to make batter, since there was no chance of buying a loaf of bread that week.

'Sarah, pop over to Mr Elliott and see if we can have four-pennyworth of flour chalked up. Ask him real nice, love.' She didn't suggest when it could be paid back because she already owed him fivepence. If that failed, maybe Sarah could take a cup round to Mrs Munn and borrow some. Eliza hadn't asked her for anything for a bit but they were all so nearly in the same state of need that to borrow off neighbours was a last resort.

'There's no shame in being poor, but it's a great inconvenience,' was the local saying.

CHAPTER 11

The Disgrace of John Ruddock

The following week John began coming in for his tea an hour later than usual. Eliza was uneasy but forbore from asking about it.

Day by day a small pile of bricks grew in the corner of the wooden cottage on the Heath.

'Where's he getting them from?' Tom asked Sarah.

'It must be something like Mrs Munn's pig muck,' said Sarah cryptically.

Tom looked shocked.

'Well, he said Farmer Green had got three ox-waggons of bricks, didn't he?'

'There'll be trouble if Green catches him,' said Tom.

'Yes,' agreed Sarah grimly.

The day after this conversation, John was laid off at half past two, which didn't displease him because he had a small bag of cement tucked under some sacks in a dark corner of the barn and he could hardly wait to fetch it and get off to the Heath to start building the chimney stack.

'Well, there's one thing I don't need to thieve and that's the sand,' he chuckled as he made his way to the barn.

'May as well slip in one or two bricks,' he thought and cautiously crept up to the pile. He had always taken them under cover of darkness but the yard seemed deserted. He quickly dropped four bricks into his sack, shouldered it and slipped back to the barn. He bent down to uncover the cement and paused, thinking he heard a footfall, but there was no sound so he added the bag to the sack and strode to the barn door. One step outside he found Farmer Green waiting beside him. He turned panic-stricken and found Jones, the farm bailiff, standing on the other side of him.

'Let's see what you've got in your sack, Ruddock,' demanded Green.

'T'only odds and ends, a bit of wood and rest of my baviour,' said John sullenly.

'Right! No harm us seeing then.' Green nodded to Jones who stepped forward, took the sack from John's trembling hand and tipped it out on the ground.

'I can see why you didn't finish your dinner if that's what your wife gives you,' said Green sarcastically. 'How long has this been going on, eh? How many of my bricks have you had?'

The colour ebbed and flowed in John's face as he glowered from one to the other of them like a cornered animal.

'We'll have to see what the Magistrate's got to say about this. This is what all your grand ideas about the rights of working men come to, is it? I suppose your friends at The Bell would be proud of you, and that good-for-nothing wife of yours.'

Ruddock swore and swung his arm back to punch Green in the face, but Jones caught it and hung on until he was felled by a chest blow from Ruddock's free arm. Ruddock was a powerful man and half as heavy again as Jones, so Green expected serious damage and Ruddock took to his heels, leaving the farmer bending over the stricken man.

Tom and Sarah found him huddled in a corner of the new cottage with his head between his knees when they went up to the Heath after work.

'What's the trouble, Father?' asked Tom diffidently. John groaned. 'Are you all right?' John shook his head.

The children exchanged helpless glances and sat down

by him to wait. After a bit he raised his head and muttered:

'I've lost me job.'

'Why?' asked Sarah.

'Green caught me with some bricks and stuff.'

'You'll get work with someone else,' said Sarah encouragingly.

'I think I've killed Jones.'

A look of horror passed over Tom's face.

'What, the Farm Bailiff?' asked Sarah incredulously.

John nodded.

'What did you do to him?' she asked.

'Knocked him down as hard as I could.'

'Did he look dead?'

'Didn't stop to see.'

'I shouldn't think he's dead. Come on, Tom!' she cried, jumping to her feet. 'We'll go back to the village and find out, Father. We'll come back straight away.'

John threw his head back to rest on the wall in a gesture of relief, eyes half closed. He was a handsome man by village standards, with a straight nose, red full lips and cheeks and dark arching brows partly hidden by unruly straight black hair.

'Little Sare's that quick-witted she'll grow up a very capable woman,' he thought appreciatively.

As they reached the square they saw a knot of women talking excitedly and their mother just going into the cottage door with Bobby in her arms and Tize clinging tearfully to her skirt. They ran up, panting for breath. She looked haggard with anxiety.

'Where's your father? Do you know?'

'Up the Heath,' they whispered together.

'He's knocked Jones the Bailiff down.'

'Is he hurt bad?' asked Sarah.

'No, just bruised, which is a mercy for us, I suppose. Do you know what he were up to?'

Tom and Sarah exchanged wary looks.

'Well, I'm bound to find out. *They* all know,' Eliza said bitterly, nodding towards the group of women in the square.

'Green caught him with some bricks,' said Sarah.

'Just as I guessed. The man's a fool.'

The children were shocked to hear her say that, although her looks often conveyed it.

'I knew this Heath business would lead to trouble. How can I pay the rent next week? What are we going to eat? What's to happen to him?'

'We'll think of something,' muttered Sarah uncertainly.

They went into the cottage and tied up the door. Eliza sat down on her stool, covering her face with one hand, elbow on table, while she comforted Tize with the other.

'I don't know who we can ask.'

'Miss Hall,' suggested Sarah.

'No. They've done enough for us and this will mean serious trouble in the Vestry. We mustn't ask them.'

There was a tap on the door.

'See to it, Sare,' said Eliza wearily.

'It's Mrs Lyle, Mama.'

'Oh, Martha! Come in.'

Martha Lyle was a tall, imposing woman of indeterminate age, probably about fifty. She wore her tawny hair in a bun and had a robust reassuring manner.

'Sorry to hear about the trouble, Liza.'

'I just don't know what to do.'

'Where is he now?'

'Up the Heath.'

'He'd best stay there for a bit and you don't tell anybody. Say you don't know where he's gone.' She looked hard at the two older children. 'Remember that. You don't know where yer father is.'

'Where can he stay? He ain't done the hearth and chimney yet.'

'Will the Lunnons or the Nursalls have him?'

69

'I dunno. Don't want to get nobody into trouble.'

'They could keep quiet easy enough. No-one knows much of what goes on among all them trees and bushes up there. Perhaps he'll arrange something for himself.'

'Not John, no,' replied Eliza curtly, 'and what about us? I'll owe Mr Barnstable three weeks' rent next Saturday and Mr Elliott ninepence.'

'Don't worry, dearie. You just stay here and I'll be back with a nice hot cup of tea and we'll think out something. We've both got a decent thinking piece on our shoulders, Eliza Ruddock, and we've still got some bottles of Yarb beer.'

Eliza smiled weakly.

'You're a good friend, Martha.'

'Just going up the Heath, Mama,' said Sarah as she and Tom got to their feet.

'Wait! Better take him some baviour. I've got two oatcakes and a little bit of cheese. Come straight back.'

'Yes, Mama.'

The new cottage was empty when they reached it but they hung about outside the strange collection of abandoned vehicles and clutter which surrounded the Nursall home. Harry soon noticed them and called them in.

Mary Nursall came out to greet them. She was rather ineffectual about her dress and house management. In fact, when she lived in the village it was a standing joke that when one of the women apologized for the untidiness of her home, the visiting friend would say 'Well it bain't in quite such a sorry state as Mary Nursall's, dearie,' and they would both giggle, but not unkindly because Mary was well known for her generous, happy nature.

'We're looking after him, my dears. Come along in and see him.'

At that moment she looked as if she had been disturbed while getting up and certainly before she had done her hair or got her felted woolly jacket on properly. It was off one shoulder and half way down her arm.

John Ruddock was huddled in front of the fire and looked up sheepishly as they were shown in.

'We've brought you some baviour, Father and Mr Jones is all right, just bruised,' said Tom.

'Ah, she's heard then?' They nodded.

'What will become of us?' he said, shaking his head miserably.

'It'll blow over,' said Harry. 'Give it a fortnight and you won't hear no more. It were only four bricks and a pound or two of cement. They won't take you before the Magistrate for that.' Harry would probably be a few years older than his wife, and rising sixty. He was handy at most things and earned their keep with a bit of jobbing gardening, joinery and general repair jobs. He never worked any longer than he needed and kept them in vegetables and eggs from the bit of ground he'd cleared around their home. The main room they were all in was roofed over with an assortment of timber planks covered in heather thatch and it rested on a variety of old conveyances and huts which had been used with great ingenuity to form the 'other services' of the homestead. Sarah had long admired this ingenuity from the outside where it resembled the stored contents in the end of a farm barn, and she was enthralled by the inside.

One side room, probably the kitchen, was formed by an upside-down farm waggon supported on old wooden boxes and crates which also served as cupboards. The room on the other side was what must have once been a very handsome coach with an ebony finish, bearing a coat of arms on the door. Its steps were permanently down now and supplemented by a box on the floor.

'That's our bedroom,' said Mary proudly as she followed Sarah's gaze and watched her eyes grow wide with astonishment.

'Yes! There's room you see because Harry's sawn out these flaps under the winders and they lets down when we go to bed.'

She demonstrated on one side and a rolled up pallet lying on the coach seat obediently uncurled on to the hinged flap, allowing an absurd clutter of objects to roll out on to the floor.

'Oh dear! Such a muddle,' sighed Mary.

Sarah quickly bent down to retrieve a boot, an assortment of single socks and other small garments, a few onions, a ladle and a gingerbread mould. Mary gathered up the rest. The pallet was rolled up, the flap replaced and the escapees were tossed in at the coach door to repeat their journey later in the evening, Sarah guessed. There was a prodigious amount of storage space between the wheels of the coach which was crammed to overflowing with such a strange assortment of useful things that Sarah could distinguish nothing in particular.

One of the remaining walls of the living-room was taken up by a fireplace, and a broken settle which looked as if it must have started life in a pot-house, and on the other side was the porch through which they had entered. It was an old hen-house, the nesting boxes making exceedingly useful places to store small items like stoneware jars of preserves and salt, fruit, vegetables, sickles, clippers and an incongruous shoed horse hoof containing pens and inkpot.

The floor was probably virgin sand but it was covered by a layer of dead bracken which ensured that smaller straying objects were rarely found. The furniture was a cluttered-up table, three stools and a few upturned boxes.

Mary and Harry had no children.

'What do you think of our house, then, Sarah?' asked Harry, his blue eyes twinkling in the rushlight.

'It's lovely. I've never seen one like it.'

'I'm sure thou baint,' chuckled Harry.

'Do you know where our front door is?'

'No.'

'It's t'other side of the bedroom, of course. Coaches always have two doors, you know, and that's h'our family crest h'of course.' He finished the sentence in a mock 'county' drawl and laughed heartily.

Even John seemed to cheer up a bit.

CHAPTER 12

Friends in Need

The family in the tiny cottage on Aspley High Street fed better than usual the week following John Ruddock's disgrace. However poor one's own lot, it is morale-boosting to slip along to an even needier neighbour and insist that they accept a little bit of this or that left-over because 'it's bound to be going off if it baint be eaten this very evening.' The bread-line economy of this little community seemed to foster an amazing solidarity, embracing all the working people, providing they never gave themselves airs about being any better off than their neighbours. The general feeling was definitely against nonconformity of any sort. A child that won a prize for exceptionally good progress at school was discouraged almost as much as one who was found shoplifting. To be exceptional in any way was seen as courting adversity and this is what condemned John Ruddock in the eyes of the village community. John and his friends who sat at the big round table in the taproom of The Bell each evening were 'askin' for trouble "stirring the pot" like that.' They should 'let sleeping dogs lie' or 'not go interfering in those things which don't concern them and nothing can't be done about anyway.'

Fortunately this attitude didn't stop a lot of neighbourly support for Eliza.

'Baint really her fault. She didn't know how he'd turn out when she married him.'

Like all reformers, the patrons of the round table at The Bell viewed this as a sign of stupid ingratitude on the part of those they were trying to help. The group was one short all the evenings of that week and they shook their heads despondently over Ruddock.

'It were a daft thing for him to do. 'E knows what a regular tartar ol' Farmer Green be,' said George Dunne.

'It were dafter to get caught.'

'It gives the Movement a bad name having fellows like that in it.'

'He shouldn't need to go thieving to live. That's what the Movement's all about,' replied George.

'Until Parliament abolishes the Corn Laws good and proper there'll be no improvement. Do you know one loaf of bread costs a quarter of a man's wage and in our grandfathers' time it only cost a twelfth? That's what Cobbett's Register says. I've got last week's here,' said the earnest young man called Dilks, who was studying at the Institute.

'He says it's partly because of them Irishmen what have been brought in to work cheap.'

'Do it say anything about these new-fangled machines, eh Jerry?' asked Dicken.

'Aye. It says they've been breakin' up threshing machines in Kent and then they went on and burnt the ol' magistrate's ricks just to learn him.'

'Good luck to them,' chuckled Philip.

'They may get strung up when they're caught,' mused Dicken.

'They'll get a trip to New South Wales out of it for sure,' said George.

'Peel's sent in cavalry in Sussex, all the way from

Dorchester and there's three regiments of dragoons in Kent,' said Jerry.

'Aye, they're taking it seriously at last and do they give us a living wage? Nay! They bring in the military. The money they're spending on them with the free quarters and their dead weight pensions would have set all to rights for a bit.'

'They deserve a revolution,' said Jerry. 'I mean we ain't wanting violence but when they act like that I'm sure tempted to yearn for their blood if that's the only way they understand.'

'It will all be *our* blood, Jerry,' sighed George Dunne.

'Aye, lad. It always is,' confirmed Philip.

Their discussion was interrupted by the entrance of Green and Dudley who strode up to the bar, scrutinizing the group as they went. They were never seen in The Bell and everyone knew they had just left a Select Vestry meeting in The Swan and been sent in search of Ruddock. They ordered beer and leant against the bar looking as innocent as they could, but an uneasy silence settled on the taproom, broken only by the clearing of a throat, the knocking out of a pipe and someone spitting noisily into the hearth.

Eventually Dudley cleared his throat and, as if addressing the room in general, asked:

'Can anyone tell me where to find John Ruddock? I've a special message to give him.' He looked towards the round table for an answer. They shook their heads and muttered negatively to each other. The Register-reader, Dilks, said boldly:

'No, Mr Dudley. No-one here has seen him for nigh on a week,' which was perfectly true but not necessarily the answer to the question. Dudley knew he'd get no better answer, so they drained their tankards and left.

'I know where they'll start looking next,' said George Dunne darkly.

'Aye. I just hope he's got enough sense to make himself scarce and not get nobody into trouble up there.'

'Maybe we should warn him.'

'How? No sense in tramping up. It will only lead them in.'

'Tell his children. Tell Tom or Sarah. Sarah's an amazing quick little wench, my wife says. *She'll* be careful.'

'Best tell Eliza Ruddock and leave it to her. She be a sensible 'ooman.'

'The Vestry's going to start evicting up the Heath if they find an excuse. It's said they've bin talking about it awhile. It's Devereux the old d . . .' He only mouthed the epithet silently and the rest snorted with shocked amusement.

Old George was right, because the very next morning at half-past eight Harry Nursall sighted Green, Dudley and Miller riding among the furze bushes on the Heath. Sarah and Tom had been up at half-past six and gone back to start their day's work with a plateful of Mary's slightly burnt porridge in their bellies. Harry knew the men would find no sign of Ruddock but he didn't want them nosing about his homestead, so he was digging the Ruddocks' garden when the three found the new cottage.

'Good morning, Mr Nursall,' called Miller cheerily.

'Good morning to yer Farmer Miller, and you sirs.'

'Whose garden are you digging, then?'

''Tis mine.'

'Oh, what's happened to your old place?'

'Oh, it be getting a bit de-lapp-ee-dated,' (he enunciated the word carefully) 'so I'm giving my wife a surprise. Think as how she'll like it?' he asked mischievously.

They had dismounted and Dudley held the horses while the two farmers inspected the new cottage.

Bert ostentatiously followed them in.

'So *you've* built this, have you, Nursall?' asked Green suspiciously.

'Aye, of course. There ain't much I can't turn my hand to.'

'No. I've seen some of your work and I'd say the standard was much better than this,' replied Miller.

'Workin' in a hurry, yer know. Want it ready for her birthday in the spring,' said Harry, looking him levelly in the eye.

'It won't be ready without a fireplace and chimney,' said Green.

'Nay,' sighed Harry, 'them ol' bricks are that expensive – half-pence each, aren't they, Mr Green?'

Green scowled at him. There was not a brick to be seen.

'Come on. We won't find what we're seeking,' he called angrily to the others, mounting his horse and moving off.

No sooner had they gone than Harry began to whistle gaily as he went back and forth between the cottage and a circular clump of furze bushes which had a narrow opening, little more than a rabbit track, winding between to a space in the centre where about two hundred new bricks were neatly stacked. When he had retrieved fifty or so, he set to work to mix some mortar and was soon building a chimney stack with great rapidity and skill. By nightfall, the chimney was virtually finished and by the next dinner time, when Mary brought him some beer and bread, he was putting the finishing touches to the hearth.

'Well! What will Eliza Ruddock think of it then?' he asked.

'Oh, 'tis beautiful. She ought to be very pleased.'

'I told them busybodies it were for you. Are you disappointed, gal?'

'Oh, get along with you. 'Course not, Harry. I

wouldn't leave our home for anything. This is just ordinary. Very nice, I mean, for a family what's got no home, but *ordinary*.' Harry chuckled and Mary said: 'But supposing them busybodies come back? I were that frightened all day yesterday. Your sauce starting while you could still hear their horses' hooves.'

'Well, I reckon if they *do* come back it will be to pull it down and they'll have to argue that through in the Vestry, won't they? Eliza Ruddock and the children will have to move in tomorrow. Tom and Sarah said when they came up early this morning. They've got to quit before Barnstable calls for the rent tomorrow afternoon.'

'How will they manage?'

'Old George Dunne and Jerry Dilks have borrowed a handcart. It wouldn't do for me to be seen helping them, down in the village. They are going to shift out at first light to Ol' Betty Munn's place because that's off the beaten track and Barnstable won't think of looking there if he decides to raise a hue and cry, and they won't be up here until after nightfall when the hullabaloo should have died down. All bin thought out you see.'

'Yes,' said Mary doubtfully.

'You should have seen little Sarah's eyes get big as saucers when she saw the chimney and hearth nearly done.'

'They'll need to find a fire lit when they come, and some nourishment,' said Mary anxiously.

'Aye. It shouldn't really be lit till the mortar's dry, but there's no help for that. It will crack something dreadful but I s'pose we can always patch it up in the summer.'

'I can keep them fed Sunday, maybe.'

'Well, there's nothing to do about it but manage the best we can and trust to providence . . .'

'At least it won't cost them anything to keep warm up here and there'll be no rent to pay.'

Harry nodded. 'Just as long as that hot-head John

keeps out of the way for a bit and don't do nothing foolish like felling trees when he gets back. If someone starts taking live wood or poaching too conspicuous we shall all be in trouble. I'm only surprised they've let us be so long.'

'Oh, Harry. Don't say that. Suppose they pulled our place down,' said Mary tearfully.

'I'd build it up again straight away – never you fear, gal.'

'It wouldn't be the same though.'

'It would be better. I'd lay my hands on another coach and you could have a best parlour to h'entertain your friends in.'

'Aye, so you would,' smiled Mary.

Harry covered up his handywork with bits of brush-wood and heather to keep the frost off and he and Mary set off across Wavendon Heath and down Red Lane to an old wooden barn full of stored hay, belonging to a farmer at Bow Brickill. There they delivered some beer, bread and a small piece of boiled bacon to John Ruddock.

'Well, it's all done, John me lad, and they'll move in tomorrow night. Ol' George Dunne and Jerry Dilks are helping them with a handcart they've borrowed,' cried Harry cheerfully.

'Oh, you're a real friend in need. I don't know how we're ever going to repay you.'

'Lie low for a bit. That's how. We'll keep our ears to the ground and see what's happening towards the end of next week and then maybe you can sneak back to your new home.'

'I'd like to see Eliza's face when she sees it,' said John sadly.

'Were you terrible cold last night?' asked Mary, changing the subject.

'Nay. Snug as snug. Hay be very comfortable stuff so

long as you have a good blanket between you and it. I'm restless, though.'

'Well, you can potter about in the frith so long as you keep away from the lane,' said Harry.

'Would you do me a favour . . . I mean, another one, of course? Could you ask Jerry Dilks to lend me some of those "Political Registers" and I'll improve myself while I'm here. Tom and Sare can bring them over.'

Harry looked doubtful. He didn't reckon reading was going to 'improve' a working man and that sort of reading might do downright harm, but he agreed to pass on the request.

Saturday morning, Tom and Sarah collected bracken for the floor, ever alert for intruders, but apart from a few groups of roaming children they saw no-one. In the afternoon they helped Mary Nursall sort some odds and ends to make the new cottage homely. They built a sort of open cupboard out of empty wooden boxes and set a couple about as seats. Mary generously gave them two matching pink lustre plates to put on the handsome brick mantle-shelf which Harry had built above the hearth.

'They'll go wonderful well with the old sugar basin,' said Sarah in delight.

She also gave them a big blue and white plate and the gingerbread mould which Harry fixed up on the wall and, later on, she came across a huge framed picture of the old King that she insisted they took.

'Well, I'd even forgot it were there under the coach so it ain't taking anything away from me, and just look here! There's a pair of ol' bellows. They've got a hole in the leather but you might be able to mend that and I reckon if you rub that ol' green dirt with some sand and water, Sarah, you'll find it's shiny brass underneath.'

Sarah's eyes shone, but she felt guilty about the terrible muddle they had created all over the Nursalls' floor. It looked as if a cyclone had gathered together a miscellaneous assortment of objects and then died just there in its tracks.

'Shall I help you tidy up, Mrs Nursall?' she asked.

'Oh no, dearie. Don't you worry. I'm quite used to it being in a bit of a muddle,' sighed Mary.

By six o'clock when the forlorn little procession arrived with the handcart, there was a fire burning brightly in the hearth, a rush light fixed to the wall, the lustre plates winking and gleaming on the mantlepiece with a passably shiny pair of brass bellows on the hearth.

'Oh my! Oh my! Oh my!' cried Eliza in delight. ''Tis so homely! Where did all these beautiful things come from? Mary Nursall! Oh, how can we ever pay her back? What a pity John ain't here when it's mostly his work.'

She sounded tearful so old George and Jerry got her bustling about supervising the unloading of the cart.

'. . . and the pallets? Oh, in here, I s'pose. Oh! Just look at the bedrooms! There's two! Oh, John! All this work.'

As soon as the table and stools were set in place, Sarah and Tom produced a covered basket Mary had given them and unpacked a round loaf of bread, the biggest slab of boiled streaky bacon they had ever set eyes on, and bottles of home-made beer. Eliza had not been allowed to leave the village empty-handed either, so they had enough food for several days.

Eliza was so overwhelmed she collapsed on to a box seat laughing and weeping at the same time.

'You are going to stay to supper, Mr Dunne and Mr Dilks? I shan't hear the word "no", not when folks have been so terrible kind to us. Sarah, run over and fetch Mr and Mrs Nursall please. Say I want them to come to supper to warm our new home and I shall be that hurt and upset if they don't. Oh, and ask them if they don't mind bringing their trenchers, and something to sit on, please.'

The party was in full swing, in fact caution had

evaporated and there was louder talking and laughter than had ever been heard on the Heath, when a tap sounded on the door.

They all froze, mouths open in mid-sentence.

The tap was repeated more loudly. Eliza's terrified eyes roved round the table and Harry was about to rise when the latch lifted and the door slowly opened.

An untidy lock of straight black hair appeared first and beneath it, John Ruddock's quizzically raised brow, and nose.

'Oh, John! Johnny!' cried Eliza rushing into his arms. 'It's lovely and I was saying over and over again what a pity you weren't here. He can stay a bit, can't he?' she appealed to Harry.

Harry exchanged glances with Mary and the other men.

'No-one will be up looking for him tonight, do you reckon?'

'Nay, surely not. If he gets away by first light it should be safe enough.'

CHAPTER 13

The New Wage-earners and Uninvited Visitors

After their guests had gone they laid Bobby and Tize to sleep on their straw pallets and Eliza was about to send Tom and Sarah in the same direction when Tom shyly drew out his first earnings from his breeches pocket and laid it reverently on the table. There was one shilling and elevenpence.

'Why, my!' cried Eliza. 'Just look at this. We have another working man in the family.'

Tom blushed with pleasure. Eliza glanced uncomfortably at John, saw his scowl and held his eye upbraidingly.

'Well, aye. That's very good, Tom. Yer mother can do with that.' He had tried hard but there was still a note of bitterness in his voice. They didn't notice Sarah but there was just a hint of resentment playing about her pointed little face, too. Mrs Munn hadn't sold her lace edgings yet. She longed to do her bit towards the family income.

The next week it was Sarah's turn. She had left the cottage about half-past six each morning with her father, who was spending the nights with them. Eliza imagined she was walking across the Wavendon Heath with him and when she arrived home tired and irritable between six and seven each evening, Eliza guessed she had been playing with her friends in the village, but Sarah wouldn't tell her. On Saturday evening Tom proudly put two shillings and fourpence on the table, explaining that although Mr Cox hadn't been over to collect up the straw plaits that week, Mr Higgins had bought them himself so that Tom had something to take home.

'I'm getting a bit faster at the plaiting,' Tom told them eagerly.

Sarah squeezed between Tom and her father and began scooping coins from her pinafore pocket and emptying them on to the table through grubby little fingers. Eliza sorted and counted them out in astonishment.

'That's two shillings and sevenpence! Where did you get it, love?' She looked worried.

'Lots of places,' said Sarah.

'Tell us exactly, Sarah.' Eliza's voice was severe and Sarah bit her lip, sticking out her chin aggressively to stop the hot tears welling up.

'Well, Mrs Munn sold my edgings for one and two-pence and Old Mrs White gave me a farthing for getting her shopping and fetching a bag of flour from the mill and Mrs Mitchell gave me a half penny for taking their Patsy over to her uncle at Water End and Farmer Miller gave me the rest for picking stones.'

'Oh Sarah, our Sare!' Eliza engulfed her in her arms. 'There was I wondering if you had stoled it and you'd been working *so* hard. It's too much, little one. We can manage without you stone picking.'

'Of course we can,' said John angrily as he slammed five shillings and sixpence down on the table

Eliza, still holding Sarah, looked at him in surprise.

'Now what have *you* been doing? I *thought* you was keeping something back.'

'I were dying of boredom in that there barn so I walked over to Wavendon and got some jobbing work with Farmer Hurst. Him that has fields out on Brickill side of village. He don't have nothing to do with Green or Miller.'

'Would you believe it! We don't need to live on charity. I have as much to manage on as I usually have now we don't need no rent.'

'What have I been telling you all these months, gal? And you had to be forced out of that hovel to come up the Heath.'

Eliza opened her mouth to say she would still rather have come up in her own time, but John's happy face stopped her.

The following week there were two unwelcome visitors to the wooden cottage, which made Eliza very uneasy about their future.

On Tuesday morning she was terrified to hear the thud of horse's hooves on sand close to the cottage door, followed by a sharp rap of a hunting crop, but she put on a brave face as she opened the door.

'Ah, good day, Mrs Ruddock,' said the Reverend Devereux, still astride his horse. 'Is your husband about?'

'No he ain't. Sorry, sir. I haven't set eyes on him for a while. I don't know where he is.'

'I see you have a nice new home.'

'Well, it ain't ours of course. Some good neighbours have bin so kind as to let us have it till John comes back because I couldn't pay the rent on the other.'

'Ha, is that so? Well, good day, Mrs Ruddock.'

Eliza compressed her lips bitterly as she watched him ride off through the bushes.

'I can't see any poor wretch going to him for help like you might have thought he were Rector for,' she said to herself.

On Thursday, Green rode up and didn't deign to dismount either. He hit the door hard with his heavy cane crop and bawled, 'Anyone in?'

Eliza threw open the door angrily. She was not a woman to be intimidated by violence. She had seen enough of it.

The two eyed each other malevolently.

'Is yer husband home?'

'No, and not likely to be. I don't know where he's gone and this ain't "home". It's just lent me by some good neighbours.'

'Umph,' he grunted disbelievingly. 'I see you've got a fireplace and chimney with a fire going. P'raps I can step in for a moment.'

'That ain't convenient, Mr Green.'

He turned his horse roughly, just touching his cap by way of farewell.

Eliza shook her head grimly.

'That spells trouble. The Vestry will be told and they'll be up evicting us, I fear. Maybe I should have let him in.'

She walked round the outside of her new dwelling looking at the chimney stack. Very little was visible above the tarred wooden roof topped with heather thatch that Harry had put on to 'keep the place cosy and

85

hide them bricks'. No, Green had merely wanted to see his new bricks and it was best that she had kept him out. There would have been no charming *that* man even with the help of Martha's Yarb beer.

The Select Vestry met that evening and Devereux began the business by referring to yet another letter from his Wavendon counterpart, the Reverend Jenkins.

'Gentlemen, I am sorry to have to tell you that we do not seem to have settled this wretched parish boundary dispute as we had hoped. There have been renewed hostilities between the contestants and other people seem to have been rather heavily inconvenienced. Perhaps you'd like to say a few words about that Mr Miller.'

'I should indeed,' said Dick Miller, flushing angrily. 'There's a whole field of my kale trampled to bits and if I hadn't have seen them straight away they'd have been all over my winter wheat as well.'

'What ever has happened? What diabolical agents do you refer to, Dick, by this ominous "them"?' inquired Vaughan with lively interest.

'Why, it's Jo Locke's beasts, that's what it is and how they came to be in my field is because Hannah Bates took down a new fence what Locke had put up across Salford Brook, allowing them to walk up or down it in any direction they pleased as if it were a regular turnpike!'

'And why did Miss Bates take Locke's fence down?' asked Vaughan, still looking confused.

'Because,' explained Devereux wearily, 'Mr Locke had got it into his stubborn head that the parish boundary ran on Miss Bates's side of the brook so he took down a bit of his hedge bounding the brook and fenced off a short section of it as a drinking place for his cattle. Miss Bates, on the other hand, reckoned the boundary ran down the middle of the stream so, without breaking *her* hedge, she removed the half of the two pieces of

86

fencing on her side of the stream and, hey presto, the cattle got into any fields which were not fenced or hedged off from the brook.'

Vaughan covered his mouth with his hand.

'You'd be laughing on the other side of yer face if they were your fields being poached up by thirty-five head of beasts in this weather. Them fields is so low-lying I can hardly run stock on them in the summer let alone the winter,' grumbled Miller.

'Sorry, Dick. Sorry, old man. It's just the way those two manage to carry on tit-for-tatting come what may, that amused me.'

'And they'll never stop, I'm afraid,' said Hall. 'I think we had better just write a sympathetic reply to poor Jenkins and hope we don't get called in again. What's been done about keeping the cattle in where they belong, I wonder?'

'I wouldn't know, but I do know that they won't be in *my* fields again because I've fenced the brook across at my boundary. Hannah Bates can do her worst as far as I'm concerned.'

'It was Jo Locke's fault for trying it on, if you ask me,' said Dudley.

'Well, don't let's start taking sides here else we certainly shall be involved,' said Devereux testily.

'Yes, let's hear all about the Ruddocks' problems now. We usually deal with the Ruddocks after Jo Locke and Hannah Bates, don't we?' said Vaughan facetiously.

It was unfortunate that Vaughan happened to be the only member of the village who had not heard about John Ruddock's disgrace, because Green, who always deplored Vaughan's frivolous manner, thought that he was making light of the affair on purpose.

He struck the table top with his fist and growled, 'That rogue must be brought before the Magistrate to answer charges of theft and assault and battery.'

'Oh dear. What have I missed?' murmured Vaughan contritely.

'Yer've missed three or four hundred of my new bricks finding their way into Ruddock's possession and my Bailiff, Jones, having the breath knocked out of him and his ribs broke by the ruffian.' Green was half standing and shouting across the table at Vaughan.

'Gentlemen! Gentlemen, please! Do let's remain calm,' appealed Devereux.

'My bricks are in that new chimney stack of his and I want them back,' snarled Green.

'I suppose we *could* pull the place down. After all, they are squatting on common land, and I've said before that we need to make an example of someone before the whole village moves up on to the Heath,' said Devereux, sounding rather more enthusiastic than he had for many Vestry meetings.

Dudley shook his head.

'At least they're off the poor relief up there and Nursall claims it's his cottage. It would be impossible to prove the bricks were yours, Fred, anyway.'

'I caught him red-handed, stealing them,' cried Green indignantly.

'Only four bricks! Well, we all know that they are probably yours but he will just insist they are Nursall's and we shan't be able to prove otherwise.'

'Hear, hear! It's better to leave them alone. At least the family is less expensive to us up there and it will give Ruddock a chance to show his worth,' said Mr Hall.

'His worth. Ha, ha! We all know *his* worth,' cried Green.

'It would be very difficult to find some men to pull the place down,' mused Devereux.

'I'll do it myself. *My* men will do as they're bid,' said Green.

'No, that wouldn't be wise. The members of the Vestry must not be directly involved.'

'I can see a way it could be done,' said Green, addressing himself to Devereux.

'No, no! We mustn't evict them. They've had enough hardship and they're doing us no harm up there,' pleaded Hall.

'No harm! What are they living on, I should like to know? Pheasants and hares, that's what. And how about all the wood in that shack? It's been felled on the Heath. That's against the law.'

'I'm sure the wood's not green. It will be made from seasoned planks.'

'Oh? How are you so sure of that, Mr Hall?' insinuated Green.

'Gentlemen! Order please! I think this meeting had better adjourn. We seem to be in poor odour tonight.'

CHAPTER 14

The Eviction

By the end of January, John Ruddock had rejoined the family and was getting a bit of jobbing work over at Wavendon now and again. Eliza was just making ends meet with John's earnings supplemented by the children's and the odd rabbit and pheasant that John 'found lying about'. These worried her so much, she would rather have done without them.

'If one of the Duke's gamekeepers catches you, John Ruddock, you'll be in jail and we'll be in the workhouse.'

'They won't catch me. There's enough game around for all of us and I ain't seen anything of them on the Heath.'

'They caught Fletcher last year, didn't they,' she replied.

Sarah and Tom visited the Red House and returned with about fifty raspberry canes, four young apple trees, two plum seedlings and a pear and a cherry. John was delighted.

'My – we'll have a regular orchard!'

Sarah supervised where they were planted and John was perplexed by the large size of the muck heap they had ready for use.

'I can't think where all this muck's come from, because I only took a couple of bags from Green. I reckon old Harry put it here for us.'

Tom and Sarah looked at each other and smiled.

Eliza had settled down and was taking a greater delight in her new house with each day that passed. Mary Nursall was forever rummaging about in her store places and then running up eagerly to the little cottage with a piece of sprigged cotton for curtains or cushions, or a little mat for the floor, and odd plates and a vase. Eliza soon gave up feeling beholden to her, since Mary got so much pleasure from watching their home grow cosier and more comfortable day by day.

'I *am* glad that you came up here, Liza. Do you know, I were really quite lonesome before, because we Heathers are so spread out and the Lunds are nice folk and Betty Inwood too, but I somehow just didn't feel I could pop in and out so free as I can with you.'

'Well, I'm glad now. It was a big risk to take but it seems to be working out all right and John's bound to get more work in the spring and summer. It's good having a place what's really your own and you and Harry have been so good to us. It do look real homely now, don't it?' Eliza carefully plumped up the cushion she had just finished sewing and put it tenderly on one of the upturned boxes.

January had been a bitter month and February came in cold and wet, but the Ruddocks were well fed and warm.

One evening, John and Eliza were sitting happily in front of a roaring fire listening to the rain beating against the shutters and the wind rattling and whining down the chimney, sending puffs of wood smoke into the room. The children were all in bed.

'It do seem a pity to go to bed with the fire burning so bright, don't it?' said Eliza.

'Aye. Let's just sit up until this log's burnt down.'

They sat quietly for a minute or two.

'Was that a voice?' asked Eliza.

'No. It'll be the wind in the birch trees.'

'No it ain't. It's nearer. It's men talking,' declared Eliza, wide-eyed with alarm.

'Aye. There *is* someone out there. Hear that! Sounds like they're carrying tools, unless it's a horse harness. I'll go out and see.'

'Be careful, John!'

'Don't be daft, gal. No-one's going to harm me.'

Eliza sat trembling for a few minutes and then she heard John's voice challenging someone. There seemed to be no reply. She rose and crept to the door.

'This is a fine time to be traipsing over the Heath with all these tools. You must be up to some'at,' shouted John indignantly.

'Aye, we be up to some'at as you shall see soon enough,' growled a gruff man's voice that she didn't recognize. She caught glimpses of a lantern flickering between men's legs. There seemed to be five or six of them.

'He says we be up ter some'at. Ha, ha, ha!' guffawed a high-pitched voice which belonged to a tall lean figure staggering in the flickering light as he leant back to drink from a bottle.

'Take that off him. He's had more than enough,' snarled the gruff voice.

'Aye. Whatever you say, master. Give it here, yer tippler,' said a slurred voice sarcastically. There was a scuffle and the taller man was relieved of the bottle by the other who put it straight to his own lips, but was immediately felled by a short stocky man who hadn't spoken. Several gutteral oaths were shouted.

'Give it up. Get on with yer work! Here, take this pick-axe and get started, yer drunken lot of oafs,' shouted the gruff voice.

Eliza, peeping through the door, was rooted to the ground in terror. Someone kicked the door open wide and the lantern was raised, highlighting five coarse-featured faces leering in at her. The effect of ale and the flickering light distorted them grotesquely: staring protuberant eyes, sagging jaws, gappy teeth and unshaven jowls.

'Where shall we start?' asked one.

'It don't matter. The winders; break down the shutters and the door.'

John found his voice at last.

'The first man as lays a finger on my house will wish he hadn't.'

'Get on with it, Jake,' growled Gruff to the tall man.

'Aye. You've got the axe,' said another.

He raised it, and as the first window frame shattered he was felled to the ground by John. The short stocky man hurled himself at John's back, throwing his arms round his throat but, jerking forward, John tossed him against the broken window and he fell on top of his companion who was trying to rise.

Gruff caught hold of the axe and laid into another window as a fourth man levered off the door with a crowbar and a fifth knocked John down with a side blow to his jaw.

Eliza, to her surprise, found herself breaking a crate over the head of the fellow with the crowbar, but he was a giant of a man and the broken pieces of wood fell from his shoulders without any effect.

Eliza stepped towards the struggling threesome on the

ground but as John rose she remembered the children and began to fight her way towards the back room. They were crouching terror-stricken in the corner. Tom had hold of Tize and Sarah was trying to restrain Bobby, who was bawling loudly.

'Out through the back door,' gasped Eliza.

'Where shall we go, Mama?' shrieked Sarah hysterically.

'The big furze bush,' said Tom.

'Yes. Come on, Mama, quickly. Tom knows where the hole is.' They stumbled over tree stumps and struggled blindly through brambles after Tom, who had Tize under one arm and Bobby, still bawling lustily, under the other. He found the way in and they reached the concealed space in the centre scratched, bleeding and gasping for breath.

'Be quiet, Bobby,' hissed Sarah.

'Hush, Bobby. The nasty men will hear you. Give him me, Tom. Sh-h, little one. Be quiet or they'll find us,' soothed Eliza.

The dry bracken from the floor and the heather thatch had been set alight along with the door and the roof planking. The wind fanned the flames first one way and then the other until a wild bonfire was all that remained of their little home.

'Come on! That's done,' shouted Gruff.

'Yer 'ouse will be warm enough for you tonight, Ruddock,' guffawed the sarcastic one.

'Where is the bastard? I think he's broke me jaw.'

'He's lying over there.'

'Better pull him further away. Be bad for us if he got himself cooked.'

'Best pull up them fruit trees, too,' said Gruff as the flames flared across the garden.

Two men stepped over and began hauling out the apple trees.

'They're pulling up the trees,' screamed Sarah.

93

'Stay, Sare. You can't stop them,' said Tom, but she tore away from his hands and was through the bushes in a trice, belabouring the men's legs with a stick she had grabbed. Her eyes were wide and her wild hair, torn clothing and anger transformed the small child into a demon of fury.

The two men left the rest of the trees and hurriedly followed their retreating companions.

John slowly opened his eyes and dreamily watched the birch branches flailing across the starlit sky. He turned his head to gaze uncomprehendingly at the leaping flames. An excruciating pain in his neck made him wince and his head throbbed voilently. He let it roll back and found himself looking into Tom's face.

'You all right, Father?'

'Dunno. Where am I?'

'They've burnt the cottage down.'

'My God! Where are they? I'll have them.'

'No. Lie down, Father. They've gone.'

'The children! Where's Sare and Tize and Bobby? Where's your mother?'

'We're all right. Honest. We're all all right. Just be still. I'll get Mother.'

Tom rose and found Harry Nursall standing beside him.

'Are ye all all right?' asked Harry anxiously.

'Yes. They're in the big furze bush.'

'Good, good. I told Mary you'd take them there, son. I daren't come because I knew there'd be too many for us and they'd have just took our house down as well, and then we'd have nowhere. Did you see who it were, Tom?'

'No, but Mother said she didn't know any of them.'

'I reckon they came from Wavendon. Anyhow, to work. Yer father's all right here for a bit. We'll go and get Eliza and the youngsters and then come back for him. Nay, John! Lie down. Just stay put, man. We'll be back as soon as we've got the little ones safe.'

CHAPTER 15

Recriminations, and Sarah Leaves to Seek Her Fortune

The Select Vestry met the following Thursday evening.

'I hear Ruddock's new place on the Heath was burnt down Tuesday night,' said William Hall gravely.

Devereux and Green exchanged glances.

'Hm, yes,' said Devereux noncommittally.

Hall looked steadily at Green.

'They were evicted as we arranged,' said Green shortly.

'I don't remember the arrangement. Who did it?' asked Vaughan. Even his manner was more serious than usual.

Devereux cleared his throat awkwardly.

'Some Wavendon men, I believe.'

'Aye,' said Green. 'Some labourers that were laid off for the weather and could use a bit of ready money.'

'So we have to get unemployed men from another parish to do our work, do we?' asked Hall.

'It would have caused ill-feeling against our own men, you know,' said Devereux.

'Yes, it would,' agreed Hall bitterly, 'and I understand from your good colleague, the Reverend Jenkins, that it has caused ill-feeling in Wavendon, too.'

'Er, yes. There does seem to be some awkwardness,' sighed Devereux.

The rest of the committee looked at him expectantly so he slowly drew a letter from his breast-pocket.

'I received a letter from Jenkins this morning, gentlemen, which I shall read to you.

Dear Hugh,

I am afraid the eviction of one of your parishioners and the destruction of his cottage on Wavendon Heath has caused some ill-feeling among my flock. I believe that the undertaking was at the instigation of your Select Vestry Committee and I confess I am surprised you did not consult us about it.

I did my best to defend your action on the grounds that the building was so close to the parish boundary that you may have mistakenly thought it was within your own, but using our men and, in particular, those whose reputation leaves a lot to be desired, rather went against you.'

'On *Wavendon* Heath?' exclaimed Dudley.

'It must have been a close thing. Probably right on the boundary,' said Green.

'Did you know that?' asked Miller.

'No. It never occurred to us that it might be,' said Devereux.

'Well, they can't do much about it, can they?' said Miller.

'I suppose they could rebuild it for Ruddock,' suggested Vaughan.

'What, pay out for that!' said Green derisorily.

But, strangely enough, that is what happened.

William Hall was a good friend of Cyril Jenkins. They shared an interest in incunabula and it seemed likely that the major part of the expense for rebuilding the cottage rested with Hall but the bricks and timber were ostensibly carted up to the Heath at the expense of Wavendon Parish. Ruddock had become quite popular with his new workmates there and his battered state and

96

homeless family aroused so much sympathy that several skilled men devoted their evenings and one or two Sundays to rebuilding the homestead so that, when Eliza moved in for the second time, the brick and timber home was beyond her wildest dreams. The only thing she lacked after Mary Nursall had stalwartly supplied the furnishing once again, was the peace of mind that they were safe. She was no longer quite so terrified of eviction, but John's poaching and wooding worried her a lot. She also worried about Sarah who produced more money each week than she could possibly earn by making lace.

Farmer Miller was a busy man and left his head cowman to deal with the boys who did odd jobs about the farm but he did notice the small shock-headed girl arriving to collect her crow-scarer just before first light on a bleak March morning.

'That child looks very young. Have we run out of lads in the village?'

'She's not so young, just small, and there's no keeping her away. She do the job well,' reassured the cowman.

For several hours Sarah would solemnly patrol the seeded fields swinging the rattle with a strident clatter that sent the rooks flapping heavily to perch on a bare ash tree in the hedgerow. There they would change weight from one foot to another and stretch a wing, but keep their light eyes on the child as she stumbled across the furrows, her feet getting heavier and heavier with the cloying clay. They watched, lurking like so many dark shades from the underworld, until she stopped by the hedge to prise the clay off her boots and warm her numb fingers in her armpits. Then they would launch themselves off and glide to the further end of the field to resume pillaging. Sarah would sigh, compress her blue lips and set off to scare them away again.

Martha Lyle spoke to Sarah when she called with a message from her mother.

'Are you stone-picking for Farmer Miller still, Sarah?'

'Aye, but it's more crow-scaring now.'

'It's grievous hard work for a pittance.'

Sarah shrugged and frowned.

'I think it's a shame you left school, dearie. You were so quick at your bookwork and sums.'

'They don't pay you for going to school,' said Sarah.

'Well, no, not now, but you'd be paid in the end, you know. You could get work in a shop perhaps. Folks always need someone that's good with reading and writing and doing sums. Your mother could manage all right with you earning a bit from straw plaiting and I'd give you the twopence for the teacher. Shall I speak to her and see if you can start next Monday?'

'Right,' said Sarah noncommittally.

'Good! You can pay me back when you get that job, can't you.'

Good fortune seemed to be moving a little closer to the family on the Heath and the most notable events of the next five years were the births of two more children: William, named after Mr Hall, and Mary, named after Mrs Nursall. Mary was a puny, delicate baby who caused Eliza much anxiety and made her even more grateful for the robust vigour of her eldest two. Tom was now a strapping young man of seventeen, taller than his father, but Sarah had not changed so much. Her enormous tawny eyes still shone disturbingly alert from her small triangular face, which was framed by a halo of bushy light brown hair. The hair was tamer than it used to be, but her rebellious, ambitious spirit was not.

Martha's advice had proved sound. In two years' time Mr Cox, the manager of the Leighton Buzzard hat factory, saw Sarah's potential and advanced her a little money so that she could collect up the straw plaits for him and keep a modest commission for herself. She soon stopped plaiting and spent the mornings helping the teacher with the older pupils. They stolidly resisted learning anything not connected with the close horizons of their lives . . .

'Well, just pretend that it's blackbirds' eggs in three different nests.' Sarah persevered irritably with the arithmetic.

'Where be the nests, Miss?' asked the urchin with guarded interest.

In the afternoons and evenings and often much of the weekends Sarah trudged from village to village collecting plaits and arranging for deliveries of new straw. Her employer, Frank Cox, was a small, neat man of thirtyish with thinning sandy hair and ginger whiskers. He was not good-looking but he was always impeccably dressed and drove a smart pony trap. He was quick and clever, like Sarah, but, as her seventeenth birthday approached, a niggling distrust crept into her feelings towards him which seemed quite unjustified, since he had always treated her fairly.

'You've done well this week, Sarah!'

'Yes. I went over to Ridgemont yesterday. There's plenty more wants to start plaiting there if you can get the straw to them.'

'Hm. We've got about as much as we can do with at the moment. It would be all right if I took a few more girls on but they'd be that much more trouble. I'm hard-pressed to manage by myself as it is.'

He regarded Sarah thoughtfully.

'How about you coming over to the factory? You could find someone to learn the collecting up before you left.'

'What? To sew hats?'

'Well, you'd best learn how it's done to start with but I shouldn't keep you doing that too long. You could see to the order books for me. That would give me time to see to more girls.'

Sarah shook her head.

'My mother wouldn't like it.'

'Why? You'd be earning good money. I'd see you were better off than you are now, and it would save all this trudging about the countryside.'

'She wouldn't like me living away!'

'You could live with me. My – er – wife would look after you.'

The slight hesitation as he said 'wife' was not lost on Sarah and the reason for her new distrust of the man became clearer.

'I do a lot of orders for London hatters, you know.'

'Do you take the hats up to London, then?' asked Sarah.

'No, I usually send them by carrier unless there's an urgent order and then I might send it by the *Wonder* but that eats up the profits. I have to go up regular myself to get new orders, of course.' He watched Sarah intently as he sorted the next card to play.

'Now, I'd take *you* up by the *Wonder* if you wanted to come. You'd show the hats off a treat and you could keep the order books straight. You've never been to London have you?' he finished triumphantly.

Sarah bit her lip in suppressed excitement. She knew he was set on this scheme and she wondered if she would be able to make sure the lures he dangled before her materialized.

He drove his advantage home.

'Good start for a clever young woman like you. There's a great deal going on in London. You just ask your mother and tell her I'll look after you right, eh?'

This meeting took place in Cecil Higgins's house which was where the local plaiters got their straw supplies, and Sarah walked home slowly, considering whether to accept Cox's offer. By the time she had turned off the sandy lane and caught a glimpse of the thatched roof and chimney stack rising out of the bracken and furze, her mind was made up.

Eliza was nursing Mary by the fire. Although she was

anxious about the fretful baby today, the five years seemed to have moved in reverse for her. She had put on weight, her shining hair showed no sign of grey yet and her cheeks were plump and rosy. Only the deep lines running from nostril to mouth chronicled the hard times she had seen. There was still not a penny to spare and Mr Elliott was still owed sevenpence, but with Tom and Sarah working and Tize doing some plaiting, he would certainly get paid at the end of the week, *and* there was a plump pheasant in the pot. Personally she would be relieved when it was all eaten and the carcase buried in the garden, because there was no way one could disguise the succulent smell of pot-roast pheasant if an uninvited visitor happened to call. The windows were tightly shut and Eliza looked up sharply as Sarah lifted the latch.

'It's only me, Mama. Ah, pheasant!' smiled Sarah.

'Aye, Lord be grateful. I get that edgy when it's cooking and you can't hear anyone coming on this sand.'

'How's baby?'

'Oh, she's mangy today. It's a tooth bothering her. Just look at that red patch on the poor mite's cheek.'

Sarah nodded politely but hardly glanced at the baby.

'Do you think Tize could collect up the straw plaits for me, Mama?'

'She's only young and she'd get all the money muddled up.'

'I could help her sort it out each weekend and she don't mind walking.'

'Why, where be you going?' cried Eliza.

'Mr Cox has offered me work at Leighton.'

'You bain't working in no hat factory, me girl.'

'I'm going to look after his ledgers as soon as I've got to know what's going on.'

'It's a *terrible* place. I always remember Mr Barnstable saying what a bad lot of girls he had there.'

'Ha, Mr Barnstable! There ain't much he'd approve of. He's one of them preachers at the Chapel.'

'And no worse for that, me girl,' responded Eliza sharply.

'He said he'd pay me well.'

'He didn't say how much, did he, and he didn't say how you'd earn it either, did he?' said Eliza darkly.

'He said I should get quite a lot more than I get now and I could live in his house and his wife would look after me.'

'I never knew he were married.'

'Oh yes,' said Sarah with more conviction than she felt. 'He said I could go up to London to get the orders sometimes.'

'Lunnon!' exclaimed Eliza. 'I don't know that I hold with *that*.'

Sarah smiled at the way her mother disposed of the great capital.

'It's a good chance, Mama. I may be able to set up on my own when I've learnt about it. I might make a lot of money.'

Eliza surveyed her doubtfully and thought of the village girls playing 'Poor Mary'. It wasn't much of an inheritance for one's daughters.

'You may be right, but you're too young to know all the troubles you might be taking on.'

'I'm always careful and you've had troubles enough.'

'Aye,' sighed her mother. 'You're nobody's fool, Sarah. See what your father says.'

'Huh! *He* won't let me go. You've got to be on my side, Mama. You know what he's like,' pleaded Sarah urgently.

Sarah broached the subject after tea when John had relished his pheasant and was washing it down with a pot of Yarb beer.

'There's no daughter of mine going to work in them factories,' he said firmly.

'I wouldn't be working in the factory, Father. He wants me to do the ledgers.'

'She'd be good at that, you know, John.'

'I'm surprised at you, Eliza, encouraging your daughter to join them strumpets.'

'It's likely not as bad as Mr Barnstable said, and anyway, she'd be in the office, wouldn't she? It's a good chance. She may not get another.'

'She'd be better off with a good man.'

'It depends how much he earned,' said Eliza quickly and wished she hadn't as soon as it was out of her mouth.

'Oh yes! Well, you have been unlucky, but yours ain't beaten you yet, has he? And you ain't *quite* starved, have you? There's not many honest men that earn a deal of money but it ain't our fault, it's the corruption of society.'

This apt quote from the *Political Register* calmed him down a bit. Eliza and Sarah exchanged wary glances.

'I'm not obliged to stay, Father. I can always quit if I don't like it there,' pursued Sarah.

'And where would you live? That will cost you a pretty penny.'

'He said his wife would look after me. I expect they'd just take a bit for my food. I'd be home each Saturday night.'

'Ugh.' John fidgeted, eager to get off to The Bell and Sarah assumed her victory, but her complacency was shortlived because Tom rose and followed his father out, looking darkly in her direction. He didn't usually leave the cottage in the evening and Sarah knew it was the easiest way for him to register his disapproval.

Sarah and Tom were still staunch companions in their few leisure hours and confided their hopes and fears to each other. Tom was working at a fuller's earth mine on the edge of the Heath, not far from the cottage.

'The earth's fetching a good price now. Mr Jenkins

said he be putting our wages up come Michaelmas,' he told his sister.

'Not before time, neither. You ought to earn more than you do for all that digging and humping them sacks about. I bet you move twice as much as the other men.'

'Well, aye. I s'pose so,' said Tom with a note of pride. Sarah shook her head at his hopeless affability.

'Mind you, I shall have a mine of my own one of these days,' he challenged her.

'You! You'd be too soft by half to do that,' she teased.

'Oh no, I shouldn't. I'll start one as soon as I can afford a cart and cattle to get it down to the turnpike,' he insisted.

The following Saturday afternoon found Eliza, Mary Nursall and Sarah kneeling round a small box which Mary had sorted out. They were packing Sarah's scanty wardrobe and a few 'odds and ends ter make yer room homely', as Mary said.

'There must be something magic about your place, Mrs Nursall,' laughed Sarah. 'It don't matter how much you give away, there's always still plenty more left.'

'Aye, dearie. That's just how they say a loving heart should be!'

'Yer two dresses ain't smart enough,' worried Eliza.

'Well, maybe I've got something set by . . .'

'Oh no, Mrs Nursall. Please don't worry. I shouldn't dream of taking clothes from you,' said Sarah hurriedly, hoping Mary didn't guess why.

'No, them'd be too big by half and I'm not handy at altering and yer mother ain't got the time.'

'I'll manage until I've got a few weeks' wages and then I'll have a piece of stuff made up.' Sarah's eyes sparkled at the thought of a dress made specially for her.

Tom was to see Sarah and her box down to the turnpike and safely stowed with the carrier that evening. He had been avoiding her all week since the heated discussion with their father. Mary Nursall returned to the cottage to see Sarah off and, with her typical generosity, wrapped a coloured woollen shawl round her shoulders.

'Oh Mary, it's lovely. You really shouldn't have,' said Eliza tearfully as Sarah thanked Mary and kissed her goodbye.

'Goodbye, Mama. It will be next Saturday before you know where you are and I'll be back again.'

'I do hope it's all right, love.'

'Of course it will be. You wait and see. Bye bye.' Sarah waved gaily to the tearful group in the doorway, and William, with a sound sense of occasion, began to bawl.

'I'm that worried about her, Mary. Just supposing it's like John says,' sobbed Eliza.

'You're very quiet, Tom. What do you think of me going?' asked Sarah as they made their way down the lane, Tom shouldering her box.

'I don't like it.'

'Why?'

'Girls should stay at home.'

'Nonsense! Lots of girls go into service when they're only ten or eleven.'

'That's different.'

'Why is it?'

'Well, they're going to a proper big 'ouse, ain't they.'

'I'm not going to be anyone's servant, though.'

'It just ain't proper,' said Tom stubbornly.

Sarah was more upset than Tom guessed, because they had never disagreed over something serious before.

CHAPTER 16

Eliza to the Rescue

Sarah and Tom walked the rest of the way to the turnpike in silence. The Leicester coach was just breasting the brow of the hill bound for Woburn and, as the road levelled out, the coachman cracked his whip so they passed at a spanking pace. The bottle green lacquer coachwork gleamed and the name 'Unicorn' was lettered in a gold curve on each door. The guard raised his horn and treated the admiring youngsters to a quick ascending scale.

'Is that going through Leighton?' asked Sarah with shining eyes.

'No. It'll be the seven o'clock at the Goat going to Lunnon,' said Tom knowledgeably.

'That's how I'll be travelling soon,' said Sarah. Tom turned to look at her.

'You'll be earning a lot more than what Cox'll pay you, then!' he said mockingly.

Sarah withdrew her eyes from the receding coach and pursed her lips defiantly.

'Yes, I reckon so and perhaps you'll do the same with your earth mine.'

Tom grunted and turned towards Aspley Hill.

'Here's the carrier,' he said shortly.

It was a dispiriting sight after the 'Unicorn'. Alfie Hedges slouched over the rump of his heavily-feathered skewbald cob as it picked its way down the rutted lane. Catching sight of his fare, Alfie 'gipped' and slapped the reins on the broad shaggy back in front of him. The cob's ears pricked dutifully but his pace only quickened to almost, but not quite, a trot.

'Well, here we be, Missy. All ready to take ye on to

106

Leighton.' Alfie made it sound a long way off, like London or Leeds.

'What time will we get there?' asked Sarah with a note of despondency in her voice.

'Oh, no time at all. Let's see. It mun be about seven o'clock; let's say half past at Woburn, half past eight at Heath and Reach. Do it easy by nine, me dear!'

'Bye, Tom.'

They stood looking at each other gravely. Each knew that the moment they turned away their childhood interdependence would be over and they would face the grown-up world alone. Tom hated change of any sort and his lack of confidence made him resentful towards Sarah. To her, life was a challenge that she relished but at this moment her excited anticipation was quite overwhelmed by the sadness of leaving Tom. She perhaps misinterpreted his gloomy expression a bit and, pulling herself together with an impatient wriggle, she pushed him playfully and hopped up beside the carrier.

'I'll be all right, Tom. You see if I won't,' she cried jauntily as the cob moved forward. As it broke into a rare trot, Tom lifted his hand, but he didn't smile.

Mr Cox was waiting in the yard of the Black Lion when they arrived and gave her a warm welcome. He carried her trunk the short distance to his house where she was greeted more coolly by a sharp-featured girl of about twenty whom Cox introduced simply as 'Alice'. Sarah's attic room was small but it seemed as lonely as a barn when she settled down to sleep in a proper bed for the first time in her life.

'I'll put Mrs Nursall's pictures and books up tomorrow and it will be my very own room,' she reassured herself.

The sounds of wagon wheels and horses' hooves on cobbles woke her the next morning instead of the lusty singing of birds and crowing of cockerels that she was used to. For the first time ever she regretted that Bobby and Will were not rolling about on top of her, locked in mortal combat, while Tize screamed at them to stop.

She dressed and went downstairs. Alice, in a soiled lace-trimmed negligée was preparing breakfast.

'Oh, didn't you want yer hewer of 'ot water for washing?' she asked disparagingly.

'Yes. That's just what I come for,' replied Sarah promptly. Alice looked sharply at her and poured the water from the black kettle on the hook.

'You can get it yerself tomorrow, can't yer.'

Sarah nodded coolly. She had seen a basin and ewer at Mrs Nursall's but it seemed to be treated as an ornament there and its possible function hadn't occurred to her.

Alice insisted that she and 'Frank' went to church. Sarah thought he seemed a little surprised but he invited her to come with them. She declined with the excuse of unpacking and enviously noted Alice's tight-bodiced blue dress and matching pumps. She was determined to have clothes like that as soon as she could manage it. She wondered how much they cost and how much she would earn.

As the day dragged on, Sarah became increasingly aware of Alice's muted hostility and retired miserably to bed quite early in the evening. Some time in the middle of the night she was awoken from a dream in which Tom was imprisoning her in a tiny wooden coop with no windows. He was hammering the last plank into place when she realized with a start that someone was banging on her attic door. 'What is it?' she cried.

'It's yer mother!' screeched Alice.

Sarah bounded out of bed and down the stairs in her old flannel nightshift.

There, in the parlour, was Mr Cox looking sleepily astonished in his nightshirt and cap, and Eliza pale and trembling, cowering in a space between the bureau and a jardinere.

'Mama!' exclaimed Sarah.

Eliza caught her breath and covered her mouth.

'Mama! What are you doing here? What's wrong?'

'N-nothing, love,' whispered Eliza. 'I . . . I just thought . . . Well, yer father said . . . He came back from The Bell a bit excited, like he do, you know . . . and he said as how he thought . . . in point of fact . . . he said he were certain . . .'

'There were something dreadful happening to me!' completed Sarah in exasperation.

'Yes . . . Oh, I *am* sorry, love.'

'However did you get here?'

'I waited till he were asleep and I couldn't rest and I thought I could only get me peace of mind back by coming to see, so . . .'

'You walked all the way! Oh, Mama!' wailed Sarah, softening suddenly.

They clung to each other, sobbing.

Alice compressed her mouth irritably, tossed her head and went back to bed.

Mr Cox looked on with increasing impatience.

'We ain't got another bed for yer mother,' he said shortly.

'Oh, I know. Of course not, sir. I've got to get back to see to the little ones,' sobbed Eliza.

'You can't walk back. It's eight miles,' said Sarah.

'It's me own fault.'

'Can we borrow your pony trap, please Mr Cox?' asked Sarah.

'Have you ever driven one?'

'Well, no. But I'll manage,' she said earnestly.

'Oh no, Sare. I can walk.'

'You'd better make your mother some tea while I get dressed,' said Cox bitterly.

'I'm ever so sorry, Sare. I were in such a state when yer father said you'd be sold and all that and it were all my fault for encouraging you,' whimpered Eliza.

'You just come upstairs and see my room.' Sarah bundled her up to the little attic.

'Oh, ain't it nice. All by yourself,' said Eliza.

'Yes. *All by myself*, Mama, and I start work tomorrow, remember? And you just put all that nonsense out of your head!'

'Yes. I will. I promise,' said Eliza contritely.

Cox drove Eliza home so that Sarah could resume her night's rest. He bore up well against her plaintive stream of apologies and left her with commendably good grace and the assurance that he would see no harm came to Sarah.

'He's a *real* gentleman, is Mr Cox,' declared Eliza to John the next evening.

''E must be to turn out in t'middle of the night to bring home a crazy 'ooman like you,' John replied, squeezing her shoulders affectionately.

CHAPTER 17

Coaching up to 'Lunnon'

Although John and Eliza's anxiety was now allayed, it was not entirely unfounded. Sarah soon came to realize that she was a member of a ménage à trois which Cox would have happily converted to a ménage à deux with the elimination of the nagging Alice. He made no formal acknowledgement of this, but Alice's manner towards Sarah became increasingly hostile and she lost no opportunity to flaunt her superior experience of clothes and manners before the younger girl. This goaded Sarah into a fierce determination to learn all she could about elegant living.

'I suppose you must be really wanting to get back to yer mother?' hazarded Alice with contrived concern.

'Oh no. Not at all. I much prefer to be hindependant,' replied Sarah loftily.

'Hindependant, eh?' sniffed Alice. 'Why, you ain't earning enough at the 'at factory to be anything like that.'

'But I'm earning that much more than what you are,' said Sarah maliciously.

'Ha. I don't *need* to earn. An experienced woman don't keep herself.'

'I think I'll manage without *that* sort of experience.'

'Oh, just you try, madam,' retorted Alice viciously. 'If you want nice clothes and more comfort than what you've got, there ain't too much choice for a girl.' She flounced out of the kitchen, slamming the door and Sarah pondered. It was true. She had worked hard for nearly two months and been able to take even less back to her mother than when she was at home. Eliza told her not to worry, she must spend a bit on herself but Sarah hadn't done that because she knew her mother was spending money on medicine for baby Mary. The mite had almost ceased to grow at all and Eliza looked constantly strained with worry as the baby grizzled feebly.

Not long after the exchange with Alice, Mr Cox was talking to Sarah about taking some of the new season's bonnets up to the London warehouses.

'You said I could go to London to help you,' reminded Sarah.

'You haven't got much experience yet, Sarah, and whatever would your mother do? I certainly shouldn't take her home from London in the middle of the night!'

Sarah smiled good-humouredly.

'I don't think even *she*'d walk that far. She don't hold with London though.' Sarah smiled at the visions of horror a trip to 'Lunnon' would conjure up in Eliza's mind.

'I don't think I shall tell her till I get back.'

Cox raised his eyebrows in surprise.

'But I shall need some smarter clothes,' pursued Sarah, unabashed. 'P'raps if you gave me three weeks' wages in advance I could get a seamstress to make up two dresses for me.' She gazed at him winsomely.

'You're a saucy wench and no mistake!' he laughed.

'Well?'

'All right. Ask Alice who makes her dresses and be sure you get some good stuff. I don't want to waste me money on trash, and you'll be going to meet people who know what's what.'

'Oh, thank you, Mr Cox,' cried Sarah ecstatically. 'I wonder how much they'll cost, about?'

'Don't you worry your pretty little head too much about that. You've got the measure of them ledgers amazingly quick and I was intending to raise your wage. I'll pay for a coat and a skirt and I'll lend you money for a dress. How's that? Can't cost overmuch to dress a tiny bit of a thing like you,' he teased, slipping his arm round her waist. She wriggled away smiling evenly.

Two weeks later, several of Sarah's dreams came true.

Just before half past six on a raw drizzling morning, she stood in the yard of the White Horse at Hockliffe watching the ostler and stable boys change the 'cattle' on the Shrewsbury to London *Wonder*. This was performed with amazing speed and Mr Cox stepped forward to hand her into the coach. She was complacently aware of his satisfaction with her new outfit as she settled herself gingerly into the cushions, careful to make sure that the full skirt of her new coat was not creased up underneath her. She smoothed the stiff folds of her satin skirt and peeped over it to catch a glimpse of her slippers as she neatly crossed her legs. On her head was a trimmed straw bonnet which the sewers at the factory had delighted in making up to 'suit' her. Her high spirits and pluck made her popular with most of the girls, who were full of envy at her good fortune, but not resentful. Even those a good deal older than Sarah seemed to accept her favoured position with Mr Cox and Sarah kept quiet about the humble home she had just left. One of the reasons for this acceptance was Sarah's dedicated attention to the way she spoke. She had begun by copying Alice but her quick ear had soon revealed that there were better models among the local gentry who sometimes came to look at the hats in the little warehouse showroom. Mrs Newbold, the milliner and dress maker, spoke very genteelly and Sarah listened to her carefully each time she went for a fitting.

Mr Cox was travelling economically beside the coachman and Sarah sat by the kerbside window, facing backwards. As she smoothed some barely visible wrinkles from her kid gloves she examined her fellow travellers through her modestly lowered eyelashes. Opposite her were a middle-aged couple with their daughter, who would be a little older than Sarah, sitting between them and on her left were two young men. She was gratified to find her interest returned in full measure, particularly by the mother and daughter, while the better-looking of the men leant forward to adjust the window, and turned to ask her if she found it too draughty.

'No, I am not at all cold, thank you,' she simpered.

Mind you, her companions had been on the coach for nearly nine hours so that any change in their confined scene would have been worthy of attention. Sarah gazed out of the window, cultivating a look of much-travelled boredom despite her excitedly pounding heart. She wove romantic fantasies around the young man by the other window, who would hand her out of the coach and beg her to accompany him to undreamt of places where the young and smart of London must gather. 'Cremorne, you must go to Cremorne', cried the better informed of the factory girls.

'Where's that?' Sarah had asked.

'Why, it be where the young bloods go. It's a pleasure garden. All the trees are full of coloured lights at night, and they drink champagne . . .'

'And they go there because them ladies what ain't ladies go,' tittered another.

'Ooh, yes. You watch your step, Sarah. Be sure you've got a good escort. I s'pose you'd best ask Coxy ter go with you! Lunnon's a dreadful wicked place.'

Sarah smiled in excited anticipation.

She would have liked to talk to the mother and girl opposite her but she had noted their refined accent, so she decided to say as little as possible. It was hard for her; Tom and her father always teased her about her incessantly busy tongue. In the meantime the six passengers jolted and tossed against each other travelling at an incredible twelve miles an hour along one of the fastest turnpike roads in the country. The countryside sped by until they reached St Alban's and another change of horses. The coach party went in to eat a late breakfast at the Saracen's Head. There was a moment's confusion, as Sarah thought that the young man of her fantasy was competing for the chair she had chosen but she quickly concluded he was holding it for her to sit down on. It seemed a rather pointless gesture since the chair was unlikely to make a bid for freedom but she smiled divinely at him. Mr Cox conversed in a lively manner with the father, while the mother and daughter inquired about Sarah's state of health which, she assured them briefly, was excellent. Their voices sounded even more well-bred than the Reverend Devereux's and Sarah replied to their other questions with monosyllables and smiles. She evaded details of what they would do in London and glanced uncomfortably towards her employer. The innkeeper's wife and maids brought them devilled kidneys, thick slices of bacon and a joint of cold beef, all of which they had to dispose of in great haste since the coach only stopped for twenty minutes. Sarah was astounded by the quantity of food and drink and the cavalier treatment it received. She firmly dispelled a fleeting thought of wrapping up two kidneys in her pocket handkerchief for later and allowed herself to be escorted to the coach on Cox's arm. He nodded approvingly at her, so she imagined she had passed her first test of social acceptability.

As they neared London, Sarah could no longer conceal her excitement.

'Have you never been to London before?' asked the daughter in surprise.

'Neow, never!' said Sarah, off her guard.

'No, I never have,' she repeated carefully, even prefixing the 'h' to 'have', which she rarely did.

The young man leant towards her in a friendly fashion.

'This is Highgate Hill,' he said. 'Hampstead Heath is to the right.'

'I shall not attempt to repeat that,' thought Sarah to herself.

'Look, that is Fenton House where Sir Ralph Beckett lives.'

'Oh, charming!' said Sarah, a little surprised at her own choice of expression.

The streets were becoming full of carriages. There were pony chaises and Hackney carriages, and a particularly smart phaeton passed with a coiffured beauty who was waving to some acquaintances. She was not so very young, Sarah noted.

'Oh, I do believe that is Harriet Wilson,' cried the daughter in excitement. 'See her monogram on the carriage door. How sophisticated she looks.'

'Really?' said the talkative young man with interest. 'Do you know her?'

'No, of course not,' she replied, looking a little shocked. 'But everyone talks about that book she wrote ages ago.'

'Oh yes, of course. I have heard of that.'

'What is it about?' asked Sarah, unable to contain her curiosity.

'Oh . . . about . . . herself. It's an autobiography, actually,' replied the daughter rather evasively.

Sarah appealed to the young man but he averted his eyes.

'This is Archway Hill. We'll soon be at the Angel in Islington,' he said.

'Is that where we stop?' asked Sarah.

'It is indeed, and of that I shall be mightily grateful. Except that I shall miss your company of course,' he added hastily.

As they drew off the road into the forecourt of the Angel the cracked voice of an old ostler announced their arrival.

'The *Wonder*. All the way from Shrewsbury. On time, too. The *Shrewsbury Wonder*.'

Sarah was quite bewildered by the confusion of the noisy scene as she stepped from the coach. There must have been twenty other coaches just arriving or preparing to depart. Fractious horses pawing the cobbles; coach boats open for loading in portmanteaux and parcels; trunks and boxes being strapped on top. Stable boys cursed at the horses as they strove to harness them up. Muddy, sweaty teams were being led off to the stabling and sleek, high-mettled horses pranced out to replace them. The wheezing croak of the aged ostler continued from the inn doorway.

'The *York High Flyer* about to depart. Make way for the *Flyer* there.

'The *Leeds Flyer* and it's a quarter past twelve. Time for the *Union* to be off.

'The *Stamford Regent*.

'The *Truth and Daylight* . . .'

And there were people everywhere, jostling and hurrying this way and that. Porters with small trunks on their shoulders tripped over abandoned packages;

116

people searched for lost parcels, lost friends, lost coaches . . . and above all, the deafening clatter on the cobbles of horses' hooves, carriage wheels, the black-smith cold-shoeing, coach poles dropping as the teams were unharnessed.

Sarah had never seen or heard such pandemonium. She thought her head would split.

'Come on Sarah! Don't stand there like a lost thing,' shouted Cox. 'Can you carry your small bag and these hat boxes. I'll bring the rest. We must hire a carriage.'

Dazedly Sarah followed him out on to the street, eager to escape from the cacophony, but there was no escape. The street was only less confusing because there were just two directions of movement and it was hardly any quieter.

'There are so many people!' exclaimed Sarah plaintively.

'Yes. Well it's London, ain't it,' replied Cox testily.

They alighted from the carriage at the lodging house in Aldersgate where Mr Cox usually stayed. The land-lady greeted him brusquely.

''Allo Mr Cox, sir. Nice ter 'ave yer again. We're burstin' at the seams 'ere. I've 'ad ter put yer both in the nice big room at the front, first floor.' Cox glanced apprehensively at Sarah but she was still overawed, and Mrs Briggs's strange accent made her slow to digest its content.

They were shown up and Mrs Briggs bustled about drawing the curtains and checking the water in the ewer while Sarah put her bag down by the single bed and Cox put the others down by the double one.

'Well, you know you'll be comfortable with me, Mr and Mrs Cox. Anything what you want, you just ring for. Breakfast's sharp at eight and if you want supper 'ere you tell me at breakfast. We don't do it no later than nine o'clock.'

Sarah wondered where the bell was to ring and

suspected Mrs Briggs took care to see she wasn't troubled by that sort of thing nor by the niceties of whether it would have been more respectable to have left them unmarried and occupying two of her rooms instead of only one. Anyway, Sarah couldn't claim to being a stranger to sharing bedrooms although she knew that some of their Aspley neighbours took the trouble and expense of sleeping their teenage son or daughter with a couple who had a spare room. Mary Nursall offered to have Tom but Eliza preferred to keep him under her own roof.

'Well, I think I shall unpack and change,' said Sarah pointedly. Cox muttered something about unpacking too and discreetly kept his back turned towards her.

She put on a sprigged muslin gown that Alice had lent her in a rare mood of sisterly affection. She had to pouch the bodice over the tie to keep the hem just off the ground.

'You look very pretty in that dress.' Cox had completed his unpacking and turned to survey her. 'We'll have some food and then I'll show you some of the sights,' he said, helping her to arrange a shawl about her shoulders.

'What, in an inn?' inquired Sarah.

'No. We'll go to an eating house.'

'Ah, yes. That will be lovely,' said Sarah, her eyes sparkling.

CHAPTER 18

The First Impressions of London

Gradually Sarah became a little more accustomed to the noisy bustle of people and carriages. They ate a late lunch in a restaurant off Cheapside and then walked through St Paul's Churchyard which was surrounded by a variety of shops. Cox pointed out two straw hat warehouses that they would pay a professional visit to in the morning, and he conducted her up the steps into the cathedral. He was amused by her dumbfounded astonishment at its colossal proportions. The Red House at Aspley was the largest building she had ever been in before. They strolled along Fleet Street with Sarah stopping to gaze in every shop window until they reached St James's Park which delighted her with its lake and ducks and elegant strollers.

'Oh! Just look at her dress and that 'at. Ain't it a picture! It's got a stuffed bird on,' cried Sarah, quite forgetting her elocution.

'You shouldn't keep looking so hard. Can't you do it a bit more careful. It's rude to keep staring at them ladies like that,' complained Mr Cox. Sarah looked contrite and made an effort to be more restrained in her admiration of the heavy brocaded silk and satin that rustled by.

'I'll set up in millinery one of these days. You could make as much profit on a hat like that as on a dozen straws, even our superior range,' declared Cox.

Sarah's perceptive eyes were rapidly forming new tastes. Her green satin skirt already seemed plain and crude against the stylish elegance of muted fawns or smoke greys trimmed with cerise and saffron.

Despite his embarrassment, Frank Cox couldn't help indulging Sarah's naïve delight and they drank tea in an expensively exclusive coffee-house overlooking the park. Sarah prattled on unabated about the garb of each passer-by.

After tea, Mr Cox suggested they should return to their lodging to rest but Sarah declared herself not a bit tired and entreated him to continue their sightseeing, so they eventually arrived at Regent Street just as it was getting dark. The lights hanging from the arches of the curving colonnades were already lit and Sarah was in raptures about the fairyland scene. All the ladies walking in the park had swished by on the arms of their escorts with great dignity but here they stood about in groups of two or three talking and laughing vivaciously. One or two quieter girls were alone and quite modestly dressed in the sort of style which Sarah had travelled in that day. Their faces were mostly made up with rouged cheeks and there was an ever-changing fragrance of cheap perfume as they passed.

'Are you good-natured, love?' inquired a rather common-looking young woman, catching hold of Cox's arm. He seemed embarrassed and, disengaging his arm, he turned to draw Sarah towards him.

'No thank you,' he muttered to the young woman.

Only a few yards further on Sarah paused to look in a window brightly lit by oil lamps and Cox walked on to be accosted by another young woman with the same nonsensical enquiry.

'Good-natured?' puzzled Sarah. 'Why shouldn't he be good-natured?' She guessed they must be begging but Cox gave them nothing.

The curving crescent with the high arching colonnades and prosperous shops behind them shone bright with lamps and the gay flutter of beautiful dresses and animated faces. Groups of young men, some in officers' uniforms and all immaculately dressed from their high-crowned top hats and yellow gloves to their shiny leather pumps or boots, stood talking and laughing with confident young beauties. The shop windows were full of flounced parasols, ribbons, gloves and silk stockings in every imaginable shade. There were coffee shops and eating houses filled with young men and women and a sprinkling of older men. Elaborately adorned and glazed, cold roast fowls and huge aitch-bones of roast beef graced those windows. Sarah was dazzled by the opulent luxury and the carefree manner of the people enjoying it. She stood lost in admiration of a particularly large skirt in coral pink and primrose gauze supported by a multitude of petticoats until her eye was caught by a lilac feathery cap, perched saucily on a mass of tight black curls. Just beyond there was a romantic cavalier hat draped with jade green ostrich plumes and, close by, the owner of a manly thigh in skin-tight buckskin tapering into shining black knee-boots. A bejewelled silver-knobbed cane tapped against faultlessly tailored fawn breeches set off by a cutaway double-breasted frock-coat in bottle green.

'Sarah! Sarah! Do stop gawping and come on. I am worn out even if you're not,' called Cox irritably. He waved down a Hackney carriage and helped her in, with her head still turned to gaze at the entrancing scene.

'Why did those girls ask you if you were good-natured?'

'Why? Because they were prostitutes, of course.'

'What? All of them?' asked Sarah in amazement.

'Most of them.'

'Not them really smartly dressed ones?'

'Oh yes, certainly them.'

'Not that beautiful lady with the huge feathers on her hat, talking to them army officers?'

'Do stop contradicting me, Sarah. Yes, yes, and a very expensive one. More than those young bloods could afford, I'll wager.'

Sarah gazed at him unbelievingly.

'But they were all laughing and happy and ever so well dressed.'

'They wouldn't do much trade if they were miserable and untidy. Don't you believe all that nonsense about "poor fallen women". It don't apply to that class of whore. Did you see Harriet Wilson drive past near Hampstead?'

'The one what wrote a book?'

'Yes. That book was all about her life as a prostitute,' laughed Cox.

Sarah shook her head, quite bewildered.

When they reached Mrs Briggs's lodging house, Mr Cox asked for sandwiches and tea in their room. The order was received coolly by a sullen serving girl but it was eventually delivered. Sarah hardly spoke as she tried to adjust her dazzling impression of the gaiety of the London streets into some sort of new reality. Her limited experience hindered her and she felt a new sense of respect for Frank Cox, with his matter-of-fact acceptance of this amazingly different life. She was also aware of how dependent she was upon his protection and guidance, which was a quite new sensation. The old Sarah had always understood exactly how her village community worked and her early experience of its harshness had trained her to miss no opportunity to turn the course of events to her own or her family's advantage. She couldn't help a slight resentment at the way Cox treated her as little more than a wilful child, and he certainly lacked any romantic appeal for her, but she was reasonably sure their relationship would continue to be honest and this was all she could hope for.

'Aren't you tired, Sarah?' he asked.

'Oh, no! I could have stayed in Regent Street all night.'

'Ha! I daren't think where you would have ended up if you'd done that. Your mother is not entirely wrong. London can be a dangerous place for a young country girl.'

Sarah raised her chin resentfully.

'Don't you venture out on your own, my girl,' responded Cox severely. He watched her unobtrusively as she prepared to go to bed and thought better of his inclination to suggest that she shared his. There was time enough to draw her round to it, he thought.

CHAPTER 19

The Initiation of a Hat Stand

The next morning Sarah was so anxious about the challenges of the day that she could hardly eat anything.

'Where's that healthy appetite of yours gone, Sarah? Aren't you feeling well?' inquired Cox solicitously.

'Oh yes, I'm quite well. Just not hungry.'

'You look a credit to the firm. If you're not sure what to say just keep quiet and you'll manage fine.'

Sarah was a little piqued that he had diagnosed the cause of her nervousness so promptly.

'Of course. I shall manage perfectly well,' she said haughtily and her employer smiled.

They stepped out into the fine sunny morning and walked briskly to St Paul's Churchyard. Sarah felt resplendent in her new pale yellow dress and pelerine crowned by an elaborately beribboned bonnet. Cox carried a small tower of hat boxes.

The first warehouse did not look very imposing from the outside, but inside it was spacious with a row of counters set in arched alcoves, reminiscent of the bazaars and arcades that were popular in Piccadilly and Oxford Street. Sarah was graciously ushered in by the manager, but the leaning tower of hat boxes which followed her caused them to be hurried to the back of the shop where the two men became busily engaged in sales talk. Sarah's dignity suffered when her bonnet was removed for examination and bought, together with two similar ones and orders for several dozen more. Cox supplied her with another hat which she complained did not match her suit, but a suitable substitute was found which the manager declared looked 'splendid' and he ordered some of those.

Frank Cox was aglow with professional satisfaction as they walked along the crowded pavement to their next assignation.

'You did magnificently, Sarah. I knew you would,' he said gleefully. 'Just fancy, orders for over four dozen hats!'

'I was only a hat stand,' declared Sarah.

'But what a beautiful one!'

They met with almost equal success at two other establishments and returned to Aldersgate empty-handed.

'I'm only wishing I could have brought more samples. We shall have sold out by tomorrow.'

'Do we have to sell them? Couldn't we just take orders on them until the last afternoon?' asked Sarah.

'Well, they like to have something in their hands and I've always done it that way but maybe we'll be able to get more orders like you say. Your pretty little face and dark curls certainly sells hats, Sarah.'

It wasn't only good salesmanship that prompted Sarah's suggestion but also the unthinkable indignity of having to return on the coach hatless.

'I think we shall be daring tomorrow. We shall try our hand in Piccadilly, Sarah.'

'Where's that?'

'It's where there are some high-class milliners. They don't usually buy in straws except perhaps some Italian Leghorns for making up themselves, but with the samples we've got left and our very persuasive hat-stand, I think we might succeed.'

The next morning found Sarah being ushered into a small but exclusive milliner's in the new Burlington Arcade. Frank Cox only carried three boxes with him and when he spoke he was identified as an attendant of a potential customer, so he had to declare himself more plainly.

'May I speak to the manager or make an appointment

to see him if it is inconvenient at the moment? I have some exceedingly superior bonnets made upon a fine straw foundation which I am confident he will be interested in.'

The man and woman exchanged wary glances.

'I am the acting manager,' said the man, eyeing Sarah doubtfully. 'We normally make all our own millinery, Mr . . .'

'Mr Cox, and may I introduce my assistant, Miss Ruddock.'

'Pleased to meet you, madam.'

'Delighted, I'm sure,' said Sarah, smiling divinely as she extended a gloved hand.

Summoning all her courage she broke the awkward pause that ensued with:

'You do have some exceedingly handsome hats,' and continued carefully '. . . but personally I should find many of them – perhaps not that little cap there, but most of them – rather too formal for taking an early morning stroll in, say, St James's; certainly too formal for a warm, sunny day, you know.'

The quality of her elocution and expression could hardly be faulted. Frank Cox was speechless with admiration.

'Yes. Madam may have a point there,' remarked the manager. Frank Cox rallied.

'And of course there is no obligation whatsoever if you would allow us the pleasure of showing you a few of our new season's exclusive designs. One you may notice displayed to advantage already.' Cox made a gallant flourish in Sarah's direction and she defensively caught hold of her hat brim but managed to redirect the action to that of adjusting the angle slightly, as she smiled beguilingly. The acting manager smiled back and bowed to her while Cox hastily removed the lids of his boxes and placed their contents in a row on the counter.

The assistant picked up the first one and examined it carefully.

'What is your opinion, Miss Jones?'

'Well, I think the young lady has a good point. They are well sewn but the style is a little . . . er . . . rural undoubtedly, but even that has a certain appeal for the summer.'

'We do have more . . . *sophisticated* styles for the autumn and winter, of course,' reassured Sarah, with little regard for the truth but a great deal of satisfaction that the correct word had supplied itself so promptly.

Cox and Sarah left empty-handed with a dozen more orders in the book and Sarah had managed to retain the hat she wore.

'So long as those hats sell, as I am sure they will, we have just made a very valuable new client – and we shall celebrate this evening. Where do you want to go, Miss Ruddock?'

'To Cremorne.'

'The Cremorne Gardens in Chelsea?' queried Cox, a little taken aback.

'Yes! Have you never been?'

'Well, no; but that's no obstacle. I daren't think what your mother would say, though.'

'Well, she don't know . . . I mean, she doesn't know, does she?' replied Sarah gaily.

'You are a wicked girl but very good at selling hats.'

CHAPTER 20

An Evening in the Cremorne Gardens

After they had rested, Sarah and Cox set out from Aldersgate and walked down to the river. A little way along the embankment they found a water-cab waiting by some steps beneath an arch on which a notice announced that the boat was bound for Chelsea.

'Oh! Are we going to Cremorne by boat?' cried Sarah. Cox swung his cane jauntily and laughed.

'We are indeed. We are doing everything in style this evening.' He bought the tickets and helped her into the boat. They made their way to the front and sank into plush seats covered by a canopy of draped maroon velvet. The sun was sinking into cushions of purple and orange cloud resting on the horizon and, quite suddenly, the broad expanse of the rippling Thames began to glimmer like a molten gold causeway reaching to their feet.

Sarah wore her new best dress for the first time. It had a well-supported full skirt of white muslin printed with lilac and green flowers and enormous padded puff sleeves. There was a little satin apron chequered with lilac ribbon to match the print and on her head was an elaborate nonsense of lilac and white satin ribbon tied in huge loops and bows which the girls at the hat factory had delightedly created for her. She drew Mary Nursall's shawl closer against the cool river breeze as a boat passed, crowded with respectable-looking parents and children.

'They will have spent the afternoon at the Gardens,' said Cox.

'Oh, do families go?' asked Sarah with ill-concealed disappointment.

'Only in the afternoon. The company changes amazingly at dusk.'

'Ah,' said Sarah complacently. Cox smiled and shook his head.

They were rowed past the new Houses of Parliament and on under Vauxhall Bridge, and soon caught sight of coloured lights which developed into a fairy-tale scene of huge overhanging elms mysteriously festooned with red, yellow and green lanterns, reflected in the dark dancing water of the river. A group of smart young men and women were gathered by the landing stage to note the new arrivals as they laughed and chatted. Sarah stepped saucily out of the boat, showing rather more slipper and ankle than was necessary, and took Cox's arm. A small boat followed them in, rowed noisily by two young dandies escorting four or five laughing girls. Sarah so wished she was one of a party like that.

'Shall we have a drink before we explore this Isle of Delights, Sarah?'

'Yes please. What sort of drinks do they sell?'

'Perhaps you'd like a sherry? I shall have bitter beer.' They sat down on a rustic seat beneath a large green lantern hanging from the branches above and Sarah sipped, wondering how long it took to acquire a taste for sherry, as she avidly absorbed every detail of the passing scene.

'There are some beautiful dresses, even better than in Regent Street, aren't there? Just look over there at that tall fair lady in that lovely dress with the low draped bodice. I think it must be deep cream. It is certainly silk. Look how much stuff there is in the skirt!'

'Can you hear that music?' asked Cox.

'Do you think there is dancing?' Sarah's face glowed with excitement.

'Let's go and see,' smiled Cox.

They passed lawn after smooth green lawn bordered by beds of red and pink geraniums from a greenhouse. Sheltering under the huge plane trees were kiosks selling drinks and posies and trinkets. Every so often a miniature Grecian temple, illuminated in pink or green, would float into view between the bushes.

Following the sound of music they eventually arrived at a huge platform where six or seven couples revolved slowly, face to face, in the shocking intimacy of the new waltz, and many more stood or sat around the edge. Although the scene seemed gay enough to Sarah, everyone behaved with great decorum, particularly the ladies and she again found it impossible to imagine that any were as unvirtuous as Cox had insisted. There were one or two older people about, mainly men, and some on their own who looked rather sad and lonely. She could sympathize with them because she too felt an outsider, but whereas she was perfectly confident that her time of gaiety lay ahead, they were mourning a youth that was gone.

'May I have the pleasure of this dance, please?' asked Frank Cox as the orchestra started a faster tune.

'Oh, certainly,' said Sarah, her confident tone belying her anxiety about what she should do with her feet. Cox perceived her worry immediately.

'It's quite easy for you. You just move in time and nobody can see your feet, but this is the first time I have tried to waltz!' Sarah pursed her lips and they launched themselves into the gathering throng where she was soon floating gracefully along in time to the music with head held high. The orchestra stopped playing all too soon for Sarah but Cox was quite out of breath as he escorted her to a seat a little way from the platform. She had hardly arranged her skirt before a young man diffidently approached them and addressed Cox.

'Good evening! My name is Beddoes. I wonder if I may make so bold as to enquire if the young lady in your charge will be so kind as to favour me with the next dance?' He had turned towards Sarah as he finished this speech, apparently assuming that Frank Cox was a chaperon rather than an escort.

'I am Cox.' They shook hands. 'And this is my friend, Miss Sarah Ruddock.' He slightly emphasized 'friend', which unnerved Beddoes a little.

'Would you care to dance with this gentleman, Sarah?' enquired Cox austerely.

'Why, yes. It is so kind of you to ask,' answered Sarah demurely.

Sir Walter Beddoes was not as easy to dance with as Cox and he was not very good-looking; rather chinless and pale, but his voice was well-bred and his clothes faultlessly tailored and matched.

'I don't believe I have seen you here before!'

'No, it is the first time I have visited Cremorne.'

They spoke inconsequentially about the gardens' attractions until the orchestra stopped playing, when Beddoes suggested that Sarah and Mr Cox might care to join his friends. Sarah eagerly accepted on both their behalves. Fortunately Cox seemed less churlish than she had feared and allowed Beddoes to shepherd them to the far side of the dancing platform where his party occupied a rustic alcove flanked by rose bushes. He introduced them to Lord Frederick Plaice, exhorting Sarah to call him Freddie, which the sandy-haired youth readily endorsed, and to Nancy, Valerie and Raymonde. The three young ladies smiled hospitably, but Sarah, with her sharp senses, thought she detected a glimmer of mistrust in Valerie's and Raymonde's manner. Fair Nancy was affably giggly and spoke with an undisguised London accent. The elegant Valerie spoke in a pseudo-refined tone which Sarah reckoned she could better herself and the dark, sultry Raymonde spoke breathlessly with a hint of an Italian accent which Sarah suspected and Cox knew to have originated much nearer Chelsea than Italy. Freddie had jumped up immediately he had been introduced and now returned with a trayful of sherries for the ladies and whisky for the men.

'Oh, how wonderful, Freddie,' fluted Valerie.

'Too divine,' breathed Raymonde.

'Come and sit by me, Sarah, and we'll have a regular gossip,' ordered Nancy: 'You nivver gets *us* spirits, do you, Freddie?'

'You couldn't carry them, my dear. Just look how inebriated you are on one or three sherries.'

'Oh, nonsense! I'm just enjoying meself. Ain't that what we're 'ere for?'

'Of course we are,' said Frank Cox gallantly, 'and I'll let you sip my whisky.' This was accomplished with some squealing and giggling.

The next three hours passed blissfully for Sarah. They gossiped and drank and danced until Frank Cox was nodding off to sleep so often that it became embarrassing. Their new friends saw them into a carriage and waved them off to Aldersgate after arranging to rendezvous at Vauxhall Gardens the following evening. Sarah had also arranged to meet Nancy in a coffee house in Piccadilly at noon the following day. She had mutely appealed to Cox for permission but he seemed too sleepy to care.

CHAPTER 21

The Hard Light of Day

Frank Cox was tetchy at breakfast and complained of a headache.

'That was appalling rubbish they were selling as whisky last night. You'd never have guessed from the price, mind you.'

'Where are we working today?' asked Sarah.

'I thought we would get a carriage to Kensington. I have one client there and a couple more that I should like to interest.'

'You remember I have arranged to meet Nancy in the Gainsborough at twelve o'clock.'

'You're meant to be earning your living, not gadding about with trulls, you know, Sarah.'

'She isn't! She's a nice girl!' cried Sarah indignantly.

131

'The two ain't necessarily exclusive,' retorted Cox irritably.

'I thought twelve would give us time to work in the morning and then the afternoon as well,' pouted Sarah.

'We'd best get on our way then.'

At half past eleven Sarah assured Cox she could manage alone, so with some misgivings he put her in a carriage, gave her some money and arranged to meet at the lodging house at four o'clock. His headache was severe and he was relieved at the prospect of a sleep.

At Piccadilly, it cost Sarah some courage to enter the splendidly decorated coffee house on her own and her confidence was tried a little by finding no sign of Nancy, but she sat down with dignity and ordered a cup of coffee with an impeccable accent. There were heavy plush curtains in a dull red draped back from the centre of the tall arched windows and matching flock paper on the walls. Each table was set in a small draped alcove with a brass ornamented gas lamp in a wall bracket.

Nancy soon arrived, flustered and apologetic.

'There was this dreadful sailor and I just couldn't bundle him out,' she explained.

'Where was that?'

'In the place what I lives in.' Sarah couldn't quite understand but didn't press the point. Nancy looked older and far less carefree than she had last night. It was partly her clothes which were not very new and the rather random way they were put on. Her hat and shawl were askew and she wasn't wearing a tightly-laced corset.

'Why are you smiling, Sarah?'

'You just made me think of an old friend of mine.'

'Is she nice?'

'Oh yes, very nice. Much older than you though.'

'That don't sound like much of a compliment. Mind you, I do feel pretty old today. In fact I feel damned sick.'

'Oh dear. Do you think it was the drink last night? Mr Cox wasn't feeling well this morning and he said that was why. The whisky was bad.'

Nancy laughed. She had a very attractive way of throwing back her head and laughing with such natural abandon that it was infectious.

'*He* certainly ain't suffering from the same as what I am. I'm afraid it's a penny-royal-tea job for me an' slippery elm if that don't work.' Sarah looked puzzled.

'There, you really ain't one of us, are you dearie! I told Val and Raymo that you weren't but they wouldn't 'ave it. They're worrying about keeping their precious gentlemen. Well, they may talk nice and have plenty of the useful stuff but it takes so long making them part with it that I'd rather settle for less well-bred gents myself. They're usually more dependable, too.' She lowered her voice confidentially.

'Now that gentleman of yours . . . He's straight, dearie. Nothing fancy, but a man of the world and got a good business. He'll treat yer fair.'

'He's just my master, you know . . . I don't have any soft feelings for him,' said Sarah a little sharply.

'No? Well I'm just giving you a bit of good advice, Sarah. Don't rail at me.' Nancy looked hurt.

'No of course not. I'd just rather be independent. That's all I meant.'

'If he's yer master you don't hexactly 'ave hindependent means, do yer? If he wants to give you a bit more money you have to earn it and I've seen enough of you, me gal, to guess as how you knows exactly what you want, and it's pretty expensive,' teased Nancy, pushing Sarah playfully.

Sarah considered this carefully.

'Do you – er – earn – a lot of money?'

'Well, I keep meself comfortable. I could if I wanted but I'm sort of lazy.' She smiled beguilingly. 'Well, that's *my* bit of hindependence, see? I don't work no more than I feel like. Now Val and Raymo they is much more 'ardworking than what I am and they make a big effort to collect the nobs. Like them two last night. They'll probably go right to the top, yer know.' Sarah was nonplussed by this professionalism. She looked hard at Nancy to see if she was serious and she undoubtedly was. There was real respect in her voice as she talked about reaching 'the top'.

'A real nice little 'ouse off Regent Street, all to themselves with a maid or two and twenty quid a month spending money. That's what they'll end up with, I shouldn't wonder. I won't 'cause I don't entertain that class of gent but I'm 'appy . . . 'cepting I'm going to be sick just now – mind, Sarah love! Let me out quick!'

She stumbled to the door and just reached the gutter before she spewed up. Sarah hurried after her solicitously, barely giving a thought to the indignity of their departure.

A waiter followed them out with a worried look but Sarah quickly realized that it was their coffee bill and not Nancy he was concerned about. She settled with him.

'Shall I take you home, Nancy?'

'Neow. I'm all right now but it will come on again. Let's walk in the air for a bit. Let's go to the Park.'

Sarah felt very drawn towards this honest extrovert. She had such a child-like innocence about her which seemed so strange under the circumstances. Even her round face, a little puckered and jaded, framed by fair curly hair, had the appeal of a rather tired eight year-old's. Her smile was sweet and she listened to her companion with full lips parted to reveal pearly childish teeth. She seemed very vulnerable.

It wasn't long before Nancy began to droop again, so they left the park and trailed through the back alleys of Bond Street until they reached a terrace at the back of Regent Street which seemed reasonably genteel. The middle house was somewhat grander and had a portico over its shiny black door which was embellished with a large brass knob and knocker. Sarah was surprised when Nancy rang the bell.

'Come and have a cup of tea, love. It will be quiet enough and Mrs Butler won't mind. Mrs Butler is our – sort of landlady,' explained Nancy seeing Sarah's bemused expression.

The large hall inside was furnished as a reception room in a similar sumptuous style to the Gainsborough but slightly faded and well used.

Nancy sank down gratefully into a deep armchair and motioned Sarah to do the same. The neatly capped maid who had let them in was about to go downstairs.

'Oh, Joan! Do please get me a pot of tea, love. I'm feeling that bad,' wheedled Nancy. Joan shook her head sympathetically and disappeared below stairs as an imposing lady of about forty-five emerged from a room off the hall.

'Oh, Mrs Butler, this is me friend Sarah popped in for a cup of tea. Well, she really brought me back because I was feeling a bit poorly.' Mrs Butler nodded and studied Sarah carefully.

'Good afternoon, Miss . . .?'

'I dunno. What's yer name, Sarah?' giggled Nancy.

'Ruddock. Sarah Ruddock. Good afternoon, ma'am.'

Mrs Butler smiled coolly and called down to Joan to bring three cups up. She poured out the tea when it came and asked Sarah about herself almost as if Sarah was seeking employment with her.

'And how *is* the hat business, Miss Ruddock?'

'Quite well. In fact, we are doing very well for new orders in London.'

'Good! I'm glad to hear it. You are a lucky young woman to have choices, aren't you?'

'Er – yes,' said Sarah uncertainly.

Nancy left hurriedly, looking very ill and returned a

few minutes later breathing heavily. Mrs Butler looked severely at her.

'I told you to get yourself seen to last week,' she said.

'Yes, I know. It was so dreadful last time I can't sort of pluck up courage.'

'Well you must. You know it will be worse the longer it's left. It will probably be the last time you'll need to do it.' She spoke with detachment rather than unkindness and, rising, went into her room to return with a packet which she placed on the table in front of Nancy.

'Immediately Miss Ruddock leaves, you take this money round to Dr Gill. You know the rules, Miss Glover.'

'I'd better go now. I've got to be back at Aldersgate for four,' said Sarah.

'I'll walk along a bit with you,' said Nancy eagerly.

'What did she mean about the rules?' asked Sarah when they were outside.

'Me job! I'm out of me job if I don't get it done right now. No money. Nowhere to live.'

'Oh, that's cruel.'

'Not really. She's pretty good to us. She'd no need to give me the money. After all, it's really me own fault for being careless.'

'You can't help it in your job, though, can you?'

'Yeah. You can always use a vinegar sponge. That's what most girls do. It were that busy sometimes and the vinegar makes yer sore and I couldn't be bothered, yer know.' She wrinkled her nose and smiled apologetically.

'Just lazy; that's me, like I told you. Anyhow, I'm paying for it now, ain't I?'

Sarah shook her head doubtfully. 'How far is it to Dr Gill's?'

'Only round in Eastgate.'

'I'll see you there.'

'Oh Sarah, thanks. You are a chum. You've no idea how *awful* it were last time!' Nancy reached for Sarah's hand and they walked close together in silence till they reached a shabby little court. There was a board bearing some hardly distinguishable names on the wall by a door virtually devoid of any paint.

'This is the doctor's,' said Nancy with a shudder. 'I shan't get to Vauxhall this evening. Tell them I'm sorry.'

'I'll call round to ask Mrs Butler how you are tomorrow, Nancy.'

'Thanks love.' They embraced tenderly and Sarah walked away as the door was opened by a very old and dirty looking woman.

She walked all the way back to Aldersgate with her mind fixed on poor Nancy and the ordeal she was undergoing at that very moment. She arrived at a quarter past four to find Mr Cox having some tea. His sleep had revived him and dispelled his headache, so he was in a good humour.

'Well, here's my little hat-stand! Come and have some tea and one of Mrs Briggs's delicious cakes.' (This was for the benefit of the proprietress who was tidying up the dining-room. The cakes looked indifferent.)

'I've had some tea, thank you.'

'What's wrong with you, Sarah? Have *you* got a headache now?'

'No, not at all. I'm fine.' Her pale cheeks and abstracted expression belied that, and Cox was puzzled.

'Well, how does our pretty Nancy earn her living then?' he teased.

'As you said,' said Sarah shortly.

'Oh, we've been learning the not-so-pretty facts of life, have we then?' he bantered.

Sarah turned abruptly and ran out of the room and up the stairs. She threw herself sobbing on to the bed, praying that he wouldn't follow her.

CHAPTER 22

Sarah is Taught a Lesson

They met Valerie, Raymonde, Freddie and Walter at the Vauxhall Gardens, but all the glamour had turned sour for Sarah. The girls had decided that she was not a threat to them and did their best to give her a cheerful time, but the flirtatious, light-hearted banter that had charmed her the night before suddenly seemed menacing. The vision of Nancy's pale crumpled face kept floating into her mind and all she wanted to do was to go to the terrace to see whether she was all right. She pleaded a headache and they left soon after ten o'clock. Walter Beddoes went with them to find a carriage and insisted upon getting their Leighton address. He urged Sarah to call upon him in Manchester Square and pressed a card into her hand while Cox was boarding the cab. Sarah responded politely, longing to be alone.

Back in their room, Cox undressed but, after his afternoon rest, he seemed reluctant to go to bed, much to Sarah's discomfort.

'It's been a successful trip, hasn't it? You've enjoyed it, haven't you, Sarah?' She murmured an assent as she stepped out of all but one of her petticoats.

'I wish you'd tell me what it is that's upset you. I'm a man of the world. You won't be able to shock me very easy.' He spoke softly as he engulfed her in his arms. Her body went rigid and it was all she could do to stop herself striking out at him.

'Why don't you come into my bed, little hat-stand, eh? I'll calm you down and make you forget your troubles, my sweet.' He was stroking her unruly brown hair. 'I'm very, very fond of you, Sarah, you know.' She placed her hands on his shoulders and pushed him away.

'No, please, Mr Cox. I've got a headache. Please leave me alone.'

He looked annoyed and she thought he would persevere, but the wildness in her huge tawny eyes warned him off.

He flounced into bed, flapping the covers irritably.

'I've spent a lot of money giving you a good time, my girl. You ought to think on that. You take rather a lot for granted. I've been very patient but a fellow expects fairness. Most men wouldn't have waited as long as me, you know.'

Sarah loosened her corset, crept into bed and lay curled up tensely, her hands over her face, hoping he wouldn't bother her again.

They had just returned to Aldersgate about four o'clock the next day when Sir Walter Beddoes sent his card up. Sarah went downstairs to meet him.

'Ah, Miss Ruddock. So I have found you in at last!'

'Have you called before then?'

'Yes, I have been positively haunting the place. Did your worthy proprietress not tell you? I came as soon as I was dressed just after noon, I believe. Yes, it *was*, because I looked at my watch when the good lady said that you usually returned about four o'clock; so here I am again.'

Sarah offered her hand graciously as he spoke and wondered where this preamble was leading.

'You are astir very early it seems, Miss Ruddock. What do you do with yourself? Have you been driving in the Park?'

'No-o,' said Sarah, eyeing him doubtfully. 'I have been visiting some shops in Bond Street and Piccadilly.' She mentioned the location hopefully to indicate the superior quality of the shops.

'Ah. You young ladies are always shopping. You must

139

take me with you tomorrow. I shall rise particularly early for the occasion.'

'I don't believe you would enjoy that very much,' lisped Sarah sweetly. Beddoes admired her twinkling smile but didn't detect the hint of sarcasm. 'And we are going back to Leighton tomorrow.'

'Well, I insist, positively insist, that you come out to drink coffee with me this very moment. Perhaps I should ask permission of that uncle of yours?'

'He is resting just now but I shall tell him where I am going, if you will excuse me, Sir Walter.'

Sarah found Cox sprawled across his bed fast asleep, so she changed quickly into her sprigged muslin gown, or rather, Alice's gown, and left him a note to say that she would return about eight o'clock.

'Oh, how charming you look! You will not be offended if I call you Sarah, as I presumed to do last night, will you?'

'No, of course not.'

'Where shall we go to drink our coffee? Have you been to Almack's in King Street? It will be rather quiet there so early in the evening but that will allow us to chat nicely, won't it?'

'Oh yes, that sounds fine,' smiled Sarah gaily.

Almack's rooms *were* quiet. There were only two other couples and a group of four middle-aged men who seemed to be discussing business. The red plush curtains were ponderously draped around the windows on one wall and around elaborately cut mirrors on the other three. There were cut glass chandeliers and carpets on the floor which Sarah skirted round with awe until she saw that Sir Walter and even the waiters walked upon them as unceremoniously as if they had been strewn rushes. She tentatively trod upon one to reach the table Beddoes had selected, lifting her skirt and feeling faintly horrified at the way her slippered feet sank into the soft pile. She wondered how they kept so clean and bright.

Beddoes noticed her awe with amused satisfaction. He was becoming tired of the brazen sophistication that Valerie and Raymonde assumed on all occasions and found Sarah's ill-concealed innocence quite refreshing.

'I do not understand how you can bear to return to that dismal village of yours. Will you not find it impossibly boring after the novelty of London, eh?'

'Yes, I fear I shall,' sighed Sarah.

'Why return then? Why not stay here?'

'But I have nowhere to live.'

'I am sure we could find you somewhere.'

Sarah shook her head sadly. She did not realize how transparent her defences were. She thought Sir Walter still assumed that she had independent means. She craved for the life of glamorous excitement that beckoned. Walter Beddoes was old by Sarah's standards, but he was only twenty-eight. The soft lighting gilded his wavy fair hair which was parted in the centre and swept across each temple. Even his angular nose and receding chin were not too pronounced as he smiled kindly across at Sarah. She lowered her eyes discreetly as the waiter delicately arranged the cups, coffee jug and wafers in front of them.

'I can put at your disposal a small suite of rooms in a neighbourhood that is quite superior to Aldersgate and you should have no expenses,' he murmured persuasively.

Sarah raised her eyes.

'Do you mean live in your house?'

'Well, no! Not quite proper, I fear!' He laughed and Sarah realized with annoyance that she had committed a breach of etiquette.

'No, not Manchester Square,' he chuckled. 'The mater would be somewhat scandalized. No offence meant, of course, my dear. You know how irritatingly respectable mothers can be. I have the lease of a rather pleasant villa in Tothill Street where you could be very cosy and within an easy distance of St James's Park. We could walk together there when the weather was fine, or ride in my phaeton and in the evening we could visit the different Assembly Rooms. I could introduce you to the Argyle and even the Clipstone Hop when you wanted to be really daring.' He raised his brows enquiringly.

'It sounds very tempting, Sir Walter.'

'So why are you about to make an excuse?'

Sarah hesitated. 'No expense'? Did he mean that he would actually give her money to live on? She visualized her mother's furrowed brow and worried eyes: 'Lunnon! I don't hold with that!' and Nancy appraising her friends' future: 'Twenty quid a month, I shouldn't wonder!'

'Mr Cox depends a lot on me.'

'Oh, does he? Yes I see, I think. He is not really your uncle, perhaps?' Beddoes was regarding her keenly but she could not quite gauge his expression. Her answer to this question was clearly important but she was not sure what he wanted her to say, so she plumped for honesty.

'No! Nancy just guessed that. I work for him. He owns a factory and we are in London to sell the straw bonnets that are made there.' She waited apprehensively to see what effect this change of status would have. To her relief, his face relaxed again.

'Ah, just that?'

'I am not sure what you mean, Sir Walter.'

'Your relationship with Mr Cox is purely a business one, is it?'

'Yes, purely business. Hats, that is.' She added the last phrase to make quite sure there was no misunderstanding. She was surprised how rapidly their conversation had progressed from trivial gaiety to this rather tense exchange.

'I am sure you are very good at selling hats. I should certainly be inclined to buy any that I saw you wearing, but I am also sure Mr Cox could find someone else to help him, and think how you would enjoy living in

London, keeping me amused, my dear. That is skilled work, too, you know, because I am so easily bored.'

'I should have to be well paid for it then,' laughed Sarah.

Again the calculating expression which she could not quite fathom swept briefly across his face.

'I am not quite sure when you are teasing me and when you are serious. I am not even sure how old you are. You look very young.'

Again Sarah plumped for honesty. 'I am nearly eighteen.'

'Ah. Well how much do you think this highly skilled job is worth? How much do you think you should cost me?'

It was Sarah's turn to wonder whether or not he was serious.

'I hope you are not intending to "buy" me. That may be quite proper for straw bonnets, but I should not approve of it for myself at all.' A note of warning had crept into Sarah's voice which was, intentionally or genuinely lost upon him.

'Oh, you are a tease, Sarah. Yes! I shall buy you, just like a delightful, beribboned, bewitching straw bonnet. Tell me your price.'

'Terribly expensive!'

'Oh dear. I shall have to barter. How tedious,' he sighed.

There the matter dropped, leaving Sarah wondering whether she had just rejected a golden egg or closely evaded capture.

A string trio had now begun to play an overture from a popular operetta, and more people began to arrive. Sarah decided from their dress and bearing that the men at least were very affluent. There were two high-ranking military gentlemen who were treated with great respect by the waiters. The women were young and beautiful and almost certainly not wives. Sarah's eyes missed nothing. The ladies seemed gay and happy. They were lavishly dressed. Why should she have any doubts about joining them? She thought of Valerie and Raymonde. She had probably just been offered the prize they were seeking. She would be very unpopular there if she accepted it, but this did not bother her unduly. Nancy! How could she have forgotten Nancy?

'Sir Walter, I must go now. I promised to visit a . . . friend.' She did not want to discuss Nancy's plight with him.

'Oh! Very well, then, Sarah. Where may I take you?'

'I am not quite sure of the name of the street but Regent Street is quite close.'

'I can't leave you to walk alone there.'

'It will only take me a minute to reach the house. Please don't worry. I shall take a Hackney carriage back to Aldersgate.'

He drove her to her destination without further enquiry.

'Goodbye, Sarah. You will consider my proposal and let me know tomorrow, won't you. I shall not be miserly towards you, you know.'

The scene at the impressive black door was no longer quiet, as it had been the previous afternoon. There was a group of young gentlemen pushing in past a burly door-keeper who was at pains to keep out two drunken sailors. Sarah slipped in unquestioned and found a merry male company filling the hall under the watchful eye of Mrs Butler.

'I've come to see how Nancy is, please, Mrs Butler.' That lady drew Sarah to the bottom of the stairs, her face grim.

'She's very bad. Do you want to see her?' she asked quietly.

'Well, yes, if she's well enough,' faltered Sarah with a sinking heart.

'Come on then, quickly.'

144

She took Sarah up to a small garret at the very top of the house. It was sparsely furnished but clean, and propped up on some pillows lay Nancy. She looked like a white marble effigy. Her delicate hands lay on the counterpane looking almost transparent with the blue veins standing out plainly.

Sarah stood transfixed in horror until Nancy opened her eyes. They seemed startlingly blue and large set against the dark shadows around them. Her almost colourless lips stretched into a weak smile.

'Oh, you've come, Sarah. I've bin wondering whether you would all day.'

Sarah knelt down and took one of her hands. It was cold.

'I'm sorry. This is our last day in London and we've been so busy.'

'It don't matter. You've come now, love.' Nancy's voice managed to capture some of its usual cheeriness.

'Was it very bad?'

'Neow. Not really. It didn't hurt half as bad as last time but I knowed from the old chap's face that summat had gone wrong.'

'Will you be all right?'

''Spect so, me gal! It will just take me a bit longer to get on to me feet again, I s'pose.' Her brave cheerfulness seemed exhausting and she shut her eyes.

'You're tired. I'd better go.'

'Neow, Sarah. Just stay a bit and hold me hand. Tell me what it was like at Vauxhall last night.'

Sarah prattled on, making the evening sound so gay and lively until Nancy's smile faded and she was sure she was asleep. She tucked the limp cold hands under the coverlet and smoothed the pillow and sheet, then crept downstairs. The roar of male voices and laughter became louder at each landing. Mrs Butler looked up at her questioningly as she reached the hall.

145

'Will she be all right?' whispered Sarah.

'She's a strong girl,' said Mrs Butler non-committally. 'She'll be well looked after. I guarantee you that.'

Their eyes travelled over the carefree noisy crowd of men, young and old, far outnumbering the girls in sight and then met and held one another's gaze for a moment, united in impotent bitterness.

Sarah returned in a carriage, feeling helpless and somehow bereft. She found Cox already in bed, reading a journal and she gave him the small amount of change left. He scrutinized her face but she turned aside.

'So have you been thinking about what I said?' he asked in a neutral voice. Sarah didn't answer.

'I'm sorry I lost my temper last night, Sarah. I am really fond of you, my dear.' He was feeling his way carefully and his effort to warm his voice made it sound unbearably ingratiating to Sarah but she tried to control herself. She even remembered Nancy's words, '. . . he'll treat yer fair, he will.' She began undressing. He waited until she was in her corset and shift and then slipped out of bed and gently drew her towards him. Her stomach had turned to stone and her throat contracted so that the scream in her chest could not force its way through.

'Relax, relax, my little hat-stand,' he murmured, holding her head against his chest. He bent and slipped his arm beneath her knees to lift her. The scream forced through, a strangled, guttural cry and, to her surprise, she watched Cox reel across the room, trip and fall heavily against the chest standing at the foot of his bed. She must have hurled him there in an involuntary frenzy. Horrified, she stood rooted to the spot struggling to get her breath. He slowly pulled himself up on the chest, glaring at her malevolently.

'So this is all the thanks I get for looking after you; spending my money so free to give you a good time. This is your gratitude, madam, is it? Madam – ha! More like a vixen! I wonder if your cubs are worth that much fight, eh?' He laughed nastily, his face white with rage.

Sarah suddenly came to life. She pressed her curled fingers to her cheeks, defensively.

'I – I'm sorry. I didn't mean to. I didn't know what I was doing. Leave me alone! Please let me be!' She finished in an hysterical wail.

'My God! Don't you worry. I won't touch you again in a hurry. You may live to regret it, though!'

CHAPTER 23

Sarah Learns Her Lesson

Sarah and Cox hardly exchanged a word at breakfast the next morning. Cox was nursing his wounded pride and bruised shoulder while Sarah thought miserably of Nancy. They had packed their bags, and the *Shrewsbury Wonder* left the Angel sharp at a quarter to one.

'Please may I call to see how Nancy is?' Sarah asked eventually, in a small contrite voice. Cox gave her a bleak glance and grunted. She thought he meant 'no'. After a pause she said:

'She is desperately ill.'

'Ugh. Why is that?'

'She went to a doctor to get an abortion on Thursday and it's gone wrong.'

'You'd best not have got yourself mixed up in that sort of company.'

'You were happy enough to join them the other night,' flared Sarah.

'I wasn't at a brothel, was I?'

'No. That would cost you money!' Sarah regretted the words immediately they were out of her mouth. Why could she never curb her sharp tongue?

Cox jumped up, nearly knocking his chair over and left the dining-room.

'Whatever now?' thought Sarah. 'If I'd not upset him he might have taken me there. I've no money. I won't get back in time for the coach if I walk.'

Walter! She ran upstairs to get the visiting card. Cox must have gone out. She hastily pinned on her hat, flung a shawl round her shoulders and ran towards the embankment until she found a Hackney carriage.

'Twenty-four Manchester Square, please,' she commanded.

'Supposing he's not at home?' she worried. 'Bound to be at home at this time in the morning. He may have gone away to stay with friends, though . . .' However would she placate the driver when she told him she had no money? She flushed at the thought of the undignified scene that would surely ensue.

The carriage stopped outside an imposing terrace house and she sprang out and up the steps. A well-groomed butler answered her knock. Just a fleeting glance of apprehension passed across his face at the sight of the flushed young lady with a slightly crooked hat tied precariously to a mass of wiry brown curls. Sarah returned his look of enquiry haughtily and wished she had her own visiting card.

'Is Sir Walter at home, please? I should like to see him for a moment, if it is convenient.'

'Do step inside, madam. I shall inform Sir Walter that Miss . . .?'

'Miss Ruddock,' supplied Sarah graciously.

Walter appeared with alacrity, wearing a red brocaded jacket. He looked delighted to see Sarah, who rapidly explained how ill Nancy was, but not the reason, and how sure she was that he would want to know, so she had rushed here to tell him. She proposed that he accompany her to visit Nancy.

'What? At Mrs Butler's establishment?' he asked, with raised brows.

'Yes. That is where she is,' replied Sarah a little irritably.

'Of course. Shall we do it after dinner?'

Sarah explained about their impending departure and eventually managed to imbue in him some sense of urgency, but he took an exasperatingly long time to get ready. Sarah heard the door knocker sound and strained her ears to listen. It was her driver and she bit her lip wondering whether the butler would come in to ask her for the fare, but the door shut so he must have settled it or asked him to wait.

At last they were travelling towards Mayfair in Walter's phaeton. At his suggestion they stopped at a florist's in Piccadilly and chose a huge bunch of carnations and lilies, which Sarah carried through the shiny black door. The maid regarded them austerely and went to fetch Mrs Butler, who came out in a morning coat with her black hair loose and no make-up on.

'We've brought these for Nancy,' said Sarah, desperately searching her face for some indication, but it was quite expressionless.

'She died at half past three this morning. She was not alone.' The colour drained from Sarah's face.

'Sit down, Miss Ruddock. Perhaps you would care to wait in the parlour for a moment, Mr . . .?'

'Beddoes, ma'am.' Walter laid the flowers he had taken from Sarah on the table and withdrew, following the maid.

'Remember, please, Miss Ruddock, that this would not have happened had she not put this unpleasant business off for so long. She would have been perfectly well if she had had it done a month ago.'

Sarah had no idea why she made this point so firmly. It seemed irrelevant now.

'And also remember where I am should you ever need me. I always have a place for a sensible girl like you.'

Sarah raised her eyes. Now she understood and she prayed fervently that she would never need Mrs Butler.

Walter solicitously helped Sarah back into the phaeton. It was hardly necessary because, although a little pale, Sarah was coldly calm but he drove her back to the lodging house and even insisted on driving her and Cox to Islington.

He waited with Sarah in the bustle of the Angel's yard while Cox supervised the stowing of their luggage. The noise must have been as great as at the beginning of the week but it made no impression on Sarah now.

'Have you made a decision about my offer, Sarah? I have hardly slept all night. Your face haunts me.' Sarah turned away.

'I can't,' she said.

'You can't decide or you can't accept?' he asked earnestly.

'I can't decide. Please don't press me now,' she cried brokenly.

'No. I am sorry. It is most sad about your friend.'

Sarah rounded on him. She had thought of Nancy as his friend too. He seemed to be not in the least disturbed.

'When you come to a decision, just write to me and I shall drive down to rescue you from the dismal muddy countryside. You will do that? Promise me, Sarah. You will write soon?' he implored urgently as Cox walked towards them.

'Yes, yes,' said Sarah impatiently.

She was relieved that Frank Cox was travelling on the outside of the coach. She took only a cursory note of her companions inside and spent the first part of the journey gazing unseeingly out of the window as she reviewed each event of her stay in London. It seemed more like 'her life in London'. During that five and a half days she had encountered an utterly new way of life, had naïvely enjoyed its pleasures and had had shown to her the

150

price. The subdued Sarah who returned could easily have been five and a half years older.

As they sped between the pale chalk banks near Dunstable a sudden yearning for her home struck Sarah and she guiltily realized that she had not spared a thought for the family in the little cottage on the Heath, all her time in London. When they alighted at the White Swan in Hockliffe, Cox's temper seemed improved, so Sarah ventured to ask him if she could go home since it was Sunday the next day.

'I'll get back to Leighton tomorrow evening,' she assured him.

'Oh, so you do intend to return to the humdrum hat business then, do you?' he asked sarcastically.

A retort sprang to Sarah's mind but she managed to keep her lips closed.

'I want to see how my mother is,' she pleaded.

'It don't matter how I am, does it?' he said peevishly.

'There'll be Alice . . .' suggested Sarah and wished she hadn't.

'No there won't be, actually. I told her to find herself another position while I was in London. She was getting too free with her tongue for my liking.' He announced this angrily, looking hard at Sarah. She turned her head away and a mirthless smile formed on his lips as he watched his message reach its mark. He then added:

'And *you* can go where you like as far as I am concerned.'

Sarah considered this veiled threat but her yearning for home had become so strong she decided to gamble.

'I shall be at Leighton by half past nine,' she said firmly. Please would you take my bag when I've changed my shoes.' With an enormous effort she touched his arm affectionately and gave him a radiant smile.

'Right you are,' he said guardedly. 'I *do* prefer my girls to be "good natured".'

CHAPTER 24

Sarah Makes up Her Mind

As she strode along the Woburn Turnpike, her spirits began to lighten. She wished she had taken off some petticoats when she changed her shoes but she soon accomplished this behind a bush, rolled them up, placed her hat on top and tied the bundle neatly with her hat-ribbons.

Perhaps for the first time in her life Sarah consciously noticed the details of the 'dismal' countryside in which she had been reared. She saw the furled shoots of dogs' mercury and cuckoo pint thrusting up among the gnarled roots of the hawthorn hedge. She broke off and chewed some of the bursting thorn buds. 'Bread and cheese' was the odd name the children called the apple-green sprouts, but they no longer had any flavour and she felt a ripple of nostalgia for a childhood which had had more compensations than she had ever realized. She saw a hen blackbird flit quietly away ahead and, when she reached the spot, she quickly found the nest with one azure egg blotched with brick brown. It was such a miracle of shape and colour lying in its earthy cradle. The tree branches were still bare but they each etched a distinctive pattern against the sky; the elms bushy-tipped with swollen buds; the beeches waving delicate fans, and the coarse-twigged ashes. She remembered the games the little girls played in the yards and the seasonal succession of tops, marbles and 'pin-a-sights'.

Her reverie was interrupted by the Northampton coach cracking by in a cloud of dust. She passed the time of day with the toll-gate keeper who was enjoying an evening pipe in the doorway of his little square house and soon she was passing the high arched entrance to the yard of the George clattering with coaches and horses. Woburn Square seemed comparatively tranquil, graced by its new Gothic market-house and Regency terraces. There was a tattoo of iron-shod hooves issuing from the yard of the Goat and a four-horse farm waggon waited outside the Magpie, then the peace of the fields again. She could see the woods skirting the Woburn edge of Aspley Heath on the rising sandhills.

She turned off the Turnpike up Longslade and cut through to the sandy lane, walking faster and faster until, as the light began to fade, she ran up the heather-clad bank and into the top edge of the cottage garden. She was imagining her mother's surprised face giving way to a delighted welcome, but a moment later she stopped short at the sight of Tom leaning against the back wall of the cottage. He had his arm round Bobby's shoulders, and Bobby's head was pressed against Tom's chest. Sarah froze. She could see Bobby's shoulders heaving and hear his muffled sobs. She didn't want to know what was wrong. She couldn't bear another trag-edy today. She suddenly longed to be in Bobby's place; to feel Tom's comforting arm around her; to be able to indulge in supported grief. She walked slowly towards them. Tom heard a twig snap and looked up. His grave face barely registered surprise.

'What's happened, Tom?' she asked bleakly.

'It's little Mary. We've just bin to bury her.'

'Oh! Poor Mama.'

'Yes. She'll be glad you've come,' he said flatly.

Despite her sadness, or perhaps because of it, she noted the old familiar things as if for the first time. She heard that Tom's voice was now a deep baritone, that he stood over six feet tall and that Bobby, who had turned away in embarrassment, was growing into a finely-featured lad with Tom's fresh complexion but darker eyes and hair. She left them and went round to the living-room. Eliza was nursing William and comforting Tize who knelt by her. Their eyes were swollen and red. Mary Nursall was at the fireplace pouring some hot water into the teapot and John was pacing up and down the room in his regular state of frustrated helplessness. Tize saw Sarah first and took William off her mother who rose to embrace Sarah.

'Oh, I do wish you'd come sooner, love. I kept sending to Leighton for you,' she said reproachfully.

'I'm sorry, Mama. I've been away.'

'Bin away! Where 'ave you bin?'

'I went to London to help Mr Cox get orders for the summer straws.'

'Lunnon!' Eliza's face looked even more worried.

'I am sorry about Mary, Mama. I should never have gone if I'd known.'

'I s'pose it were a blessing really, like the Rector said. She'd nivver 'ave bin a strong child.' Eliza sniffed abjectly into her wet hanky.

'No. It's all for the best, dear. It's the good Lord who decides these things,' said Mary Nursall consolingly.

'The good Lord! More like a bad government,' muttered John, but the women ignored him.

'. . . but we did do our best for the poor wee mite, didn't we, Liza? No-one can say as we didn't do our best.'

'No, Mary. I'se ever so grateful for the way you sat up with me. There weren't no-one else 'ere ter do it.' Sarah recognized the reproach again.

'Come and 'ave a cup of tea,' said Mary.

'Yes, Sarah. 'Ave a cup of tea, love. I don't know where our Tom and Bobby be.' She looked round anxiously.

'They're out in the garden. I'll fetch them, Mama.'

John didn't go out that evening and after the children had gone to bed, Sarah and Tom left their parents sitting in front of the fire and strolled up the lane.

'What have you been doing, Tom?'

'Same as usual.'

She hoped he'd ask how London was, but they walked on in silence.

'How's Father getting on?'

'He's on as a roundsman again.'

'But it's getting to be busy?'

'Aye. He's upset Farmer Hurst at Wavendon now and ole Jo Locke at Lower End's bin putting it around that he's a Luddite.'

'Luddite! That's all over now!'

'I dunno except it's a bad ole name.'

Sarah thought Tom was blaming his father rather than the trouble-makers.

'At least he's got the courage to say what he thinks.'

'It don't do us no good though. Mr Perkins won't give me a rise like Rogers Jones what's not bin working so long. He says he's doing me a favour keeping me on when me father's a bad un.' Sarah's loyalties became stretched now.

'I bet you're the best worker he's got,' she cried indignantly.

'Yeah. Likely so,' said Tom bitterly. 'And the other thing is poaching. He's telling Mama that Harry gets them rabbits and pheasants off the Duke's gamekeeper. He don't! Father's got five snares up here – there's one just yonder – and I know he's got two gins over Red Lane. He's likely got a lot more.'

'He'll get caught sooner or later!'

'Yeah. Then what? Jenkins will sack me and all we'll have is Tize's plaiting.'

'And my money.'

'Umph,' snorted Tom contemptuously.

'I'll get more now,' said Sarah with unjustified confidence.

'How?'

'Well, Mr Cox says I'm good with his ledgers and he'll

155

give me a rise, and he want me to . . . look after his house.'

Tom rounded on her.

'I don't know just what that might mean but you ought to be here looking after us.'

'Mama does that.'

'She needs you. She's been sending to Leighton for you all week.'

'That was because of Mary.'

'Father says Cox will make you into a fallen woman.'

'I thought you didn't hold with what your father says?'

'I daresay he's right this time. You're certainly talking fine and fancy.'

'Tom! I only do what's best for the family. You know that! I'll be able to earn a lot of money soon. Just give me time.' Sarah's voice was high with hurt and indignation.

'I can earn the money. There's no need for you to cheapen yourself in a factory.'

'You don't seem to be doing *that* well,' snapped Sarah and regretted it immediately.

He turned to face her. Although it was dark, she could visualize him standing in the angry frustration of not being able to express himself, just as he had done as a boy, but he was now a tall man glaring down at her. Now, as then, she came to his rescue with her agile mind and tongue.

'What you need, Tom, is your own business, then it won't matter what they say about Father. You must have spades and shovels and a horse and cart and someone to help you.'

'Yeah, that's all I need,' he said with heavy sarcasm.

'We'll manage it between us. Just you see.'

'I don't want money as you've earned off that Cox fellow.'

'Why? I've been working for him for years.'

'Not living with him, though.'

'You're allowing yourself to suppose too much, Tom.'

They didn't mention money to each other through the next day but Sarah was hurt by Tom's coolness towards her. She knew he was doing her an injustice at the moment but she was oppressed by the decision she had to make and there seemed to be increasingly little choice. What grieved her even more than submitting to Cox was the fact that Tom's presumptions would then be correct. She had always looked up to Tom, and his opinion of her was deeply important. She turned the problem over and over and always there was one insuperable conclusion. They needed money, her mother and the children and Tom all needed the money which only she could earn in sufficient amounts. The only way to earn it was to keep right with Cox. If she did that she could gradually bring him round to expanding the business and allowing her a stake in it or even, perhaps, lending her money to start up on her own. The only alternative was Sir Walter Beddoes; or Mrs Butler, of course. Sarah shuddered.

She said good-bye to her parents.

'I am sorry I haven't brought you anything, Mama. Mr Cox will be paying me for helping him in London and I'll get over as soon as I can.'

'Don't you worry, love. You must spend a bit on yourself. We'll manage somehow. I don't need to buy any more medicine for the poor little mite now,' she said tearfully.

Tom walked down the hill with her but said very little apart from enquiring if she had enough money for the carrier.

'I suppose you've got money for Mr Hedges?'

'Oh, yes,' she lied.

At the Red Lion at Leighton she asked the old man to wait a few moments while she went to fetch some, but he refused.

'Nay. Don't you let that worry you, girl. I'll do it

157

happily for tha father. Whatever they say about John Ruddock, he's a brave man. Him and his friends talk the way things should be. It's only a pity there's so little chance of it coming about.' Sarah thanked him fervently.

As a child she had accepted the local opinion about her father and his ineffectualness in coping with the family's problems, but now she was beginning to allow him a grudging respect. Every day brought fresh injustice to the poor people that she lived among. As a child she accepted these unquestioningly as the way life was, but her spirit rebelled when she had to suffer them in order to survive.

There seemed no alternative now, because Sarah was, above all, a survivor.

CHAPTER 25

Sarah Strikes a Bargain

Sarah plied the knocker on Mr Cox's front door feeling apprehensive about her reception. The position of her family was as fragile as ever and she had to be 'good-natured' to Frank Cox whatever it cost personally. A coarse-featured girl of about twelve in a shabby white cap, opened the door and stood surveying Sarah sullenly. Sarah impatiently stepped past her into the hall.

'Is Mr Cox in?' she demanded.

'Neow. 'E said to say 'e wouldn't be long, Miss.'

Sarah went in search of her bag. The bed in her old room was unmade, with a dirty night-shift thrown across it. There was a crude plaster model of a pig, cracked and chipped, on the chest and a frayed skirt and petticoat inside it. She found her belongings in her box in the bedroom where Cox and Alice had slept and her London bag on top of the chest there. The top two drawers were empty and so was half the wardrobe. What should she do? What *could* she do? However tempting Sir Walter's offer was, London was a long way away and no sum of money had been mentioned. It was a gamble and she had seen the sort of competition she had if Beddoes failed her. No! Rather the devil she knew. She would have to work hard here but she could do that and she would be able to tell Tom how she earned her money or, at any rate, how she earned some of it. She winced and then, making a firm effort, she drew herself up, tossed her head haughtily and unpacked her bag and box into the empty drawers and wardrobe, her lips compressed bitterly. The room was drab and cheerless, although it had a good window overlooking the street. She thought she would like to get some floor cloth and curtains, and then she thought of the expense, and then she thought of how much less they might be bought for with a little care and influence and how much change that might leave in her pocket. Frank Cox would pay for his pound of her flesh – no doubt of that!

She gazed out of the window, her elbows on the sill and a faraway expression in her eyes. The main trouble with fuller's earth was its weight. Tom must have a horse and cart and those came expensive. She'd no idea how much. The fullers who needed the earth were mainly in Gloucestershire or Yorkshire and the journey to get it to them was long and expensive but they had no source nearby so the price was good. Capital! Capital! That elusive commodity with which all was possible and without which one carried on making it for other people. If Sarah had some, how could she best spend it? Tom had no head for figures. He would soon fall victim in the cut and thrust of business. Sarah couldn't manage his affairs because she would be too busy making the money. Her mind began to explore other avenues. She had remembered everything she had seen in London. She had been in and out of so many gown shops, linen drapers and cloth merchants pricing this and that, and she had shrewdly noted that a straw bonnet or a gown in a stylish bazaar in Piccadilly could cost four times as much as in a St Paul's Churchyard warehouse. Yes, 'style' was the all-important ingredient. If Sarah learnt the rudiments of dressmaking she was confident that her keen eye and judgement would take her far in the world of fashionable outfitting. If Cox would lend her money for rent and stock why should she not start her own business? She had no ambition to compete with the local tailors working for the poor and a pitiable profit. No! She was planning no less than to dress the Rector's wife. Mrs Devereux was always arrayed elegantly. She certainly didn't go to the local dressmakers. She went to London and to Piccadilly or Regent Street, which was a long way. At that moment there was nothing about the coming summer fashions, either in the materials or the style, on which Sarah was not a dependable authority. All she needed to do was to travel up to sell Frank Cox's hats two or three times a year and return with a stock of stuffs and knowledge to keep a couple of seamstresses busy and the wives of the local gentry well supplied. Having captured the Rector's wife, her clientèle would follow naturally. She could think of plenty! Mrs Vaughan, for whom even Sarah felt a fleeting pity. The Headmaster's plump wife dressed in the most appalling but expensive way. Sarah could satisfy her own pity and purse by vastly improving that worthy matron's appearance. Miss Hall! Well, she couldn't make money from Miss Hall, but that lady's tastes were so plain and practical anyway and she would be sure to help Sarah by putting in a good word to her friends.

By the time Frank Cox returned, Sarah had planned her future and greeted him ebulliently, flying down the stairs and depositing a friendly kiss on his cheek. His natural caution bade him beware but his loneliness and desire won through so he responded warmly and they sat down together in great good humour to eat some appallingly prepared food.

'Who is this girl?' asked Sarah, distrustfully pushing some gritty cabbage to the side of her plate.

'She is called Verity,' stated Cox.

'Where did you find her?'

'Oh, she's one of a large family in a yard off Church Street.'

'It's a pity her mother didn't teach her to cook.'

'She only needs some guidance, Sarah. I am sure you can supply that.'

Sarah delicately removed a mass of unchewable and unidentifiable meat from her mouth, shaking her head uncertainly.

'Verity verily looks dirty, sullen and stupid,' she said.

'Well, I shall give you the housekeeping money, Sarah, and my leave to do exactly as you think fit . . . so long as I am made comfortable.' He added the last bit warningly.

'All right. That's fair,' said Sarah. 'But I won't be able to work so much. I shall have to stop at four o'clock each day. I should like to make this house more cheerful too. May I have money to buy floor cloth for the bedroom, please, and some stuff for curtains. I shall ask Mrs Newbold to show me how to make them up.'

'Can't we pay her to do it?'

'I should like to learn to sew. It may be useful. You were talking about starting to make hats, you remember?'

'Well, yes. I think Madam du Prêt in Crofter Street would teach you that better.'

'Yes, the Mantua maker,' said Sarah eagerly. 'And if I improved the appearance of the sitting-room and dining-room we could perhaps begin to entertain a little.'

'Yes. That could be good for business,' declared Cox enthusiastically. 'There are a couple of hatters in Luton I do a little trade with and I should like to do more. I

161

knew you would come round to being sensible, Sarah. I see you have unpacked. Shall we go to bed?'

Sarah acquiesced with a sigh. She would plead indisposition tonight and tomorrow she would buy a bottle of vinegar and a large sponge. Tom should never find out for certain and it was for his benefit that she did this. What would Nancy have said? What would Mrs Butler say? They were the people who really understood. She did have choices but not many and this was not one of them.

The next two months passed quickly for Sarah. They took on several more girls at the factory to get the London orders completed in time. The hats were boxed and sent up by carrier with Cox coaching up two days later to supervise their delivery. Sarah would have liked to have gone but it was not necessary, and the factory supervisor had recently been sacked when Sarah's books proved he had been embezzling on a small scale but frequently.

'You'll have to stay and keep the place in order, Sarah. Since you said I didn't need to replace Bates there is no-one else to do it.'

'Yes. I realize that, but you don't pay me nearly as much as you paid Bates, Frank.' The intimacy of their relationship allowed her to call him by his first name in private. She always referred to him as 'Mr Cox' in front of the girls.

'You must have change from the housekeeping, surely?'

'Not very much and you wouldn't want me pennypinching on that to make up my wages, would you?'

'Well, no. How much do you think I ought to pay you? Remember I pay all your keep.'

'You paid Bates thirteen and sixpence a week. I think with some deducted for keep you should give me at least twelve shillings and sixpence.'

'Women aren't paid the same as men.'

'I do not understand why.'

'Because – because they aren't so strong.'

'And how did Christopher Bates use all this strength?'

'Well, his particular job didn't require it but . . .'

'But – but. I am doing his job and I am keeping the ledgers – and I am keeping your house. I think you had better pay me fourteen shillings, Frank. You are getting a very good bargain at that!'

'My, you certainly have the best head for business I have ever seen on the shoulders of a woman!' said Cox with grudging admiration.

'Fifteen shillings a week and I shall start training two girls to sew hats. They shall make copies of some of the ones we saw in London.'

'I can't remember what they were like well enough to copy them.'

'But I can!' said Sarah confidently. 'Well?'

'Well what?'

'Fourteen shillings a week, for the moment.'

'For the moment?'

'Well, if I set up a hat-making business for you I shall deserve more than that.'

Frank Cox settled for the fourteen shillings a week before the rate rose even higher.

Sarah knew that she could make that up with some housekeeping change and the odd gratuity she was given by clients coming to the factory.

Sarah visited the family on the Heath each Sunday that she could manage but these became less and less frequent. Eliza would have liked to see more of her but she was pleased that Sarah's work was flourishing so well. Tom was still working very hard for his eight shillings and sixpence a week and gave almost all of it to his mother. He was resentful that Sarah contributed so much, although Eliza was always careful to conceal just

163

how much it was. She enjoyed being able to buy little luxuries like milk and cakes for the family.

'Have a piece of plum cake, Tom.'

'Hmm. How did you manage to buy this, Mother?'

'Sarah gave me a little bit yesterday and now poor little Mary's not needing nothing . . .' Eliza's voice trailed off brokenly and Tom didn't pursue it.

CHAPTER 26

Trouble on the Heath

It was one Tuesday evening that John got taken poaching. He was making his way home through one of the Duke's new plantations when a gamekeeper stepped out on the path ahead of him.

'Good evening! Let's be seeing what you've got in that bag.'

''Tain't none of your business.'

'I'll be the judge of that.'

John turned his head furtively as he considered running for it.

'You'd best not do anything you'll regret, Ruddock.'

The use of his name subdued John and he handed over the brown blanket bag. The gamekeeper emptied out a tangle of rabbit snares and a small spring trap.

'I uses them in the hedges over at Farmer Hurst's where I work,' said John aggressively.

'Let's have your coat off then.'

'No. You ain't got no right.'

'Oh yes I have. You're trespassing and you ain't got nothing to hide anyway, you says.'

The man knew John's reputation for violence and was relishing the interview almost as little as his captive.

John made a desperate bid to push past him but the

gamekeeper caught him by the wrist, tripping him up with his foot at the same moment so that John went sprawling face down on the path and the carcases of a plump pheasant and rabbit flew out of his long overcoat and lay incriminatingly limp among the pine needles. The keeper picked them up and frog-marched John down to the turnpike where he sent a message to the watchman who helped drive John to Woburn gaol in his cart. The news was not long reaching the village and the Heath and Tom returned home grim-faced for his supper.

'What is it, Tom? Do you know where your father is?'

'Yeah! He's in Woburn gaol.'

'Oh, oh. What is it? Poaching?'

'Yeah.' Tom sat down heavily with his head between his hands and his mother put her arm round his shoulders.

'He only does it to help.'

'Help! Perkins will know by tomorrow and then that's me out.'

'Oh surely he won't, love? You're his best fellow.'

Tom snorted contemptuously.

'Oh no, he can't! It will mean the workhouse. Oh, Tom! We can't! We can't go there. All my life I'se dreaded that. Think of poor little Willie and Bob and Tize. He can't do that to us,' wailed Eliza.

'It's Father what's done it.'

'No, don't blame him, Tom,' she sobbed.

Tom got to work early the next morning, just before half past six. Perkins was late and Tom hung about the yard kicking clods of earth and throwing stones at birds to relieve his tension. As soon as the master arrived he called Tom over to the shed that served as an office.

'Well, Ruddock. I hear that father of yours is in trouble again. Good and proper this time. He got off light over them bricks.'

Tom, standing erect and grave, didn't deign to answer.

'Ain't you got a tongue in your head, man?'

Tom merely lowered his eyes. Had he pleaded with Perkins about his mother and the little ones facing the workhouse he would probably have kept his job, but Perkins resented his silence and proud bearing.

'You'd best look for another job, Ruddock,' he said, glowering at the Herculean youth, fully expecting him to break down and beg not to be dismissed, but Tom raised his eyes steadily to his master's face, touched his forehead and strode out of the shed. He strode on down Leighton Hollow without pausing and along the turnpike towards Wavendon. He applied for work at the Sawyer's and the brickyard, but to no avail. He avoided Hurst's farm but tried the other two near Wavendon and then turned towards Simpson, Milton Keynes and Great Brickhill and back through Bow Brickhill. At each farm the reply was either 'no, no work here', or, when Tom asked how much he would be paid, they offered eight shillings or less, a week. When he shook his head they suggested that he be taken on as a roundsman.

He arrived home utterly exhausted just after eight o'clock that evening, having eaten nothing all day. The children were in bed and Eliza raised red-rimmed eyes as he came in.

'Oh Tom! You look worn out, love. Where have you been?'

'Looking for work.'

'Yes, the Rector said Mr Perkins had told you to go.'

'And no-one will pay me a proper wage.'

'We'll have to go then,' she said hopelessly.

'I'll get work, Mother. I won't stop until I do.'

'But it won't be in time,' she sobbed. 'Rector came round this afternoon and said he'd send a cart for us tomorrow at eight o'clock. He said it would be best so as we shan't be a burden on you while you're looking for work. He said you'd best leave the Parish and go to Bedford or Luton. Oh Tom! I said about Sarah and he said it was no use depending on a young girl's wage.

Anyways, I've been thinking it over and it ain't fair to take all her money. She needs it to set herself up proper. Don't let her know what's happened, Tom. Promise you won't!'

Eliza started to cry even louder.

'Oh, Mother, don't!' begged Tom brokenly, putting his head in his hands. 'I'll go round tomorrow and say as I'll take eight shillings if they'll have me.'

'No, love. You were right not to. It ain't enough. We'll go and then you won't be worrying. Rector's right. Promise you won't tell Sare?'

Tom was too tired to argue any more.

The cart came at half past eight in the morning. Eliza had spent two hours packing their few clothes in an old bag along with some odds and ends which she kept changing her mind about and unpacking, only to pop them in again a few minutes later. She gave one last look round the little home that she was so proud of, wondering whether she would ever see it again, and then ran to get a jar off the mantelpiece and stow it in the bag. She looked at the children huddled together by the door. Tize was hugging a tattered rag doll that Mary Nursall had made for her and Bobby was carefully supporting something inside his jacket.

'What you got there, Bobby? Show me.' He reluctantly drew out something wrapped in a piece of green velvet.

'Show me, love. It ain't your toad, is it?'

Bobby revealed the small warty face with its liquid gold eyes gazing intelligently up at them.

'Oh, you can't take that, love. He wouldn't like it there. It would be cruel. Go and put him back in his hole.' She only wished they all had some chance of 'liking it' there.

'Can I keep the piece of velvet, Mam?'

'Yes, love.' He returned from the garden rubbing it comfortingly against his cheek.

Willy, with a belligerent expression on his face, was clutching a fir cone.

'I'se keeping it,' he said firmly.

'Yes, love. I expect they'll let you.'

The carter expressed his impatience by taking the bag off Eliza and putting it in the cart, then he helped them in, lifting Willy and his fir cone in last.

Tom stood wretchedly in the doorway.

'Goodbye. I'll come for you as soon as I've got work,' he called.

Eliza waved abjectly and the man slapped the cob's rump and pushed the cart to get it moving through the deep sifting sand.

CHAPTER 27

The Union Workhouse

On Monday morning, while Cox was still in London, a message was brought to Sarah that there were two men waiting in the office to see her. She was surprised to find the carrier, Alfie Hedges and her father's friend, George Dunne. One look at the sombre expression on their faces alarmed her.

'Hallo, Mr Hedges and Mr Dunne. What has happened?'

'It's yer father,' said Hedges.

'In quod,' said Dunne.

'Oh – oh. What for?'

'Poaching!' said Hedges.

'Well, he was caught by a gamekeeper with a pheasant and a rabbit and some snares about him,' explained George, carefully avoiding unwarranted judgement.

'Oh dear. What are we going to do?'

They didn't answer her but shifted uneasily.

'Tom's got the sack,' volunteered Hedges.

'What?' exclaimed Sarah aghast.

'On account of his father being in gaol, they say,' said George miserably.

'How about my mother and the children?'

'Taken them off to the new Union Workhouse at Woburn.'

'The workhouse?' cried Sarah incredulously.

'Aye. Rector said it were best because there were no-one to support them,' said George bitterly.

'When did this happen?' demanded Sarah.

The two men looked at each other helplessly.

'Well . . . John, now, he must have bin taken last Monday.'

'Nay, Tuesday, Alfie, because it was the day after Bill brought the register over from Bedford.'

'And we heard about Tom on Friday . . .'

'Why didn't anyone send for me?' interrupted Sarah angrily.

'Well, I reckon yer mother and Tom didn't want to worry you.'

'Worry me! Too proud, more likely. Poor, poor Mama. I must get there. Can you take me quickly please, Mr Hedges? I must just call at home to get some money. Come on, quickly.'

'Well, begging your pardon, Miss, I don't see any need to rush round like scalded cats.'

'Nay, a bit of brain work so as to decide how best to tackle it is all that's needed,' said George.

'We'll do that as we go,' snapped Sarah.

She made Hedges whip up his old cob to a speed it hadn't achieved for many a year as they jolted towards the Woburn Union Workhouse.

Every so often the two men glanced uncomfortably at Sarah's wrathful face and then thought better of their inclination to say something. She was really in anguish at the thought of her mother's degradation. One of

Sarah's earliest memories was the expression of abject horror which passed across Eliza's face at the mere mention of the 'workhuss'.

Before the cart had properly stopped on the newly paved front yard of the Union, Sarah jumped down and hurried across to the heavy studded door. She hauled hard on the stirrup-shaped bell pull and heard the hollow clang which reverberated deep inside the building die away, and no other sound. She waited a few moments and then pulled again. After a long pause she heard unhurried slip-shod footsteps approaching. The bolts were drawn back and the door opened just wide enough to reveal the puffy pale face of a stout woman in a soiled linen apron and shapeless shoes with the heels trodden down.

'What is it?' she demanded curtly.

'Could I see Mrs Ruddock and her children, please?' Sarah's words were in the form of a question but the tone of her voice made it a command.

'No you can't. No visitors till Saturday.' The door began to close but Sarah stopped it with her foot.

'I've got to see her. I'm her daughter,' Sarah cried angrily.

'Visitors two till four on Saturday,' snapped the woman.

'I must see them. I've come all the way from Leighton. There's no need for them to be here.'

'You'd have to see the Master.'

'All right. Take me to him.'

'You will have to come back at nine o'clock in the morning, I am afraid, Madam,' she enunciated sarcastically.

'Why can't I see him now?'

'He's not about and he only sees people in the morning.'

'Let me in!' cried Sarah, but in her frenzy she moved her foot and the door slammed to.

In a bare stone room on the farther side of the central courtyard, Eliza was sitting on a bench with four other women making plaits from a huge heap of gleaming pale straw on the floor. Her eyes were red and her face pale and bleak.

'He'll be all right,' murmured one of her companions. 'All my three got it last winter and they're running round as gay as larks now.'

'Yes. They be up and down that quick, the little uns,' said another woman soothingly.

'If only they'd let me be with him,' said Eliza.

'Get on with your work there. No gossiping,' said the stout woman, returning from opening the door to Sarah.

'Can I see my little boy at supper-time?' pleaded Eliza.

'Matron don't like them to be disturbed. They're better left quiet.'

'But he'll be wanting me,' Eliza sobbed.

'You can go to see the others for a moment at five o'clock as long as you don't get them all upset.'

'Thank you,' murmured Eliza.

'I'll stay here till the Master comes back or someone else comes. There's bound to be someone and they won't keep me out then,' declared Sarah.

'You'd be better coming back with us, lass,' said George. 'We can have a council of war with the chaps this evening and see what's best to be done.'

'No! I'm getting my mother and the children out of here tonight. Whatever is Tom doing?'

Alfie and George shrugged helplessly.

'You go home. I can come and get you if I need to.'

'It's a long walk.'

'I've done longer often enough.'

Hedges and Dunne reluctantly left Sarah sitting on a stone staddle with her small bag beside her. After about

171

an hour, a line of men came straddling along the road with spades and pickaxes. They were mostly old and some were so frail they were struggling to carry their tools, let alone wield them, but there were one or two younger men as well. The blank, hopeless expression on their faces was the same, old or young. The man in charge of them rang the bell and looked down in surprise as Sarah appeared at his elbow. She had calmed down and had time to consider her tactics.

'Are you by any chance the Union Master?' she enquired archly with eyes wide.

'Neow, Miss.'

'Do you know when he will be back, please?'

'Well, I can't say as I do because I just take these men up to mend the turnpike. I'm delivering them home like – if tha can call it a home,' he added jokingly, jogging her with his elbow. 'We've been doing the edges up by Potsgrove Lane today.'

The stout woman in slippers opened the door and the roadman said, 'Now perhaps you can tell this young lady when the Master will be back?'

'I've told her already,' she replied coldly. 'Nine o'clock tomorrow morning. He won't see no-one tonight.'

'I'm not going till I've seen him,' announced Sarah as the last old man slipped in through the partly opened door. The woman banged it closed in her face.

'I shall ring the bell all night if he doesn't see me soon,' screeched Sarah.

'You'd better not,' came the faint reply.

Sarah retired to her staddle.

Eliza slipped into the children's wing at five o'clock. She found William first, standing sullenly by himself, wearing a Union shift. She engulfed him in her arms, but to her distress, he seemed quite detached and kept his eyes firmly averted from hers.

172

Tize ran up and threw her arms round her mother's shoulders.

'Oh, love. They've cut your beautiful hair off.' Eliza held her away to look. She was dressed in a straight striped tunic of blue and grey drab, like all the other girls, and her hair was cropped close to her head. She looked embarrassed and began to sob.

'There, there, dearie. It will grow again real fast. You see,' comforted Eliza. 'Hush lamb, you mustn't. They'll send me away if they see you crying.'

Tize did her best to stifle her sobs.

'Is William all right, love? He don't seem right.'

'He's all right, I think.'

'Is he eating his food?' whispered Eliza.

'Yeah, yeah, he's eating.' Eliza didn't look reassured. When she crept back to her place, tea was over and the women were sewing clothes for the children. Eliza shuddered at the thought of coarse brown twill chafing the toddler legs that the breeches were intended for.

'You've missed your supper, Liza,' whispered the woman next to her, sadly.

'Yes, but I managed to see Will and Tize, though.'

'They all right?'

'William don't seem himself. He won't look at me. Tize says he's taking his food. He's pining and fretting I 'spect.'

'No talking down there!'

After a pause Eliza whispered, 'They've cut all her beautiful curls off. She looks *that* forlorn, poor wench. I wish I could get to Bobby. I'se going to try.'

'Be careful, Liza.'

Eliza waited until the supervisor was taking in the sewing and locking it up in a chest, then she crept away down the corridor. She wasn't sure where the infirmary was. She wandered up and down the long corridors in each wing, then, with her heart pounding, and looking furtively from side to side, she ran up the main staircase on to the first floor and resumed her search. Somewhere at the back of the building she paused at a large door in a Gothic arch. She thought she could hear a child crying. She pressed her ear to the keyhole. She could! It was Bobby crying! She knew it was Bobby. She tried the door but it was locked. She tapped timidly. No-one came. She knocked hard, hurting her knuckles on the metal studs. Footsteps sounded and a woman's voice demanded to know who was there.

'It's me! It's Bobby's mother. Please let me in, just for a moment.'

'No. You shouldn't be *here*,' said the shocked voice.

'Please.'

'No. I've sent for the doctor. He'll be here soon.'

'Please let me in,' cried Eliza, her voice rising hysterically.

'No, certainly not. You're disturbing the children. Go back to your dormitory at once.'

Eliza's heart was bursting. She gasped; she gave a strangled cry and then a louder one. She opened her mouth wide. She could hear someone screaming. They screamed and screamed, just as she wanted to, but she was sure it was not herself.

Sarah rose from her hard seat. It was dark now and she moved towards the door thinking she could hear some-one screaming, far away inside the building. She reached the door and listened. It was her mother! She could hear her mother screaming, screaming. She threw herself at the door, hammering on it with her fists and then grabbed the bell lever and pulled and pulled. She didn't hear a chaise drive up but, as the door opened, she turned to find a large man muffled up in a cape by her side.

'Oh, Doctor Fisher!' cried the stout woman in surprise.

Sarah pushed past her and ran along the corridor and

up the stairs towards the screaming which suddenly subsided in a muffled gurgle. She turned a corner and saw her mother dripping wet. One of her arms was held by the Matron who had an empty ewer in her hand and the other arm was held by the Master of the Union.

The doctor and the stout woman arrived close on Sarah's heels.

'What's the trouble?' asked the doctor.

'Just a case of hysterics,' said the Matron defensively.

'I thought you said it was a sick child?'

'Yes, yes, it is. This is its mother.'

'Oh dear. Well here I am to see him now, my good woman,' said the doctor comfortingly, patting Eliza on the shoulder and then drawing out his handkerchief to dry his hand.

'Take her back to the dormitory will you, Mrs Smith,' said the Master.

'No!' cried Sarah. Eliza's glazed face suddenly broke into life as she recognized Sarah.

'Is this – er – person with you, Doctor?' inquired the Master.

'No, no, not at all. She was ringing the door bell rather vigorously when I came.'

'She's been worrying us all evening,' said Mrs Smith severely.

'That's my mother,' said Sarah aggressively.

'Bobby's crying in there,' wailed Eliza. The Matron and Master stepped towards her again.

'Oh dear,' said the doctor. 'I think, perhaps, if you promise to be very calm, Mrs . . . er . . . Mrs . . .'

'Ruddock,' said Sarah.

'Yes . . . if . . . er . . . if you do that perhaps you may watch me examine your son – and your daughter may, too,' he said haltingly.

The Master, the Matron and Mrs Smith all looked affronted but had to let the doctor have his way. They followed him into the infirmary. There was an oil lamp burning at the far end but its light didn't penetrate to the high vaulted ceiling, and arching shadows rose and fell on the stone walls, dwarfing the line of beds. Only three or four were occupied by small forms and most of them seemed miraculously asleep. Even the one that Matron led the doctor to was perfectly quiet.

'You see it weren't him crying at all. It was another child what she heard.'

'Yes,' agreed the doctor as he uncovered the limp body. Bobby coughed several times and turned his head fretfully at the disturbance.

'Could we have a lamp here, Matron, please?'

Bobby's face and abdomen were covered with the angry blotches of measles. The doctor felt his forehead and feet and tapped his chest.

'Bobby, love,' murmured Eliza as she took his hand, but his eyes continued to gaze unseeingly at the ceiling.

'Will he get better, Doctor?' she asked.

'Well he hasn't got a temperature now,' he replied evasively. 'In fact, I think a hot water pot might help, Matron. See that it's well wrapped, though. He must have this medicine every three hours. Prop him up to give it to him – don't dose him lying down and I shall come back in the morning, unless you send a message.' He added the last phrase in a quiet aside to Matron who nodded and he glanced at Eliza to check that she hadn't heard, but Sarah had. The three officials followed him to the door.

'What shall we do about the mother and sister?' asked the Master.

'I think they could stay with him if they don't disturb the other children, don't you?' He appealed to Matron.

'Since he's so bad, I suppose so,' she said heavily.

Eliza and Sarah crouched by the side of Bobby's bed. Sarah did her best to prepare her mother, hoping against hope that he would rally, but his breathing became more and more laboured until it came in gasps with long intervals in between.

'He seems to be deep alseep,' murmured Eliza hopefully.

Sarah shook her head, despondently.

After an interminable time the gasps stopped altogether and he died peacefully at a quarter past six.

Matron took them to her room and gave them tea.

'We did all we could, you know, dearies,' she said to the weeping pair. 'Measles is a dreadful thing. There's four other little ones in here now and I am sure the two-year-old and the four-year-old won't come through. It's a hard job but we do our best for them and they gets good nourishment when they're able to take it.'

'Yes, thank you, I'm sure,' sobbed Eliza. 'If only they let me be with him yesterday. He weren't that bad on Sunday, Sarah. He just had them spots and a fever.'

'It wouldn't have made any difference, Mama.'

'Maybe not but he would have known I cared.'

'He knew that I'm sure, Mama. We must get you and Tize and William home.'

'Oh yes, but what about Bobby?'

'I'll see to it all. You stay here with Matron while I go to see the Master.'

CHAPTER 28

Tom Finds Work

While the sad drama at the Woburn Union was taking place, Tom was sleeping on a hay rick at Ridgemont. He had called at more farms than he could remember during the past three days. He had been loath to ask for work nearby where his father was known, so he had started at Little Brickhill and on through Woburn to

Eversholt. He couldn't face calling at the workhouse and told himself that they wouldn't let him in anyway. He would return to take the family home on Sunday when he had work. But everywhere the response was the same. The farmers received the strapping young man warmly. Yes, they reckoned they could use him, after all it was getting close to hay time, but as soon as he asked about the wage they became defensive. They all wanted him as a roundsman. They urged him to register with the local Select Vestry for poor relief so that they would pay half his wage and the Parish would pay the rest. This Tom was adamant he would not do. He couldn't tell them that he had seen his father a victim of this system all his life; that he was asking to do a steady job of work for them, not just for the haymaking but right on through the winter when there were only worzels and swedes to be chopped for the cattle and buildings to be repaired. He would have nothing of the poor rate. He wanted a fair wage week in and week out through the year and he would earn every penny of it twice over. No, he wasn't able to explain, so he just looked at his worn boots, sighed, raised his eyes steadily to theirs, touched his cap and, bidding them 'Good day', turned and strode out of the farmyard. Most of them watched his receding broad shoulders and springy stride ruefully. If he had turned round and begged them to take him for nine shillings a week rather than ten shillings and sixpence they would have relented. After all, they told themselves they were not hard men; a fellow had to earn enough to eat and farming was hungry work. But Tom knew only too well that five people could not live on nine shillings a week, so he carried on walking.

It was just the same at Husborne Crawley and Brogborough and when he reached Ridgemont in the evening he gave up for the day and curled up exhausted on the haystack. He had no food left now and he was ravenously hungry when he woke up. He climbed down off the rick and brushed the bits off his clothes, splashed his face in a nearby pond and ran his fingers through his curly hair, which served the dual purpose of drying his hands and smoothing his hair. He set off to find the farm with a sinking feeling that the day ahead would prove as fruitless as the last two. It was only seven o'clock when he tapped at the farmhouse door. Before it opened he could smell bacon and toast cooking. His empty stomach curled up painfully. A girl of about his own age opened the door.

'Is the farmer about please?' he asked.

'Well, he may be in the cow byre,' she smiled coyly and pointed. 'Come back if he ain't and I'll help you find him,' she called after him.

'Who's that?' asked her mother.

'A man come to see Father. Wanting work I shouldn't wonder.'

'Yes, there's too many of these vagrants about now.'

'He ain't a vagrant!' said the girl indignantly.

'Oh. How can you tell?'

'Well he didn't look like one. He was young and strong.'

'Ha! That don't prove much,' said her mother acidly. 'Do get on laying the table, Rosie. We'll never get anywhere with you standing there day-dreaming, and there certainly ain't time to go traipsing about helping a young man look for your father.'

Tom duly found the cowman, who didn't know where 't'Master might be biding', so the smell of bacon and toast drew Tom reluctantly back to the kitchen door. The farmer's wife opened the door this time and directed him to try the paddock and the orchard but he drew a blank again. Rosie opened the door to him.

'I'm sor-sorry,' stammered Tom. 'I can't find him nowhere and I badly wants to see him.'

'Well he'll be back for his breakfast any time. He can

come in and wait, can't he, Mother?' she called over her shoulder.

Tom didn't hear an answer and doubted whether the girl had, but she asked him to step in and take a seat by the fireplace. There was a huge open pan, sizzling with so many curly crisp rashers of streaky bacon that Tom thought there must be an army to feed concealed about the place. Rosie tossed them into a heap to one side and began breaking eggs into the hot bacon fat.

Plop-sizzle; plop-sizzle; one, two, three, four . . . Tom watched, mesmerized. As each one was ready she deftly lifted it out on to an iron tray to drain and then began soaking up the fat with hunks of home-made brown bread. Tom began to feel dizzy and the griping pain in his belly became quite bad. When he turned round he was surprised to see the long oak table behind him had filled up with a crowd of chattering children, while four or five farm hands were washing in the scullery. They trooped in, deferentially greeting Mrs Tennant, the farmer's wife, as they took their places at the table.

'You ain't wiped your boots proper, Matthew,' she complained. 'Just look at that cow-muck on the floor.'

'Sorry, ma'am,' said the young cowman in confusion. He rose to remedy the offence.

'And you'd better wash your hands again when you've finished,' warned Mrs Tennant. 'As if it ain't bad enough having to put up with him always smelling of them cows all over without having muck on his boots,' she muttered irritably.

Rosie seemed to be making sure that Tom should savour the way she carefully loaded each wooden platter before passing it to her mother to set in front of the breakfasters. He had the utmost difficulty stopping himself reaching out and taking one as it passed just in front of him. He sat on his hands.

Rosie's father came in. He was a genial looking man in his early fifties, strong and stocky, greying at the temples and with a rather florid face due mainly to a life out in the wind and rain, but plenty of rich food and drink had also contributed.

'This young man's come to see you, Father,' said Rosie.

Tom half rose. 'After your breakfast will do well, sir,' he said faintly.

'Good,' said Tennant, sitting down and rubbing his hands in anticipation.

'Come on, Rosie. Don't take all day with them bacon and eggs. I've done half a day's work already and I'm famished.'

Tom had felt a bit light-headed as he stood up. He didn't remember feeling like that before. He wondered if he was becoming sick.

After an unbearable length of time for Tom, Tennant rose from the table and stepped towards him.

'Now young fellow-me-lad, what can I do for you?' he asked jovially, holding out his hand.

Tom rose and took it and to his surprise the farmer began to sway drunkenly from side to side and then rose up towards the ceiling, towering over him. Tom closed his eyes for a moment to take a firmer hold on the situation and when he opened them found he was lying on the settle with Rosie's face close to his.

'What have you had for your breakfast?' asked Mrs Tennant severely.

'I ain't had nothing, please ma'am,' said Tom apologetically.

'Where have you come from?'

'Aspley . . . well, that is, I did live at Aspley but I'm looking for work, ma'am.'

'What did you have for your supper last night, then?'

Tom wished she would leave him alone. He rose feebly on one arm and felt giddy.

'He's ever so sick, Mama!' wailed Rosie.

'Nonsense, he ain't had anything to eat. That's all.'

'I'll do him bacon and eggs,' said Rosie eagerly. Tom gasped at the prospect.

'No! I'll make him some gruel first and then we'll see how he is,' said her mother firmly. Tom did his best to think how much better it was to have gruel than nothing, but the sight and smell of bacon, eggs and toast were still monopolizing his senses.

Tennant had been looking on in concern while his womenfolk made these decisions.

'What's your name, son?' he asked.

'Tom Ruddock.'

'Ruddock . . . mm . . . Ruddock? I seem to have heard that name somewhere.' Tom's heart sank, but Tennant appeared unable to remember the connection.

'So you want work?'

'Yes please, sir.'

'Why can't you get a job in Aspley?' Tom swallowed miserably. 'I'd have thought they'd be wanting a strong youngster like you.' Tennant was scrutinizing him closely.

'I have tried, sir. I've tried all over but they don't want to pay me a full wage and I ain't going to be a roundsman for any man.'

'No, neither you should,' said Tennant gently. 'Where were you working?'

'Oh, leave him alone, do. The boy's famished. Wait till he's got some vittles inside of him,' said Mrs Tennant, handing Tom a bowl of gruel and a spoon. He tried to get up.

'Oh no, me lad. You get that into you on the settle. We had enough trouble putting you there. It took four men to shift you from the hearthrug.' Tom looked amazed.

Rosie was sitting at the table having her breakfast with her round blue eyes fixed on Tom's face.

After the gruel and two cups of sweet tea they let Tom get up and he declared himself to be perfectly well.

'There! What did I tell you,' said Mrs Tennant triumphantly to Rosie. Tennant had gone back to his work, telling Tom he would see him later.

'I'm ever so glad. Can I do you some bacon and eggs now, Mr Ruddock?' Rosie asked. They both looked at Mrs Tennant for approval.

'Yes. I expect he can manage them,' she said, much to Tom's relief.

'Oh, I never thought as how I'd be eating bacon and eggs for me breakfast,' he said, smiling broadly at Rosie.

'It must be ever so long since you ate anything. Didn't you have nothing for supper?' Tom shook his head.

'Nothing at dinner time?' Tom shook his head.

'And breakfast yesterday?' Tom thought hard.

'Ah, yeah. I had a little bit of bread I'd got in my pocket.' He looked so dolefully at her that Rosie wanted to take him in her arms and kiss him better but a quick glance at her mother supervising the washing up in the scullery made her think better of it.

She was a really pretty girl, Tom thought. She was fair and plump with the firm whiteness of a fattened pullet plucked and trussed for the oven. Tom had admired them in the butcher's shop window when he wasn't even hungry. He couldn't help comparing her to his clever sharp-tongued sister who had nothing plump and white about her. What little there was of her was dark and springy and quick, more like the wild black kittens at the bakery.

Tennant returned after Tom had breakfasted and found him and Rosie sitting on either side of the big kitchen table presumably talking politely about the weather and such, but he did notice that they both unaccountably blushed as he came in.

He found Tom unduly reticent about his family and recent employment which bothered him, but Rosie gave him such a beseeching gaze that he agreed to take Tom on for two months at ten shillings and sixpence a week.

183

'It will be a long walk for you from Aspley,' he said doubtfully.

'Don't you worry, sir. I shall be here at six o'clock each morning,' said Tom gratefully. 'And thank you very much for the breakfast. I'm sorry about all the trouble.'

'No trouble!' said Rosie fervently.

Tom strode back towards Woburn feeling more elated and happy than he could remember for years. He was no deep thinker but he did find it a little unaccountable. After all, his father was in gaol and his mother and brothers and sister were in the workhouse and all he had was a job for two months, a full four miles away from the cottage on the Heath.

CHAPTER 29

Woburn Gaol

John was allowed out of gaol in the company of a guard to attend Bobby's funeral, which took place in St Botolph's graveyard. It was an overcast, windy day with scurrying clouds and squalls of rain. Tize kept her mind off what was happening by watching the odd dead leaf, dredged from secluded corners, pin itself briefly against the Rector's black skirts as he stood beside the neat rectangular hole. The speed and wretchedness of Bobby's death had deprived them of time to adjust and even Eliza stood mute and numb. He was laid close to his infant brother and sister as Eliza had wanted, although the Matron and Master at the Union had tried to persuade her that a parish funeral would be more sensible. Sarah undertook to pay the expenses, although George Dunne and a group from the round table at The Bell pressed fifteen shillings into Eliza's hand. It was collected from John's comrades in four parishes to help her over an 'ockard time' they said. Eliza thanked them fervently, knowing that it had meant many weary hours of tramping from door to door. The family, apart from John and poor Bobby, were united in the cottage that evening.

'You shouldn't have accepted their money, Mam,' said Tom.

Eliza looked up from her mending, unhappily.

'And why not?' asked Sarah.

'I don't hold with the likes of them!'

'They're well-meaning people,' said Eliza reproachfully.

'They've caused *us* enough trouble with Father.'

'That's nonsense!' exclaimed Sarah. 'Just because they can't change anything doesn't mean to say they're bad for trying.'

'It's only trouble-making talk.'

'You ought to think for yourself instead of passing on ready-made judgements from other people,' rejoined Sarah angrily.

'Sarah! Tom! Stop it! Just think of poor Bobby.'

The two glowered at each other but remained quiet until Eliza went to bed.

'At least they do something *real* to help,' resumed Sarah.

'We could have paid for the funeral.'

'Yes. I said I would at the workhouse. I didn't notice you there, Tom.'

'I didn't know, did I,' blustered Tom. 'How was I to know when I was tramping all over looking for work? Anyway, they wouldn't let Mother out until *I* got there, would they?'

'No. I'm sorry Tom. My tongue ran away with me. What's the work like? Is Tennant a fair man?'

''E's not half so bad,' muttered Tom, still angry.

'It's a long way to walk.'

'I manages.'

'Mother says you don't get home till nine o'clock usually.'

'No, I stay to supper.'

'Do you get something docked off your wage for that?'

'No.' Tom began to thaw. 'They're very good. They feed us real well and I get all the meals that the young chaps living in get. Rosie, that's the daughter, she does most of the cooking and she's real good.'

'Oh. How old is she?' asked Sarah, not missing the brief flush on Tom's face and the way his eyes fell.

'She were eighteen last June and she's got curly hair, all yellow, and . . .' Tom stopped in confusion, seeing Sarah's grin.

'And big blue eyes?' she prompted.

'Er, yeah.'

'And she's quite short and plumpish?'

'How do you know?' he burst out.

'Oh, ha, ha,' laughed Sarah. 'I don't need to. I just know *you*, Tom.'

There was a pause. The expression on their faces became grave as their thoughts reverted to their parents.

Sarah broke the silence.

'What are we to do about Father?'

'I don't know as there's much we can do.'

'He was standing there by Bobby's coffin looking so forlorn and helpless. I wanted to comfort him but when I went up he just hung his head and with that man beside him I couldn't think what to say. We must go to see him.'

'I ain't going to that place.'

'Tom! He is your father.'

'He got himself in there. Everyone kept telling him and now look what's happened to Mama and Bobby.'

Sarah shook her head miserably.

'He's not bad. He just doesn't look ahead. He gets so upset seeing Mama without enough food for the children and he wants to give her something so badly he just hopes it will be all right.'

'Ugh,' grunted Tom sullenly.

'I think we ought to go and see Mr Dunne and Jerry Dilks and the others and talk over what's to be done.'

'Ha; that ain't doing much.'

'It's better than nothing, but they mustn't think we want any more money off them.'

'No, we've took too much charity off them already,' said Tom hotly.

'Tom! . . .' Sarah exploded, and then thought better of starting another argument.

Bobby's funeral was on the Thursday so Sarah set off to walk the eight miles to Leighton as Tom set off for work just after five on Friday morning.

'I've written a letter to Mr Dunne, Tom. Will you put in under his door as you pass, please?'

'What have you said?'

'Just that I should like to visit Father tomorrow afternoon and could he arrange that if anyone needs to be told. I've said I'd like to talk things over with him too.'

'Shall I tell Mama?'

'Well . . . no, don't say anything. I've told her I shall be home tomorrow evening. There's no point in her walking to Woburn with Will, and we can sort things out better without her. You know how awkward Father will feel. I said I'd be at the gaol at four o'clock. I'm hoping Mr Dunne might come.' She waited hopefully for Tom to say that he'd come but he just took the letter and said goodbye.

When Sarah walked into the little walled forecourt of Woburn gaol she was pleased to find George Dunne and Jerry Dilks waiting for her.

'They says we can talk to him for fifteen minutes,' said George.

'Can we all go in?' asked Sarah.

'Well, they said only one, but I reckon as how this might smooth the road.' He opened his hand to reveal a sixpence. Sarah smiled her gratitude and the constable accepted it with a look of abstraction on his face. He opened the door and turned away to his desk as if too pre-occupied to take any notice of them.

John Ruddock stooped by a stool on the far side of a deal table in a bare room lit by high slit windows. His straight black hair was longer and more unkempt than usual, framing his pale, bearded face. There were dark shadows beneath his dull eyes and the prison shirt hung from his shoulders limply.

'Cheer up, Father,' cried Sarah embracing him.

'Aye. We've come to get you out of this, me lad,' said George jovially. John shook his head miserably.

'Mama's well. Tom's got a new job with Tennant at Ridgemont. They seem good people. He's a lot happier than he was at the mine.' Sarah carefully avoided saying how much he was earning. John nodded dully.

'Come on man! Pull yourself together. Sit down,' said George, setting an example.

'He must keep his side of the table,' muttered the constable from the door.

Sarah took the other stool and Jerry remained standing awkwardly.

'Do you know how long they'll be keeping you, Father?' He shook his head.

'It's over two months to quarter sessions,' said Jerry.

'Perhaps a local Magistrate will deal with it,' said George.

'How can we find out?'

'Write to somebody?' ventured George.

'If we wrote to Bennet, the Duke's steward, he'd know all about it, what with it being the Duke's land he was caught on and His Grace being a local Magistrate into the bargain.'

'Aye! Good thinking, Jerry. He's said to be a very fair man is Bennet.'

'I'll warrant you write a good hand, Miss Ruddock,' said Jerry.

'Yes. Why don't you write and then you can say how upset your mother was to be sent to the workhouse and all about poor Bobby, bless him, and how little Willy's pining for his papa.'

John shot to his feet.

'Stop all this, George Dunne. She ain't writing begging letters like that for me. I'd rather stay in this wretched place.'

'Quiet there,' bellowed the constable. 'Keep yer voice down Ruddock, else they'll have to go.'

'John, John! Calm down. We only be trying to get you free quicker, man,' hissed George. 'Eliza needs you. You've got to support them. Tom's only taken on for two months, you know, and you can't let them go back to the workhouse.'

'No. God forbid!' said John hoarsely, slumping back into his chair.

'Yes, let me write, Father. I'll only put in as much as seems necessary. You don't want to stay in this place. It smells awful. Where are they keeping you? What are they feeding you on?'

'I'm in one of the bigger cells, they say, but it ain't much and neither's the food. But the terrible boredom is the worst. A man just sits and thinks and worries about his family.'

'Did they give you them *Northern Stars* and *Registers* I brought, Mr Ruddock?' asked Jerry earnestly.

'Nay, I've had nothing.'

'Ah. They must have destroyed them.'

'More than likely, Jerry lad. Anyway, we'll try to collect up some more and do a bit of palm-greasing when we bring them next time.'

'Thankee. I'm always in your debt, my good comrades.'

189

'You'd best be going now,' called the constable.

'Bear up, Father. We'll manage something,' said Sarah.

'Aye. Depend on us and try to keep cheerful, man,' said George, clapping John's shoulder.

John could hardly begin to keep what he hadn't got and he looked wretchedly miserable as he shambled back to his dirty cell.

Bennet read Sarah's pleading letter sympathetically and John's case came before a Magistrate three weeks later. He pleaded guilty to killing the pheasant and trespassing but claimed the rabbit was caught on the common and he was released with a fine of five pounds to be paid in weekly instalments by Michaelmas.

CHAPTER 30

Sarah Sets to Work

Back at Leighton, Sarah set about earning her fourteen shillings wage and more too.

She spent two nights a week working with Madame du Prêt, the milliner and Mantua-maker. The lady's English wasn't very good and she could only show Sarah by example how to do things, but she was amazed at how quickly her new pupil learnt.

'Ah! The neat leetle fingers! You will be a great one, *ma chèrie*, a very clever maker of *les chapeaux*.'

Sarah was not so satisfied with the progress of her three hat-makers back at the factory, though. They had made nothing between them that she would dare to send up to London yet, but, if perseverance could win the day, it would be won.

Frank Cox found himself entertaining mixed feelings about Sarah's capacity for hard work. He could not complain about the value he got for his money and she was now manoeuvring towards another rise. He knew he would eventually have to give in, because there was no winning with Sarah. If he had been honest, and sufficiently analytical, he would have realized that what really bothered him was the steady erosion of his authority. He would tell his girls in the factory to do something and a year ago it would have been promptly done, but now he found them saying, 'Yes, sir. Shall us just go and ask Miss Ruddock, sir?'

It was the same at home. Verity was now a clean smart scullery maid who served a part-time cook and a maid, and none of them did anything without asking Sarah. They would even hesitate to bring him a tray of tea if it interfered with a task she had set them.

'This is a slip of a girl of seventeen,' he reminded himself. 'What the deuce will a man do with her in five years' time? How much worse in twenty years' time when she has lost her looks, too.' Frank Cox would mull this over each time he reviewed his temptation to propose to Sarah. He was not the meekest of men and the prospect of life-long subordination did not appeal to him.

He had been musing along these lines on the evening that Sarah inevitably raised the question of a rise in her wages.

'Frank?'

'Yes dear?'

'Are you pleased with the way the house and factory are running?'

Cox sighed resignedly.

'Yes, of course, dear.'

'Do you realize how hard I am working?'

'Yes. I should really rather you didn't. Not quite so hard, at any rate.'

'Oh, really!' said Sarah in surprise.

'Well, I feel we ought to have a bit more time to enjoy each other's company.'

'Oh . . .' She regarded him keenly for a moment and decided he probably meant 'in bed'. 'Men!' she thought contemptuously to herself.

'The extra trade must be bringing you in a lot more money.'

'Yes, and a lot's going out on the household expenses,' he countered.

'Ah! Do you want me to sack Cook and go back to Verity's meals, again?' inquired Sarah sweetly.

'Heaven forbid,' muttered Cox.

'I have such a lot of expenses helping my mother and paying my father's fine, you see. There isn't much left over for me to buy clothes for myself and I have to keep looking smart, don't I?'

Cox watched her with an indulgent smile as she demurely smoothed her fine brocade skirt of a deep plum colour. The bodice was skin-tight about her bare eighteen inches of waist, and the tight sleeves were generously puffed and ribboned at her elbows. A large square collar edged with cream lace set off her eyes and hair to perfection.

'Of course. How much do you want?' he sighed.

'Seventeen shillings?'

'That's more than three times the amount I pay my youngest factory girls.'

'And I'm not worth three times as much?' She looked sideways at him, brows raised and eyes huge.

'Just about, I suppose. Seventeen shillings a week,' agreed Cox wearily.

'Of course, you ought to pay your girls at least eight shillings,' commented Sarah swiftly.

Cox looked up sharply. 'I have as many as I need.'

'Perhaps that's *not* the only consideration.'

'Oh, we've joined the revolutionaries now, have we?'

Sarah smiled tolerantly. She thought of her father and George and Jerry. Well, perhaps *she* would make sacrifices too one of these days but she would only do it from strength. When she was secure herself she would not be satisfied with talk. She would see that something was done to improve their lot. How, she didn't know, but there must be a way.

'You know that hat shop we talked about?' she asked.

'Which hat shop?' asked Cox sharply.

'To sell the hats I'm making. What I was wondering was whether I shouldn't start it in Aspley Guise.'

Cox adjusted himself to the idea of Sarah's shop as rapidly as he could.

'Why Aspley Guise?'

'Because there is a very wealthy clientèle there. It would save them going up to London, wouldn't it?'

'*If* our hats were as good.'

'They will be and, furthermore, I think we should make gowns too. We could bring the stuff back from London each time we go up to sell bonnets and I can look around and make note of what is in fashion.'

'And the dressmakers?'

'Well, Mrs Newbold has two apprentice seamstresses at the moment and I have been learning about patterns. It is cutting out the cloth that is really skilled. The seamstresses just sew what they are told. If I could spend two weeks at a dressmaker's in London – Madame Follett in Bond Street, say – I should manage, I think. We could start with simple day gowns and then gradually master the others. Really, country tastes are generally simpler than in the city. And, we should make the hats to match the gowns, of course.'

'Of course,' said Cox without conviction.

'Frank! I know the very place. It is up for sale on the Square at Aspley!'

'I don't know whether I have the capital.'

'Perhaps we could rent it.'

'It would be better on the Northampton Turnpike. How about Woburn?'

'The shop would cost a lot more there, and I believe

193

the Woburn ladies would travel to Aspley. I don't think coach passengers would have much time to be fitted for dresses.'

'I'll think it over,' he said. Sarah rose and joined him on the chaise longue. She draped her skirts carefully over the back rail and put one arm round his neck while she stroked his side-whiskers.

'You're very good to me, Frank.'

He sighed. How was he going to survive this turmoil?

Within a month Sarah had her shop. There was one room over the main part where she planned to live, and a small room built on at the back for her seamstresses. She would have to take the ladies upstairs to be fitted, so no expense must be spared to make it elegant. Frank Cox's pocket grew lighter by the day, but Sarah justified each expenditure and he had to confess that she managed exceedingly well.

They stood upstairs surveying the old stone cross in the centre of the Square through the velvet draped window. Sarah's bed was masquerading as a settee in plum coloured velvet which matched the curtains and on the floor was a slightly worn but beautiful rug donated by Lucy Hall.

'Do you like it, Frank?'

'Very nice.'

'Is that all?'

'It will suit well. There doesn't seem to be much room for me, though.'

'Oh, you wouldn't want to live *here,* Frank. It's too far away from the factory.'

'Yes, I see. Who keeps me company in Leighton Buzzard, I wonder?'

'If I had a pony chaise I could visit you on Sundays.' Sarah's voice sounded so wistful. Frank Cox had more sense than to think it was for him.

'Yes. I expect I shall manage well. I always did.'

'Of course you will,' said Sarah confidently.

'How about a name for the shop? I think something with a French ring – Boutique? Salon? Yes – "Sarah Lacelle's Salon". I mean, "Ruddock" really isn't quite the thing.'

'It's not your shop, my girl.'

'No – but – "Cox" is nearly as bad as "Ruddock". I mean, can you imagine one lady saying to another "My dear, you *must* go to Cox's for that afternoon dress". But "Now Lacelle's Salon is *the* place to go, my dear."'

Cox laughed at Sarah's impersonation of extreme gentility.

'Frank?'

'Yes,' he sighed.

'If you were to *lend* me the money for my first stock and enough to run it for six months, I should start paying you rent and gradually pay you back all you lent me. How is that?'

'You are very confident this will work, aren't you?'

'Yes! Completely! I shall make it work.'

Cox believed her and it seemed a good opportunity to regain control of his life. He could not claim that he hadn't enjoyed Sarah. His life had never been so packed with excitement and activity, but enough was enough and when he did come round to proposing to a woman, she would be young and pretty and empty-headed and *he* would make all the decisions.

CHAPTER 31

The New Businesswoman

John's fine was paid mainly by Sarah but his confederates at The Bell collected nearly as much and delivered it with the usual tactful formula,

''Twill tide Mrs Ruddock and the little ones over an

ockard patch.' Sarah and Eliza suspected a lot of the money had come out of George Dunne's own pocket but they accepted it gratefully and never revealed to John or Tom how much it was.

In 1839 the Chartist movement was at last gaining the support of more skilled craftsmen. It seemed a modest enough demand: a vote for each man (women's suffrage had been reluctantly abandoned to give success a better chance); confidential ballots; any man eligible to become a Member of Parliament (a means test was applied at the moment) and payment for serving as a Member. The People's Charter merely laid down the bare essentials for parliamentary democracy but it was opposed by the ruling classes with a vehemence born of fear – the fear of a bloody revolution in the French style. A Mr Gammage was coming to Aspley to speak about the history of the 'Movement' and John submerged his grief and recent tribulations in busying himself with arrangements for the meeting.

'How many people are you expecting Thursday week, Father?' inquired Sarah.

'Well, it's difficult to say. There were two hundred at a meeting up in Leeds last week and over three hundred went to Manchester to listen to Fergus O'Connor.'

'Aspley Guise isn't quite Manchester and I doubt if Mr Gammage is going to draw the crowds like Mr O'Connor. Anyway, the Halls' threshing barn won't hold above a hundred, will it?'

'No, but we shall only have seats at the front for the women and the old uns. We can pack a lot in standing. You will be coming won't you, Sare?' he inquired earnestly.

'I'm terribly busy getting the shop ready, Father. I mean, I shall *try*, of course, but I'm not quite sure.'

John looked disappointed. Sarah felt conscience-stricken because she knew he wouldn't ask Eliza or Tom to go and she did want to support him, but she was no longer a free agent, if indeed she had ever been one. In the eyes of the village gentry it was unfortunate to be discovered a Methodist, but to have Chartist sympathies was unforgivable. Although she shared her father's opinions, her business depended upon the approval of the gentry and they must never find her out. She winced at the thought of her father's contempt; and this was not her only disloyalty! She had rented a pew in the centre of St Botolph's church and was steeling herself to occupy it each Sunday morning.

Just before his arrest, John had been carrying a petition from door to door. It read: 'The body of every parish church belongs of common right to all the parishioners. Abolish rented pews!' Sarah playfully reasoned with her father that since he would never dream of going to the parish church, and disapproved of people who did, it seemed hardly a cause to involve himself in.

'It's the principle, Sare!' he said staunchly. 'It is just one of the symbols of the domination by the gentry of the working people who toil to keep them.'

Well, she planned to get adequate payment for her toil and if she had to appear to join the gentry to do it, then so be it. She was only grateful that the Heath was nearly two miles from Aspley Square, but she felt so guilty about her gratitude.

One of her first clients was Mrs Vaughan. Miss Hall was her very first, of course. Sarah invited her to see the arrangements and admire how well her carpet suited, before the large silver letters proclaimed the establishment to be 'Miss Lacelle's Salon'. Mary Hall ordered a hat. Sarah doubted that she needed one but Miss Hall insisted and also left Sarah to choose the style and colour. In answer to Sarah's earnest enquiries about the garments it would be worn with, Miss Hall declared that if she liked it, she would wear it with all her dresses and coats and she was certain she *would* like it because Sarah was such a very clever young lady. Sarah shook her head in perplexity.

The Classical Academy was only a few doors away from Sarah's shop, and Mrs Vaughan, the headmaster's wife, timidly peeped in on the first morning that Sarah opened.

'Oh, Mrs Vaughan! How good of you to call,' cried Sarah encouragingly. 'Do please come in.'

'Well, I don't really think I need a hat, but I should like to ask your opinion about altering a dress. I fear it does not suit me. At least my husband declares that it doesn't and I am sure I don't know. I am not a good judge of these things, I fear.'

Sarah felt sorry for the stout young matron. It was difficult to conceive a garment that really would suit her, but she rose to the challenge when the orange, grey and black check silk was produced. The checks were huge and the predominant colour was bright orange.

'I believe, I truly do,' said Sarah gravely, 'that a plain material would do you most justice. I wonder if we could use this splendid quality silk to trim a dark grey dress?'

'You mean . . . cut it all up?'

'Well, the skirt would make an excellent petticoat and might peep out at the hem of the dress; then just imagine a loosely draped bow at the throat, or perhaps a ruche – yes, a *ruche* to reflect the touch of colour at the hem!'

Sarah had lifted a bolt of grey shot taffeta on to the table and was holding a fold aloft with one sleeve of the dress ruffled across it.

'A . . . roo?'

'A ruche! Look, I have a drawing of a lovely style, copied from *The World of Fashion* this very season.' Sarah swiftly produced a large drawing that she had laboriously made.

'Oh, that does look most becoming. I wonder if I might bring my husband in to see what he thinks?'

'But of course. Some gentlemen do have excellent

taste and, after all, it *is* them we try to please with our appearance, isn't it?'

Theresa Vaughan gazed uneasily at Sarah but her face was such a study in sweet composure that her remark must have been quite innocent.

Sarah was not quite as composed as she seemed. Studying the retreating figure of Theresa Vaughan she wondered if she could ever capture a hint of 'becomingness' with such an unpromising subject. Well, now was no time for a faint heart. She just wished her second commission could have been a little easier.

The next day Mr and Mrs Vaughan returned. Sarah had seen the head of the Academy a few years before, but she had been too young to take much notice of him. Now she was impressed by his jaunty good breeding. He was dressed informally but tastefully. His cutaway jacket and breeches were stylish and well made and, unlike his unfortunate wife, he had a figure to do his tailor justice. His wavy brown hair was greying at the temples which, combined with his straight profile and neatly trimmed whiskers, gave him grave distinction. Despite this, Sarah could not help being intrigued by the cynical rise to his brows and his humorous mouth which suggested a youthful irresponsibility quite incompatible with his position.

Sarah curtsied sweetly to them and tripped away to get her drawings.

'Isn't it all so charmingly decorated, dear?' inquired Mrs Vaughan.

'Yes, most charming; even down to the proprietress.'

'Oh yes. I thought you would notice that,' she replied with a hint of ill-humour, but her husband laughed and gave her shoulders a reassuring squeeze.

Sarah returned. Yes, he approved the pattern; he was sure Miss Lacelle's judgement was sound. They both approved the grey shot taffeta, which was fortunate because Sarah's stock was small.

During the rest of the week Sarah received a small but steady stream of ladies who wanted to look at her new shop and who bought a few ribbons or a pair of gloves. She was gratified by their admiring compliments on the decoration. She had a single walking-out costume displayed which she had designed and cut under the guidance of Mme du Prêt. It was her main advertisement and she didn't plan to sell it until she had a worthy replacement. She would ask a quite exorbitant price if anyone inquired, but no-one had yet.

Early the following week Mr and Mrs Vaughan returned. Sarah could not quite understand why it was necessary for Theresa to bring her husband on this occasion.

'Good afternoon, Mrs Vaughan. Good afternoon, Mr Vaughan. I am so pleased you have managed to call today because we need to see that we have the tucking in the bodice quite right. Perhaps you would care to step upstairs for a fitting, Mrs Vaughan. Please do you mind waiting for Madame here, sir? Do please take a seat.'

The tucking was far from right but Sarah deftly released a gusset here and inserted a few pins there and fixed on a piece of the orange check silk down the front of the bodice to give an impression of the final effect.

'Oh yes!' cried Theresa in delight. 'That does look splendid! May my husband just creep up to have a quick look?'

'Why, of course.' Sarah anxiously inserted a few more pins to conceal the improvisation at the bodice back and invited Francis Vaughan to come upstairs. He cast a swift glance round the room before surveying his wife.

'Ah. I do believe that is the most becoming dress that I have ever seen you wear, my dear.'

'Oh good. I thought you would like it. I can't wait to show it to Beatrice. She has such good taste in these things.'

'Perhaps Mrs Devereux would like to accompany you

to the final fitting? We should be ready by Monday,'
said Sarah.

'Could she really? What a good idea. I shall ask her if
she can.'

As the Vaughans walked up the High Street, Sarah
pirouetted about the shop in a dance of delight. Her
plans were reaching fruition sooner than she had dared
to hope. She skipped upstairs and fetched the dress
down to the back room.

'Temperance! Ellie! Just think! Mrs Vaughan is bringing the Rector's wife, Mrs Devereux, with her on
Monday. We must work all Saturday and Sunday to get
this finished and those other two dresses if we possibly
can. I shall help you with the sewing and I shall go round
to Mrs Wilmot now to see if she could come too. It is of
the utmost importance that we make a gown for Mrs
Devereux. She is so well connected, we might have Lady
Hethrington next!'

Temperance and Ellie did their best to share her
enthusiasm, but as soon as she had gone, Temperance
said in dismay:

'I'se told Billy Lunnon as I'd go to Woburn with him
on Sunday afternoon and I'll have to go to chapel in the
morning else me mam and pa won't let me go out.'

'Yeah. Me mam said I was to go to see me Grandma
after chapel and they won't hear of me missing that.'

'I wonder if she will pay us more?'

'If she pays us well they mightn't flinch so bad but
what about working on a Sunday!' They exchanged looks
of horror.

It was a problem which had not occurred to Sarah in
her excitement and she was exceedingly exasperated
when they told her.

'Of course I shall pay you extra. I'll pay you . . . one
shilling each for working late on Saturday and *two*
shillings for Sunday. Three shillings extra. That's nearly
half as much again as your wage!'

The girls shook their heads unhappily.

'Us'll tell our mams that. They may come round all right, Miss.'

'Well, I suppose *I* ought to go to church. Yes, Mrs Devereux and the Rector must see me in church. Look, you two go to chapel and I'll go to church and then we shall come straight back here and change. You bring some old clothes on Saturday and no-one will know that we're working. We shall sew and sew until we've finished and I shall pay you three shillings extra each.'

'Yes, Ma'am,' they mumbled.

'I ain't got no other clothes, Ma'am.'

'Oh, Ellie, really!' Sarah had no right to get cross. It was so little time since she would have been in the same predicament, but she had suddenly found herself on the master's side of the bargaining table with all its worries. The girls acknowledged this when they sullenly qualified her with the 'Ma'am' instead of the 'Miss' at the end of each sentence. She found this irritating too.

'I shall cut you out a dress. What stuff would you like?'

Ellie rolled her eyes.

'That ging . . . ging . . . whatever you calls it.'

'The striped gingham? Why, yes! I shall cut you out a pretty little frock in that, Ellie, and you shall sew it up at home tonight. Look, I'll draw you a picture of it.' The girls watched her swift pencil strokes with moon-round eyes.

'Oh, you ain't half clever, Miss,' cooed Temperance.

Sarah smiled and shook her head.

'Temperance, I can't do one for you this week. You bring something to wear Sunday and I shall cut you out one just as soon as there's time.'

'Thanks, Miss. We'll make it right for Sunday somehow, but Lord 'elp us.'

CHAPTER 32

Going to Church

Sunday was one of the most glorious June days that ever dawned. Sarah looked out from her upper window. Some toddlers were playing round the cross in the centre of the Square with the sun glancing off their hair and white pinafores. Sparrows were squabbling over sand baths nearby and chaffinches flitted and piped among the lush young leaves of the horse chestnut, which overhung the path near the Academy. It still bore its pinky-white candles which gleamed in the sunlight. Sarah stepped out from the door of Miss Lacelle's Salon with the untroubled serenity of the weather-house lady on a fine day. The air smelt fresh and exciting with just a hint of woodsmoke and lime blossom. She carried a leatherbound prayer book, confidentially supplied by Mary Nursall, and a furled parasol Frank Cox had bought her in London. Her kid gloves were from her new stock, which she regretted, but they exactly matched her primrose yellow dress. Lilac ribbon decorated the bodice of the dress and secured her bonnet beneath her chin. She had sat up until after midnight making the hat, which she had barely begun when Temperance and Ellie left exhausted at half past nine. It was in yellow silk with a pendulous pale ostrich feather which bounced gently up and down as she walked, and floated as she turned.

Her poise was soon disturbed by the side gate to the Academy opening just ahead of her and a crocodile of small boys beginning to pour out under the anxious supervision of a young master.

'Ratcliffe, Smith! In line please, in pairs – *pairs* I said, sir! Can't you count that far, Jennings?'

Sarah had to wait patiently. The agitated young man cast her an apologetic glance which distracted him just long enough for one twelve-year-old to buffet his neighbour into the road.

'Eddison, desist! Jilks, back in line, sir.'

He fell in behind the fourth form and the older boys lounged nonchalantly after them. Two prefects treated Sarah to an impudently approving stare. Her face hardened but immediately composed itself as Mr and Mrs Vaughan appeared at the main gate following the family procession of two little girls, one boy, the governess and the nanny.

A fleeting glance of uncertainty passed across Theresa's face when she saw Sarah but Francis Vaughan smiled gallantly.

'I am so sorry my entourage has impeded your progress, Miss Lacelle. Do allow me to make amends.' He proffered Sarah his free arm which she accepted with a radiant smile and so arrived at the church door bringing up the rear of an impressive procession. She released Mr Vaughan's arm there and explained that she had her own pew, before any hint of embarrassment ensued. She noticed the look of relief on Theresa's face.

Sarah made her way down the aisle just ahead of the Vaughan family. Her eyes were lowered demurely but she was quite aware of the rustle of interest among the congregation. A wizened old woman, Mrs Jones, whom Sarah knew well, moved past her with surprising alacrity and opened the pew gate for her. It was the way the old soul earned a valuable few pence each week but, unfortunately, Sarah had not anticipated this extra expense and only had her threepenny piece for the collection inside her glove. She beamed benevolently into the old lady's face to atone, and was disconcerted to see its swift change from an ingratiating toothy smile to beady-eyed malevolence. She had certainly recognized Sarah Ruddock. Sarah consoled herself by considering what an excellent situation her pew was in, just beyond the edge of the new gallery which had been put in to accommodate the pupils from the Academy. As she knelt to pray she wondered again why such a pew had been available for her, but the explanation became clear as soon as the service began. Some small objects began to fall from above touching her shoulders and bouncing off her hymn book. Soon one landed on the shelf in front of her – a dried pea! Sarah was not unacquainted with pea-shooters and pursed her lips as she surmised that the prime target was probably her hat and its plume. She shook her head gently and dislodged a few peas. Mercifully, the supply of ammunition ran out towards the end of the Venite and she enjoyed a brief respite for the first Lesson. During the second Lesson, paper pellets began to rain down on her and these grew in size until small darts began to arrive for the Creed, at which point there were some muted whispers and scuffling in the gallery above and the bombardment ceased. She spent the Collects furtively shaking and nodding her head in an attempt to disengage debris. She could not possibly remove her hat and the thought of issuing from the church with it adorned with paper darts made her wrathful. She decided to bring her inconvenience to the notice of the young master early on Monday, and Mr Vaughan the following week, if her persecution continued.

As it happened, there were no embarrassing adornments on Sarah's hat as she shook hands with the Reverend Devereux at the church door and the serene expression on her face suggested to any onlooker that the service had afforded her only peaceful solace. She smiled and nodded to a lady who had visited her shop during the week and who was now revealed to be Mrs Miller, the wife of Dick Miller the farmer.

'Oh, do meet my husband, Miss Lacelle. This is the

lady who has just opened the new salon on the Square that I told you about, dear.'

Miller extended his hand smiling and Sarah took it, looking him in the face with a slightly challenging expression, but it seemed lost on him.

'So you are planning to make our Aspley ladies fashionable, are you, Miss Lacelle?'

'Oh, I am sure they don't need me to do that!'

'Well, we menfolk would be obliged if you don't tempt them too much, please. It's hard on our pockets, you know.'

He smiled down gallantly at her and had clearly not paid much attention to the grubby, shock-headed little girl who had spent so many hours stoning his fields and scaring off the rooks. Well, a new identity suited her purposes, she thought complacently.

CHAPTER 33

Sarah's First Callers

Temperance and Ellie were waiting at the door for her when she returned from church. Ellie was proudly showing Temperance the new frock which she had just finished sewing up before she went to chapel, despite her mother's admonitions. The three of them stitched hard until after eight o'clock that evening and then Sarah delivered Mrs Vaughan's dress to Mrs Wilmot, the village seamstress, who had undertaken to put the finishing stitching in early next morning. Sarah returned to the salon exhausted. She had only just settled into an armchair lent her by Frank Cox, intending to look at some French fashion journals borrowed from Mme du Prêt, when there was a tap on the door. She sighed as she rose. To her surprise it was the young teacher from the Academy standing timidly on her doorstep.

'I do hope you will excuse my presumption in calling, Miss Lacelle, but the behaviour of my pupils this morning has caused such distress to me. The guilty boys have been given extra Latin homework for tomorrow. I thought you would like to know that.' He spoke quickly and nervously with a clipped, interrogative accent that was strange to Sarah. She couldn't think how the Latin homework could concern her unless it was a particularly effective deterrent, but he seemed anxious that she should reassure him.

'Won't you step inside for a moment, sir?'

'Oh, well, no. Kind of you it is, but I must trouble you no longer . . .'

'It is no trouble. I should be most pleased, Mr . . .?'

'Griffiths. Dafydd Griffiths my name is, Ma'am.'

He had somehow stepped in as he introduced himself, despite his assurances and had soon accepted a seat on the other side of Sarah's hearth. He was of medium height but slightly built with an apologetic stoop to his shoulders which made him seem smaller. His thick hair and deep-set eyes were dark and his nose long and angular, but his face had a lively expression reflecting a quick intellect despite the general self-effacing manner he assumed. He nervously reiterated apologies for the misconduct of his pupils until he succumbed to Sarah's gentle encouragement and began to tell her about his family and life in South Wales.

'My father was telling me,' said Sarah, 'that there had been some violent disturbances at Newport recently.'

'Well, yes. The Chartists it was now. One of their number, a man called Vincent, is in gaol in Monmouth, and it seems they may have planned to release him, but it was an ill-managed affair. Quite a small group of soldiers – twenty-eight to be precise – quelled the riot, if that is what it was, indeed.'

Sarah detected that his sympathies lay with the rioters despite his effort merely to relate the facts.

'Yes, and they opened fire and killed twenty-two men and wounded many more, I'm told.'

'You are well informed, Miss Lacelle. Is it that your father has some interest in these matters?' he asked cautiously, watching her face. Sarah eyed him with equal caution.

'Yes, he does read about them sometimes.'

'I believe there is a gentleman coming to Aspley this week to talk about the history of the Movement.'

'Yes, his name is Mr Gammage. Will you go to the meeting, Mr Griffiths?'

'Well, there. So awkward it is! I fear Mr Vaughan would not approve of me going,' he sighed.

'No. I have the same problem. People like us cannot afford to displease our employers, can we?'

Griffiths looked at her keenly, his shyness forgotten.

'You would like to go to the meeting, then?'

Sarah smiled. 'I do hope you are not sent to spy on my sympathies, Mr Griffiths?'

'My goodness, no. Believe me. As you have probably guessed already, I am a supporter of the People's Charter myself, but one has to be so careful. A wicked thing it is that one cannot be honest about supporting such an eminently good cause. There is no violence intended by most of the leaders. The violence is committed by the methods of suppression.'

'Yes, that is what my father and his friends say, but there are those who want violence and they cannot be held back much longer. They say that as well.'

'Yes, we can only hope for success when the Charter is debated in Parliament next month. Everyone is impatient with these delays.'

'My father is helping to arrange the meeting on Friday but please do not tell anyone about these connections of

208

mine, Mr Griffiths. I am sure it would do my new business no good. But I do feel like . . . a . . .'

'Defector?'

'Yes, perhaps,' answered Sarah, not knowing the meaning of the word. 'I wish I was able to support him.'

'Yes, indeed. You have decided me. My mother and father would never miss such a meeting, nor indeed my two brothers either. I shall go and represent us both, Miss Lacelle!'

'What about Mr Vaughan?'

'He will probably not get to know and even if he does, I doubt whether he would ask me to leave my post. He depends a great deal upon me . . . And now I must go and leave you in peace. You have been most kind, Miss Lacelle. I can hardly start to tell you how much you have cheered me up. It is lonely that I am here, so far from my home and family and it has been such a comfort to discover a confederate so close.'

'You are always welcome, Mr Griffiths, and when you come to tell me all about the meeting I shall allow you to call me Sarah instead of Miss Lacelle, which is so formal.'

Dafydd Griffiths was only the first of Sarah's callers from the Academy. On the following evening she opened her door in response to a bolder knock and was surprised to find Francis Vaughan on her doorstep.

'Oh, Mr Vaughan! Do step in, please.'

'Thank you,' he said, stepping in with alacrity as if he would rather no-one caught sight of him there.

'I have come, Miss Lacelle, to apologize most profoundly for the deplorable behaviour of my pupils in church yesterday morning. I fear I only learnt about it this morning from Mr Griffiths.'

'Oh, please do not worry. Boys will be boys, won't they. I expect they get a little bored with the long service.'

'You are really too kind. I must confess that it is by no means the first time it has happened.'

'Won't you take a seat?'

'Well, I really only just came to convey my apologies but yes, just for a moment perhaps. You have such a charming and cosy establishment here . . . Yes, well, as I was saying, Mrs Gerome used to sit in that pew. Do you know her? A most worthy and particular elderly lady who wears . . . well, I was tempted to say "bizarre", but at any rate very large hats decorated with all manner of things . . .' Sarah smiled encouragingly.

'And I do mean all manner of things. Silk butterflies, for instance, and fruit and even stuffed birds!'

Sarah giggled, anticipating the irresistible nature of such a target for the boys.

'Well, last autumn there was considerable interest in the Academy for the art – or should I say skill – of toxophily and some of the young men became very proficient, but what I failed to discover until too late was that some of the younger scoundrels were manufacturing miniature bows with arrows to match, and the upshot,' (he paused with brows humorously raised for Sarah to register the pun) 'the upshot was that one of these weapons was smuggled into church. When Mrs Gerome emerged at the end of the service that morning, to shake hands with the Rector, the stuffed bee-eater on her splendid hat was neatly transfixed by a quivering arrow for all but the poor lady herself to see.' Sarah found the tale so funny that she abandoned any sort of affectation and laughed helplessly.

'So you see, you really escaped quite lightly, didn't you.'

Sarah quelled her amusement and put on her most severe expression.

'Well, Mr Vaughan, I was so cross yesterday that I decided to complain to Mr Griffiths first of all and if I suffered any more insults next Sunday I decided I should storm round to the Academy and complain bitterly to the Headmaster. And I shall!' She threatened him with a wagging index finger. 'I am made of sterner stuff than Mrs Gerome. I have paid for my pew and I shall not dream of relinquishing it, so be warned!'

'My! What a very determined young lady!'

'Yes!' agreed Sarah, but she allowed her face to relax into a mischievous grin and they laughed together.

Before the end of the week Mr Vaughan again called on Sarah one evening. His ostensible reason was to pay for his wife's dress. The final fitting had been made in the presence of Mrs Devereux, who was careful not to express open enthusiasm for Sarah's proficiency but was, nonetheless, impressed, as Sarah's keen senses detected.

The dress was due to be collected the next day after a minor alteration and Sarah could think of no good reason why Mrs Vaughan could not bring the money herself. Sarah had planned to copy some drawings from the French journals before she returned them to Mme du Prêt but she did not really mind, since Francis Vaughan's vivacity and capacity to amuse were welcome after a hard day's effort trying to please all and sundry. Mind you, she reminded herself, it was excellent that she *was* being required to please all and sundry. Her new venture seemed very successful. Vaughan reclined in her armchair showing no inclination to hurry away to his duties, so she made some hot chocolate (a luxury sent over from Leighton by Cox) and they chatted easily about this and that. Sarah was gratified that he so evidently enjoyed her company and the comfort and taste of her room, but a small voice which she tried to shut out insisted she should be wary. She could not afford to have any gossip of a compromising nature circulating in the village, and she had not been born and bred there without knowing how very insubstantial an event could set the tongues wagging. She knew they had already begun about her appearance in church and her pew. How long before that news reached the Heath?

As Francis Vaughan returned to his house he passed Dafydd Griffiths leaving by the side gate and vaguely wondered where he was going to so late in the evening. Sarah had only just carried the cups out to the scullery when there was his light tap on her door, and so her whole evening was taken up with entertaining gentlemen. She had to confess reluctantly that, compared to Vaughan, Griffiths was rather boring, although his loyalties commended themselves to her more. She rather hoped he might fall for an ardent female Chartist at the meeting the following evening. As she crept wearily into bed with no work done she found herself reflecting that entertaining gentlemen in an establishment like Mrs Butler's had the two great advantages that they paid their way and you were free to catch up on sleep during the morning.

CHAPTER 34

Disloyalty Discovered

The prevailing mood in the cottage on the Heath was bleak. When John returned from prison, he had quietly removed Bobby's stool but Eliza had demanded to have it back by the table so that they would remember him at each meal. This oppressed Tize and her parents dreadfully. The only member of the family who seemed unperturbed was William. Apart from being too young to share their grief he was gifted with an exuberant and extrovert nature which had the advantage of taking Eliza's mind off her dreary preoccupations because he was always in trouble of one sort or another. Tom was rarely at home except on a Sunday. He returned from

Ridgemont late and so tired that he just tumbled into his bed, so that Eliza had no company in the evenings except Tize, and John briefly before he left for The Bell.

'I reckon Tom bain't going to be around much longer,' said John one evening with the feeling that something said must be better than the gloomy silence they were enduring.

'What do you mean?' cried Eliza in alarm. John's tactless choice of subject matter in suggesting that she might be losing yet another son struck on a raw nerve.

'Be still, woman. I only meant that he seems sweet on that girl of Tennant's.'

'Well, yes, and what of it, John Ruddock? They can't marry when all he has is a month's more work, and can you see a rich farmer like Tennant having our Tom marry his daughter? Not that he ain't a very fine lad of course. I'm not meaning he ain't but marriages are made by money in them circles. It's nowt but puppy love, anyway.'

Poor John! Even his most innocent remark seemed doomed to draw wrath upon him from some quarter. He tried again:

'I wonder how that daughter of ours be getting along? We bain't seen much of her since she opened that fine shop.'

'Oh, don't start finding fault with our Sare, now. She intends to make something of her life. She allus has, ever since she were a tiny mite. I don't want to stand in her way. She always helps with what she can.'

'Liza, I don't neither,' said John earnestly. 'She's got a good head on her shoulders and she'll help the Movement when she can spare the time.'

'Not if she's any sense at all, she won't! That would spell trouble for her just like it has for you.'

'We ain't put on this world to avoid trouble. We're sent to fight it and stop it happening to folks. Sarah will stand by them as knows what's right.'

213

'Is she going to the meeting tomorrow?'

'Well, if she has the time, but she's very busy with the shop.'

'More fool her if she does.'

'Why?' shouted John indignantly.

'Why? Can you see Mrs Vaughan and Mrs Devereux going to buy things at her shop if they know she's a Chartist? Use your head, John Ruddock.'

John hung it instead. He did not want to believe this of Sarah. Eliza was not usually so cruel to him, but the death of Bobby, the absence of Tom and Sarah and the nightmare of the workhouse made her nervous and irritable.

Tize had been sitting silent and unhappy during this dialogue and she decided to turn it to a lighter vein.

'They says Sarah went to church on Sunday and she looked ever so nice. She were wearing a beautiful hat with one of them big fluffy feathers in it.'

'Church?' spat John.

Eliza looked sharply at Tize to try to stop her saying more but the girl's eyes were downcast as she fidgeted with a woooden spoon on the table.

'They said she went to church with Mr Vaughan the Headmaster of the school. She walked up to church holding his arm, like. She do seem to be getting on well, don't she?'

John had risen. He bent across the table, his black hair falling over his flushed face.

'You say she went to church, girl?'

Tize drew away in consternation. This was not the effect she intended.

'Well, she's got to, ain't she, John? I mean, she do have to keep up appearances with them gentry what's going to buy things in her shop,' cajoled Eliza.

'Mrs Jones, the pew opener, says she's got her own pew, too,' volunteered Tize consolingly.

'Her own pew, has she? My God!'

214

'Don't use that sort of language here, John.'

He paced up and down the room running his hands through his hair.

'Why have I raised serpents? Why do other men have wives and children as helps and comforts them while I rear vipers in my nest?'

'Oh John! Tize, love, stop looking forlorn and go out to play,' wailed Eliza, bundling the innocent bearer of bad tidings out of the cottage.

'Did you know about this, Eliza?'

'Only Mary let something drop about a prayer book for Sarah but . . . what do it matter? Pull yourself together, John. Can't you see she's got to. She ain't doing it to hurt you. She ain't even doing it because she likes it.'

'What's a man or woman got left if they've no principles to stand by? Real principles ain't what you can trade in when they're inconvenient. We ain't good enough for her now, Eliza.'

'She said she wanted us to go up to see her shop next week when you've finished with your meeting.'

'I ain't going. I don't care for her making something of herself that way. I should think more of her if she were home here with us, helping you. And I shan't think a great deal of you if you go to see this fine shop of hers, Eliza Ruddock.'

CHAPTER 35

Comfort from a New Friend

The next evening, Tize had still not fathomed out how she had precipitated the trouble between her sister and her parents, so she called upon Sarah and told her all about it. The poor girl suffered a vicious shaking which made her teeth clatter. Sarah relented a little as the tears began to roll down Tize's cheeks.

'Oh, I'm sorry. You just don't understand do you, girl?' cried Sarah petulantly.

'No. And I ain't going to stay and be treated like this, neither,' sobbed Tize, escaping by the scullery door.

Sarah shed a few tears of self-pity herself. She was neither fish, flesh nor fowl, now. She was unacceptable to the villagers she had grown up amongst because she had advanced herself. She was unacceptable to her fellow tradesmen because, firstly, she was a woman and, secondly, she catered exclusively for the gentry. And now even her parents disowned her. Tom had never approved of any ambition she had ever had and that hurt her most of all, because she still longed for him to be the stolid dependable ally of her childhood. A light tap on her front door compelled her to wipe her cheeks and pull herself together.

Dafydd Griffiths stood there with an expression of grave concern on his face.

'Please excuse me intruding but I just thought that maybe there was some trouble you were having.' He could see clearly from Sarah's puffy eyes that he was right.

'Oh, why was that?' asked Sarah shortly.

'Well . . . the young lady who just collided with me in the street . . . seemed upset . . . and . . .' he stammered.

'That was my sister,' sniffed Sarah.

'Oh dear, family trouble is it? Can I do anything? I should be so happy if I could.'

Sarah was torn between exasperation and gratitude.

'It is kind of you, Mr Griffiths. Do step inside. It's just that Tize, Eliza that is, was telling me that my parents wouldn't have anything to do with me because she, the foolish girl, had told them all about me going to church and my pew.'

'Oh, and they would rather you were at chapel, is it?'

Dafydd could understand this sentiment, since his parents would hold the same.

'It's just my father. He doesn't actually go to chapel but he doesn't approve of church and particularly not of the Rector, and he takes a petition round for signing against rented pews, so you see I was hoping that they wouldn't hear about all that until I had made good and could explain it to them.'

'Oh dear, oh dear. Do you think I might act as mediator?'

'Oh no! It's good of you to offer but it will pass. I was feeling rather low spirited you know, and this was the last straw.'

'Now I can see a very simple thing I can do to help. If you can forgive me being here at all, intruding on your sadness. Perhaps you will tell me why such a talented and successful young lady is feeling low spirited for I believe that whatever I say or do not say, a trouble shared is a trouble halved. Indeed, there is a Welsh saying exactly to that effect, so true it is.'

Sarah smiled weakly as he took her shoulders and gently propelled her into the armchair. He drew up a small chair and sat down at her side expectantly.

'I was just feeling sorry for myself and that was a hard lesson I thought I had learnt when I was very young: that one must never feel sorry for oneself, you know.'

'Yes. So I tell myself, but I often don't listen. Tell me the reason for this outburst of self-pity.'

'I just do not belong anywhere now. It has always seemed so clear to me that what my family needed was some money and so I work hard to earn it and, believe me, I have worked very hard since I was small; then no-one is grateful. No-one at all! My brother Tom disapproves of me; my parents disapprove of me and all the village people I grew up among disapprove of me. No-one wants to know me now!' she sobbed, despite herself.

'None of that is really true. Perhaps it *is* disapproval

217

as you say, but it is not deep disapproval. It is more a distrust, an envy perhaps, that will not last if you stand firm by what they all know is right. I understand because I am in just the same position, see?'

'Why?' asked Sarah.

'Well, I am a miner's son and all my parents seemed to want was that their children should better themselves, so that we boys should not be miners and the girls should not be miners' wives and sisters and, because I was gifted with being good at my books, I got a scholarship to Newport Grammar School. Now I thought Mama and Dada and all my friends would be very happy to see me there but no! And why? Because "Thou shalt not be different in any respect". Only conformity is safe. It is written in huge invisible letters over every terrace doorway: "To be one of us you must be as we are",' he intoned in deep rectorial tones. Sarah laughed.

'So what happened to you?'

'Well, all my old friends stopped playing with me, as if they thought I was too elevated; the boys at school would have nothing to do with me because I was a miner's son and my parents had to keep apologizing for me because they were being ostracized. I mean they were still encouraging me, you know, but it was a rather apprehensive sort of encouragement as soon as I got to the grammar school, and I know full well that they won't be telling the neighbours much about my post here in this very respectable school.'

'Oh dear, what a pity.'

'So would you agree that we have a lot in common, Miss Lacelle?'

'But I am more guilty than you because I have betrayed the things that my father is fighting for. Not that I want to – I don't – but I am weak enough to abandon my principles for less worthy things, am I not?' asked Sarah earnestly.

'Perhaps because you consider earning money to help

your family your first duty? Now, if that is so, you can easily salve your conscience because when you are a very successful businesswoman, and that might be quite soon, why then you will have so much money you won't know what to do with it and you can give it all to your father to help the poverty-stricken dependants of imprisoned Chartists, eh? There! *Rhanni trwbl, haneru trwbl –* "a trouble shared is a trouble halved".'

Sarah smiled.

'That sounds fine, but supposing, Mr Griffiths, I decide to buy myself a huge house and a smart carriage and pair and some beautiful clothes, then there will be none left for the poor dependants of the Chartists.'

'Oh, you despicable lady! I shall have to decide whether to cease visiting you or become your butler and share in your lascivious pleasures.'

'I am sure you would make an excellent butler, providing I can trust my large cellar to your care.'

'It is the butler's duty to sample each crate of wine, Madam, but I hasten to point out that I am a devout adherent of Mr Turner's principle of Total Abstinence.' This speech left Sarah rather perplexed but generally in a much happier frame of mind for Mr Griffiths's visit, and he again promised to represent them both at Mr Gammage's lecture the following evening.

CHAPTER 36

The Meeting

The only available place of sufficient size to hold the Chartist meeting was Mr Hall's threshing barn just off the Square. Lucy Hall had plans to start a school there to encourage more village children to learn to read and write, so she had collected some benches and chairs together, but many more would be needed. For weeks, the Round Table Circle at The Bell had been discussing the vexed question of how many people would come, and at six o'clock on Thursday evening the Square at Aspley Guise was the scene of the most unusual activity. Ox waggons and drays arrived piled high with a strange assortment of benches, settles, chairs and stools from the surrounding villages, while people ran back and forth from the cottages round about carrying a similar assortment of furniture. As with the building, so with the seating; it was not that it was unavailable nearby so much as who was prepared to supply it. A trifle reluctantly, Fred Price, the proprietor of The Bell allowed all his seats other than the odd stool to be carried across to the barn. The landlords of The Anchor and The Steamer were not so forthcoming, but in the interests of not alienating any customers they contributed a few seats. Harry Vane at The Swan considered his position as host to the Select Vestry meetings and refused any seats, on the grounds that his customers could not be expected to stand for three or four hours. He was rebuked by John Ruddock for this.

'You should tell your customers that they ought to be at the meeting and come yourself by way of example.'

'Talking of examples, Ruddock, I understand that some of yours ain't the sort that good working folk could be proud of.' John flushed angrily and left.

Sarah raised the edge of her curtain and bit her lip guiltily. Well, velvet armchairs were hardly suitable and she only possessed two, one upstairs and one down. Temperance was sewing late and Sarah asked her to leave by the back door with two wooden chairs to be delivered to the barn.

By seven o'clock every seat was taken and the people were still arriving on horseback, in pony chaises and on foot to squeeze into the barn. John and George and their confederates were relieved and elated by the assured success of the evening, until they began to worry that some accident might have overtaken the speaker, but he arrived by a quarter past seven, having ridden over from his home in Buckingham.

'Will thee take a tankard of beer to refresh thyself, sir?' asked George. 'Though I am afraid you can only stand over there on account of all the seats being in the barn.'

'Thank you very much, Mr Dunne, but no. I don't partake of intoxicating liquors.'

'Well, a cup of tea, perhaps? We can manage that don't you think, John?'

'Well, aye . . . of course,' said John, none so confident as he sounded.

'It had best be somewhere close, comrade,' said Dicken.

'How about your daughter's across the Square, John?' suggested Philip Wooding.

'Ah yes, of course,' said John doubtfully. 'I'll just go ahead to arrange it. You bring Mr Gammage over.'

At first Sarah was happily surprised when she opened the door of the salon to her father and then she became apprehensive when he stammered out his mission.

'Father, why didn't you warn me?'

'How was I to know he didn't take liquor?'

'Father, I'd be pleased to help you, only . . . I'd rather . . . Bring them up the passage and round to the back.'

'We ain't grand enough for your shop, then?' shouted John.

'No, it's not that at all.'

'No, it's not *that,* John Ruddock,' said Martha Lyle's deep voice authoritatively. She had just arrived at the back door herself, to see if Sarah was going to the meeting.

'Bring them round to me. The pan's hot.'

'But the people are all waiting!' cried John in despair.

'They'll be happy to wait another fifteen minutes. We must show the gentleman hospitality, and my cottage ain't far.' With her usual commonsense Martha took John's elbow and steered him out of the back door into the Square to meet the group of men.

'I should be happy if you would have a cup of tea by my hearth, sir. I am very sensible of the hardship you gentlemen face for the sake of the Movement. I am afraid you will have to sit on a box because our benches are in the barn, but you'll think none the less of us for that,' said Martha.

Nearly four hundred people tried to squeeze into the Halls' barn that evening and those that were unsuccessful waited outside. Dafydd Griffiths had taken his place early and listened with increasing admiration and pity as Gammage recounted the efforts and deprivations of the active Chartists. He told them about the Birmingham Convention in May and how they called upon supporters to withdraw their savings from the bank and convert paper money into coinage. 'What savings? What money?' called some good-natured hecklers, who were greeted by laughter. He called upon them to do no business with non-Chartist tradesmen and urged them to abstain from work and intoxicating liquor for the 'Sacred Month' if this was called for. He told them how the police had been summoned to break up the meeting in the Bull Ring but had been repulsed by the crowd of many thousands (general cheering ensued) and how the military had then been summoned and succeeded in dispersing the crowd (general booing), but riots in the city continued for several days. He told of the strikes in the South Wales ironworks and how the furnaces had died down and the black smoke ceased erupting from the chimneys for the first time for many years (cheers!); but on a sober note he reminded them that no work meant no money and no food and talked of children starving and babies suckling blood instead of milk. He forecast the crippling effect on the country's economy if the strikes spread to Lancashire and Yorkshire and, nearer to home, the framework knitters of Leicester. But there was no cheering now for, although his audience were country tradesmen and labourers and had never set eyes on a mill, they had sufficient imagination to know that, imprisoned in a city away from the life-giving soil, when a man's wage stops so does his family's food. There is no escape. Voluntarily to court this retribution takes a courage of the highest order.

He finished by describing the two wings of the Movement: the Moral Force led by William Lovett and the Physical Force led by Fergus O'Conner.

'If we are Chartists then we get our principles from the Bible. We shall avoid violence for as long as we can, but if our peaceful quest for democracy fails, then there is nothing left but to support our brothers in this struggle for justice by opposing violence with violence.'

The cheers and clapping were not the wild mindless accolades of rhetoric now but the gestures of people who foresaw the grim realities of their struggle.

The vote of thanks was given by James McKay, a Woburn tailor, who mentioned the 'Memorial of Congratulation' that had been sent to O'Conner last May, when no bloodshed was incurred in the Birmingham Conventions, advocating the Moral Force. It was signed by over fifty local Chartists. The vote was passed unanimously as was the pledge to support the Charter.

To the relief of the local group, Mr Gammage declined further offers of hospitality and, mounting his horse, rode off to Woburn, where he was resting on his way to address the straw hat makers of Luton the next day. Dafydd approached the group bidding the speaker farewell, since he was curious to meet Sarah's father. They warmly invited him to join them in carrying the seats belonging to The Bell back to their place, which he dutifully did.

'It is important to get the right things done first, and a pot-house without any chairs is a sad place,' joked John, who was feeling very elated. 'You must join us for a tankard of beer now and tell us about yourself.'

'My name is Dafydd Griffiths and I work at the Classical Academy.' He was reluctant to confess his profession in this company. '. . . And I should like very much to join you but I hope I shall be excused for drinking water.'

'Of course you will, comrade.'

'You are a countryman of the stout ironworkers we have heard about this evening, aren't you?' asked George Dunne.

'Yes, indeed. I am proud of that, although it is they who are making the sacrifices. Which one of you gentlemen is Mr Lacelle, may I ask?'

They looked at each other blankly.

'Oh, I see I have made a mistake, but you must know him surely?'

'Can't say that we do,' said John slowly. The explanation for this question had occurred to others of the group but when John was reluctant to acknowledge himself they let it lie.

'Well, I must return home now and I hope I shall have the pleasure of meeting you gentlemen again. Goodnight,' said Dafydd.

As he walked slowly across the Square, he felt ill at ease about Sarah's motives. She seemed to have been seriously misleading him for some reason he did not yet understand.

He tapped on her front door, wondering whether to challenge her or not, but inside he found Martha Lyle already giving an account of the meeting, so he made an excuse and did not stay.

CHAPTER 37

A Memorable Journey

It was barely three weeks after Mrs Devereux had accompanied Mrs Vaughan to Lacelle's Salon for the final fitting of her dress that she arrived to collect one of her own. Sarah insisted that she should try it on just to make sure that the fit was perfect, as indeed it was. Sarah, Temperance and Ellie had developed their skills apace and had encountered very few problems with this day dress and cape of fine white checkered cotton, printed with tiny purple, red and green flowers. The full long sleeves were gathered and generously puffed just above the elbow and then gathered into a wide wrist band. It was a practical rather than an eye-catching dress and, Sarah surmised, a test for future orders of a more elaborate nature.

'This seems very satisfactory, Miss Lacelle,' said Beatrice Devereux, a trifle grudgingly.

'Yes. I think we may be proud of the fit, Ma'am,' said Sarah, 'and it was so wise of you to allow me to point the bodice. My friend, Mr Cox, assures me that points are quite the thing in London at the moment. I think they will become longer and more pronounced next season.'

'Indeed? Well, I shall need a new evening dress for the autumn. Could your establishment cope adequately with that, do you think?'

'But of course. Evening dresses are quite a speciality of ours,' lied Sarah. 'What sort of material had you in mind, Mrs Devereux?'

'I hadn't really considered. Might you show me a selection to choose from?'

'Of course. I need some new stock. I think I might

make a visit to London and I shall bear Madam's commission in mind.'

Sarah was gratified to see Mrs Devereux's new dress displayed to the congregation the following Sunday. She was sure that the restrained good taste must commend itself to the older ladies and it was their patronage that she needed. The salon had fast become a fashionable place to meet for the daughters and young wives of well-to-do families in Aspley and the surrounding country-side. It was rare for there not to be two chaises waiting in the Square any morning and sometimes the shop was so crowded Sarah wished it had been twice as large. But the young ladies tended to buy small articles or lengths of material to have made up at home by a visiting seamstress. It was their aunts and mothers who were likely to place the large orders.

Sarah's proposed visit to London was a delightful idea but she was so busy that she could hardly see how it could be done. Temperance and Ellie would have floundered behind the counter for all but the simplest trans-actions and it would be a pity to shut the shop. She racked her brains for a stand-in . . . Her mother and Tize and Mary Nursall? No: even if they would come, they would be totally overawed by the patrons, and Mary's deficient dress sense would set the business back severely . . . Martha Lyle, her old friend and mentor? Well perhaps that was just possible. Martha would have no particular sympathy for the business but she was sensible and would not be overawed by the ladies. Sarah set off to ask her, and Martha reluctantly agreed to spend a couple of days working with Sarah to see if she thought she could manage. The next problem was the coach fare which was a colossal one pound ten shillings each way, and Sarah needed every penny of her takings to buy the new materials. This problem was solved in the most unexpected fashion.

Quite late one evening, Sarah answered a knock on

her door and found, not Dafydd Griffiths but Francis Vaughan on her doorstep.

'Good evening, Miss Lacelle. Forgive my interrupting you, but I believe I may be able to be of some assistance to you, perhaps.' She invited him in and asked if he would take some hot chocolate, which he accepted.

'Now my wife tells me that she believes you intend to visit London to purchase some materials. Is that so?'

'Why yes. I do.'

'Well, materials are very heavy and may prove awkward on a coach, and since I am driving up to London to see to some business and to collect a friend who is coming to stay with us, I wondered whether you might honour me with your company? I shall travel fast by post-chaise, but I fear I shall be alone,' he said apologetically.

'How kind! That would be extremely convenient for me, Mr Vaughan. I shall bring a companion. How long will you stay in London?'

'Would three days be sufficient for you?'

'Yes, an admirable length of time.'

Sarah was loath to take Temperance or Ellie away from the salon when they were so busy, but the other possible companion was Tize and she preferred not to have the details of her connections in London relayed to the Heath. She decided that Temperance was the most resilient of her helpers and would cope with the novelties of London the best, but Temperance's enthusiasm did not sway her parents and days of protracted negotiation and persuasion followed. Sarah had to send them the letter from Mrs Briggs confirming her room booking in an attempt to convince them that she would not allow their daughter to be whisked away to a house of ill-repute, where her unsullied virtue would be sold for an enormous price. Sarah was sufficiently observant and uncharitable to remark to Martha that she doubted whether the virtue in question would remain unsullied long, and written evidence that a fair proportion of its value would be paid to Temperance's parents, might have been more effective in gaining their consent. Anyway, grudging permission was eventually given and Temperance became so excited that the sewing work suffered badly.

'Temperance! Ellie! Grace! Do stop chattering and get on with your work,' screeched Sarah for the fourth or fifth time that hour.

Mr Vaughan was to collect them from the salon at six o'clock on Monday morning. At ten to six Temperance had not arrived and just before six, Vaughan and Temperance's younger brother arrived simultaneously.

'Please miss,' stammered the boy, 'our Temperance ain't well. She's bin terrible sick all night and me Mam says she can't go to Lunnon.'

'Oh dear!' cried Sarah in consternation.

'What bad luck!' said Vaughan. 'Is there no other lady who could accompany you?'

'None that I can think of and certainly not immediately.' Sarah was close to tears.

'Well, is a companion really essential? I shall promise to behave with the utmost decorum and I *am* the headmaster of a very reputable school.'

Sarah's doleful expression cleared rapidly.

'It is your reputation that I am partly concerned with, Mr Vaughan, but if you think it is satisfactory to dispense with a chaperon, I am perfectly happy to travel alone with you.'

'In you get then, Miss Lacelle.'

They stopped at the Sugar Loaf in Dunstable to change horses and have breakfast. When they crossed the yard to return to the chaise they were amazed to see a middle-aged cripple sitting in a miniature waggon drawn by three large foxhounds. The waggon had no need to be very long for the man had no legs, but it was

228

well sprung on large wheels and fitted with a whip-holder, boat and lamps.

'That's Ol' Lal,' said an ostler, 'and 'e can't 'alf move in that there little cart of his and no mistake. He'd leave them new cattle of yours behind.'

'I don't believe it!' declared Vaughan.

'Try him, sir! You just try him.'

Ol' Lal was showing off his equipage by running his dogs in tight circles in the middle of the forecourt of the inn. He wore a jaunty cap with a long yellow feather in it which emphasized the reckless expression on his grinning pock-marked face.

'Yah-ho! Come on me beauties!' he called in a high voice, cracking his whip above his head. He also used his whip hand to steady himself on a bar which held him in place, since his lack of legs made him unstable. He held the reins of his three steeds skilfully in his right hand.

Sarah was fascinated.

'Do you fancy a wager, Lal?' called Vaughan.

'No, don't,' begged Sarah. 'He'll get hurt.'

'No he won't. That's the way he makes his living, I'll warrant.'

'Aye, I'll take you on, sir, though it ain't quite fair on you,' cried Lal, wheeling his dogs about to bring him alongside Vaughan and Sarah.

'Half a sovereign?'

'You ain't much trust in them cattle of yours, have you!'

'Oh yes, I have. You'll not beat us. Make it a sovereign.'

'Right. You may as well give it to me now.'

'No. I'll throw it to you if you deserve it. Can you catch it?'

'Never fear.' He pulled off his cap and twirled it in the air with his whip, tossing it back on to his head in one movement.

'Come on then, Miss Lacelle,' cried Vaughan.

They pulled out into the St Albans road at a canter, and the coachman was soon springing his team into a gallop with his whip cracking over their flattened ears. Their drumming hooves made a deafening noise and the chaise pitched from side to side like a storm-driven ketch. Sarah, clinging on for dear life, hung out of the left-hand window and Vaughan out of the right.

'This is quite amazing!' shouted Sarah.

'Yes, poor beggar, but he's coming on. Look! And we're going nearer twenty miles an hour than twelve.'

'He can't do it.'

But on he came, steadily gaining. His lips were stretched in a wide grin, exposing his irregular blackened teeth, and his whip cracked over the hounds' heads.

'Ya yip! Yip! Yip!' he sang. 'Up Trojan, up! Come on Rocket! Rocket! Yip! Yip!'

He let out a 'Halloo-oo' of triumph as he drew alongside Vaughan, his leading hound level with the haunches of the back pair of horses. He tore off his cap and held it inverted a moment for Vaughan to toss in the sovereign which was miraculously caught and tipped into his mouth. Holding it between his teeth he began to pull abreast of the leading pair of horses.

'There's a coach coming!' screamed Sarah.

'Watch yourself – coach coming up!' yelled Vaughan. The *Independant Tallyho*, bound for Birmingham, was coming towards them at a gallop, late for its Dunstable schedule. Vaughan's coachman steadied his beasts as fast as he could without rolling the chaise and Lal pulled ahead of him with a handsbreadth separating him from being trampled by one team or the other. Vaughan just had time to see the look of horrified consternation on the *Tallyho* coachman's face before they thundered past and he sank back into his seat. Sarah was still leaning out of her window watching Lal as he sped ahead and turned off into a left fork, turning his hounds about smartly so that he could crack his whip and yell as the chaise passed. Sarah laughed and waved to him as a fair damsel might have saluted her tournament champion.

'Well, I never expected a bit of sport like that,' declared Vaughan, replacing his hat on his head.

'Sport! We might have ended up in the ditch if the *Tallyho* had been a moment earlier and goodness knows what would have happened to that poor wretch!'

'My dear girl, there was no need to hang out of the window shouting if you were so terrified.'

'I am sure you couldn't hear me shouting.'

'But don't deny it. You are not the stuff that timid beauties are made of. Not that you ain't beautiful, of course; merely, not timid.'

Sarah smiled. She was not sure how to respond to this display of boisterous high spirits.

'Is this not a rather strange way for a respectable headmaster to behave? What would your pupils have said if they could have seen you?'

Francis Vaughan threw back his head and laughed.

'Oh Lord! They would have loved it, but I don't behave like this at home, you know. I lead the most exemplary of lives and it is appallingly boring. So stiflingly boring I don't know how to bear up sometimes. I find myself living from one day's hunting to the next and the summer is quite desperate. You won't repeat this, Sarah – sorry – I mean, Miss Lacelle. You won't repeat this to anyone in the village, will you?'

'No. Of course not,' she laughed.

'Were you offended by the slip I made when I used your first name?' He leant forward and took her hand, his face lowered and turned aside so that his clear blue eyes gazed appealingly up at her.

'This man is dangerous,' thought Sarah, lowering her eyes and considering the matter gravely to conceal her excitement.

'No, not at all. I find "Miss Lacelle" rather too formal for my liking.'

'Does that mean I may call you Sarah?'

'Yes.'

'Excellent. My name is Francis and you may call me "Fran" while we are alone,' he smiled roguishly, looking exceedingly handsome and young.

Sarah was silent a few moments and then betrayed her thoughts by asking, 'Does Mrs Vaughan go hunting?'

'My goodness no. She is certainly not the athletic type of woman. Why, do you?'

'Oh dear, no. I have never learnt to ride.'

'Should you like to?'

'Why, yes. Very much!'

'You would look devastatingly charming, mounted, in a well-fitted riding habit.'

'Until I fell off.'

'Became unseated, young lady. The best people *never* fall off.'

'Oh – "became unseated",' enunciated Sarah in her mock-county accent, 'but I am sure the effect is equally undignified.'

Vaughan roared with laughter and patted the small gloved hand which he still held.

'You and I shall get along famously, Sarah, and I shall undertake to become your riding instructor next summer. That, at least, will be something to look forward to when the hunting season ends.'

'I find it hard to believe that your life is so boring with all those naughty little boys you have to care for.'

'Well, between you and me, they are very often nasty rather than naughty and I do not care for them over much sometimes. I only wish the same could be said of some of my masters!' He added the last sentence quietly and Sarah was not sure what he meant.

'Is Mr Griffiths fond of the boys?'

'Ha, ha! Well, not in the way I meant. Not that I am

aware of, at any rate. No, he is a dependable fellow, Griffiths. Of course, he came to apologize to you, didn't he? Has he called again?'

'Ah . . . oh, yes. He did call again,' she said vaguely. Vaughan looked at her hard, but she steered the subject back to the boys.

'Now, shooting arrows at old ladies' hats in church I call naughty, not nasty. How are they nasty?'

'Well, in a multitude of ways which I trust a well brought up young lady like you could not begin to contemplate, but they are also bullies and show great cruelty to each other and any of their teachers who are in the least sensitive and not careful enough to conceal the fact. Poor Dafydd Griffiths suffers somewhat but he is learning to cope. He will probably make a good teacher when he learns never to show his Achilles heel.'

'What is that?' Sarah meant the classical allusion, but it was to her credit that Vaughan still assumed she had had the benefit of a genteel education.

'Well, I expect it is his background. He has never actually told me about it but, despite his excellent education, I strongly suspect that his origins are humble and the young men have a nose for such things. You see, his Welsh accent gives him an advantage which he would not enjoy if he was of humble English origin because his accent would betray him immediately. Why are you smiling, Sarah?'

'Nothing, no reason, really,' said Sarah.

They soon reached St Albans and dined gaily at the Old Red Lion while the horses were changed and, two and a half hours later, Vaughan set Sarah off at Mrs Briggs's in Aldersgate, arranging to pick her and her purchases up on the following Thursday morning.

CHAPTER 38

Young Love

Tom was having a more trying time than Sarah with the opposite sex.

Farmer Tennant had nothing to complain of as far as Tom's work was concerned. He arrived early each morning and did three men's work with relish during the day. He was good-natured, dependable and intelligent enough to trust but not enough to suffer from boredom and frustration. At meal times he spoke very little and often didn't respond when spoken to because his normally keen blue eyes had taken on a dreamy abstraction and were forever directed towards Rosie.

Rosie's work did suffer. Her mother was exasperated with her for letting the porridge burn almost every morning while the breakfast eggs were usually over- or underdone and she would be found 'mooning about' in the orchard watching Tom scything when she ought to have been preparing the vegetables for dinner.

'You'll have to get rid of that young man, Robert,' said Mrs Tennant. 'I can't do with Rosie mooning about and not doing her work proper.'

'Oh, it will pass. He's a good worker.'

'That's what you said near two months ago and it's only got worse.'

'We were the same when we were young, I 'spect.'

'Yes, but we could get it out of our systems by being wed.' Tennant looked at his wife doubtfully. It saddened him to hear marriage spoken of in terms of remedial medicine, although he feared it might be somewhere near the truth in their case.

'Well, they are a bit too young for that.'

'It could never be considered, Robert. Not seemly at all!'

'He's a good sound lad, Nell.'

'But no family and no money,' she replied, scandalized.

'No, I s'pose you're right, dear,' sighed Tennant.

Tom would not have been surprised if he had overheard this conversation. He did little to encourage Rosie because he knew he would be unacceptable as a suitor and he didn't wish to jeopardize his job, but he suffered keenly.

'Tom?'

'Yeah?'

'Can't you stop that scything just a minute and talk to me?' said Rosie plaintively. She had spent a pleasurable ten minutes standing against an apple tree watching the golden ripple of shoulder muscles and the rise and fall of his abdomen as he gracefully swept away the swathes of grass, naked to the waist. Had *she* the benefit of a classical education, the name of Adonis might have risen to her lips, but Rosie was rather more earthbound, by nature, anyway.

'Tom, can't you stop scything a minute and come and talk to me?' she asked again.

'Er, yes, only I'se got to get it done before supper.'

'Oh you work too hard, you do.'

'It's a good job one of us do.'

'Ha. You want me to go back to the kitchen, do you?'

'No, Rosie. I didn't mean that. 'Course I didn't.'

He smiled down at her full, pouting lips and the long dark lashes above her imperious blue eyes. He couldn't help his own falling to the firm white mounds that bulged slightly above the tight band round the low-cut neck of her summer dress, but he blushed for this.

'Tell me about your sister.'

'Which one?'

'Sarah, of course.'

'There ain't much to tell,' said Tom shortly.

'She's got that "Lacelle Salon" in Aspley, hasn't she?'

'Yeah.'

'Don't you get on with her?'

'Er, yes. Our mother says we was very close when we was children.'

'Why won't you talk about her now?'

Tom blushed and shrugged.

'Have you quarrelled?'

'Yes, a bit.' Rosie looked interested.

'What about?'

'Oh don't keep on, Rosie. She's different to me, that's all.'

'Can I meet her?'

'I don't think you'd get on well. She's sort of . . . clever and . . . quick, like.' Rosie looked puzzled.

'They say her shop is lovely. I should like to meet her, Tom.'

Tom's only answer was to begin sharpening his scythe and so Rosie went back to her work.

Rosie carried on badgering Tom about visiting Sarah and the shop. Tom could not deny that spending a holiday afternoon with Rosie would suit him, so when Farmer Tennant declared a day off for the Cherry Fair in Woburn and offered to drive his family and farm hands over in the big waggon, Rosie suggested that they ask her parents' permission to walk home from Woburn, making a detour to visit Aspley. Rosie's mother was disapproving but by early afternoon she was in a relaxed holiday spirit, helped by her husband treating her to dinner in the George – quite the finest of inns on the Hockcliffe-Newport Turnpike.

'Well, don't be all night about it,' she said.

Farmer Tennant beamed good-naturedly. 'I trust you to look after me daughter proper, Ruddock, and no bad behaviour, Rosie,' he called after them.

'Fancy saying that to your own daughter, Bob,' reprimanded Nell Tennant as they stood side by side watching the young couple walk, well apart, down the Newport road.

'That wench would lead Tom Ruddock on as much as her mother did me,' teased Tennant.

'And I'm sure that weren't much,' snapped Nell primly.

'No; I shouldn't mind a bit more now,' he said slipping his arm round her waist.

'Oh! Robert Tennant! At your age, too.' Nell softened suddenly and they strolled back to the Fair feeling more tender towards each other than they had for years.

Tom's and Rosie's paths converged steadily until they reached the lane to Mount Pleasant when Rosie stumbled against Tom and he put his arm out to steady her, and kept it there in case she stumbled again. They stopped in the shade of a sycamore tree on the crest of the hill. Not a word passed between them but somehow they found themselves in each other's arms, and kissing seemed the only appropriate means of communication. They climbed over a gate and meandered quietly among the fields, their arms round each other's waists, enjoying the deepest tranquillity of mind they had ever experienced. They didn't care at all where Aspley had hidden itself, so long as they didn't find it too soon.

When they eventually did reach the Square, they found Martha Lyle shutting up the salon. She told them that Sarah was in London and let them in to have a quick look round.

'Lunnon!' exclaimed Rosie fervently. She was full of admiration for the beautiful wares and the elegant decoration and she left even more determined to meet Sarah.

Tom received her raptures coolly and was grumpy as far as Husborne Crawley where they had a quarrel and made it up exquisitely in the fields on their way to Ridgemont.

After this outing together, Tom regarded their relationship much more seriously. Rosie was always in his thoughts and his ineligibility nagged him relentlessly. He even began to lose his appetite, which the Tennants noticed first and Eliza as soon as he began to lose weight, which he did rapidly because of his age and the heavy demands of his work. If he had been more articulate he could have reassured his mother by telling her the reason, but all he did was to come round to the idea that perhaps Sarah could help him decide what to do, if he could bring himself to visit her.

CHAPTER 39

Sarah is Introduced to Some New Business Speculations

Sarah's life was becoming more complicated by the hour but, by and large, she found this exhilarating and her appetite remained unthreatened. One of her first bits of business on reaching London was to order some visiting cards from a printer near St Paul's Churchyard.

> Miss Sarah Lacelle
> Aspley Guise
> Bedfordshire

they were to proclaim, in Gothic lettering framed on a cream-laid card embossed with gold.

She collected them on Wednesday morning and decided to try them out by 'visiting' Sir Walter Beddoes, which she did by Hackney carriage. On her arrival in Manchester Square, she neatly wrote on the card 'Formerly Sarah Ruddock, at present resident at 104 Aldersgate', gave it to the carriage driver to deliver and then had him drive her back to Piccadilly to gather up her orders. When she returned to Aldersgate just before four o'clock, she found a bunch of red roses with Sir Walter's card waiting for her. On the card was written 'Please come to Vauxhall tonight if you are able. I shall call at half past eight, hoping you can oblige.'

'Excellent,' she murmured and went to seek a vase and a maid to iron and goffer her evening dress. As she rested on her bed, she thought sadly about Nancy. 'Ah, well, the last thing she would have wished is that I should forgo an amusing evening on her behalf. I must enjoy it for her, too.'

Sir Walter arrived on time, impeccably mannered and very attentive. When dusk fell, they were waltzing in a fairyland of coloured oil lamps which illuminated the drooping tree branches, heavy with summer foliage now. The sultry breeze wafted an ever-changing medley of fragrance to them: night-scented stocks, roses and musky perfume. It contrasted so much with the multifarious stench of the London streets which Sarah had distastefully endured all week. She bantered on light-heartedly to Walter whose eyes hardly left hers. He seemed disinclined to talk, and as he handed her down the steps from the dancing platform she was wondering whether the evening was going to be as amusing as she had hoped.

'Just fancy meeting the lovely Miss Lacelle here!' declaimed a cultured male voice nearby.

Sarah spun round to find Francis Vaughan sitting at a small table with another man of about his age and a strangely dressed young woman.

'Miss Lacelle, allow me to introduce Miss Nina Poginski, the renowned dancer, and Dr Matthew Crisp, the renowned . . . no I shall not tell you. He must prove himself,' laughed Vaughan, probably a little drunk, thought Sarah.

'Charmed, I'm sure,' curtsied Sarah, sweetly. 'This is

239

my good friend, Sir Walter Beddoes; Mr Francis Vaughan.'

'May we have the pleasure of joining you?' inquired Beddoes.

'But of course. We shall be delighted.' And so they spent a very gay evening drinking, dancing and laughing. Sarah was very animated and so confident it was hard to believe that barely three months had passed since her first visit to Vauxhall. The three men vied with each other to keep her amused and seemed hardly to notice poor Nina, who fortunately was not particularly bothered since her mastery of English did not allow her to join in the conversation much.

Long after midnight they sauntered to where the carriages were waiting and when he found the others had come by Hackney, Sir Walter kindly undertook to drive them home. Sarah was gratified by the ripple of admiration that greeted his smart newly-lacquered chaise with its doors embellished by a family crest.

Dr Crisp was the friend whom Vaughan was taking back to stay in Aspley and they called to collect Sarah and her large parcels the following morning.

Sarah wasn't sure that she liked Matthew Crisp. He was of medium height and build, about thirty-five, with dark hair receding at the temples, spectacles and clean-shaven except for a small neat moustache. He seemed a reserved, almost secretive man, which confirmed Sarah's suspicion of the night before that he and Fran were somewhat drunk. When he did speak to her his tone was patronizing, as if he considered talking to a woman rather a waste of his intellect and time. Sarah gathered that they had been friends ever since they were at a school called Eton College. Their personalities seemed in total contrast.

'So how are your youthful charges progressing, Fran?'

'Bad as ever. It always seems to be the brightest

youths who are the most trouble. It's the way of the world, I suppose.'

'Yes. I must give you some good advice sometime. I have recently been reading a very interesting treatise in German by Dr Moll.'

'Really. What is his interest?'

'A study of *Libido sexualis*!' Crisp lowered his voice so as not to offend Sarah, who was gazing demurely out of the window and not missing a word.

'Well, do try, old chap, but I suspect I can tell you quite a lot about that, within the confines of my area of experience, of course.'

Crisp smiled humourlessly. 'Hot baths must be severely restricted. Too stimulating, he says.'

'Well, how interesting. That seems to be something my scoundrels have failed to discover. They have a perfect antipathy to water, hot or cold.'

'And your other business interests. How are they progressing?'

'I have managed to obtain a bit more land for tree-planting. Unfortunately, it's at a premium and I have serious Ducal competition. The wily fellow keeps fencing in a bit more and the Vestry seem loath to point out that it is common land as firmly as they would to me.'

'Oh – common land! That is normally considered fair game for enclosing, surely?'

'It's more difficult here because we have squatters building their wretched hovels all over it.'

'Evict them!'

'There's been talk of it but some are paying quit rents and some may be able to get freehold possession. You can't throw them out.'

'How is that?'

'Well, it's partly a question of possession being nine-tenths of the law; a sort of *loi-agraire*. If some elderly pauper has lived there long enough he can claim a freehold title by getting a friend to sign an affidavit that he has been living there for as long as he can remember – and their memories are appallingly short on these occasions – and then, when he is secure, he will perjure himself shamelessly by swearing that all his neighbours have been living there as long as he has; then they all get a freehold title. There is a regular metropolis growing up on the Heath since the new Poor Law Act. Before that, the Select Vestry was responsible for allocating the poor relief to paupers without property but now, when it means living in the workhouse to get relief, they all go and squat on the Common.'

'How interesting! Tell me, Fran, if they have rights to the land, then they can sell it, eh?'

'Yes, I suppose so.'

'And if you or I buy it off them legitimately, then it's no longer common land.'

'No. It can't be, can it?'

'All that is needed then is the gleam of some new golden sovereigns.'

'Ah! You don't know our villagers. They may seem stupid enough most of the time, but if you try buying something off them then their mild moist eyes suddenly begin to glitter and their minds become needle sharp, as do their tongues and their arithmetic.'

'I defy even you to strike a good bargain, Mat.'

'Is what he says really true, Miss Lacelle?' appealed Crisp.

Sarah looked confused. She had been listening to this dialogue with a variety of emotions chasing each other through her mind. They began with indignation and ended with anger. She had not yet analysed why she felt so upset, when the sentiments that Vaughan expressed were by no means new to her.

'Ah, forgive me, Miss Lacelle. You have not been following the gist of our conversation. It must be infinitely tedious for you to have us discussing business concerns. Come Fran, we must be as amusing as we were last night.'

'That will be nigh impossible, Mat, because I am totally sober this morning. Anyway, I believe you do Miss Lacelle an injustice. She is quite a shrewd businesswoman.'

'Really?' Crisp raised his supercilious brows as if he considered this very unlikely unless his friend was referring to the most common woman's profession.

'What business venture do you aspire to, Miss Lacelle?'

'I run a milliner's shop for a businessman in Leighton Buzzard,' she said coolly.

'Oh yes; and is he doing well?'

Sarah opened her mouth to retort but caught her tongue between her teeth and held it in check.

'Yes, he is doing quite well,' she said acidly.

Francis Vaughan looked at her narrowly. He detected her anger but was not sure of its origin. He decided she must have been upset by Crisp's tactlessness.

Sarah's return to the salon was like a conquering hero's with spoils of war. Temperance and Ellie begged her to open all the parcels so they could see the new stuffs that they would be sewing. She had brought a small present for each of them. A silk scarf for Ellie to go with her new gingham dress, and some fancy stockings for Temperance. She had paid quite a lot of money for a fine wool shawl for Martha Lyle, in gratitude for much more than looking after the salon for three days. Martha seemed touched.

'You shouldn't have spent your money on me, Sarah! You should have bought some more stuff.'

'No, Mrs Lyle. I wanted you to know I hadn't forgotten who made it possible for me to be where I am.'

'Go on with you! All I did was know when I seed some native talent and make sure it weren't wasted.'

'I am grateful, anyway,' said Sarah briskly.

'Tom and his girl, Rosie, called to see you on Tuesday. They'd been to Woburn Cherry Fair.'

'Really! Oh dear. I am sorry to have missed Tom.'

'They'll call again. I told them when you'd be back.'

'What is Rosie like?'

'She seemed to know her own mind, I'd say, but that's what Tom needs, ain't it?'

'Is she pretty?'

'Oh yes. May not wear well. Will go to fat I'd say.'

Sarah laughed. 'You sound as if you were passing judgement on a horse, Mrs Lyle.'

'I sometimes think that's all we are. Beasts of burden to please men.'

'That's not the way I see myself – nor you.'

Tom called in late on his way home one evening the following week. Sarah was relieved he had missed Dafydd Griffiths, who had just gone.

'Tom! How nice. Why, you've got thinner! Are you well?'

'Yeah,' said Tom, scowling.

'Come upstairs and see where I live. I was sorry to miss meeting Rosie Tennant. You will bring her over again, won't you?'

'Yeah. S'pose so.'

'Sit down and tell me what you've been doing and then I'll make us hot chocolate.'

'There ain't that much to tell.'

'You and Rosie went to the Cherry Fair at Woburn?' prompted Sarah.

'Yeah. Well, everyone went. Tennant drove everyone over in the big waggon.'

Tom closely examined a snag on the thigh of his breeches and Sarah resolved not to say another word until he told her why he was there. She had already decided, a little sadly, that it was not merely a social call. The longer the silence continued, the more difficult it became to break it. Eventually, Tom said: 'Why ain't you saying nothing, Sarah?'

'Because I was waiting for you to tell me what *you* had come to say, you goose.' Tom smiled sheepishly.

'It's about Rosie and me.'

'Mmm?' said Sarah encouragingly.

'What can I do, Sare?'

'I'm still not sure what the problem is.'

'Well, her mother and father wouldn't bear the thought of me wedding her, would they?'

'Ah! Have you asked them?'

'No. 'Course not.'

'Is it . . . er . . . I mean, you don't want to marry her quickly, do you?'

'Not particular . . . No! 'Course not!' he said vehemently, as he realized the implication of Sarah's question.

'Oh, well, there's no problem then. Given a bit of time they and loads of other parents will be *begging* you to marry their daughters.'

'Me? Why?'

'As soon as you have your own business and are making a lot of money.'

'Don't mock, Sarah.'

'I'm not. Stay on at Tennant's until next spring. Tell him at Christmas that you'd like to leave. Perhaps wait until after spring sowing and say you'll do a bit of jobbing for him at hay-time if he needs you – just so he doesn't feel you've let him down. Then, throw up banks round the larch spinney on the edge of Tidbury Hill, where Joe Clarke said there's bound to be good fuller's earth, you know, and start digging.'

'Oh easy! Make me fortune in a couple of weeks, shall I?' scoffed Tom. Sarah ignored him.

'Perhaps you'd better start putting that bank up now.

Someone else is going to if you don't.' Sarah well knew who might.

'I ain't got no spade.'

'Father won't be needing his in the evenings, unless he helps you, of course. Couldn't you borrow a spade and barrow off Tennant? You may as well tell him what you're up to as long as it doesn't get back to the Select Vestry. Tidbury will be in Wavendon Heath.'

'No. It's just in Aspley Heath. The boundary goes up the lane from our cottage.'

'Be careful not to let it get about what you are doing, Tom,' warned Sarah. 'Not till you've got a bit of money for fencing and bribing.'

Tom looked alarmed.

'Don't worry, Tom. We'll manage. Leave that to me. I'll get a shovel and barrow by the spring.'

'I didn't come here asking favours,' he said sternly, rising from his chair.

'No, I know you didn't. You came to ask my advice and I've given it you and I am not usually wrong, Tom, am I? Answer me, Tom! *Am* I usually wrong?'

Sarah had taken the points of his waistcoat in her fists, which were as high as she could conveniently reach, and was pummelling his stomach with her knuckles.

'Leave off, Sarah. You're tickling,' he chuckled.

'Well?' She gave him another knuckling.

'No, you are not wrong usually. You are nearly always right. Leave off, will you, Sarah, do!'

CHAPTER 40

A Misunderstanding, Plans and Proposals

Dafydd Griffiths never confronted Sarah with his failure to find her father and his visits to the salon were becoming almost daily events. He usually looked in for a chat quite early in the evening. He seemed rather withdrawn the next night.

'Is there anything wrong, Mr Griffiths? You seem rather low-spirited.'

'No – nothing wrong,' he said abruptly.

Sarah sighed. She felt loath to repeat the struggle she had had with Tom yesterday, particularly when Dafydd usually displayed a perfectly easy loquacity.

'I have had several visitors this week,' she volunteered cheerfully.

'Yes indeed. I noticed.'

'Oh, which one did you notice?'

'The very well-favoured fair giant who visited you after I left yesterday.' Sarah took one look at the tortured expression on his face and burst out laughing.

'It is spying on me that you've been!' she teased in a fair rendering of a Welsh accent.

Dafydd continued to look wretched and hung his head. Sarah was compelled to pat his shoulder consolingly, which made him leap to his feet.

'Forgive me, Miss Lacelle. Please do forgive me. It is absolutely no business of mine. I have behaved disgracefully and am ashamed. Perhaps one day you may understand something of the feeling which goaded me, but I hope not. Jealousy is bitter indeed.' He snatched up his hat and began to hurry to the door, but Sarah got there before him.

'Mr Griffiths, do calm yourself. It was disgraceful of

247

me, too, laughing at you, but when you understand the joke, I am sure you will also laugh. However, before I share it with you, there is just one thing I want to say . . . Oh, please don't look so wretched!'

He just shook his head miserably.

'You have been a good friend to me. I look foward to you calling in for a chat. I do really and I want you to come, but please don't feel you *own* me. No-one can ever do *that*, Mr Griffiths. Now, guess who that well-favoured fair giant was? I am very proud of him. It isn't every girl who has such a handsome brother.'

'Brother!'

'Yes, that is Tom whom you have heard me talk about.'

'But he is not in the least like you.'

'No, I am painfully aware of that. When I was a little girl, the women used to say to my mother, as if I was deaf: "What a pity poor little Sare isn't like her brother. Wouldn't it be nice if she had blue eyes and rosy cheeks and curly fair hair," and I used to be sure my mother thought so too. But she always used to say: "Everyone's different; what suits some don't suit others, and look at her lovely big eyes."'

'Oh, she was right. I wouldn't have one hair of your head changed. It's so lovely that you are,' laughed Griffiths, transformed in a twinkling. Sarah was quite amazed and attributed it to a particularly effervescent Celtic nature which was new to her.

The next evening, a knock on her door brought Francis Vaughan with his friend Dr Crisp.

Sarah invited them in rather formally and did not intend to take them upstairs, but she saw Vaughan glance uneasily at the windows, so she had to lead them up.

'Perhaps you would be so kind as to bring that chair up, please, Mr Vaughan. I am not furnished for visitors, I fear.' She hoped such a hint might limit their stay but

248

Crisp was too absorbed in his own importance and Vaughan preferred not to notice.

'What a very elegant sitting-room you have here, Miss Lacelle,' said Crisp. 'Patronizing as usual,' thought Sarah.

'Are you enjoying your holiday, Dr Crisp?'

'Why yes. I am quite impressed. The air is so relaxing, don't you find? It strikes me as an exceptionally healthy place.'

'Yes, we are very healthy, are we not, Sarah,' quipped Vaughan.

'But seriously, Fran. I think the place has possibilities – business possibilities, I mean.'

'Bottled air, three shillings and sixpence a suck?' suggested Vaughan. Sarah smiled and Crisp ignored him.

'My business is to make sick people think that they feel better and healthy people think that they feel sick, and I believe I could persuade both sorts to come here rather than have the expense of a holiday in a continental spa town. Imagine: "The sandy pine-clad hills of Aspley with their petrifying mineral waters offer the convalescent or weak-chested an exceptionally mild, relaxing climate combined with the invigorating effect of gentle exercise in balmy air and scenery of exceptional beauty."'

'Petri . . . what did you say?' inquired Sarah.

'Petrifying, turning to stone, my dear Miss Lacelle. Have you not seen the famous ladder?'

'Oh that; surely you haven't actually seen it?'

'Well, no, but I have it on excellent authority that when it was dug up it exactly resembled stone! Haven't you seen it, Fran?'

'No, not in the . . . er . . . stone, so to speak. Anyway what is so healthy about that? Do you propose to defy the ravages of time by prematurely burying your patients and petrifying them?'

'You may well scoff, Fran, but when I have published my letter in the *Lancet*, that is a new medical journal, and people come flocking to take up residence in your quaint, secluded village, you may wonder whether you could profitably sell them some land to build a house on.'

'Ah, that is why you were so interested in the property rights of our squatters, was it?'

'I have only just formulated this plan over the last two minutes but – yes – yes! There you are, it is a ready-made situation and he who benefits is he who puts one and one together and makes four hundred and two, eh?'

Fran laughed heartily.

'Sarah, I am sure you will have no difficulty in believing this now, but *this* is the man, who when at an age of so-called innocence, sold sealed copies of a map showing "guaranteed easy to accomplish and well-concealed short-cut for the forthcoming cross-country challenge cup race" to his fellow runners for one penny each and made an outrageous profit.'

'Until, Miss Lacelle, an ignoble boy whom he had been pleased to call his friend, bought one, copied it and began to sell it for three farthings!' concluded Dr Crisp.

Sarah had to join in the uproarious laughter in spite of her feelings. Still chuckling, Vaughan said:

'Well, Mat, if you like Aspley so well, why don't you buy yourself a house here, eh? You could travel down for a week or two whenever your practice could spare you. The hunt is an excellent one and Sarah and I could keep you amused in the summer.'

Dr Crisp didn't answer immediately. He seemed to be turning over the idea and considering it from various points of view. Eventually he said:

'Who would look after it in my absence?'

'It should not be too difficult to find a housekeeper.'

Vaughan's face suddenly lit up as he turned to look at Sarah.

'Miss Sarah Lacelle! Why not? You haven't enough room here have you, Sarah? You need the two rooms for your business. I can't think how you manage to live in such a confined space.'

Sarah returned his gaze gravely as one thought succeeded another. Her first was that she had spent most of her life sharing a room half this size with five other people. Her second was that she did need more room for the business. Her third was that if she was to manage Crisp's house entirely at his expense, then maybe she should consider the deal. The last thought ran along the lines that if she was to live in luxury without paying any money what was she expected to pay with. She transferred her gaze to Crisp and sighed.

Vaughan's and Crisp's thoughts ran along similar lines but rather in the reverse order to Sarah's. Vaughan, for instance, considered how much more convenient it would be for him to visit Sarah if she had an establishment which offered more seclusion. He always felt furtive as he waited for her to answer his knock, fearing that the village tongues would start to wag, with dire consequences for his position.

Crisp coolly calculated the relative cost of his long-standing ambition to own a comfortable, indeed, perhaps an elegant establishment complete with its mistress of obvious personal charm. Should it be situated in the country or in London? He considered the possible cost in financial terms and in erosion of respectability and came to favour the country on both counts. He also considered the advantages of a base to develop the new business venture which he had just outlined to his friends.

'Well, yes. It is a possibility that has certain attractions. We must talk it over. Have you anywhere in mind? Is there a well-appointed villa for sale?' he asked.

Sarah and Vaughan exchanged glances again.

'Is there not one up Woburn Lane?' asked Vaughan.

'Yes, I believe Mr and Mrs Brown's old house is available.'

'That would suit well. It has the privacy of a large garden,' said Vaughan.

'Well, you must take me to see it,' said Crisp.

CHAPTER 41

Sarah Takes Mr Nursall in Hand and Visits the Villa

At the first possible opportunity Sarah shut the shop early and hurried up to the Heath. Only her mother and William were in, and they greeted her in delight.

'Oh, Sarah. How well you look. We've heard such stories about your fine shop.'

'You haven't come down to see it, Mama,' said Sarah reproachfully.

'Well, no, but you know how it is, dear. I'se that busy. There's all the washing and mending and Willy's such a little scamp.' She hid her embarrassment by playfully chasing him around the room, to spank him, much to his merriment.

'Mother, there's lots of cottages up here now. How many of them pay quit rent?'

'Quit rent? I don't rightly know. I believe the Keens and Perrys do. They've been here longer than most. Harry Nursall will know.'

'Does he pay?'

'Oh no, I don't think so.'

'He and Mary have been here as long as anybody, haven't they?'

'Yes, but they wouldn't like to be thought of as being sort of regular, you know. Harry is particular about being his own master. He wouldn't like to think he were here because the Vestry allowed it.'

Sarah chuckled. She admired the spirited independence of Harry and Mary Nursall.

'I think I shall pop over and see how they are, Mama.'

'Yes, you do that, dear.'

'I shall be back quite soon.'

They were both in and greeted her warmly. She didn't mention the shop or invite them down because she knew they wouldn't come, but she chattered on inconsequentially for a while and then asked:

'Mr Nursall, do you know how many folks up here pay quit rent?'

'Quit rent!' he laughed. 'Only the slack-twisted uns.'

'Did you know that you could sell the land as yours if you've not been paying rent?'

'I can't see how that would benefit us, young lady.' Harry spoke a little stiffly.

'Well, if someone was determined to get the land anyway, it would mean you had something in your pocket instead of being evicted for nothing.'

'But we ain't been evicted yet, have we?'

'No, Mr Nursall, but I have been listening to people talking and I fancy it may change soon.'

'Aye. I've been afearing as much. There's too many come up. Must be nearly half the working men in the parish lives up here now.'

'Oh, Harry, don't say that,' wailed Mary.

'What people have you been alistening to, Sarah?'

She looked at him keenly for a moment and decided he and Mary were best taken into her confidence.

'Let it go no further than these four walls.' She glanced around and smiled. 'Well, let it go no further than the side of this coach, that chicken shed and the inside of this waggon.'

'Stop your teasing, girl, and get on with it,' said Harry.

'Mr Vaughan, the headmaster of the Academy and a friend of his called Dr Crisp from London would like to own land up here. They plan to sell it again for a lot of money for people to build houses on, I think. In fact, they are planning to attract a lot of gentry here because it's so healthy. Now do you see what will happen?'

Mary looked anxious and Harry sighed heavily.

'I know you don't like the idea of getting deeds for something you think is yours by rights, but I think you should set an example. You've been here long enough to do it without trouble, then you can help the others to get their rights. What do you have to do?'

'Get one of them affidavits sworn by someone else, saying that they can remember you living here for years and years or that it were given to you by a relative what they can remember living here, and a lot of silly nonsense it is,' growled Harry.

'Yes, I know, Mr Nursall, but you don't want to see them all thrown off and men that have plenty of money already make a lot more out of it?'

Harry shook his head disconsolately.

'Well, I wanted to warn you. It means doing it soon, before the Vestry realizes what you're up to. I for one would like to get in the way of anything that benefits them.'

'And me, girl. We'll think it over, shall us, Mary?'

The following morning, a note arrived for Sarah from Francis Vaughan asking her to meet Crisp and himself at the Browns' villa in Woburn Lane at eleven o'clock. She slipped off, leaving Temperance behind the counter, and found the two men already there. Vaughan had decided it would be imprudent to call for her at the salon.

They were shown round the empty house by a caretaker who was none other than sharp Mrs Jones, the pew opener. Sarah wasted no smiles on her on this occasion, merely reflecting that in spite of Vaughan's prudence, their activities would be part of the gossips' dinner-time menu. As far as the house was concerned, however, Sarah was soon sharing Vaughan's and Crisp's enthusiasm. It was ideal for the use they had in mind. On the ground floor was a large reception hall, a well-proportioned drawing-room with large windows over-looking the south garden and an adequate dining-room next door to the kitchen, as well as a small breakfast-room on the east side. On the first floor there was a sitting-room, bedroom and dressing-room for Sarah, together with two other bedrooms, and in the attic a spare bedroom and accommodation for three servants. Sarah became more and more animated as she planned the furnishings.

'Oh, what beautiful windows!' she exclaimed in the drawing-room. 'Can't you just imagine draped pink velvet curtains to echo the rosebuds in this charming wallpaper; and I think the rug should be moss green. Do you think you shall afford a rug, Dr Crisp?'

'Well, the main room surely deserves a rug. Yes, I think you shall have your moss green rug, Miss Lacelle.'

'If you could take me to London, I know the very place where the curtain and chair material may be purchased most favourably and we can make them up in the shop.'

'This will cost you a pretty penny, Mat! I think I shall have to make a donation and in return I shall expect to relax here sometimes when you are away, my friend.'

'That sounds fair. You know, only last night he was deploring how he was obliged to live with his work, Miss Lacelle! It is difficult to relax when one is at the beck and call of masters and pupils.'

'It is indeed,' said Vaughan feelingly.

'Yes, it must be a great strain,' agreed Sarah, hoping the touch of irony in her voice wasn't noticed. The two men had clearly been planning their ménage, cosily centred upon her, as a shared asset. Well, so long as her benefits were well-defined and provided for, she would not complain. She was now confident that she could take care of herself.

They admired the large garden which had been neglected for a season.

'I could find a good gardener for you, Dr Crisp,' volunteered Sarah. Her first thought was Tom, but she quickly realized that he would not relish her being in such a compromising position, nor would her father. Harry Nursall, perhaps?

They finally inspected the stables and carriage-house where there was a pony trap.

'I suppose this is to be sold with the house?' queried Crisp.

'Yes. Exactly suited to Sarah's requirements, I should think. You could use it for delivering clothes and to carry out fittings in ladies' homes, couldn't you, Sarah?'

'Well, yes! That would be very good. I could send up to London for stuff and collect it from the Woburn coaching inns, too.'

'She needs a neat little pony for this, Mat.'

'A sturdy strong one would be safest, perhaps,' said Sarah, estimating the number of sacks of fuller's earth that might be fitted into the trap.

'You two are being exceedingly generous with my purse,' complained Crisp.

'I shall provide the pony myself, Mat,' said Vaughan.

'To begin with, I think we should go to visit Mr Brown's attorney to see whether I can afford the place.'

'Yes. The down-to-earth businessman as ever, Mat,' said Vaughan, clapping him on the shoulder jovially.

CHAPTER 42

Harvest Time

It was now harvest time and all the men were afield early. The women and children followed a little later when their homes had been set in order and the dinner packs tied up in their check or spotted cloths. Some of the women followed the reapers to bind up the sheaves and set them in shocks to dry but most took their children to glean, or 'leaze' as they called it, in the fields which had been reaped.

This particular season the weather had held fair and the empty villages brooded peacefully in the late August sunshine like abandoned ships in a billowing sea of gold and green. The apple harvest promised to be prodigiously good and the trees in the cottage gardens and small orchards were bowed down with fruit. The worcesters were beginning to 'blush up', the cox's orange pippins grew round and brown and the mammoth bramley seedlings swelled by the day. The bees hummed busily on Michaelmas daisies. Pot marigolds shone like miniature gold and yellow suns exhaling their special pungent odour which blended with the fragrance of apples and the warm smell of dusty roads, and took some undertones from the 'muck hills', to compose the perfume that is peculiar to sunny summer villages.

Martha Lyle had grown a marrow of such stupendous size that its fame was spreading beyond Aspley. Those who were not labouring to bring the harvest home until dusk, sauntered over from New Town and Husborne Crawley of an evening, to lean over her gate and behold it in its moony yellow splendour, handsomely ribbed with green. Even Sarah made a short pilgrimage one evening, although giant marrows normally failed to interest her in any way.

'Do you know, Sarah,' confided Martha, 'I've got fond of that vegetable! I almost feel as if it was me child. I even find myself *talking* to it.'

Sarah giggled. It struck her as a really comical confession coming from the 'no nonsense' Martha.

'Have you been out leazing, Mrs Lyle?'

'Oh yes, most days. I started off at Green's sixty acre but he's such a mean ol' man. He wouldn't let us on until they'd finished stooking and then the ol' crows had taken most. I've bin working Farmer Miller's fields since. I was thinking of you picking up stones on a cold wet November day, going up and down like me, and what a sorry sight you looked then.'

'Yes, I didn't enjoy it, but needs must.'

'Aye. You was only sorry *looking*, for the rest you was as tough as a piece of horse hide.'

'I suppose I still am, but I've just wondered lately.'

'Why's that?' asked Martha in surprise.

'I don't rightly know. A sort of loneliness as if I want someone with me.'

'I hope it ain't anyone in particular?' said Martha fixing her eyes on Sarah's.

Sarah didn't reply immediately, which was unusual.

'No. No-one I could possibly consider at any rate. Well, I must get back. I've two dresses to draw designs for by tomorrow.'

Martha watched her go with some misgivings.

It was Tom's first harvest as a farm hand and he was enjoying it. He had been doing a bit of scything all season so there were no stiff muscles down his back and his power and stamina soon had him promoted, beyond his years, to be the 'King Reaper' who worked just ahead of the other men, setting the pace and the rhythm. His wide-brimmed straw hat was essential protection against the sun, but it was decked out with a garland of bindweed and poppies to designate his royal status and there were few men and women who didn't pause to smile at his easy grace and the breadth of his scythe sweep which defied any challenge. Some of the young women paused quite a long time but Tom seemed supremely indifferent to anything except the job in hand, which only enhanced his regal dignity.

It was a busy time for Rosie and her mother as well, because the men could not return to the farm for their breakfast and dinner and provisions had to be taken to them. Harvesting was the heaviest work of the year and a good farmer like Tennant knew it didn't pay to work hungry men, so towards half past eleven the reapers would begin to scan the edge of the field by the cart track at each stroke of their scythes, impatient for a sight of Rosie and Nell Tennant in the pony cart. Eventually, when they had done at least one field width more than they had hoped, the cart would rock into sight, its springs compressed by the gargantuan amount of food and barrels of beer and cold tea slung around its sides.

'Right you are, Tom lad! May we break?'

'Let's just reach the turn,' smiled Tom, and his word was their command.

While the men produced their pots and filled them at the barrels, Rosie and her mother spread a cloth on the stubble and laid out the hunks of fresh-baked bread with thick slices of streaky boiled bacon draped over them and mustard pickle or pickled onions and walnuts. The jobbing men who didn't live on the farm brought their own, or a member of their family did, and it was usually a much more meagre allowance, but Rosie saw to it that the left-overs found their way to the needier. However urgent the work the dinner hour was sacred and most of the older reapers were soon lying down in the shade of the hedge for their forty winks while the youngsters sought other gentle diversions. Tom, for instance, sat patiently by the pony trap until the cloth and barrels had been tidied up and stowed.

'I've brought you summat, Tom,' whispered Rosie. 'Let's go up the lane and I'll give it to you.'

They sauntered away, well apart, contriving to reach the lane together as a matter of coincidence and Rosie gave Tom a slice of plum cake which had been kept sealed up since Christmas.

'I must get more flowers for yer hat, Tom. Them ones is all withered with the sun.'

'Yeah. It's that hot!'

'Bend down for me to get them off.'

'Shall I take it off?'

'No, I'll manage if you sit down here.'

'Shall you sit down here too, Rosie? Them flowers don't matter yet.'

It seemed sensible to leave picking the new flowers until the very end of the dinner hour else they would be limp before the Reaper King resumed his place. Rosie and Tom's conversation was not sufficiently instructive to report, so we shall fill the hour by wandering along that sunny August lane. It had been created a thousand years or so ago to serve the needs of the farming people and ever since then man and nature had worked together to keep the place not only convenient for travelling between the fields but a home for a myriad of plants and animals and a deeply satisfying sight for the occasional human eye that was susceptible to such things. The wheat fields were down on the plain where the earth was well limed and held the moisture, so the lanes and hedgerows were abundantly supplied with a great variety of plants. There were not so many flowers in the shady parts beneath the crab apples, holly and field maple but, where the hedges had been laid, the ditches were filled with wild mint and hairy willow herb while the drier banks supported an exuberance of scabious, tufted vetch and hard knobby knapweeds, large and small, which were aflutter with butterflies – small tortoise-shells, cabbage whites, peacocks and painted ladies. There were isolated clumps of St John's wort and wild succory and, in the short grass on either side of the cart tracks, bloomed a profusion of smaller flowers – white and purple clover, may weed, silver weed and the delightful shell pink flutes of bindweed. Where a bit of ditching had been done the previous winter, the piles of tossed earth were vibrant with poppies, the delicate little orange four-petalled ones and the scarlet and blood-red flounces of the field poppies.

As it turned out, it was fortunate for Rosie and Tom that there was such a profusion of flowers to pick.

'Oh, Rosie! We've forgotten the time. Quick! Come on! They'll be waiting for me.'

'I ain't done your flowers.'

'Us'll have to pick some quick, as we go.'

CHAPTER 43

Wedding Plans, Short and Long

The autumn passed in a whirl of exciting activity for Sarah. Her business expanded so much that she took on two more girls and had to build another lean-to shed in the yard to accommodate the stock of cloth which she was wisely increasing in advance of the orders. Frank Cox called in regularly to see how the shop was going. Since he did not mention his loneliness at Leighton, she guessed that her domestic vacancy had been filled. She was concerned to find his attitude towards her hardening, though. She had nearly managed to pay back his loan, but as Cox saw the business beginning to flourish he steadily increased her rent.

'Why should you expect even more rent, Frank, when

I don't bother you with the business at all?' asked Sarah indignantly.

'Why? Because I have to get a return on my capital. Let me remind you that you are only able to behave as if you are your own master because of my capital.'

'I know, but I have no chance of ever running my own business while I am paying so much of the profit to you.'

'I have to consider *my* expenses, too, Sarah. I am getting married and I have a house to buy. I might have to sell this shop if I can't raise enough money!'

He drew a hand-written card from his waistcoat pocket and laid it on the counter proudly.

Mr and Mrs George Lands of Heath and Reach are pleased to announce the engagement of their daughter Josephine Maria to Mr Frank Cox of Leighton Buzzard . . .

'Oh, how wonderful! I do congratulate you. I remember the young lady. She used to come in to buy bonnets with her large Mama who wore the peppermint green and bright pink tulle dress all summer!'

Frank Cox turned up his eyes in exasperated admiration.

'What a memory you have, Sarah. You will remember the young lady's dress too, then?'

'No. Do you know, I can barely remember any detail of the young lady. She was overshadowed by her mother in every way. Quite a formidable woman!'

'Yes,' sighed Frank. A fleeting wave of nostalgia overwhelmed him as he recollected the stressful excitement of life with Sarah. The women he encountered never seemed to strike a happy medium of character.

'She is rather a quiet young lady, Josephine, but very eager to please.'

'How fortunate for you. I hope you find her mother equally satisfactory,' said Sarah mischievously. 'I am sure you will have a very tranquil marriage. I believe the Lands are quite rich, as well?'

'Yes, passably,' said Frank tersely. He didn't wish to go into details of the generous marriage settlement he expected.

'And who is making the wedding gown?'

'Well, I did suggest you. I really did, but they always go to a London fashion house.'

'What a pity. I haven't been asked to make a wedding gown yet.'

'Perhaps you will make your own soon?'

Sarah looked at him sharply. 'Oh no, not yet, Frank. There are a lot of things I want to do before that.'

'You make it sound like the end of life. I thought most young ladies regarded it as the beginning.'

'Everyone to their tastes, and I suspect marriage is not to mine at the moment.'

Frank laughed. 'I only hope it proves to be to mine.'

Tom followed Sarah's advice and explained his plans to Farmer Tennant. Rosie was not at all pleased.

'Tom, we won't see each other every day. Don't you care?'

'Yeah. 'Course I care.'

'Why go away, then?'

'Because like I've said, I want to be me own master and earn enough to . . . well . . .'

'Well what?'

'Well, you know why.'

'Not really. Tell me, Tom.'

'I want to wed you.'

'Oh-ah, Tom. Mind, there's someone coming. Come right into the barn. Come on quick, Tom. Up the back on to the hay. They'll never see up there.'

'Your father sent me to lift some turnips.'

'Turnips is all you think of.'

'No it ain't, Rosie. Honest. It's nearly always you.'

263

'And when it's not me or turnips it's your sister Sarah. Was it really your idea to go and dig holes in the sand, or was it hers, eh, Tom?'

'Well, I always meant to. It was what I was doing before I come here.'

'Yes, but it was her idea, wasn't it?'

'Well, I did call and ask her what she thought about us and . . . and . . .'

'What business is it of hers? It don't matter what she thinks. It's "Sarah this" and "Sarah that".'

'It was you who kept badgerin' me to take you to see her.'

Rosie sniffed. The visit had left her with the distinct impression that Sarah wanted to keep control of Tom, and Rosie recognized a girl who was used to getting her own way when she met one. There was not room for two of them in Tom's life.

Tennant told his wife about Tom's plan.

'Mm. Well, the proof of the pudding is in the eating, Robert.'

'But he can't get by on his own. He hasn't a tool to his name. Where's he going to get spades and barrows and waggons from? I think I'll give him a day off a week while we're slack. I can easily spare him through the winter and I'll lend him a good spade and shovel and a barrow, then we'll see what he's made of.'

'You're soft. He won't need much more, will he?'

''Course he will, woman. He doesn't know how deep he's got to dig before he strikes the earth, and then he's got to bag it and cart it down to the turnpike. He won't even be able to pay a carrier to start with, but he's a hard-working fellow and as strong as a horse.'

'Well our Rosie's set her heart on him and she's used to getting her own way. She's got a soft father to thank for *that*, too.'

Robert Tennant laughed good-humouredly.

* * *

Tom's father was full of support for the enterprise as well.

'That's a good idea, son. Be your own master and dance to your own tune. That's what I've always wanted to do but I never will now.'

'You could help me, Father. Mr Tennant says he'll lend me a barrow and spade and shovel. You've got a spade. That's all we need till we strike it.'

'You'll need some'at to shore the sides up if you have to go deep.'

'Oh yeah! I hadn't thought of that. I'se going to need a lot of wood shuttering,' said Tom dejectedly.

'Would dead branches do? We could get plenty of they and the odd live one might drop off.'

'Oh no, Father! You're no use to us in gaol.'

'Mr Hall?'

'He's done so much. I don't want to ask him.'

'Our Sarah's doing very well at that shop.'

'I ain't asking her,' said Tom firmly.

'She gave me a real good sum of money for the relief fund for the families of them Chartists what are in prison. Do you know, they've had Lovett and Collins in gaol for nearly three months for organizing the great petition.' Tom turned away defensively and his father's face fell.

'I'll help you dig, Son. 'Course I will. When shall us start?' he asked earnestly.

'We'd best start banking round.'

'Where?'

'Side of Tidbury where Mr Clarke said.'

'Shall us ask him and Harry Nursall to come and puzzle out just the right spot?'

'Yeah, maybe.'

Late in the afternoon of Tom's first full day digging, he heard the thud of horses' hooves. For a split moment his heart missed a beat as he involuntarily recalled the terror of the ghostly riders, but when he straightened up there were only Graham Dudley the builder and Francis Vaughan approaching.

'Good day,' said Dudley. 'Ain't you working for Farmer Tennant over at Ridgemont?'

'Yeah,' said Tom, rather sullen in his embarrassment.

'You look busy,' commented Vaughan in a friendly tone.

'Yeah.'

'What are you banking off then?' asked Dudley.

'Just a bit of ground,' replied Tom, blushing.

'You going to start growing some vegetables, then?' inquired Dudley.

'Yeah,' said Tom, brightening.

'Soil will all get washed away and it ain't even south facing,' said Dudley aggressively.

Tom looked perplexed.

'Aye, you can't tell these youngsters,' spoke up a familiar voice from Tom's side. He spun round to find Harry Nursall had materialized from some furze bushes nearby. A look of profound relief passed over Tom's face.

'Thou tell them that here or there is the right spot and they just h'ignores you and goes their own way and learns hard. Still, I guess we all had to do it, eh?'

Harry's homespun philosophy and leisurely delivery seemed to leave the two riders less than satisfied. He shifted his pipe to the other side of his mouth, settled comfortably on the handle of Tom's shovel and began again.

'You know, I allus remember the time when I was a little 'un and me dad – he were Henry Nursall from Water End. Your father would remember him well, Mr Dudley. You know, if I be not mistaken, my father used to work for thine. Aye, it must be about . . .'

'Well now! Most interesting, Mr Nursall,' interrupted Dudley rudely.

'But we really must be getting along now,' interposed Vaughan with better grace. 'Good day to you, my lad! Good day, Mr Nursall.'

'Huh,' sighed Tom in relief.

'Now what were them two bastards poking around for?' mused Nursall. 'They bain't just taking the air. I wouldn't be surprised if that danged Select Vestry ain't sent them to see what we be up to.'

'What will they do, Mr Nursall?'

'Make trouble.'

'What shall us do?'

'Nowt. Just carry on, me lad. We'll fight 'em somehow. Come on! Get on with it!' Harry picked up the shovel and began to throw up the bank beside Tom.

Francis Vaughan called on Sarah that evening to acquaint her with the progress of the house purchase.

'We should be able to take possession next month, Sarah! Mat will be able to celebrate Christmas in his new home if you can organize the furnishings by then.'

'Yes, it should be possible, apart from this being a very busy time for me. We've had orders for three dresses this week, all to be finished by Christmas.'

'Oh dear! We shall have to manage without you. I thought I should go up to London to help him choose his furniture. It would have been good if you could have come too.'

Sarah's face was a study of frustration.

'Oh, I must . . . I should love to and I could buy some more stuff for the shop. Could we perhaps manage it in three days if we set off very early in the morning and arrived back late at night?'

'Yes, or even the other way round. We could get to the Red Lion at St Albans one night and be in London early the next morning.'

'Yes, let's do that,' cried Sarah enthusiastically. 'Would you like me to bring Temperance?'

'No, not particularly. I always think two are much better company than three, but if you feel you *ought* to . . .?'

'It is our reputations that worry me; especially yours.'

'Perhaps you could arrange it that I do not call at the shop for you. I shall not mention to Theresa that I am taking you.'

'Did you tell her last time?'

'Yes, but I told her that Temperance was coming, as indeed I thought she was.'

'And you didn't tell her that Temperance couldn't come?'

'No! Absolutely no point. I am not a fellow for making trouble for myself,' laughed Vaughan. Sarah smiled. She was wondering how Francis had planned their accommodation at the Red Lion. She decided to wait and see.

'I shall need to spend quite a time at the villa measuring the windows and the rooms. I think I shall arrange with Mrs Jones to do it on the afternoon that we go and then you may pick me up from there.'

'An excellent plan. Our departure shall be concealed from all but the redoubtable Mrs Jones . . .?'

'And she can be made discreet with a little expense.'

'Ah. You seem to know the lady.'

'I have known *of* her for some time, and I flatter myself that I understand her rules,' replied Sarah crisply.

Vaughan regarded her with an expression of guarded admiration.

'Well, what have you been doing today?' asked Sarah gaily, contriving to lighten the mood of their conversation. 'I saw you ride through the Square with Mr Dudley.'

'We went up to inspect the state of the Heath.'

'Oh, why?' asked Sarah with studied carelessness.

'There's so many damn shacks up there now and men enclosing more of it.'

'What men?'

268

'Well, there was this tall young man, Ruddock's son, I understand, swinging a spade and tossing sand about as if it were feathers. A strapping fellow with fair curly hair. He would quite have turned your head, even your hard little head, until you'd tried to speak to him.'

'Oh! Was he foul-mouthed?' asked Sarah innocently.

'No, just inarticulate. In fact he only had one word.'

'And what was that?'

'Y-e-a-h.' Vaughan imitated Tom's solemn slowness. Sarah smiled, pursing her lips a little grimly.

'It's better than "no".'

'Oh, I agree. I agree whole-heartedly,' declared Vaughan, smiling roguishly at Sarah in a meaningful sort of way.

Sarah tried to look severe but soon started to chuckle. She found his boyish high spirits difficult to resist.

After a pause she said: 'Now tell me about these people on the Heath. How do they claim it's their land when it really belongs to the parish?'

'I am not saying many of them do yet. I merely remarked to Mat that some of them, with their wits about them, had signed affidavits claiming that they regarded it as theirs, having lived there so long and, providing they had never paid a quit rent, it would probably hold up in court.'

'I see; but what is an affidavit?'

'Just a piece of paper stating their claim and witnessed by a solicitor and a third party.'

'Would it matter if they couldn't write?'

'No. The solicitor could write it and they could sign it with a cross, I suppose. But why this interest, Sarah? What dastardly financial speculations are you about to undertake?'

'Oh. How could *I* make any? Come! I am only a poor weak woman. I couldn't own property, could I?'

'Well, it might be difficult and certainly unseemly.

269

You shall have to marry . . . But I believe I detect some Amazonian sarcasm in your tone?'

Sarah only smiled grimly in reply.

CHAPTER 44

Sarah's Change of Heart

Sarah confided her plans to Martha who agreed to look after the shop for three more days. They decided to explain her absence as a business trip, with no details of her destination, and Martha exhorted Sarah to 'take care'.

'Oh, don't you worry about me, Mrs Lyle. I can look after myself. You should know that.'

'Well yes, dear. It's just a sort of misgiving I had.' Sarah gave her a questioning glance but was too busy to pursue the matter, and on Monday afternoon she retired to the villa to make her measurements under the beady eye of the resentful old lady.

'What are your plans when the house is sold, Mrs Jones?' asked Sarah innocently.

'I don't know for sure, Mum.'

'I doubt whether Dr Crisp will need you, but he may, of course.'

'I could keep house for him, Mum.' She stepped forward, in a sudden mood of co-operation, to hold the end of Sarah's tape measure and the two came face to face when Sarah rose. They were exactly the same height and as Sarah gazed into the age-creased, putty-coloured face with its bright shoe-button eyes, she knew that although her own sweet smile and open tawny eyes would have left most people, particularly of the male sex, unacquainted with her thoughts, they concealed nothing from the shrewd, scheming Mrs Jones.

'I shall be living here myself and can supervise the house-keeping in Dr Crisp's absence. He will not be here a great deal, in fact.'

A most ingratiating smile creased Mrs Jones's face even more and exposed her gappy blackened teeth.

'Folks are very free with their tongues, Mum. A business lady like yourself cannot afford that.'

'The calculating old blackmailer,' thought Sarah.

'No, Mrs Jones, and that is why I may require a companion, but I should prefer a person of great discretion. I should need to have total confidence in her,' she warned.

'You could trust *me*, Miss.' The old lady had let the smile (if that word can be used to describe such an unattractive grimace) drop and her use of 'Miss' conveyed to Sarah that they were now at the bargaining table on equal terms.

'We shall have to see, then, won't we?' she said briskly.

Their eyes met for a moment in some sort of mutual exchange, but neither party was quite sure whether it was mutual respect or mutual hostility. Only time would tell.

The sound of Vaughan's chaise pulling into the drive made Sarah gather up her list and tape and stow them away in her bag. Mrs Jones helped her into her coat and hat, handed her her gloves and insisted on carrying her bag to the waiting vehicle. She was clearly taking her probationship quite seriously.

'Ah, the faithful Mrs Jones!' quipped Vaughan as he slipped a coin into her hand. They left her standing in the drive with one stick-like arm raised and the most unbecoming smile on her face.

'Will she gossip about us, then?'

'How much did you give her?'

'Half a crown!'

'*No*! Our reputations will be safe until that is spent.'

271

'Then we shall have to see that it is replenished in time.'

'Yes, but one needs to balance one's outgoings very nicely for the best effect. It might be better if I did that, you know. I have an understanding with Mrs Jones.'

'I shall supply you with a fund for the purpose, my dear. It is imperative that this is managed well if I am to benefit at all from Mat's new establishment.'

'I can see I shall have to come to an understanding with you, too, Fran.' It was the first time she had used the familiar name he had invited her to use.

'That won't be difficult, Sarah,' he said, squeezing her to him briefly.

Their night together at the Red Lion confirmed this.

For the first time Sarah tasted the amazing fulfilment of love. She was amazed, because her experience so far had led her to conclude that its physical manifestation was no more or less than a sordid bargaining counter which allowed women to survive in a world designed solely for the gratification and protection of rich men. One of the things that surprised her was her fervent desire that Fran felt equally fulfilled. He did seem to, but surely this experience was likely to be one with which he was well acquainted. She was again surprised that she found this reasonable surmise so distasteful and her final surprise was the immediate change in her own character. She enjoyed a sublimely agreeable breakfast in the low panelled dining-room of the old Tudor inn, floating with Fran in a dreamy world of unreality. It suddenly seemed unimportant whether they ever reached London, whether the warehouses she had planned to visit had the stuffs for dresses and curtains or the moss green rug that she had set her heart on. The usual moment-to-moment compulsions of her energetic life seemed to have given way to a creamy, dreamy luxury of idleness close beside Fran.

Francis Vaughan was the only man Sarah had met

with the sensitivity to reach her. Her father, Tom, Frank Cox and Sir Walter could not and would not even try, because all that was important to them was the physical and mental impact of Sarah. Dyfedd Griffiths maybe could, but he was too earnest. To have allowed him into her soul would have been never to let him out. He would have demanded to possess her, if she had, and she did not want to hurt him, so her defences were at their highest and prickliest for Dyfedd. Fran was so different, in that he combined sensitivity with a great delicacy which forbade him to intrude and a lightness of touch which forbade him to bore and an irresponsible youth-fulness that protected him from worry. Sarah found herself regretting some of these apparent virtues, par-ticularly the last, and that disturbed her most of all.

These were some of the thoughts which occupied her mind during the following two days. These and the corollary of how she could return to shoulder the urgent demands of her life, which so affected the people who depended upon her when she was abjectly in the power of a man whose birth, age, education and social loyalties were so different from her own. She once again felt the cruel pangs of feeling a traitor to the people and things she knew to be right. She would now also feel a traitor to Fran if she continued to conceal her birth and loyalties.

Despite Sarah's uncharacteristic passivity, they got Crisp's approval for the purchases they wished to make and, with Sarah's guidance on where to go and what to choose, they successfully completed most of the purchas-ing and arrangements for delivery. Vaughan entered into the enterprise with enthusiasm and they behaved rather like children, equipping a doll's house in their own make-believe world. Eventually they were springing along the turnpike, homeward bound.

'I have been worrying about you a little, Sarah.'

'Oh, why?' she asked, breaking out of her reverie.

'For the very reason that you have sat here beside me for two hours and hardly said a word. I have been wondering whether you are unwell or whether I had come to form a totally wrong impression of your character, somehow. Where, for instance, is that lively little virago who was hanging out of my carriage window a month or so ago shouting wild encouragement to that cripple we were racing?'

'I don't know, Fran, I really don't,' smiled Sarah. 'In fact, I am every bit as worried as you.'

'Well, well! What shall I make of that?'

'Perhaps you should try to guess,' she suggested.

'Perhaps it is that I have changed and you can think of nothing to say to me?'

'No, I don't think so. Do you feel as if you had changed?'

'Just a little perhaps.'

'How?'

'Well, I wonder whether this plan of ours for Mat's new villa will be a success.'

'We have arranged for the furnishings.'

'Yes, the physical ones we have. It is the living one that I am becoming doubtful about.'

'What do you mean?'

'You, child, of course!'

'I have only offered to live there as a custodian, so to speak.'

'Yes, but I think he would have every right to be offended if your duties stopped there.'

'Right?' queried Sarah with a hint of her old fire returning.

Vaughan searched her face, smiling first with amusement and then sadly.

'Well, I suppose it *is* your decision, Sarah, but let me warn you that he expects more of you at his convenience.'

'Oh, I know! I suppose I must turn down the chance

to live in those delightful rooms we have been planning,'
she said bitterly.

'That would be a pity, wouldn't it, Sarah? It would
make it well nigh impossible for us to spend any time
together, and you had no such doubts when we left,
surely?'

'No. But I have changed, as you have noticed.'

He made no answer but to kiss her passionately.

CHAPTER 45

Christmas Cheer

Sarah settled down more quickly than she had expected
when she arrived back at the salon. They had so many
orders for Christmas dresses and pelerines that she had
to begin saying that they would not be ready until the
New Year. There was not a single moment to be
misspent in daydreaming. She had to pay Mrs Wilmot to
cut and make up the curtains for the villa. When Dyfedd
called of an evening, he found the salon as busy as
during the day and soon gave up. Vaughan did not call
and Sarah guessed he too had acquainted himself with
the frenetic activity, although she could not quite banish
a niggling doubt that he might not even have bothered
to find her. Of course, she reminded herself, he would
be spendng time at the villa.

'You seem to be spending a great deal of time getting
Dr Crisp's new house ready, dear,' commented Theresa
Vaughan one suppertime.

'Yes, there is a lot to do. You must come up to see it
soon, Theresa. Wait until next week and then the
curtains should be up and all the furniture arrived.'

'Is Miss Lacelle making the curtains, then?'

Vaughan detected just a shade of contrivance in this question.

'No, Mrs Wilmot is making them.'

'Oh. I expect Miss Lacelle is very busy with new dresses for Christmas?'

'I couldn't say, my dear. Dresses are somethng I don't order for Christmas as a general rule.'

'Don't be silly, Francis. I am sure she is busy. She is making Beatrice a red velvet evening gown and I believe Mrs Miller and Mrs Dudley are having dresses made.'

'How *did* all these good ladies manage before Miss Lacelle opened her shop?'

'Oh, I believe they didn't have so many new dresses, not Mrs Miller and Mrs Dudley, at any rate. Beatrice always bought hers in London, but Miss Lacelle's prices are very reasonable, you see, and it's *so* convenient.'

Francis Vaughan was finding this conversation rather tiresome. He almost had the impression that Theresa wished to confront him with Miss Lacelle and knew of no other way to do it. Eventually he took the bull by the horns.

'Would *you* like a new dress, Theresa?'

'Well, yes. If you don't think it would be too extravagant,' she said doubtfully.

'No, you have just told me how reasonable Miss Lacelle's prices are.'

'She couldn't do it in time for Christmas. She has closed her orders for then because she is so busy.'

'Oh, why did you need to ask me if you already knew how busy she was?'

'I didn't, dear. I told you,' said Theresa reproachfully.

Vaughan shook his head irritably.

'Go in and order a new dress to be ready as soon as possible, do!'

'But should you not like to choose the stuff? I should only want a dress that you liked.'

'Oh, I do wish you had a bit more confidence,

276

Theresa. Most ladies would be so pleased when their husbands suggested that they had a new dress they would be off to the shop to choose it the next moment.'

'Francis, I just know that you have a better judgement than I have when it comes to things like this. Why, I can't even draw a tree. You know how dreadful I am at painting, and you were so pleased with the grey taffeta.'

Vaughan laid aside his book and surveyed his wife's puffy troubled face with a sense of hopelessness. He was not an unkind man and he was patient, as far as men seem capable of being that. It was largely because of these assets that he was a good teacher, but he found his wife unattractive to look at and so intellectually stultifying as to be sometimes unbearable. She managed the house admirably. She was even a comforting surrogate mother for the smaller boys, but he did wish she would not trouble him or, if she did trouble him, at least some element of interesting surprise might be introduced. He could not remember Theresa ever surprising him, not even mildly. Sarah, on the other hand, was a constantly challenging enigma to him. He felt compelled to try to understand Sarah and each time he thought he had, she eluded him yet again.

He became aware of Theresa's voice.

'. . . so Francis, that is what has been worrying me,' she ended earnestly.

'Oh dear!' sighed Vaughan to himself.

'In what way exactly, dear?'

She looked at him sharply.

'Why, in exactly the way I have explained. You are so irritable lately.'

'Ah. I'm sorry, my dear. I expect I am working a little too hard, what with Mat's new house to be ready for him by Christmas Eve.'

'Isn't that what I just said. Do please let me.'

'Let you?'

277

'Let me do the house for you. Really, you see you can't remember anything from one moment to the next!'

'There isn't much to do,' cried Vaughan in alarm.

'But you said it would be a week before you would let me see it.'

'Not necessarily. Do come to see it now if you would like to. The curtains are not finished yet, though.'

'There, you sound quite *cross* again,' cried Theresa tearfully.

What was worrying Sarah, whenever she had a moment to consider it, was what was happening on the Heath. Ever since she had found out about the affidavits, she had been wanting to speak to Harry and suggest a visit to Woburn to find a solicitor. It was several weeks since she had seen anything of her family as well. She had given up hoping that her mother would call to see the shop but, to her surprise, three days before Christmas when the salon was full of ladies waiting for fittings and Sarah didn't know where to turn next, she caught a glimpse of Eliza and Tize hovering timidly by the door. Sarah cast her eyes heavenwards in dismay and then, pulling herself together, she excused herself from conducting a lady upstairs, called Ellie in to take her place, hissing that she would be back as soon as they had the dress on, and shot out to the door to arrest her mother and sister, just as they had abandoned their plan to come in.

'Mama! I'm so pleased you've come,' cried Sarah, kissing them both. 'It is a pity you have found us so busy, but do come in, do.'

'Well, Sarah, I hardly dare. There are such a lot of fine ladies in there.'

'No-one finer than you, Mama. You creep in and I shall find you a corner to sit and look at my drawings while I see to fitting a lady upstairs, and then I shall take you up to show you.'

'Oh, oh,' wailed Eliza. 'It's so lovely.'

'It's even better upstairs. Come on. Over here. Look, you'll be all right looking at my drawings here.'

Sarah squeezed them into a tiny corner under the stairs and thrust a sheaf of dress designs at them, which they could hardly hold in their agitation.

Eliza held out a parcel to her, quite speechless with shyness.

'For me, Mama?'

'Yes. It's only a little plum cake for your Christmas dinner, love,' she whispered.

When Sarah returned downstairs they had fled.

'Oh why, oh why could they not have come all these weeks when I could have shown them everything,' she grieved silently.

On Christmas Day, despite her exhaustion, Sarah went to morning service. She could not stop her eyes fixing themselves on Francis Vaughan's back whenever the service required the congregation to stand. It was the first time she had set eyes upon him since he put her off in Woburn Lane on their return from London. She noted the way his thick brown hair waved behind his ears and his smart, full-skirted grey coat fitted his broad shoulders without a wrinkle. Why were these details of special significance to her? He was only the best dressed man in the congregation by a small margin! Why did she will him to turn his head to view the handful of scholars that remained in the gallery? (These were just the few lonely boys whose parents were abroad.) He didn't, and so she tarried in her pew, dropping and retrieving her gloves and prayer book until the Vaughan family had filed down the aisle. He didn't glance towards her but, as they passed, he looked down at his wife and murmured something. It seemed a look of tenderness to Sarah, and she found herself suddenly hating Theresa Vaughan. She wished the wretched woman had been more worthy of her envy. How humiliating to have such a totally unremarkable woman for one's rival! Would Theresa be aware of the pressure of his arm supporting her? Would she notice that glance of tenderness? No! How very profligate of her.

Sarah's angry frustration at least fuelled her flagging body and she hurried back to the salon, changed into a plain walking-out dress and stout shoes and set off for the Heath with some cold roast chicken and some nuts in her bag.

Eliza was just serving up a spit-roast goose, which little Willy had spent the morning turning this way and that over the fire. They greeted her with some surprise and just a hint of coolness, although Sarah did wonder whether that impression was created by her own over-wrought state.

'My, I thought you would be too busy in your shop, Sarah,' said Eliza. She always said 'your shop', as if implying that it was only important to Sarah.

'Even I don't work on Christmas Day,' said Sarah reproachfully.

'No, of course not. But you've probably been to church, haven't you?' suggested John with more than a hint of animosity. Sarah merely raised her brows. She decided not to thank her mother for the plum cake in case their visit to her crossed her father.

'I've brought some cold chicken and some nuts,' she said, placing them on the table.

'You need not have. We've plenty,' said John ungraciously. Sarah wondered why she had returned to the bosom of her family when she might have gone to her room to rest.

'Where's Tom?'

'Oh, he's at the farm. Rosie Tennant wanted him to be there today,' sniffed Eliza.

'I don't rightly remember how me son Tom looks any more,' said John sarcastically.

'Oh, go along with you, John Ruddock! But he is at

the farm mostly now,' conceded Eliza sadly, '. . . and what with poor little Bobby not being here . . .'

'Eliza, remember what we said,' said John sternly.

'Yes, I won't say it again but it's just that it is Christmas, you know.' She sounded close to tears and Sarah was tempted to compare their mood with the cheerful crowd she could imagine around the Tennants' table. That led her to wondering about how dinner would be at the Classical Academy today. The Headmaster would be carving an outsized turkey and joking gaily. Was Dyfedd Griffiths there? She didn't know; her observation of the congregation this morning had been so limited. Dr Crisp certainly wasn't at church with them, but he would surely be invited for lunch.

'It's very, very good!' declared Willy with his mouth full.

'Yes, it is, love. It's cooked beautiful, ain't it,' appealed Eliza.

'Yes. Did you turn it?' asked Sarah.

'Yes. All day. All by myself,' said Willy, his rosy cheeks bulging even more than when his mouth was empty.

Sarah glanced at Tize, hoping she might follow Willy's good example of cheeriness, but she had reached the stage of gawky adolescence when one's own silence seems somehow to lessen the excruciating embarrassment of one's family's chatter. Sarah couldn't remember passing through such a stage herself and Tom had rarely been in any other.

'Well, tell me what you are doing, Father.'

'Not a great deal that matters.'

'How's the Movement going?' Eliza glanced at her apprehensively. 'Dyfedd Griffiths keeps me informed a little.'

'Oh, yes,' responded John, brightening up. 'He's a useful young man. We need a few educated fellows like him.'

'His family are supporters. They are miners but they live near the Welsh ironworks.'

'Oh, it's *terrible*, the suffering. They started striking in the summer, but now there's most of the Lancashire mills and the Yorkshire ones idle, too. They say there have never been so many chimneys without smoke coming out of them for as long as folks can remember. And the Leicester framework knitters, starving.' He shook his head miserably. 'We thought with all *that*, the Government would crumble. We all thought they'd be bound to listen. It ain't as if we want anything unreasonable, is it, Sarah? It makes yer feel bad to be sitting down to a meal like this when there's so many without.'

Eliza flung down her knife and fork.

'Now I ask you? Is this the way to talk? It's your fault, Sarah. You started him off. Since we *have* got a middling good dinner, and since if we did go and throw it away in the garden it would do no-one any good, and since me and Willy have spent all day getting it ready for you . . .'

'No, no – stop, Liza.'

'Yes, Mama. I'm sorry. We won't talk about that any more.'

John and Sarah exchanged looks of penitent confederacy.

CHAPTER 46

New Year Resolutions

Theresa Vaughan had ordered her new dress a couple of weeks before Christmas and Sarah had promised to get it made for the New Year. Theresa had been so diffident about the stuff and style that she had ended by begging Sarah to make the decision for her. She returned for a fitting after Christmas.

'Oh, that does look nice. Do you think it is bright enough for a party?'

'Well, yes. I am sure it will suit and be useful as a day dress too. Are you going to a party?'

'Yes. We have been invited to the house of a friend of my husband's. He has only just moved into it, so he wanted to see in the New Year there.'

Sarah suddenly felt a yawning gulf of disappointment open up inside her. She found it difficult to continue talking lightly to Mrs Vaughan. It was unreasonable to feel like this, she told herself. How *could* she have been invited? Even had she already been living there, she would not have been able to go. She wondered how he would arrange the catering, but he could pay for the food and drink to be delivered from Woburn, she guessed. Francis Vaughan had still not called, but she saw him ride out with Crisp each morning. They would have been hunting the day after Christmas, of course.

'. . . will it be?' Sarah realized Mrs Vaughan was speaking to her.

'I'm sorry?'

'Will it be ready for Friday, please?' Theresa seemed always to be talking to people who were not listening, lately.

'Oh yes. I shall see that it is,' replied Sarah austerely.

She gathered that most of the families of the members of the Select Vestry had been invited, as the ladies came in to make frivolous little purchases. Fran must have been busy proclaiming Dr Crisp's reputation, since they were all a-twitter with excitement and surmises as to whether Lady Osborne would be there, and perhaps even Sir Geoffrey Hethrington and his lady. It seemed possible that the entire Christmas hunting field had been invited. Sarah wore a sour face all week.

'I do wish she'd stop finding fault with me all the time,' complained Temperance.

'She's as bad with me,' said Grace.

283

'And me. But she must be terrible tired. Just look at the way she's been at it since long before Christmas,' said Ellie.

'Yes,' they agreed. 'She seemed out of sorts when she came back from that trip. She must be terrible tired.'

Sarah was sitting despondently in her room on the eve of the New Year, imagining the riotous gaiety in progress up Woburn Lane, when Dyfedd called.

'Oh, it *is* pleased to find you in, I am. I thought you would be out tonight, perhaps.'

'Oh no! Why did you think that?' asked Sarah bitterly.

'Well, so many parties there seem to be. Mr and Mrs Vaughan have gone to Dr Crisp's, and the boys are having a small one of their own with the servants.'

'Should you not be there?'

'I have been. I am the only master in residence, so I must not be away long, but I find the noise oppressive, and I believe the boys find my presence so. So here I am, to wish you a very happy and prosperous time next year!'

'Thank you. And I wish you the same,' Sarah smiled wanly.

'I believe you are low-spirited, Miss Lacelle?'

'I am tired. I have been working very hard.'

'Ah, yes. To be sure. I must not keep you.'

'No, do stay please, Mr Griffiths – just until your duties summon you. I *am* feeling rather low and I should like you to cheer me up.'

Dyfedd's earnest face became transformed with pleasure.

'I shall apply myself to that task with great dedication. Now, how shall I begin?'

'Well, the expression on your face has given you a very good start,' laughed Sarah.

He did try to be amusing and Sarah was grateful. She couldn't help just wondering how it was that Fran always managed to be rather more amusing with no apparent effort at all. After all, they were both intelligent men. Perhaps, intellectually, Dyfedd was the better. She suspected that, although most of the difference was undoubtedly character, Fran's background in a superior sort of English school must contribute as well although, she remembered, it had worked no miracle on Dr Crisp, but both those men were infinitely more self-confident than Dyfedd Griffiths.

He did undo a lot of his effort when he paused by the door of the salon as she saw him out and, perhaps gaining a little courage from the dim lighting, took one of her hands fervently between his own.

'Forgive me making a confession to you, Miss Lacelle, since it is, indeed, so close to a new year. I sometimes delude myself into such happiness by imagining what a wonderful year it would be if a certain lady came to feel she could in any way return a little of the respect and deep admiration I hold for her.'

Sarah drew her hand away as gently as she could and suppressed several unkind quips that rose to her disrespectful lips.

'Mr Griffiths, that sentence is too long for me quite to understand, but I do wish you a very happy New Year.'

She feared that his step on the path as he walked back to his duties sounded lighter than it had any right to be. She thought she had phrased her reply to convey total neutrality, but perhaps his powers of delusion were exceptionally well developed.

The next day Sarah visited the Heath again. Tom and her father were working on Tidbury Hill, and she decided to call on the Nursalls before she went to survey the new enclosure.

'Hallo, Mr and Mrs Nursall. We have a beautiful day for the first of the year.'

'Indeed we have, Sarah, and it is good to see you. Your mother says the shop is so busy. I do hope you don't work too hard, dearie. You do look a little pale.'

Sarah smiled, grateful for their concern.

'So, are you here to bully us about them affidavits?' asked Harry.

'Yes, that's it, Mr Nursall.'

'What shall us do?'

'I think we should go to Woburn to see Mr Day, the solicitor, and see if he will arrange to draw up several, then when we know how much it will cost, we can start talking to people like Mr Goodall and Mr Giles. How about Mr Perry and Mr Jenkins? They've been here a long time, too.'

'Nay. They pay quit rent. They are hand in glove with the Select Vestry. They got that money and pistols for being watchmen. It is best they don't hear nothing of this, Sarah,' replied Harry sternly.

'Right. We have to be careful and do this very quietly then. How much will it cost, do you think?'

'I ain't no idea. Have you, Mary?'

'No, I don't remember anyone having anything done by one of them there solicitors,' said Mary distrustfully.

'It should be cheaper by the dozen,' laughed Harry.

'Well, that is what we tell Mr Day,' smiled Sarah. 'Shall we go tomorrow?'

'How about yer father?'

'Well, we haven't been here long enough, have we?'

'Supposin' it was my land what I'd banked round when I first come and then I gave it to yer father?'

'Yes! Well! Could they prove otherwise?' asked Sarah, brightening.

'Nay, I don't see as they could. Furthermore, the Daltons and Butchers live pretty close by. I reckon as how I gave some land to ol' Jack Dalton and Tom Butcher, if they're happy ter have it off me.'

'You have been generous, Mr Nursall.'

'Aye, it's me nature, but some of it were for exchanges, mind you, gal,' Harry cautioned her gravely.

'Ah, yes,' cried Sarah, delighted with his inventiveness. 'What did they exchange it for?'

'Well, let us see.'

'Some geese, maybe,' suggested Mary.

'Aye, now I come to think of it, Jack gave me ten geese.'

'And Mr Butcher?'

'He gave us this chicken coop what's our kitchen and has bin ever since this long while,' said Mary.

'Yes, that's it,' cried Harry, 'and very useful it's bin too.' They all laughed heartily.

'Well, this bit of nonsense has brought the roses back into your cheeks, dearie.'

'Yes, Mrs Nursall. It's done me the world of good and it isn't just nonsense, quite the reverse. You wait and see. I wonder what we exchanged ours for.'

'A whole lot o' trouble,' responded Harry speedily.

'Oh no, Harry! You are a miserable one. A great deal of good friendship.'

'It certainly won't have been anything worth money,' declared Sarah wryly.

'Friendship is beyond price,' declared Mary sweetly.

CHAPTER 47

Sarah Considers a Woman's Worth

Having completed her urgent orders, Sarah felt justified in taking a little time off, and so she met Harry Nursall at the bottom of the sandy lane and they walked to Woburn together. They had agreed not to mention their expedition to John and Eliza until they discovered how the land lay. When they entered the elegant Georgian house facing the cobbled square, they were shown into the office of Day's younger partner, Malin. As soon as

287

Harry had acquainted him with what was required he looked a little worried and fetched in his senior, who was a thin stooping man of about sixty.

Day listened to what his partner had to say and surveyed Harry over his spectacles.

'Aha. Aspley Heath is parish common land, is it not?'

Harry looked intensely stupid, allowing his lower jaw to drop, but said nothing.

'I hope you *have* been working this land for nineteen years, Mr Nursall. You are required to swear to that on the Holy Bible, you know, and perjury is a very serious sin.'

'Oh yes. I understand that, sir, and I have been on that land, living and digging, for a full nineteen years.'

Day still seemed dissatisfied. 'Would this young woman be your daughter?'

'Oh, no. She's me friend or you might say the daughter of me friend.'

'Oh,' said Day, peering over his spectacles at Sarah as if he suspected her of some particularly degrading relationship with the old man before him.

'Then it might be more appropriate if she waits outside.'

'Why should it be more appropriate, Mr Day?' demanded Sarah, speaking for the first time.

He turned to look at her in surprise. Her command of the Queen's English seemed to unnerve him.

'Because *ladies*,' he clearly doubted that this was appropriate either, 'because ladies are not commonly involved in legal matters.'

'I fail to see how my presence could interfere with the legal matter in hand, particularly when I am here because my family now occupies some of Mr Nursall's land.'

'They do, do they? Then perhaps your father should have come to see me,' said Day coldly. 'Who is your father, by the way?'

Sarah opened her mouth, white with fury, but Harry shook his head at her and began to speak with slow deliberation.

'Well, he's me old friend John. Him and his wife Eliza and their little girl – that would be the younger sister of this young lady here who has been so good as to keep me company and it's quite a long drag up them sand-hills . . .'

'Yes, of course, Mr Nursall, thank you. Now I think I shall have to take some advice on this matter, particularly since the land belongs to the parish.'

'Oh yes, of course. And whose advice will you take, Mr Day?'

Day looked at him sharply.

'I hardly think that need concern you, but I shall naturally consult someone who administers the parish.'

'Well, it were only an idea what I had. No-one has interfered with me bit of land so I think I shall not bother with affi . . . affidavits when it do seem rather complicated. I am sorry to have wasted you good gentlemen's time,' mumbled Harry, beaming round benignly and radiating rural simplicity at its most harmless.

They walked several hundred yards down Woburn High Street before Sarah exploded.

'A woman doesn't seem to have many rights when it comes to the law, not even to be treated civilly.'

'Nay, none probably, but don't upset yourself, Sarah. It ain't worth it. You goes and does or says summat that does you more harm than good. You've got as hot a head as your father.'

'Yes, I know. I always regret what I say when I'm cross, but you were wonderful, Mr Nursall. It was as good as being at the theatre. Do you think he'll tell someone?'

'Let's hope I've made him think he's no need to trouble.'

'It's likely to be Rector Devereux if he does.'

'Aye, and that puts the ol' cat among the pigeons. We should have thought this out better, gal.'

'I've got another plan, Mr Nursall. They won't stop *us* so easily.'

'Let's have it then.'

'You know this friend of Vaughan's called Dr Crisp? He has just bought the Browns' old villa up Woburn Lane, and he says he is going to write something in some papers that medical people read saying what a healthy place Aspley Heath is.'

'I hope this is a rare good plan when you reach it.'

'Be patient, Mr Nursall. This will work, I'm sure. Now, like I told you before, he wants to buy up land so that when sick people want to come and live here, he can sell it to them and make a lot of money. He can't buy bits of the Heath unless someone who owns it is prepared to sell it to him. We can own it if only we can get affidavits done. If we say we'll sell to him, it's in his interest to help us get the affidavits and he must know solicitors in London that would do it.'

Harry was silent.

'Don't you think that would work?'

'Aye. It is the only way we'll get them done, perhaps.'

'Well?'

'Me and Mary won't sell our land to no-one.'

'No,' agreed Sarah, 'but you only have to *say* you will. You can change your mind.'

'It don't seem quite straight.'

'I think a lot of people would be happy to sell their land if he paid enough.'

'Would he, though?'

'He'd have to if he wanted it.'

'Nay, Sarah. I don't want none of it. It ain't worth paying with your peace of mind. I came along so far with you on account of your father and mother and them others, because I can see there will be trouble, evictions and the like, but I think we just have to hope for the best now. We gave it a fair try, gal, didn't we?'

Harry finished by clapping her shoulder playfully to let her know that he wasn't offended, but Sarah didn't like letting go once she had hold of an idea.

'Do you know if Father and Tom are working on Tidbury today, Mr Nursall?'

'Yes, they said last night they would be. Tennant has given Tom another day free. He seems a very accommodating man, does Mr Tennant. I shall go and give them a hand. Are you coming?'

'Yes! It will be best not to mention where we've been.'

'Depend on me, gal.'

Sarah went straight to Tidbury Hill while Harry went to fetch his spade. She paused to watch and think for a bit before she interrupted them. Tidbury was a steep shoulder of the Heath set at right angles to the main ridge. A slightly smaller shoulder ran out parallel to it so that the two were separated by a secret sheltered valley whose sides were covered with rabbit warrens and patches of short turf surrounded by ling and birch saplings. Sarah and Tom had spent many happy times there, scooping out holes in the sand, with the flat brown sandstones, to make boats or covering them with branches to make dens. They lost themselves for hours in make-believe worlds which seemed more real and secure than the everyday one. She stepped lightly over the close-cropped turf on the rounded summit where the shaded sides of the molehills were still stiff with white frost, but she was remembering her childish delight with the summer flowers that grew there. There were always harebells and lady's slipper and, Sarah's particular favourite, the delicate stiff panicles of pink century which could be found nowhere else in the neighbourhood.

Sarah smiled tenderly as she looked down upon Tom. He was digging holes in the sand for earnest now, and doing it with the effortless grace that Francis Vaughan had described to her, '. . . tossing sand about as if it were feathers'. They had completed a ditch on the upper edge and a bank rising four feet high on the lower edge, enclosing a section of the open side of the hill and now they were beginning to dig a pit directed at the heart of the hill near the lower part of the boundary bank.

It was good weather for the work, since the sand was too dry to freeze hard, but it held together better than in warmer weather. Even as cold as it was, their work was so strenuous that their shirt sleeves were rolled up and the buttons opened to their waists. Tom filled Tennant's barrow and John took it down the hill, teetered along a wooden plank bridging the ditch and tipped it over the bank. By the time he returned, Tom had a pile of sand on an old door which they lifted between them and tipped in to half fill the barrow again. John had a short rest then, while Tom finished filling the barrow. He continued to dig without pause. Sarah could see how the heavy physical exercise satisfied them; they were relaxed and happy and their physical co-operation bonded them together in a way that words never served to do. She had not seen Tom and his father more at one with each other. She envied them their strength and maleness. Women's work was so much harder on the nerves. You could rarely lose yourself in the repetitive round, overlaid with worries about money and other people's needs; fitting yourself into a complicated mould to satisfy the demands of baby, toddler, children, husband, parents. And today Sarah had had full confirmation of a woman's rights so far as the law was concerned. She was of no consequence at all.

She walked slowly down the steep hillside. As she got closer to the pit, Tom receded from view and she realized that it was a good deal deeper than she had judged from higher up. They were so absorbed in their work they hadn't seen her, so she waited until they had emptied the pile of sand from the door into the barrow.

'Well, how long before you strike the earth, then?' she called.

'Sarah!' declared her father, beaming up at her. He looked more carefree and happy than she could ever remember seeing him. Tom straightened up, nodded and smiled at her.

'We shouldn't be long at this rate of digging should we, lad?'

'Dunno,' said Tom non-committally.

'You have got deep. I didn't expect it to be so quick.'

'Aye. Well it be this very good digging machine we've got on the job. Has the power of two good horses!' laughed John, clapping Tom's shoulder.

Tom smiled complacently and began to unwind the yellow-stained strips of cloth from his hands. Sarah hadn't noticed them, since they, his hands and spade handle were all the colour of the sand.

'Oh, Tom! You've got terrible blisters. Haven't you got any thick gloves?' She realized it was a silly question as soon as she had asked it.

'Neow. These bits o' cloth do the job while they keep the sand out. I'll be needing some more though.' Sand was encrusted on the watery fluid which oozed through the broken skin. She gently wiped away as much as she could and shook the bandages before she rebound his hands, trying to get a clean bit against the wounds.

'You can't go on, Tom! Suppose they go septic?'

'Must go on. They'll be all the tougher when I've been away from the digging a bit.' He grasped his spade and began to fill the barrow. Sarah winced at the thought of the pain, but Tom never flinched. She looked at her father. His gaiety had evaporated and he shook his head sadly with a rueful glance at Tom's broad shoulders.

'It's boarding we'll soon be needing, Sarah,' he said.

'Boarding?'

'Aye. Wide boards to stop the sides of the pit falling in. It's treacherous stuff this sand. Many a fellow's found his grave sudden on this job.'

Sarah nodded, a frown on her face.

CHAPTER 48

Sarah Makes a Resolution

As soon as Sarah reached Aspley, she turned up Woburn Lane and, glancing round apprehensively, she slipped into the stable block of the villa. She had remembered some old dining chairs she had noticed there. Yes! She pushed the door open wider to let in more light and pulled one down from the pile. As she expected, the worn seats were covered with leather. She pulled out two more.

The seat of one was slashed open, so she began to pull away the covering. It was still quite strong and she couldn't tear it away from the studs holding it to the seat frame. She searched for a lever of some sort. A shadow appeared in the doorway and Sarah turned round guiltily.

'Ah, Mrs Jones! Good afternoon. I am needing a piece of leather. I wonder if you know where there is a sharp knife or something I could pull these studs out with? This seat is quite beyond repair.' The old lady scuttled away and soon returned with a large meat knife. Together they struggled until Sarah had the leather off the two seats.

'What be you needing it for, Ma'am?'

'I want to make some gloves.'

'It'll be too 'ard and thick.'

'They are for heavy work,' said Sarah, eager to close the subject.

'Aha . . .' said Mrs Jones, keeping her mouth open on her rotten teeth, but the warning tilt to Sarah's chin persuaded her to satisfy her curiosity by merely asking, ''Ow will you make the 'oles for the thread, Ma'am?'

'Oh yes. I need a punch.' Sarah bit her lip in perplexity.

'I remember me ol' dad using an 'ammer and nail.'

'That's clever of you, Mrs Jones. Is there a hammer about I could borrow, I wonder?'

'Oh yes, Ma'am.' Sarah's probationary companion was soon back with three assorted nails and a useful looking hammer. Sarah smiled her approval and thanks.

'The other thing I need are some wooden boards.' They glanced around the building. There were a couple of old doors from a shed.

'They be from the 'ut what's called the summer 'ouse,' said Mrs Jones. 'That's seen better days too.'

'Is Dr Crisp in?' asked Sarah.

'Neow. He won't be back till next week.'

They went to look at the hut in the garden. Sarah tapped the boards near the ground with the hammer and they crumbled away, but the upper ones seemed reasonably sound.

Mrs Jones watched Sarah, head on one side and mouth a little open, with the beady-eyed curiosity of an old hen, but forebore to ask any more questions.

Sarah returned to the salon and cut out a pattern in paper. She placed her diminutive palm on it and screwed up her eyes critically. She wished she had Tom there, but so long as the gloves were plenty large enough she could line them with soft linen that could be replaced as it became soiled with the discharge from the blisters. It was as much as she could do to cut the leather with her shears and she only managed one set of pieces before she had a blood blister at the base of her thumb. She hammered holes round the edges and settled down in front of the shop fire to sew and lay plans.

Her problems and the possible strategies to overcome them seemed equal to those confronting a General on the eve of battle and she was determined to approach them with appropriate coolness and ingenuity. They fell into three categories and the one that she disdained to regard as the most important was, nevertheless, the one she felt the most reluctant to face: her relationship with Francis Vaughan. She would leave that until last.

The first to consider then, were the affidavits. After their encounter with Mr Day that morning, a frontal attack was clearly out of the question. A solicitor would have to be engaged by stealth. A third party would have to be bribed into helping them. Should it be Vaughan or Crisp?

Oh dear! Her deliberations had brought her round on a tight circle back to Fran! No, let it be Crisp. She might well end up double-crossing him because he should never get Harry and Mary's land, so she would much rather it was Crisp.

This decision laid the scene for the next problem. Was she to become the mistress of Crisp's new villa and, inevitably, of Dr Crisp as well? If she wanted his assistance that seemed the only way. She just wished she found the man more agreeable. She had never encountered him alone. Perhaps it was only his juxtaposition with Fran that made the man seem so cold and supercilious? She had a sinking feeling that he might prove even worse on his own.

The encounter with Day had brought another hard fact to her notice. So far as the law was concerned, she was a domestic appendage of her father or her husband or, in the absence of both, any man who sought to protect or exploit her. Sarah had known this already, of course, but it hit hard at her proud confidence in her ability to manage her own affairs. She also knew that Harry's advice was sound and no frontal attack would win this battle. Her deteriorating relationship with Frank

Cox left her at the mercy of Dr Crisp. Only the additional income that she would contrive to get as his housekeeper would enable her to satisfy Cox's demands. Besides, Tom urgently needed Crisp's dilapidated summerhouse, his tools and his pony and trap.

There was only one decision to be made. She must concentrate on the positive aspects and make light of the rest. She would enjoy being mistress of such a grand establishment. To have beautiful rugs and curtains that she had chosen herself, new furniture and, she trusted, a liberal allowance for servants and tradesmen, must be a very agreeable life. She had soon calmed herself into a state of happy anticipation, but she compelled herself to confront the problem that she had shunned. The one that seemed to resist cool consideration.

She was appalled at the way she had succumbed to Francis Vaughan's overtures. He held no material advantage for her and endangered all she had strived so hard for. How could she, Sarah, with all her toughness, give herself to a man in return for a coach ride to London and back? How could she have become reduced to envying and hating so innocent a rival as Theresa Vaughan? Sarah was ashamed of herself.

How could she, for one moment, contemplate a liaison with a man old enough to be her father, who was a respected member of the local gentry and the Select Vestry, an educated professional man of high repute and wealth? Above all, how could she have ever entertained feelings of tenderness for a man who expressed such contempt for her own people '. . . those squatters building their wretched hovels . . . they seem stupid enough most of the time . . . totally inarticulate, he only has one word . . .'?

In her agitation, Sarah had risen from her chair and was pacing about the room. She came to a halt, rigid with shame, and raised her eyes to the long mirror in which her reflection was framed. Her pale face looked haunted and she clenched Tom's glove in her hand. 'This is ridiculous, Sarah,' she murmured. 'What would Francis Vaughan say when you told him that you were reared in a squatter's hovel, that your father was a Chartist and convicted poacher and that that inarticulate giant was your dear brother?' she smiled cruelly, but the cruelty was directed at herself as much as at Vaughan. She was trying to expunge her defection to Vaughan by torturing herself with it. It worked after a fashion and she resolved that she would acquaint him with her decision and never be alone with him again.

She sat down to concentrate on sewing Tom's glove but she was trembling and her mind was in a turmoil. She had just leant forward to make up the fire when a sharp tap sounded on the door. She sprang to her feet. It must be very late. She had heard the church clock strike eleven. It could not be Dafydd and, anyway, the knock was too peremptory. She was hardly surprised when Francis Vaughan stepped swiftly across her threshold without an invitation.

He was in his shirt sleeves and an embroidered waistcoat and seemed to lack his usual genial confidence. Sarah wondered whether the pale haunted look on his face was merely a reflection of her own.

'This is a very late visit,' she said coolly.

'Yes, do forgive me, Sarah. It is such an age since I have seen you, I suddenly could bear it no longer. I had resolved not to come because this liaison seems so dangerous for us both, but I have been endeavouring to work in my study and all I can see, gazing up from the pages of my book, is your face.'

Sarah looked up at him, speechless, her eyes huge and glittering. She summoned every fibre of determination to repeat to herself the elements of the gulf that separated them. He seemed unnervingly to follow the train of her thoughts as, still standing in front of her, he asked:

298

'Do I seem terribly old to you, Sarah? I suppose I must!'

'Yes,' she replied firmly, and then an errant piece of her mind made her add, 'except when you seem much younger than me.' He smiled timidly.

'How strange! That is just how I feel sometimes; as if you have experienced so much more suffering than me. What are you doing, Sarah? I thought perhaps you would have retired until I saw the light. What is that piece of leather you're holding?'

'I am making a pair of gloves.'

'Gloves! They are so large, and what thick old leather!'

'It is all I could find,' flared Sarah.

'May I sit down for a moment, Ma'am?' he begged meekly. 'I promise I shan't disturb you. I shall just sit silent and watch you make your giant's gloves.'

'No, no!' cried Sarah desperately. 'Please go!'

He gazed down at her, fascinated by the sudden fierceness of the tiny thing he had thought he could charm at will. He felt an overwhelming desire to gather her up in his arms, but the glitter in her eyes warned him to treat her as gingerly as an aggrieved wild kitten.

'Please go, Mr Vaughan,' she insisted.

'"Mr Vaughan"! What have I done, Sarah?'

'Nothing, nothing at all.'

'Oh, is that it? I should have visited you sooner?'

'No. Your decision was quite right.'

'It's not Mat's party is it? You do appreciate that it would have been impossible to have invited you, and I do assure you it was the most tedious party ever.'

'Parties are of no consequence to me,' announced Sarah sternly. 'Please leave me alone,' immediately pleaded the bit of her mind which had escaped domination.

The expression of alarm on Vaughan's face flickered with hope.

'I am sorry I have disturbed you, Sarah. You seem as upset as myself. I suppose you are right. I must go, but maybe we could talk things over when we are calmer, tomorrow, perhaps?'

'No! Yes! Sometime,' faltered Sarah as she opened the door.

'Goodnight, Sarah dear.' His voice was full of pleading tenderness.

'Goodnight,' murmured Sarah, shutting the door on him. She ran upstairs and threw herself on her bed, sobbing violently. She had not lost, she told herself. She had not been quite vanquished.

Would she survive another onslaught, though?

CHAPTER 49

Tom is Taken Ill

Tom arrived for work on the farm the next day with his hands swollen and the palms covered with fresh scabs. He kept them out of sight and Tennant set him to shifting fifty or so sacks of grain from one end of the barn to the other. Try as he did, he could devise no way of hoisting them on to his shoulders without using his hands and after he had painfully shifted two, they were bleeding. It was bitingly cold weather and a vicious wind swept round and through the barn. Even Tom's stoical forbearance deserted him and Tennant found him crouching by the heap of unmoved sacks blowing on to his swollen red fingers. Tom leapt to his feet with stumbling apologies.

'Let's see your hands, man,' demanded his master. 'Hold them out proper, Tom!'

It was with great difficulty that Tom endeavoured to

uncurl his fingers, and when Tennant raised his horrified eyes to Tom's face he saw his eyes were brimming over with the pain.

'Well, I gives you a free day or two to do your digging and you come back ruined for work for two months,' grumbled the farmer to cover up his feelings.

'No. They won't take long to heal. Ain't there summat I can do that won't hurt so much?' asked Tom earnestly.

'Not as I can think of. It's mighty difficult to employ a handless man on a farm.'

'Maybe you should stop paying me and I'll see to me pit,' said Tom doubtfully.

'And have you coming back with your bones poking through your palms? Oh no, you stays here till you're right, me lad. Go on in and get Rosie to bind them up and I shall see what I can think of.'

'I'se sorry, sir. Thankee,' murmured Tom.

'Well, there ain't nothing wrong with his legs, thank God,' muttered Tennant.

It was lunch time before Tennant found a job for Tom, and the time passed very agreeably, since Mrs Tennant was out shopping and Rosie convinced herself that Tom's infirmity required the most dedicated nursing.

In the afternoon he was set to get the steam engine going to drive the mangel-worzle chopper and he managed gingerly to toss the worzles into the hopper with his bandaged hands.

He was woken in the night by a throbbing pain in his right hand and arm and he got up feeling feverish and sick.

The next morning Tennant took one look at his pale face and demanded to see his hands. The palm of the right one was a livid red and an angry weal was extending up his wrist. He took Tom off to show his wife.

'It's gone septic,' she said in alarm.

'He'd best go home to bed, then?'

'He'd get up to something daft. He'd be best staying here,' said Rosie.

'His mother'll want to look after him,' said Nell Tennant.

'He ain't fit to walk home,' pleaded Rosie.

She had her way and Tom was put to bed and his hand poulticed while Rosie undertook to walk to Aspley Heath to tell his mother. She had never been before so Tom tried to give her directions, which he would not have made much of a job of at the best of times and with his teeth chattering, she couldn't make much out.

'You'd best call at his sister's. She can either go herself or tell you proper,' snapped Nell Tennant, exasperated with the extra trouble and worried about Tom.

Rosie followed her mother's advice with some reluctance and called at the salon. There was only Sarah in the shop and the two greeted each other guardedly.

'I'se come about Tom.'

'Oh, what about Tom?'

'He ain't well.' Sarah dropped her reserve and looked alarmed.

'It's his hand. It's gone septic and he's got a fever.'

'Oh, that's just what I said would happen. Where is he?' cried Sarah.

'Me mam's put him to bed at our place. He weren't fit to walk home and I said I'd tell his mother.'

'She'll want to go to him and there's no-one here. I suppose I'll have to close the shop. How bad is he?'

'I don't rightly know,' said Rosie, her face puckering up.

'He walked to work this morning, didn't he?'

Rosie nodded abjectly.

'Well, he can't be so bad then, can he?' said Sarah kindly, trying to re-assure herself as well. She gave Rosie precise instructions for finding the cottage, and arranged that if Eliza insisted upon going straight over, as she almost certainly would, they would bring William over to Sarah's so that they could walk the rest of the way faster and not have the bother of him at the farm.

Dafydd was surprised to find the sturdy three-year-old romping about in Sarah's upstairs room when he called late that afternoon.

'This is William, my brother, Mr Griffiths. Tom has been taken ill at the farm. His hand's gone septic. Do you think he will be all right?' asked Sarah.

'Well, he's a strong healthy young fellow, isn't he?' said Dafydd, looking doubtful.

'Have you heard of anyone with that?'

'Er, yes. Several. It's common for men to get damaged in the mines with the picks or the trucks, you know, and the conditions down there are wet and foul.'

'Yes. Did they get better?'

'One did.'

'Only one?' asked Sarah aghast.

'Well, some of the others survived.'

'Survived! What do you mean? They must have got better then.'

'Yes, well . . . Yes they did, I suppose.'

'Tell me the truth please, Mr Griffiths.'

'Well, doctor had to amputate, see.'

'Amputate! What, you mean cut their hand off?'

'Yes. Or their arm or their leg, depending.'

'Oh, oh,' wailed Sarah.

'But, mark you, those men weren't strong and healthy like your brother. The mines don't allow that, you know.'

A gurgle made them look down at Willy who had been standing watching them solemnly. His face was puckered up and he slowly opened his mouth and began to cry. Sarah gathered him up but his comforting was interrupted by a knock at the door.

'That will be Mama, Mr Griffiths. If she asks you what I did, don't say anything. Don't breathe a word about ampu . . . whatever it is, will you?' She thrust Willy into his unaccustomed arms and left him feeling unjustly used while she opened the door to Francis Vaughan.

'Oh, no! Not now, please Fran.'

'I've got something to tell you.'

'It will have to wait.'

'No, it's urgent. Who's that upstairs?'

Before she could stop him he had bounded up to look. Sarah rushed up to find him and Dafydd confronting each other across Willy's head with looks of matching amazement.

Vaughan beat a hasty retreat without a word.

'What was *he* doing here?' demanded Dafydd.

'I don't know,' said Sarah irritably.

'You *must* know. Whatever will he think?'

'I honestly don't care, Dafydd. Perhaps that we are clandestinely married and Willy is our offspring,' screamed Sarah, grabbing the blubbering toddler from him.

Dafydd Griffiths was too shocked even to register Sarah's unusually familiar use of his first name. He too fled from the salon.

'There, there, Willy. All the silly men gone,' comforted Sarah, rocking him to and fro. She had never made much time to cuddle her small brothers and sisters and she was surprised to find how mutually comforting it was, holding the unresisting little body tight against her own and rocking gently to and fro in time to the rhythmic sucking of his thumb.

There was soon a timid tap that must certainly be their mother, and Sarah went carefully down the stairs, still holding Willy, to let her in.

'How is he, Mama?'

'He's very feverish and the angry redness is going further up his arm. It were only at his wrist this morning, they say. He didn't even show me, Sarah! He just got up and crept out before I was awake!'

304

'You couldn't have done anything, Mama.'

'I could have stopped him going and he'd be in his own place with me looking after him,' sobbed Eliza.

'They're looking after him well, aren't they?'

'Oh yes. They've got a comfrey poultice on and it's ever so grand, Sarah. He's in a great big room with huge windows and lovely curtains and his bed is beautiful, but it won't make him better any quicker, will it? He's all amuck with sweat, Sarah. His bed clothes is all wet. Just like poor little Bobby were in the workhouse.'

'Stop it, Mama. You mustn't say things like that. Tom is a big strong man.'

'It don't make no difference, dear. Mister Jones was a big strong man. It was his foot. He'd run a fork tine through it and that went septic and he was dead in three days.'

'You mean old Mrs Jones's husband?'

'Aye. I was only a girl when it happened. He was as big a man as Tom. Not so young but not old neither, and they used to say he could lift three grain sacks on to a cart together.'

'I know he'll get better, Mama.'

'I do wish he was at home. They said they'd asked the doctor to come.'

'Well, he'll see he gets better, won't he?'

'I could have made him barley broth.'

'He is certain to have the best in a farm like that.'

'Yes, I s'pose you're right. Rosie will be at his side all the time. They'll look after him better than what I could have,' sniffed Eliza, wiping her face with a piece of drenched rag.

'Oh, not better, Mama, but every bit as well and there will be no problem about paying the doctor. They say he's a very good man they've got at Ridgemont.'

The vision of him wielding a sharp axe on Tom's arm suddenly came into Sarah's mind with blinding clarity and made her shut her eyes.

'I'll get you another handkerchief, Mama. That one's wet.'

Dr Richards called soon after Eliza had gone.

'What do you think, Doctor?' asked Nell Tennant as soon as he came downstairs.

'You're doing all that can be done. Keep the poultice hot and give him these pills every three hours and these ones every four. I've written it on. Keep making him drink even if he doesn't want to. Anything except spirits. Warm barley water will be fine. He's a strong young man. We'll have to hope for the best. Now, if that redness starts moving up his arm faster, send for me. It doesn't matter what time it is. Middle of the night – it doesn't matter. Just send for me.'

'What will that mean?' asked Tennant anxiously.

'Well, I hope it won't come to it.'

'But if it does?'

The doctor looked from one to the other of them.

'Where's your daughter?'

'She's gone back to him.'

He lowered his voice. 'If it does come to a choice between losing the lad or taking his arm off, you know what it's got to be!'

'Oh, Lord forbid!' gasped Nell.

'He's a strong fellow. I think he'll get better. Just remember what I said, though.'

'Yes, yes. We will.'

After he had left, Nell turned tearfully to her husband.

'He's such a fine young man, Robert. It would be *terrible*. Just think of him reaping last harvest time. Oh, Robert, it sounds dreadful, but when the doctor was saying about a choice and what way it would have to go, I can't help wondering if he's right.'

'Of course he is, Nell. You women is too much concerned about bodies. It would be a real shame, but I

306

value that young man for his steadiness and his courage and he'd still have them.'

'Yes, 'course, dear. It would be a terrible shame though. *Him* of all the men I have ever watched reaping.'

She shook her head and Tennant smiled affectionately.

'Us won't say a word of this to Rosie, shall us?' she said.

'No, dear. There's no need yet.'

'Nor his mother. She seemed a very gentle woman.'

'No.'

CHAPTER 50

Divisions in the Vestry

The urgent talk which Francis Vaughan wished to have with Sarah was to acquaint her with what took place at the Select Vestry meeting. He was keen to discuss the implication of this for the business plans which he and Mat had laid in embryo, and Sarah was the only available person who was a party to them.

It was in the taproom parlour of The Swan the previous evening that Rector Devereux had said:

'Gentlemen, this exodus of the poor from the village on to the Heath is becoming quite insupportable. To my knowledge, four families have left over the past six weeks!'

No-one responded immediately, since he had not made clear the grounds on which he considered it 'insupportable'. Eventually William Hall glanced round to see that no-one else was about to speak, and cleared his throat.

'I think we should all value your opinion of the significance of this, Rector,' he said.

'The significance, Mr Hall, is that the village is becoming depopulated and the attendance at church is dropping. The recent Ecclesiastical Census proved most embarrassing. There were only 142 people at the morning service and 233 in the afternoon out of a parish of 1200 souls.'

'Yes, I can see you have a professional worry, but there are no empty cottages to my knowledge – no, I am sure there are none. What has happened has relieved the intolerable overcrowding because, by and large, it is the young, expanding families who have gone, and they were living in their parents' homes.'

'You have a point, sir, but I am the custodian of these people's souls and only one quarter of the parish in church on a Sunday is a deplorable state of heathenism.'

'Heathenism! Oh, a very apt pun, Rector,' chuckled Francis Vaughan.

'I assure you it was quite unintentional,' snapped Devereux, glowering at him.

'Oh, sorry, sir,' murmured Vaughan contritely.

William Hall took no notice of this frivolous exchange. He was becoming warmed to his point now.

'Well, there, Rector! One quarter of the village population you say, and I don't doubt your arithmetic for a moment, but I must beg to point out that a large proportion of the remaining three quarters did indeed attend a place of worship on Sunday. For instance, there are five Quaker families in the parish who all worshipped with myself at the Friends' Meeting House. Not very many, perhaps, but there are certainly ten or twelve families who regularly attend the Methodist Chapel at Mount Pleasant and nearly as many our Aspley chapel, while a large number of those living on the Heath attend the chapel at Hog-Sty-End.

'I believe we should be proud of our . . . I hesitate to

say "God-fearing" – a most inappropriate phrase, let us say "God-loving" little community.' His kindly face beamed round at the generally dubious expressions of his listeners.

Francis Vaughan moved his hands slightly on a sudden impulse to clap the splendid old fellow, but a glance at Devereux's face restrained him from such a provocative act. In fact, as he commented later to Sarah, if that expression truly betokened a control of heaven-hurled thunderbolts, he, Vaughan, would certainly have been struck dead on the spot. The face of the representative of the Anglican Church certainly reflected that of a God of vengeance at this moment.

'A very interesting exposition, Mr Hall,' Devereux almost snarled, 'but one which I fear would leave the Diocesan Committee appalled at the spiritual destitution and the large number of dissenters in the parish.'

Hall flushed crimson and rose to his feet.

'I find it very hard to believe what I hear, Devereux. Can you really find it in your Christian heart to accuse all these good Nonconformists of "spiritual destitution"? I . . . I . . . I am appalled, myself – utterly!'

Devereux's lips twisted angrily but he sat silent with downcast eyes as the old man, trembling and gasping, slowly lowered himself into his seat.

'I'm sure Rector didn't mean it to come out as hard as that, Mr Hall, sir. We must all allow for each other's views, mustn't we,' said Dick Miller soothingly. He was worried for the old man's health.

'Of course we should all be tolerant of each other's views, particularly in the matter of religion, Dick. Yes, indeed,' cried Hall, 'and I am sorry if I appeared to be criticizing the Anglican faith. That was certainly not my intention.' He looked steadily at Devereux, whose eyes were still lowered. Hall continued, 'And while we are talking about the poor going to live on the Heath, I should like to point out that certain landlords, I am sure

I need mention no names, will not let to Nonconformist tenants. I believe, too, that they have the unofficial "blessing", if one may so misuse that word, of the Anglican Church in this matter. Can you blame these people for seeking their own dwelling places, eh?' His tone had become steadily louder and more emotional as he spoke.

The Committee shifted nervously on their seats, but Devereux still didn't speak.

Francis Vaughan looked from one to another of them. The atmosphere was so charged that even he was deterred from trying to relieve it with one of his ever-ready quips.

Hall's face was no longer flushed, but drawn and pale.

'Have you ridden or walked here this evening, Mr Hall?' asked Vaughan in concern.

'Er . . . walked. Yes, walked, Francis.'

'Perhaps you will allow me to bring my chaise round and drive you home. It is of no inconvenience, and I fear you are unwell.'

'I do feel a little tired. I have allowed my feelings to get the better of me, I fear. Perhaps if you don't mind. It is really most kind.'

Vaughan soon returned and helped Hall out with a supporting arm round his shoulders.

Immediately they had gone Devereux drew his papers together and looked up haughtily.

'A most unfortunate outburst,' he said. 'The old gentleman is too emotional. Well, what is to be done, gentlemen? I hesitated to add before our elderly friend that some of these paupers have been taking steps to make affidavits claiming freehold rights to the land.'

'How do you know, sir?' asked Miller.

'I have been informed by a reliable source whom I should prefer not to name.'

'Have they managed it?' demanded Farmer Green in his harsh, flat voice.

'No, not as yet and I have taken steps to suggest to all the local solicitors and attorneys how undesirable it would be in view of it being parish common land.'

'Well, we'd best start evicting them quick before they finds a tame solicitor what you've missed,' said Green.

'Yes, I am afraid there is little alternative now, and the new poor law has saved us burdening the parish poor rate since they seem generally loath to go to the Union workhouse.'

'Where should we start? There's nigh on thirty families up there now,' asked Dudley.

'Well, we had better look to the ones that have been up there the longest and those who never appear in church, I suppose.'

'Do any of them come to church?' queried Miller.

'No, Mr Miller, but there are one or two whom I believe should be made an example of.' Devereux surveyed him with one brow raised quizzically.

'Who are they?' asked Dick Miller slowly.

'The Daltons and Inwoods, perhaps?' suggested the Rector.

Miller nodded, lowering his face from the Rector's gaze. He knew that both families were staunch Methodists and he couldn't approve of this victimization, but as one of the youngest members and lacking Hall's support now, he felt unable to protest.

Vaughan returned at this juncture.

'So, what action have we decided upon?' he asked lightly.

'With regret, we can see no alternative but to start evicting some of these people by way of example, and we trust the others will take note and relinquish their illegitimate misappropriation of the Common,' said Devereux in a careful summary.

'I see! When do we begin, and whom do we employ to do the dastardly deed *this* time?'

Devereux looked at him angrily. He heartily wished they had made such decisions in an appropriately discrete way before Vaughan's return. He did not like or trust him. These Cambridge men were generally unsound, and teachers not of the cloth had a devious propensity for cleverness and a total lack of respect.

'I think we should give the matter serious consideration and not do anything in haste which we might regret.'

Vaughan opened his mouth to add 'like last time', but thought better of it. He was well aware of Devereux's opinion of him and he suspected the matter would be dealt with summarily by Green and Devereux before the committee met again. He wished to know what had happened while he was away. At the door of his house, William Hall had earnestly entreated him to hurry back to the meeting and 'try to stop them evicting those poor wretched people'. Francis Vaughan preferred not to hold strong views himself, since they inevitably proved inconvenient or uncomfortable if not both, but he had grown to dislike Devereux and his autocratic ways. He had to concede the moral victory unanimously to the valiant old Quaker and for his sake he must at least acquaint himself with what was afoot. His eye lit on Dick Miller, the only other member whose opinions might be a shade radical.

As soon as Devereux called the meeting to a close, Vaughan approached Miller jovially.

'Well, Dick! Did you get to the meet on Thursday?'

'Yes, Mr Vaughan. There was some good sport. A pity you missed it!'

'Some of us have to earn our living. We aren't all gentlemen farmers, you know!'

'Ha, ha! That's a tale! Some gentleman farmer, me! No, my only advantage over you is that I can make up hunting time by working longer hours and your young gentlemen wouldn't stand for that.'

'What will you drink, Dick? Why not come over the Square and try something a bit stronger than beer?'

'I ought to be off. *I* have to get up early.'

'No, come on! Walk over to my study. I have just brought up some passably good port. Come and tell me what you think of it. I promise I shan't keep you long.'

CHAPTER 51

Tom

Sarah rose early, put on her walking shoes and set out for Tennant's farm. She had no problem finding it since she had trudged to Ridgemont many times collecting up straw plaits and knew all the farms, although she did not visit them. She tapped on the kitchen door at a quarter to seven and Rosie opened it, pale and red-eyed. She said nothing, but stood aside to let Sarah in. Sarah's mounting alarm was increased at the sight of Dr Richards talking gravely to Mr and Mrs Tennant. Sarah's frightened eyes roved from one to the other, not sure whether she could face up to asking them how Tom was. Richards stopped talking and the three surveyed her bleakly.

'I'm Tom's sister,' Sarah heard herself murmur.

The doctor smiled wanly.

'Well, I am afraid the poison is still moving up his arm slowly and I shall have to come to a serious decision if he gets any worse, but I think, I hope, we can afford to wait just a little longer. I shall return at noon unless he begins to worsen. Should the inflammation increase or should he become delirious you will find me first at Giffords at Husborne Crawley and then at the Manse at Brogborough. If you arrive before me, leave a message and I shall come straight over as soon as I receive it.

'Mrs Tennant, I want you to keep a large pan of water boiling all morning just in case I need it. I may also need a large jug and a ladle and . . . no, don't worry, I am sure you will have the other things I need. The boiling water is most important because there may not be much time.'

'Yes, of course, Dr Richards,' said Nell in a small voice. Rosie ran from the room. Mr Tennant saw the doctor out and Nell Tennant turned to Sarah.

'You'll want to come up and see your brother, my dear?'

'Yes please,' quavered Sarah.

Tom was lying with his eyes closed. His face was ashen, and Sarah was horrified at how small and thin he seemed. He had lost weight alarmingly fast, but the main reason was because she wasn't used to seeing him lying down with his body sunk into a feather bed.

Rosie knelt on the floor holding his left hand.

'It's your sister Sarah come, Tom,' she whispered.

He opened his eyes and turned them, vividly blue, to Sarah, smiling weakly.

'How do you feel, Tom?'

'A bit better, I think.'

'Does your arm hurt very much?'

'Not as much as what it did,' he said. Rosie looked at Sarah, beseeching her to say that he didn't seem very bad.

Sarah tried to think of something to say, but her mind was abjectly blank. Mrs Tennant came in with a jug of warm barley water and a pot, and she and Rosie helped Tom to sit up and have a drink.

He smiled at Sarah. 'Don't look so terrible worried, Sare. It's them that makes me seem worse with all their fussing.'

Sarah didn't know whether to laugh or cry. Two sentences in a row was quite exceptional for Tom. She almost feared it was some terminal clarity of mind advancing.

'Well, your talking seems to be getting better, anyway,' she teased.

'Yeah. That's what Father said when he come. When did he come, Rosie?'

'Last night, Tom.'

'Yeah.'

She stayed a little longer and, when she left, Rosie followed her out into the garden.

'Did me Mam and Father say anything to you 'bout Tom, Miss Ruddock?'

'No.'

'I'se so frightened. What did Dr Richards mean about a serious decision?'

'I d . . . don't know,' lied Sarah. Rosie shot her a searching glance.

'I think they're keeping summat back from me,' she said. 'How do you think he seemed? He ain't that terribly ill, is he? I mean, he ain't going to die or anything, is he?'

'No, Rosie. I am sure Dr Richards won't let him die.'

'Cross yer heart,' begged Rosie.

'Yes, honestly. I am sure he won't die,' said Sarah earnestly, as much for her own reassurance as Rosie's.

She returned to the salon, but she could not concentrate on her work and as noon approached she wandered from the back room to the front, giving incoherent directions to the girls, who couldn't make out what was the matter.

Just after twelve, Eliza, Tize and William called on their way to Ridgemont.

'I'll come with you, Mama,' said Sarah, 'but I think it will be best if Tize and William stay here.'

Eliza looked at her questioningly.

'I've been over this morning and Dr Richards was

there and said he'd come back at noon. It will be too many people if we all go,' she finished lamely.

'How was he?'

'He didn't seem too bad. He was talking.'

Eliza agreed to Sarah's suggestion, and they left Tize and William with the girls who were delighted to stop work and play with them.

The walk to Ridgemont seemed terribly long but, as they approached the farm, Sarah found herself wishing it was longer. It was not just Tom whom she was dreading to face, it was what her mother would do if his arm had been taken off.

They tapped at the door and Mrs Tennant opened it. Sarah closed her eyes momentarily and then forced herself to look straight into Nell Tennant's face.

She was smiling!

'Dr Richards has just gone. The redness has stopped moving up. I know he ain't through it yet but I'm that relieved I feel like dancing, I do,' she blurted out.

Sarah was not prone to spontaneous displays of emotion in front of strangers, but she threw her arms around Nell's neck and then her mother's.

'Oh, I'se so glad,' smiled Eliza, with tears pouring down her cheeks.

They found Tom propped up on pillows, his left hand still held by Rosie, who was looking radiant.

'There, the doctor thinks I shall start to mend,' said Tom brightly.

And mend he did, very rapidly. Nell Tennant declared she had never known any man eat so much, even in the middle of harvesting. She had become so devoted to Tom that he could do no wrong in her eyes and the rest of her family found themselves becoming almost resentful of the cuckoo in their nest. Her affection was returned in full measure and Rosie and Eliza began to feel a little jealous of Nell. But all these feelings were very trivial compared to the universal relief at Tom's

recovery. There were few in this country community
who had not seen the capriciousness of that wanton,
Death.

CHAPTER 52

Sarah Takes Care of Some Urgent Business

As soon as Sarah became certain that Tom would soon
be well, her gaiety and resilience returned and she
upbraided herself for having taken the comparatively
small problems of her life so seriously. It was four days
since Vaughan and Griffiths had come face to face in the
salon and Sarah had seen neither of them since, but a
letter was dropped through her door that afternoon. She
looked with interest at the regular flowing letters of her
name, written on the outside of the folded, wax-sealed
sheet, but she only opened it after Temperance, Ellie
and Grace had gone home.

Dearest Sarah,
　What *were* Dafydd Griffiths and that child doing
in your room? I apologize for my impertinence but
my curiosity remains unabated.
　I should still like to talk to you of that matter I
mentioned. It is now even more urgent.
　Can you meet me at the villa at eight o'clock this
evening? Please try to be there.
　Your ever affectionate, elderly friend,
　　　　　　　　Fran.

Sarah smiled and then laughed. If she were able to
feel as seriously about her momentous decision as she
did the other evening, she would not go but, in her
present state of gay excitement, she would. She even
spent most of the next hour on her toilette and stepped

out of the salon as beautifully apparelled as a diminutive duchess.

Vaughan was already there chatting easily and amicably with Mrs Jones.

'Well yes, Mrs Jones. If it is in as poor a state of repair as you say, it would be better down. How should we dispose of it? Ah, right! Most convenient.

'Good evening, Miss Lacelle. Our redoubtable Mrs Jones was just telling me how hazardous a state the old summer house is in. She says she can arrange for a man to take it down and will undertake to see it is disposed of too.' Mrs Jones grinned gappily at Sarah.

'Oh, that sounds good, Mrs Jones.' Sarah emphasized the word 'good' and looked hard at the old lady.

'We have some business to discuss in Dr Crisp's study, Mrs Jones. Perhaps you will bring us some coffee in an hour?' asked Vaughan.

'Coffee!' exclaimed the old lady doubtfully. It was a mysteriously exotic drink to her.

'Tea will do,' said Sarah.

'Oh yes. I can make yer some tea, Ma'am.'

'Well, Sarah?' smiled Fran as he closed the study door and stood leaning against it. His eloquent eyes slowly appraised her hair, her face and each detail of her figure-flattering cream dress. She meekly submitted, wondering again how he charmed her into accepting him with such unquestioning confidence.

'Well, Fran, what is this urgent business?' she said at last.

'It's all about the Heath, and the Select Vestry wanting to evict squatters and the squatters wanting to get affidavits sworn. That is what it is all about in a nutshell and it doesn't seem nearly as urgent now as it did just before you came, my love.' He stepped towards her.

'No, Fran! We are here to talk about business and that is what we shall do.'

318

'But why did you come looking so supremely *un*businesslike?'

Sarah smiled wryly. Yes, why had she; why indeed had she? she asked herself.

'The squatters need a solicitor and a witness,' she reminded him.

'Yes, and do you think it is in our interest to get these for them?'

'Undoubtedly. They can't be evicted then and they can sell their land to you and Dr Crisp.'

'Exactly the direction in which my mind was moving. But I am a member of the Select Vestry.'

'Dr Crisp and I are not.'

'Great minds *do* think alike, Sarah.'

'When are they going to start evicting?'

'Quite soon, I fear.'

'How soon?'

'Difficult to say, because Devereux and Green may arrange it between them.'

'Green will try to get his men to do it and I know some of them.'

'You do, do you? What a useful ally you are, Sarah.'

'Yes, I shall send a message through Temperance. She lives near one of them. I can call round and ask her to see that he gets it before he goes to work tomorrow, if you don't keep me too late, Fran.'

'Now why should I do that?'

'You won't, never fear. I was only teasing.'

'You are so good at that in every conceivable way.'

'Where shall you get the solicitor? I don't think one from Woburn is a good idea. It is too close.'

'You seem to have an extraordinarily powerful intuition or else some very good spies. Mat was planning to come down on Sunday. I wonder if he could not get down on Saturday or even Friday and bring one with him?'

'Yes! Can't you write to him? You could even send it

by one of the night mail coaches at Woburn,' urged Sarah.

'You *have* taken the urgency of this matter to heart, Sarah,' said Vaughan in surprise.

'Well, you will have lost all chance of that land once they are evicted,' said Sarah, trying hard to sound dispassionate.

'Yes, indeed.'

'There are paper and pens and sealing-wax in this desk,' she said, laying them out ready for him.

Vaughan sat down and began to write with Sarah watching over his shoulder. He finished the letter, sanded it and she passed him a candle for the wax, which he impressed with his signet ring. Then he swiftly slipped his arm round her waist and drew her gently on to his knee.

'Have I not obeyed all my instructions promptly and correctly, little business woman?' Sarah nodded, a strange preoccupied smile hovering on her lips.

'Why are you looking so worried then, dear?' He smoothed out the gathering creases between her brows with his finger tip. She shrugged her shoulders and smiled sadly at him.

'Don't you think I deserve a kiss?' She bent forward obediently and kissed his cheek, but he moved and held his lips to hers, which she did not resist.

Mrs Jones's knock interrupted them and Sarah rose swiftly, trying to compose herself before she was exposed to beady scrutiny. Fran slowly opened the door.

'The only thing that worries me now,' he said as they drank their tea, 'is how we contact the potential affidavit-swearers on the Heath.'

'I think I can probably arrange that,' said Sarah.

'Really?'

'Yes, but where shall it be done. You must not be seen to be involved, Fran. We need a place that the solicitor and the men can reach without drawing attention to themselves.'

'I wonder whether the chapel at Hog-Sty-End might suit? They plan to start by evicting the squatters that have been there the longest, like Nursall and then the Methodists, like Dalton and Inwood.'

Vaughan gazed at Sarah in surprise. She had risen and was standing with her fists and teeth clenched and her huge glittering eyes fixed upon his face.

'Sarah?'

'They are despicable cowards,' she cried.

'Er, yes. But it doesn't help to become emotional, my dear. Poor old Hall nearly collapsed in the meeting the other night because he got so upset about it.'

'He's a very brave old gentleman. I hope you supported him, Fran?'

'I took him home.' Vaughan was quite bewildered by Sarah's emotional outburst.

'Fran!'

'Yes, dear.'

'You must saddle your horse and ride to Woburn with that letter, while I go and see Temperance before she's gone to bed. In fact, I believe it is too late. I shall have to get up very early in the morning.'

'Yes. Just one more kiss to help me on my way.'

CHAPTER 53

Sarah Concludes Some Business Arrangements

It took Dr Crisp over a week to organize a solicitor, and on the Saturday that the affidavits were sworn in the little chapel at Hog-Sty-End, Sarah received a note from him inviting her to call at the villa that evening. He reassured her that Mrs Jones would be in residence, for propriety's sake, and Sarah happily expected that Fran would be too, but she was disappointed in this.

'Good evening, Miss Lacelle. I am so glad you could come,' welcomed Dr Crisp.

'Good evening, Dr Crisp. It is so kind of you to invite me.'

She stood for a moment in the middle of the moss green rug, complacently viewing the softly lit drawing-room, with its draped rose pink curtains and regency furniture.

'This is my good friend and solicitor, Mr Place, who has been kind enough to travel this distance to help me with a legal matter today.'

'Good evening, Mr Place. I trust your business was successfully concluded?'

'Yes, indeed, so far as we have got, it has gone remarkably smoothly. The only thing which has prevented us from completing the task is the unexpectedly large number of applicants for my services, is it not, Dr Crisp?'

'Yes. I really had no idea that there were so many settlers on this piece of land,' said Crisp.

'Oh, you mean people who have lived on the Heath so long that they wish to swear affidavits?' enquired Sarah, wide-eyed.

'Well, yes; and then there is the complication of the tortuous nature of the county boundary, so one needs to have each claim supported by a good map to decide who resides in Bedfordshire and who in Buckinghamshire,' explained Place.

'Had you got a good map?' asked Sarah keenly.

'Yes, fortunately Dr Crisp's friend had forewarned us of this difficulty so I visited the Ordnance Office and purchased several. But I believe, Dr Crisp, that if we wish to have no possibility of ambiguity, it would be wise to attach a copy of the relevant piece of the map to each affidavit.'

'Yes, but that will take time and there are still so many to do.'

'I think it would certainly be worthwhile because one should try to avoid any future doubt about this,' said Sarah eagerly. Crisp looked at her enquiringly.

'Yes, it was fortunate that my friend Mr Vaughan was so well informed, but he did not prepare us for eighteen affidavits to be sworn,' said Crisp.

'Eighteen!' declared Sarah in genuine surprise. 'That is a lot of people to have been living on the Heath for so long.'

'Well, to be fair,' said Place, 'there were really only four of them, but the cunning fellows had thrown up banks around just about the entire Bedfordshire part and quite a lot of Buckinghamshire as well. That rather engaging character Henry Nursall must have been extraordinarily energetic in his youth and Mr Lee's grandfather must have been an elderly prodigy, indeed.'

'Mr Lee's grandfather?' prompted Sarah.

'Yes. Do you realize, Dr Crisp, that since he has been dead these ten years and was an octogenarian when he died, he must have been carrying out positively Herculean tasks of banking in his late seventies!'

'I told you what an extraordinarily healthy place this was, did I not?' cried Dr Crisp, rubbing his hands gleefully. 'But I am relieved it was not I swearing on the Holy Bible to these stupendous feats of physical prowess nor the ensuing complexities of bartering pieces of land through such tortuous chains of relatives by blood or marriage. I even confess to a suspicion that, when I meet my Maker, Henry Nursall for one, will not be in evidence up there.'

Sarah began to giggle and had to resort to her pocket handkerchief to turn her wild hilarity into a sneeze.

'Oh dear, I do hope you have not got a cold coming, Miss Lacelle,' said Place with concern.

'No . . . it was only brought on by my amusement at

Dr Crisp's clever way of joking.' Crisp smiled indulgently at her.

'Well, I can only say that I did not understand the joke at all and I beg Dr Crisp to deal discreetly with moral issues in which I am professionally involved.'

'Oh, I am sorry. Do forgive my inappropriate sense of humour, for that, I assure you, was all it was,' said Crisp.

Sarah could well imagine Fran gracefully extricating himself from such a predicament but Crisp revealed no grace at all. He rescinded his implication with cold cynicism and turned to Sarah.

'Talking of "discretion", or perhaps I mean "indiscretion", Miss Lacelle, one of the reasons that I invited you here this evening was to remind you that Mr Vaughan is in a distinctly delicate situation, placed as he is on the Select Vestry Committee. Now when I suddenly had the idea that I might buy some property here, I didn't for a moment foresee that it might perhaps happen so swiftly, else I should have been more discreet myself.'

'Please do not be uneasy on my behalf, Dr Crisp. I appreciate the entire position and shall be most scrupulous to avoid letting fall any incriminating connection between Mr Vaughan and the affidavits.'

'Very good. I can tell that Mr Vaughan has been keeping you well informed,' said Crisp grimly, making it plain that he considered *that* an error of judgement too.

'And what was the other reason?' asked Sarah mischievously.

'The other reason?'

'That you invited me here this evening?'

'Oh . . . well . . . to enjoy your company of course, and I did wonder whether you had given any more thoughts to that suggestion that you should reside here as a housekeeper. The duties would be quite light, because I should not be here very much. I have *very* heavy commitments in London, of course.' He inclined his balding head and stroked his ginger whiskers in a pompously contrived manner.

'Yes,' said Sarah slowly. 'I have considered it and the problems it raises.'

'Problems?'

'Well, for instance, it would clearly be improper for me to live here alone.'

'Perhaps Mrs Jones might be persuaded to continue her duties?'

'Yes indeed, and if she would, that should be a satisfactory solution. Her duties would increase some-what, of course,' said Sarah.

'Why is that? I thought perhaps you would relieve her of some.'

'Oh no. You are only asking me to supervise and ensure that all the arrangements are to the liking of you and your guests, Dr Crisp. My living here all the time and the increased level of comfort you require is bound to make more work for Mrs Jones.' Sarah cast a knowing glance in the direction of the door as she was speaking. She could well imagine the crouching form of the old lady listening outside.

'And the other matter is the desirability of making a formal agreement on the level of comfort which you wish me to maintain and how much money I shall require to do it. I am sure a good business gentleman like yourself would be eager to have such things made quite clear at the start.'

'Er yes, indeed, and we could even call upon Mr Place here to draw up a simple agreement if you should like that.'

Sarah smiled in acquiescence, while Dr Crisp tried to decide whether this was what he wanted in order to protect his purse or whether he preferred a much more informal arrangement in which he took as much as he could get and gave as little as he could manage to in return. A steady look at Sarah's firm bearing and determinedly raised chin decided him in favour of a formal arrangement.

'Right, would you be able to do that for me, Mr Place?'

'Oh yes, it should not prove difficult, with the co-operation of both parties,' laughed Place.

It proved more difficult than he had imagined, and occupied the following two hours during which time Sarah used a combination of sweet cajolery and hard bargaining to extract a generous monthly settlement with which to pay all the household expenses and free board and lodging for herself, in return for a clearly defined list of duties. The duty about which she had the most misgivings was not stipulated, of course, although she caught Crisp opening his mouth at an appropriate moment as if he was tempted to commit this also to paper.

'Surely there is nothing more you wish to add, Dr Crisp? I assure you that providing your part of the agreement is met, you can depend upon my goodwill and co-operation.'

'Oh yes, of course.' Crisp surveyed her with some alarm. The truth of Fran's assertion that Sarah was an astute businesswoman had suddenly struck him very forcibly.

Mr Place looked from one to the other in mild amazement. He had not expected to have the pleasure of seeing Dr Crisp meet his match, and had certainly not expected it to be in the shape of a very small and young woman.

CHAPTER 54

Village News

Sarah did not feel as elated as she knew she should, on her return from Dr Crisp's. She had intended to settle for nothing less than she had done, but she found an errant part of herself perversely regretting her own success. If Crisp had stood firm and refused her terms, she should have stayed in the salon or found more modest accommodation, but what would she have achieved? She would certainly not have been able to see more of Fran. The villa was the only place she could do that, she reminded herself. On the other hand, it was far from sensible to spend more time in that way, as she had told herself so often. It boded nothing but wretchedness; certain wretchedness for her and possible wretchedness for Fran. Ah, perhaps she was on the trail of her dissatisfaction. How much did Fran care for her? Was she just a toy which he happily lent to his friend with a most distressing generosity? Did he have any qualms at all about this arrangement he had seemed pleased to make for her? It was the answer to these questions which was vexing her so much.

Vaughan called quite late on Sunday evening.

'Hallo Sarah, my dear. Shall we go upstairs?' She led the way and he kissed her affectionately at the stair top. Still holding her, he said:

'I understand from Mat that you have arranged to go to the villa?'

'Yes!' She waited sadly for his response, wondering whether he knew the formality of the arrangement.

'When will you move?'

'Tuesday evening, perhaps.'

'Shall I go up to the villa to help you?'

'I have very little except my clothes and I thought I would ask Temperance and Ellie to help me carry those up, but, so long as you keep out of sight, it would be very nice to be welcomed by someone as well as Mrs Jones.'

He nodded.

'Well, Fran. You seem grave. I thought this was what you wanted?'

'Yes. I suppose so. It will be pleasant for you to have more room and such gracious surroundings.'

'Those things do not necessarily bring happiness.'

'No. But we shall be able to see more of each other.'

'Shall we? Is that sensible?'

'No, of course it's not, but we do not seem to let that get in our way. Well, I don't, anyway. Perhaps you are trying to tell me that I should, Sarah?'

'Oh, who am I to give advice?' retorted Sarah bitterly.

'I have become obsessed by you, my love. I don't think I can give you up.'

'But you don't mind sharing me with your friend?' flared Sarah.

'Oh don't. Don't torture me, Sarah! That is precisely what I *do* mind.'

'You have never shown it.'

'How could I. I couldn't ask you to make a sacrifice for me when I had nothing to offer in return!'

Sarah buried her face in his waistcoat and sobbed.

'Perhaps I don't have to share you in that way,' he ventured. 'Perhaps you can fulfil your obligations to Mat just short of that?'

'No. Not now. I have undertaken to satisfy him. If you had made your feelings plain before, I should have made no agreement with him.'

'You speak as if you were bound by a written contract.'

'I am.'

'Oh no, Sarah! Surely even Mat would not have required that?' cried Vaughan in horror.

'It was quite mutually agreed and I can only go back on my word by withdrawing altogether. Remember, this started as your idea, Fran.'

'Oh, I know, my darling, but I wasn't really in love with you then.'

Sarah opened her mouth to say that she would change her mind and then she thought of Tom.

'No, Fran. It had better stay as it is until other sacrifices can be made.'

'What do you mean, Sarah?'

'Never mind.'

'I have brought you a small gift.'

'Oh, let me see it!'

He drew a folded piece of new hide from his coat pocket. It was ox-blood red, soft and supple, but quite thick and strong.

'That will allow you to do more justice to your giant, dear.'

'My giant, Fran?' asked Sarah, searching his face anxiously.

'Why, the enormous pair of gloves you were making.'

'Oh, darling man!' laughed Sarah. 'Thank you very much.'

'And you notice I am not jealous enough to ask any more about him.'

'Yes. I am sorry about that. I should like you to be a little jealous because he is very handsome.'

'Well, reward my tolerance and good nature, anyway.'

Sarah moved into the villa and gave Mrs Jones a substantial increase in her wage.

To Theresa Vaughan's distress, her husband began to spend more and more of his leisure riding about the countryside visiting friends.

Dr Crisp found himself engaged a great deal writing

letters to medical journals, extolling the virtues of the healthy climate and natural beauty of Aspley Guise. He also published a pamphlet, at his own expense, entitled:

On the Salubrity of Aspley Guise in the county of Bedfordshire afforded by the Felicitous Concurrence of Topographical and Climatological Features which Render it Worthy of the Attention of all Invalids and Convalescents whose Fragility of Health or Pocket Prevent them Seeking the Celebrated Watering Places of the Continent.

In this he remarked that: 'The balminess of the air and celestial purity of the water refreshing the fragrant groves of pine trees luxuriating on miniature alpine hillocks which afford the weak-chested exactly the correct challenge for gentle exercise so recommended by the modern methods of treatment, are guaranteed to evoke perfect peaceful harmony between the body and spirit.'

When he rested from the labour of authoring such prodigious progeny, he found his new domestic arrangements completely to his satisfaction.

One of the members of the village, however, was having a more frustrating time and that was Farmer Green. Devereux had agreed that if he undertook to organize the evictions on the Heath, any expense incurred would be met by the parish and Green could salvage the confiscated buildings. Towards the end of January, a day was set for the work and the only decision to be made was where it should begin. Green had come to distrust Harry Nursall's gossipy innocence.

'That man ain't as simple as he makes out,' he said to his wife one dinner time.

'Neow, you're probably right, because he is a clever builder and carpenter, ain't he? Skill like that don't usually go with stupidness.' Her husband nodded in agreement.

'I think we'll let Nursall be for the moment. Us'll start with them Dissenters.'

'Start what?'

'Evicting, that's what. Only don't you breathe a word of it.'

'Do I usually go around gossiping?' cried his wife indignantly.

On the day agreed upon, Green found four of his six men unaccountably off sick. And on the second occasion, the picks and crowbars had all mysteriously been misplaced.

The following week, Devereux received a letter from the Reverend Jenkins at Wavendon enquiring whether there was any truth in the rumour that Aspley planned to start evicting on the Heath again, so it was decided to postpone their activities for the time being.

Green's fury increased with each frustration, and he eventually resorted to offering each man an extra five shillings. Since none of them earned more than eight shillings a week in the winter, this was an incentive which none of their fellow villagers would blame them too much for accepting, but still they held back, with various excuses.

Vaughan innocently enquired about the evictions at each Vestry meeting but was answered evasively and had to be satisfied with black looks from Devereux and Green. He was surprised to learn more about Green's setbacks from Sarah.

'I am never quite sure whether being a ladies' dressmaker affords you exceptional patronage over the village gossip (which I doubt) or whether you have hidden spies of whom I am quite unaware.'

'Both are true, Fran,' answered Sarah gaily. 'I employ four local girls to sew and you remember that one of Green's men lives near Temperance.'

'Yes, but there seems to be no end to your sphere of influence, my dear. How, for instance, have you so effectively tamed that diabolical old . . .'

'Sh . . . sh!' hissed Sarah, pointing vehemently at the door which was ajar.

'Oh no! You mean we are unable to have a private conversation now?' whispered Vaughan.

'Well, only if you accept Mrs Jones as being a party to it but, as you say, I have her well under control at the moment.'

Vaughan groaned. 'Does she know *all* about us?'

'Undoubtedly.'

'I shall not relish being blackmailed.'

'That is a risk a respected member of the local gentry accepts when he behaves as badly as you, my love.'

Fran sighed and rose to close the door, peeping round it first, but there was no-one in sight.

'Come and comfort me, my darling. After all, what have I to lose now?'

CHAPTER 55

A Great Deal of Wind, Love and a Little Envy

March was soon coming in like a lion, with high gusting winds which tossed and chased the winter debris of broken shutters and branches up and down the High Street and round the Square at Aspley. Ladies crept out of their doors, holding their hats to their heads and, in frustrated fury, the wind wrapped their skirts tightly round their legs like swaddling bands. Sarah, battling down Woburn Lane with Mrs Jones's pattens clacking along in her wake, quite expected to find herself clutching at the old lady's ankles to prevent her being swept aloft.

'It's blowing fit ter turn a donkey insides out,' shrieked Mrs Jones.

'Fit to what?' Sarah shouted back.

'Fit ter . . .' Her words rose to join the plaintive cawing of the storm-tossed rooks.

On the Heath, the Duke's pine plantations looked as if a company of giants had crashed through, felling long swathes like children rampaging through a field of standing wheat. The wild nights with squalls of lashing sleet and rain were a hard test for the little wooden cottages, and not many escaped damage.

'Oh deary me,' wailed Mary Nursall one morning, 'I knew summat was happening when I dreamt I was being shipwrecked on a great big tossing boat, Harry.'

'Aye, still we might have woked up trundling along the turnpike with a mail coach pole through our bedroom. All we've got to do is push the ol' coach back again and mend the kitchen roof. Lucky that birch tree was where it was.'

'What do you think will have happened to the Whites' hut? You were saying what it was only held together by the chapel's Sunday prayers.'

'I should think the evictors could not have served them worse. I'll go down and see as soon as we have straightened up here.'

'Bring them back with you, Harry, if they ain't got much left.'

The way to Ridgemont was closed to traffic for three days while two gigantic beech trees were sawn up. They had fallen from the high churchyard at Husborne Crawley right across the road as it passed over the brow of the hill. The stocky church tower, built of beautiful olive green sandstone, brooded stoically over the ravages of yet another inclement early spring, and down in the fields a couple of miles away, the old farmhouse stood equally firm, despite the clattering of tree branches against its windows.

It had taken Tom every bit of this time to regain sufficient strength to do a full day's work and he was still alarmed at how much heavier a sack of wheat was and how much farther it seemed to cross the forty-acre than it had before.

'Don't you worry, man. You expect too much of yourself because you don't remember how bad you was, like we do,' consoled Farmer Tennant. 'Why, you're doing more than many a fit fellow already. Come hay-making you'll be as strong as you ever were!'

''Ope so,' sighed Tom.

'Are you going on with that fuller's earth pit?'

'Yeah. I'll start whenever you can spare me, sir.'

'Ha. Some fellows can't be put down,' said Tennant grumpily.

'Me sister Sarah has made me gloves. I've got them here in me pocket.'

Tom proudly drew out the soft red gloves and gave them to Tennant to examine.

'She's a clever young lady, your sister. They ought to look after your hands all right. Talking of young ladies, Tom. Have you and Rosie made any plans?'

'Plans, sir?'

'Well, you've bin thrown uncommonly close these last few weeks, ain't you?' Tom blushed deeply and hung his head. Eventually he said:

'I'se very fond of her, sir.'

'Aye. She's very fond of you.' Tom raised his eyes swiftly to scan the farmer's face.

'Might you . . . p'raps . . . if I made a thing of this pit . . . sir?' stammered Tom.

'I might indeed, Tom. And Nell and I were only saying last night that we might get more sense and work out of the pair of you if you was wed!

'Now, don't say as how I've spoken to you. Nell won't like it so well if it don't seem like her idea, but I know your worth now, Tom, and it's fair wearing me down to see the pair of you so uncomfortable.'

Tom's face was a study in radiant perplexity.

He laughed. He blushed. He picked up a stone and

threw it accurately at a gate post and when Tennant extended his hand, he nearly lifted the laughing farmer off his feet.

'One thing I can guarantee about you as a son-in-law, Tom, is that your chattering will never get on me nerves.'

'Wh . . . wh . . . what shall I do?' begged Tom.

'Oh no. I ain't a-going to tell you *that*, son, but you could try talking to Rosie for a start.'

Tennant watched Tom's fleeing figure and remembered with a sharp pang that it was exactly as he had watched him go the day before he was taken ill. He was not a church-going man, but he muttered a few words of gratitude to any God who might be listening.

Rosie and Tom were granted the rest of the day free and they set off to see the progress on the fallen trees and to visit Sarah and then Tom's parents. Such was their change in expectation that they held hands as they waved goodbye to Rosie's parents and they were soon buffeting their way up Crawley Hill with their arms round each other's waists.

Sarah was not particularly busy in the shop and she welcomed them in, immediately noticing the radiant happiness in their faces. She took them upstairs.

'Well, sit down there, do!' she said, a trifle impatient with their love-lorn awkwardness, 'and tell me all the news.'

They looked at each other and smiled and blushed.

'Oh, Rosie, please! Put me out of my misery. I know Tom won't,' pleaded Sarah.

'Me mam and father says we may wed in May!' She smiled shyly at Sarah.

'Oh that is wonderful! I am so happy for you both.' And she was, really, apart from a nasty little worm which murmured: 'Young love, ha! Innocence, ha! It's so easy for them, you see.'

'What will you do about Tidbury, Tom?'

'I shall start again as soon as Mr Tennant can spare me.'

'Don't forget to wear your gloves.'

'No. I'se got them in me pocket.' He drew them out proudly again.

'I've got some good news for you too, Tom, only don't tell anyone, will you?' She looked hard at Rosie, who nodded vigorously.

'I shan't tell, Miss Ruddock.'

'I'm not living here now. I am a part-time housekeeper for a man called Dr Crisp who has just bought the Browns' old villa up Woburn Lane. You know which one, don't you, Tom?'

'Yeah,' said Tom, wide-eyed.

'Well, there was an old summer house in the garden that's been pulled down and I've got all the boarding stacked up waiting for you to fetch it.'

Tom nodded his gratitude.

'And something else that will be very useful for you soon, Tom. I've got my own pony and trap. The pony is called "Dobs" and seems quite placid, only he's rather small and light, unfortunately, but he's bound to be some use. You must look him over when you come for the boarding.'

Sarah's eager smile began to fade as she saw Tom's face darkening.

'What's wrong, Tom?' He lowered his eyes and shrugged.

'Well?' she demanded.

'Just, I was thinking as it weren't really yours to lend, and what you'd done for this doctor,' muttered Tom.

'What do you mean, "what I've done for this doctor"! He is letting me live in his house in return for me looking after it when he is away, as he is most of the time. The pony does not belong to Dr Crisp. It was a present from one of his friends to me!' flared Sarah.

Tom raised his brow questioningly.

'And why should he not give me a pony to go with Dr Crisp's trap when he is a rich man and knows how useful it will be for my work? Why, eh, Tom? Why do you always think so badly of me?' Sarah's eyes were full of tears.

'Tom!' cried Rosie indignantly. 'I never knew you could be so unkind.' Tom leapt to his feet, looking from one to the other of them.

'Tom, I'm sorry. You always set me off, and you and Rosie were so happy when you came. Please forget what I said. Just come for the planking if you want it.'

Sarah dabbed at her eyes. 'I'm sorry, Rosie.'

'It don't matter. It weren't your fault.'

'It wasn't Tom's either. We always quarrel now.'

CHAPTER 56

Vaughan Finds Ladies Hard to Please

'You aren't going out tonight, are you, dear?' inquired Theresa Vaughan plaintively.

'I've got to. It's the Select Vestry meeting at seven. I did tell you. Don't you remember, dear.'

Vaughan's wife sighed.

'Even those meetings seem to keep you later than they used to.'

'Well, I suppose we have more business to discuss in the winter.'

'Do get home as soon as you can, please.'

'Have you something you want to discuss with me?'

'Do I need to have?' cried Theresa. 'Really, you will be asking me to make appointments to speak to you, like the boys' parents, soon!' Vaughan looked up from his book in surprise. Theresa's face was flushed and pouting, making it much more interesting than usual.

337

'I *am* sorry, my dear. You seem to feel I have been neglecting you lately.' He rose, took her in his arms and kissed her.

'Oh, Francis. Whatever is the matter?' she gasped. 'You haven't kissed me like that for . . . for . . . well, hardly ever.'

'I am sorry. I was only trying to atone,' he said helplessly.

'You don't have to apologize. It's just that I am not used to you behaving like that.'

'Ladies are very difficult to please,' he grumbled as he left the room to get his hat and coat.

Theresa was not a stupid woman, but she was innocent and unimaginative, so that right up to that moment she had not been able to say why she was uneasy about her husband's frequent absences. She still worshipped him, as she always had, in her undemonstrative way and he still treated her, as he always had, kindly but absent-mindedly as if she were a small child. He was spending more time visiting his friends, but he had always been popular and she knew he found her boring. It was only when he suddenly kissed her in that well-practised, passionate way, as if tossing her a sweet-meat, that she knew she had a rival.

She sank into her chair and gazed unseeingly at the fire. What should she do? What *did* a woman do when she knew her husband was unfaithful? Confide in a friend and ask advice, perhaps? Beatrice? Oh no, she could never bring herself to confess to Beatrice. She supposed she should try to find out who her rival was. Beatrice! Oh *no*, surely not! But who else? She was nearby, beautiful, elegant, poised. He had frequently said how he admired her dresses, her tastes, her manner, her tea. Who else *could* it be but Beatrice?

Theresa sat up straight, bristling with indignation. Her best friend! The wife of a clergyman. Someone whose conduct should be unimpeachable. Really! Theresa paused, surprised at her own reaction. She somehow expected she would crumple up against such a challenge but here she was full of fighting indignation!

Whatever would Rector Devereux say when he found out, and find out he would, Theresa would see to that! She smiled. He, who had always rendered her speechless with nervousness whenever she was in the same room with him, suddenly presented himself to her as a champion.

Theresa's champion was at that moment presiding uncomfortably over the Vestry meeting at The Swan. Vaughan, the insufferable, was just asking his usual tactless question.

'Well, still no evictions on the Heath! Have we dropped this plan?'

Green glowered at him, too.

'No, not at all, Mr Vaughan. We have merely been waiting for the most propitious moment,' said Devereux smoothly.

'I should think it might be now!' ventured Dudley. 'The state of those hovels after these gales should make the job easy.'

'What do you think, Green?' asked Devereux.

'I am ready to get it done anytime.'

'You have the equipment and the men all raring to go, then?' inquired Vaughan provocatively.

'Yes,' snarled Green.

'Well, shall we say the day after tomorrow, and I shall ride over to Woburn to warn the Master at the Union workhouse. How many people will they have to accommodate?'

'The Daltons, that's four children. The Inwoods have six,' counted Green.

'The Nursalls; there's only the two of them,' said Vaughan helpfully.

Green shot him an angry look. He was coming to dislike the man profoundly. He seemed to have an uncanny knack of raising precisely the things that were least comfortable for everyone.

'The Ruddocks. That's only two children now,' said Green nastily.

After a bit more discussion Vaughan rose.

'I *am* sorry gentlemen, but I have a rather urgent commitment, if you will excuse me. I hope you will not need my presence further?' He beamed round amicably and was amused to see the look of satisfaction on Green's face.

As soon as he left The Swan he turned away from home and stepped briskly up Woburn Lane.

'Oh dear. I do believe I have another lady feeling low-spirited!' smiled Vaughan ruefully as he gazed into Sarah's troubled eyes.

'Another?' she queried.

'Yes. Theresa is feeling neglected,' sighed Vaughan.

'Do you think she knows about us?'

'No, of course not. But I mustn't spend quite so much time here, darling. I have left the Vestry meeting so that I could talk to you and get home early.'

'What has happened there, then?' asked Sarah dejectedly.

'They will try to evict the Daltons, the Inwoods, the Nursalls and the Ruddocks on Thursday. Devereux is riding over to warn the Union tomorrow. Perhaps we should warn the families?'

'Leave that to me,' said Sarah grimly.

'Now, just tell me what is wrong with this little lady. Why so pale and dejected?'

'Oh, I had a quarrel this afternoon.'

'Who with?'

'No-one you know.'

'About business?'

'No.'

'What about? Tell me, my kitten. I must share in your

340

woes, as well.' He pursed his lips and tried to look woeful.

'Oh – you silly man. Do stop,' smiled Sarah.

'Tell me!' he insisted.

'Well, if you must know, it was my giant who I quarrelled with,' she teased.

'Was he not pleased with his gloves?'

'Oh yes, but he was cross about you giving me the leather.'

'Oh, what ingratitude when I was so generous towards him.'

'Yes it was, wasn't it. I wonder why you do give me pieces of leather and ponies, Fran?'

'Only one of each, love. I think I do it out of an abject desire to give you a material token of my love, knowing that there is nothing that you would really value that it is possible for me to give you. There. Self-appeasement, if you *really* want me to be serious!'

Sarah looked even sadder.

'Isn't it more cheering for me to be silly?' he asked.

'Yes! Let's never think about us. Love me, Fran, please.'

CHAPTER 57

Conversation Pieces on the Heath

On Wednesday night the wind suddenly dropped and Thursday morning dawned fair and mild. The proverbial lamb seemed to have chased away the lion and the field at the bottom of Tidbury was full of real ones who could at last leave the shelter of their mothers' sides and discover life in a friendlier aspect. They ventured away in jerky spurts on their long, knobbly-kneed legs, their alert little faces full of excited curiosity. The older ones attempted some standing jumps and paused, delighted with their ability, before scampering away to play 'King of the Castle' on a little knoll. Harry Nursall smiled as he watched them butt each other down and wondered for about the sixty-fifth time how such lively little creatures could mature into stolid, grass-bound sheep. He then sighed, knocked out his morning pipe against the gate post and turned back to the Heath with a purposeful stride.

Half an hour later the evictors arrived. There were only two of Green's men, the other three were co-opted from the Woburn Union workhouse, and all five looked reluctant. Green, on his horse, followed a short distance behind as if herding them on and, bringing up the rear of the uncomfortable little procession, was a carrier with a donkey cart.

'We'll start here,' shouted Green, indicating the Daltons' cottage.

Jack Dalton was already standing, arms folded, at his door. The faces of his frightened children peeped out from behind him and his wife looked out through the window.

'Dalton!' shouted Green, 'this land is parish property and we are here to turn you off it. You can have ten minutes to remove your things to this cart what will take your family to the workhouse.'

'I reckon you are wrong, Farmer Green. This land belongs to me. I bought it off Harry Nursall.'

'It weren't Harry Nursall's to sell, as well you know,' snapped Green.

'Oh yes it were. I have it all written down here,' said Dalton, waving his affidavit.

'I ain't interested in your bits of paper. Are you going to move your stuff or shall we pull the place down over it?'

'Don't you lay a finger on their place,' shouted John

Ruddock's voice. Green turned to find John and Harry Nursall standing side by side with folded arms.

'Ha! Pity you ain't got any work again, Ruddock. You'd best start getting your stuff out too. It's your turn next.'

John reddened and stepped forward with his fists up.

'Don't, John!' warned Harry. 'He can't do nothing.'

'That's just where you're wrong, Nursall. I have eviction orders here for the lot of you.'

'If Jack Dalton's bit of paper ain't worth looking at, yours certainly ain't,' said Harry calmly.

'Let's have a look at yer precious bit of paper then. Bring it here, Dalton.'

Dalton obediently walked across to Green and handed him up the affidavit.

'Ah, no. You don't take me in with this. It has ter be properly witnessed and signed and Nursall had no right to the land anyway. Day wouldn't do one for him. It ain't worth *that*!' Green tore it into four pieces and tossed them away.

'Get them pick-axes to work! Get the door down and the shutters off!'

Dalton ran back to the door of his house, pale with terror.

'What are you waiting for,' snarled Green to his men.

As they moved towards the hut, about twelve more men stepped out from the surrounding bushes and silently took up positions round Green and his men, some with their hands in their pockets, some with arms folded.

'This is your doing, Nursall! Obstructing the law it's called. You'll regret it. You'll regret it!' He turned his horse roughly, hit it smartly on the haunches and careered away through the bushes. The carrier whipped his donkey into a trot and Green's men shouldered their picks and scrambled away as fast as they could, followed by jubilant jeers.

The crowd of men, women and children who had appeared from nowhere gathered round Harry and John, uncertain whether they had really won the day or only the first round.

'What about me affidavit?' cried Dalton in anguish.

'Here are the pieces, Jack. You can stick them together,' comforted one of his neighbours.

'It don't matter anyways, because it's all on mine,' said Harry.

'He sounded as if he's coming back to wreck your place, Harry. That's for sure,' said Tom Butcher.

'Aye, and I'm not giving any of them me affidavit. I shall produce it in front of proper witnesses and then they'll have ter put their tails between their legs,' said Harry truculently.

'Will it work, Harry?' asked Mary.

'Aye. We've still got Dr Crisp, love. I don't relish doing business with him, but as long as we make certain he thinks we're on his side.'

'How do yer stop them pulling yer place down? We'd best keep guard.'

'Nay. You've got work to do. You've missed half a day now. There's no telling when they'll be back. They'll be licking their wounds and wondering whether we really have got proper affidavits. It's a good job he didn't take yours off with him, Jack.'

'Suppose Rector comes up asking for them?'

'Mmm,' considered Harry. 'If yer all trusts me with them I could ask a friend ter look after them and you can all say you ain't got them around and don't know where they are hexactly.'

'What, give them to Dr Crisp?' asked Eliza doubtfully.

'No!' cried Harry scornfully. 'There's someone we trust more than him.' Eliza looked at him thoughtfully.

'How about our home, Harry?' Mary asked in a small voice.

'You know what I said about building it better next time, love!' She smiled bravely and Harry continued:

'If they wreck that, we'll have them! No violence mind, Johnny! Hear what I say! It will spoil it all for taking them to law if we have a rumpus. Let them do their worst and then we'll string them up by their heels, eh?' He looked hard at his wife.

'Yeah . . . That's right by me, Harry. I'll be upset but we ain't got any little ones and we've good friends, ain't we?' She smiled at Eliza, who put her arm round her shoulder.

'My goodness, we do owe you a roof over yer heads, 'course we do, Mary, Harry,' said Eliza.

'John, man! Will you make sure we've got your roof, 'cause we'll be needing it, I reckon. Remember, no fight at all. Let them tie their own noose and stick their heads in it,' said Harry earnestly.

'Yeah, that's right, Johnny. You just keep cool,' cried Butcher.

'Good ol' Harry!'

'Well done, Mrs Nursall!' they all cried.

Devereux rode up in the afternoon. Most of the men were at work and Harry was taking the affidavits to a safe place. He knocked on Mary Nursall's door first and then Eliza's. They both pleaded ignorance of any affidavits and, after getting a similar reply from two or three other cottages, he left. As he was approaching the turnpike from the end of the sandy lane, he met Harry.

'Ah, Mr Nursall. Just the fellow I wanted to see,' said the Rector jovially.

'Good afternoon, Rector. This fine weather do make one feel good-natured, don't it?' replied Harry. Devereux looked a little sharply at him but his jolly open smile did not allow any suspicion of sarcasm.

'Yes . . . mmm . . . very pleasant weather for the time of year. Now it was a business matter that I wished to ask you about. I think you have lived on the Heath

345

longer than any of the other men, haven't you? How long would it be about, Mr Nursall?'

'W-e-ll. Let me think. It were me grandfather who first thought of coming up but he never made it, God rest his soul. He kept putting it off till the next season, you know, and could never quite bring himself to take the plunge and then when he were approaching ninety . . . We are a long-lived family, you see, because *his* father were . . .'

'Yes, yes, Mr Nursall, but you yourself. When did *you* come to live up here?' Devereux spoke patiently and slowly to help the old fellow follow his question.

'Yes, well, I were just getting round to reckoning it out, you see, because me grandfather died when he were ninety-two, which would be in 1788 when me father was sixty-nine, you see, and I always remember me mother saying to him . . .'

'So that was 1788 and you hadn't moved then?' said Devereux, not quite so patiently.

'Oh no! We hadn't moved *then* because I would only be about seventeen years old. Me poor father were sixty-two when I were born. Of course, me mother was a bit younger than he were . . .'

'Yes, I suppose she would be.' Devereux's patience was wearing very thin now.

'Well, funny you should say that, Rector, because she weren't that young and there *was* a woman of nigh on fifty what had twins. She lived up at Mount Pleasant. They do say the air is very clean and healthy up . . .'

'Had you moved on to the Heath in 1820, Mr Nursall?'

'1820, you say. Now let me think.' He tipped his straw hat forward and scratched the back of his head. He looked up at the Rector's face, noticing with well-concealed satisfaction that it was quite thunderous. Then, as with a sudden flash of clarity, he said,

'Nay . . . nay . . . we hadn't moved up in 1820, sir.'

'It couldn't have been so long after that though, could it?'

'N-o-o, not so long after, maybe.'

'Anyway, Mr Nursall, you wouldn't have any documents stating when you moved here, would you?'

'No. Not on me, like, sir,' said Harry apologetically.

'Nor in your house, perhaps?'

'Oh no, I ain't got any dock . . . dockiments in me house excepting me father's settlement certificate and probably Mary's – that's me wife, Mary, she were called after her mother – and we may have her . . .'

'Thank you, Mr Nursall. That's all I wanted to know, thank you very much. Good day to you.' Harry shook his head sadly.

'Pity he's in such a hurry,' he thought. 'I was planning to tell him what me mother and father died of and I might have told him about Mary's too.'

He also said to Mary, when he reached home a few minutes later:

'I do enjoy talking to the gentry, love. It's a pleasure for me. I really looks forward to it.'

'I don't expect they'd say the same for you.'

'I'm hemmed sure they wouldn't,' laughed Harry.

CHAPTER 58

Life at the Villa

Sarah was finding that life at the villa suited her very well. She and Mrs Jones had settled for mutual respect as the basis of their relationship, and Sarah delegated the daily running of the house and garden to her. This just left Sarah with the longer-term planning, the engaging and paying of servants, and Mrs Jones even carried out the reprimands, when needed, so Sarah was spared any unpleasantness at all. Sarah felt a little guilty about this but the old lady seemed quite indifferent to anyone's opinion of her except, perhaps, Sarah's.

Sarah's single dissatisfaction was that seeing Fran for an hour each evening did not satisfy her social inclination. She particularly missed the conversations with Dafydd Griffiths which had kept her informed of the activities of the Chartist movement and other things. He hadn't visited her since his encounter with Vaughan and she toyed with the idea of inviting him to the villa one evening, but she didn't relish the thought of another encounter between them. One night she was just tidying up the salon after she had been working late when his tap sounded on the door.

'Oh, Mr Griffiths! Good evening. I have been wondering whether you would ever call to see me again.'

'But how can I? You are rarely here in the evening. I have been wondering whether I might receive an invitation to visit you in your new abode.'

'There! Of course you must come. Do you know the house?'

'Yes, it is Dr Crisp's new one, I believe. Perhaps he would not like me to call?' Griffiths's eyes held the tortured expression that Sarah was becoming familiar with as he searched her face earnestly.

'Oh no, of course not. I have my own rooms and he is rarely there anyway.' Dafydd looked immensely relieved.

'I should come early in the evening, like you used to do, because I often have work to do later on. Why don't you accompany me now since I am ready to go home and I shall show you my new abode.'

'Indeed I should like to do that very much.'

Fran called in most evenings but he did not usually stay long, in order to placate Theresa who had been behaving rather oddly.

'So what has Mrs Vaughan been saying today, Fran?' This was becoming Sarah's opening line.

'Oh, it is very exasperating. This dinnertime she kept up an interminable conversation about me delivering a letter to Devereux. She would not let the subject drop, as if she felt compelled to engage me in conversation in order to prevent me seeking other distractions. I mean, if the conversation was an interesting one, it might make sense, but poor Theresa is so limited. However does she think that discussing whether Devereux was in to receive letters or not and if he was not, whether I waited for him or whether I left the letter with someone else and if I did, who was it, was it Beatrice Devereux and if so, how was Beatrice engaged; how can she think that all this could possibly interest me?

'I heartily wish I had troubled her to deliver the letter herself and then she could have checked up on all these things at first hand.'

'I am sure she wished you had,' said Sarah, rocking with laughter.

'Really, Sarah, I do not see how it is so amusing. I only wish I could.'

'It is you who are so funny, Fran, you dunce.'

'Me, a dunce! Why?'

'Can't you see?'

'No!'

'She thinks you are having an affair of the heart with Beatrice Devereux. She thinks her best friend, Beatrice, is her rival! Really, that is rather sad, isn't it?'

'No! Do you honestly think so?'

'I am certain.'

'Perhaps you are right, and right about me being a dunce as well, because now I recall all the tedious conversations we have had recently in *that* light, they do make a little more sense.

'Whatever am I to do? Poor Beatrice!'

'I am sure Mrs Devereux can look after herself,'

sniffed Sarah. 'It is your wife whom I feel so guilty towards.'

'No, Sarah, you mustn't feel that. This has been my fault entirely. You are not to blame.'

'That is not the way most people would judge it, Fran. Men are naturally inclined to be unfaithful to their wives. They can't help it, poor things! But it is the constant duty of respectable women to discourage them. Oh, it is always the woman's fault, I do assure you!'

'Oh dear, oh dear,' smiled Vaughan. 'I do believe you have been reading the writings of that infamous Miss Wollstonecraft.'

'No, I declare I have never heard of her, but maybe I should if she writes that "justice" is entirely reserved for the use of the male sex.'

'I shall make sure you don't! You are quite formidable enough on your own, my love. I find myself feeling positively frightened of you sometimes.'

'Oh dear!' sighed Sarah, pulling a face at him.

'Fran, what was in this much discussed letter that you delivered to Devereux?'

'Why do you ask, my love?'

'Because I am inquisitive, of course.'

'Well I hope you are confidential as well.'

'Oh yes. Even when I choose to act on confidences nobody ever finds out how I came by them.'

'So I have noticed.'

'Well?'

'He asked me to make a comprehensive list of all the attorneys and solicitors in practice from Buckingham to Bedford and Dunstable to Newport Pagnell.'

'Oh, we can guess why he wanted that, can't we?'

'Yes, and we also know that it is "shutting the stable door after the horse has bolted",' smiled Fran.

'You did it, nevertheless?'

'Oh yes. Not very efficiently, but well enough to keep up a semblance of innocence. I hope Harry Nursall has seen to it that the "Heathens" keep their affidavits safe. It would be a pity if they were stolen or destroyed in the evictions.'

'Yes, they are perfectly safe,' said Sarah confidently.

'And you will not divulge how you know that, will you?'

Sarah laughed and kissed him.

'Now, how would you feel if I *was* Beatrice Devereux, Fran?' she asked, changing the subject gravely as they stood in each other's arms.

'Absolutely terrified!'

'Whereas you are only mildly frightened of me?'

He nodded and Sarah smiled.

Francis Vaughan's reputation was not the only one to be suffering in the village, as John Ruddock discovered to his chagrin.

He was doing a bit of jobbing for Farmer Miller and had been sent to take one of the draught horses to be shod. Wilfred Sykes, the blacksmith, bore no resemblance to the proverbial jolly giant of his craft. He was not a large man; he was rather ill-featured, with a pronounced squint and his nature, so far as his fellow human beings were concerned, was worse than his looks. His practice was to encourage the horse minders to part with any scandalous tit-bit of gossip and to pass this on, slightly enlivened, to the very ear where it would fester best. His redeeming feature was his uncanny power over a horse; the flightiest thoroughbred would stand as gently as a placid shire while he held its hoof.

'He must whisper sweet nothings into them hemmed horses' ears what they understands, but he certainly don't do it into ours,' they'd say.

'Well, how's yer Chartist friends, eh, Ruddock?'

'Only needing a bit more help to win the day,' said John.

'Help? The only help you'll get is a ticket for New South Wales, he, he!' John ignored him.

351

'I hear that eldest daughter of yours is excelling herself.'

'Yeah. She seems to be doing quite well,' said John guardedly.

'Quite well! I'd say a schoolmaster and a doctor were doing *very* well in that line of business. Mind you, she's got a good teacher in that there Mrs Jones. She were always reckoned to be a loose 'un after her husband died.'

'What are you trying to say?' asked John dangerously.

'Nowt in particular.'

'It sounded like more than that to me. Make yourself plain, man, so we knows where we stands.'

'Hold yer noise, Ruddock. You're upsetting the mare.'

John couldn't get any more out of Sykes, but the poison had reached its mark.

CHAPTER 59

Mary Nursall Will Not be Moved

Mary Nursall was singing gaily as she cleaned her kitchen. The door of the hen house was open, letting in sparkling shafts of sunlight, and she brushed away with one of Mr Lee's new besoms, winkling out the autumn leaves which had lodged in crevices in the lower nesting boxes.

> A bunch of may I have brought you,
> And at your door it stands.
> La-la, la-la, la---la.
> It is but a sprout but it's well put about,
> La-la, la-la, la---la.

She gathered the leaves and dirt at the door and, on the last la---la, she swept them out with a flourish that sent sunbeams glancing through the shafts of light. Then she rested on her broom and looked around with deep tranquillity.

A brisk wind was sweeping the masses of cumulus clouds across the azure sky which made a backdrop for the tossing fronds of the young birch tree standing by the coach. Its silvery trunk gleamed with smooth bands of soft pink where the wild weather of the previous week had peeled away some old bark, and its short catkins radiated stiffly from the tips of its pendulous twigs. The birds were singing joyously as well. From every tangle of bramble and briar and each bare thorn and birch tree came the warbling of dunnocks and robins, the piping of thrushes and blackbirds and the repetitive percussive signature tunes of twenty great tits. Mary's tame cock chaffinch was hopping nearby, importuning her with his piercing 'pip' as he displayed his coral pink breast, so subtly complemented by his slate grey head and olive back. His drab little mate ostentatiously ignored him as she busied about the onerous priorities which seem doomed to occupy the female of the species.

Mary knew that her tranquillity arose from being a part, a yielding, unobtrusive and integral part of this community. She felt so privileged to share in the exciting busyness of spring that swelled the buds on the bushes and coupled the birds. She exalted in the prospect of the blackthorn buds bursting into snowy splendour and then the prodigious masses of may blossom, with its acrid catty smell, and of watching the dog roses unfurl immaculately pink and the little lines of fluffy fledglings, apprehensive about their first flight.

She was so preoccupied with anticipating the glories of April, May and June that she only became aware of Farmer Green and three men when they were standing in front of her. Her happy smile slowly faded as she watched Green dismount. The first thought that domi-nated her mind was that their presence there was unseemly, an obtrusive infringement of the natural well-being. They did not belong and she, the tussocks of grass, the thorn and briar bushes, resented their inva-sion. The men had frightened away the chaffinches and it seemed as if, suddenly, the bird song became strident and aggressive. Even the sun responded to their unwel-come presence by drawing a mass of cloud across itself, and the golden light faded and darkened ominously.

'Good day to you, Mrs Nursall. This land is parish property and we are here to turn you off it,' stated Green.

Mary drew herself up, affronted. The words made no sense to her.

'*You* are here to turn *me* off?' she asked incredulously.

'Aye. That's what I said.' There was just a hint of uncertainty in his voice. He had heard that Nursall's wife was a bit queer in the head. He wondered just what inconvenient form this queerness might take. His life seemed set about with unexpected obstacles recently. She certainly looked strange, even verging on the disre-putable. Her grey hair stood out in wild wisps towards most points of the compass. Her slightly protuberant pale grey eyes looked distracted and vague. The strangely nondescript garment she wore reached down to her left ankle but only to her upper right calf and a felted woolly shawl, knotted round her neck, seemed to have dragged her dress almost off her bony left shoulder.

Just to add fuel to Green's worst misgivings, a wild smile suddenly lit up her face.

'Who are you? I can't remember yer name!' she cried.

Green groaned inwardly.

'Green. Farmer Green,' he said roughly.

'And these other gentlemen?' He glanced over his shoulder nervously.

'*Them*! That don't concern you.'

'Of course it does. I can't talk to them if I don't know their names.'

'You don't need to talk to them. Just get your stuff out.'

'What stuff? What do you mean?'

'We . . . have . . . come . . . to . . . evict . . . you!' He shouted the words slowly in her face but she didn't flinch; she just tipped her head to one side and shook it in a dismissive way as a scarecrow might reject the application for nesting space of an importunate robin.

'Oh no,' she said, 'you can't evict me.'

'And why not?' sneered Green.

'This is me 'ouse. I have lived here years.'

'We . . . are . . . going . . . to . . . pull . . . it . . . down,' he bellowed.

A fleeting look of anger swept across Mary's face, and then she said calmly:

'Well, if you must, I can't stop you doing *that* but you ain't evicting me because I ain't a-going!'

'You've got to go if you've no place ter live!'

'Oh no. Don't you worry yourself on my account. I shall manage. I . . . ain't . . . going . . . see!' She raised her voice just a little at the end to match Green's mode of communication.

'Ha. Just see what yer husband has to say about that.'

'I can tell you now, Mr Green. He always agrees with me. We . . . ain't . . . going!' She had never attempted to shout at anyone before and she was quite pleased with the satisfying firmness of intent it gave.

Green tossed his head in exasperation.

'Get on with it then. Don't stand gawping there like – like a line of nincompoops.'

'Where shall us start?'

'The door. Get the door down and . . . and the winders.'

'It ain't got no winders!'

'What does it matter! Just break it up!'

'What? Not the coach?'

'Yes,' roared Green. He grabbed one of the pick axes and began to hack frenziedly. He broke down the porch and the inside wall of the chicken hut. He drove the pick axe through one window of the coach and gashed open the door. Masses of miscellaneous objects began to roll out of hidden recesses and cascade down from the tipsy shelves and nesting boxes and fall from hooks on the roof as that began to collapse. He set about the upturned waggon but it was too solidly constructed and his temper, strength and breath all ran out together. He stumbled free of the debris and thrust the pick axe back at the men who were standing awe-struck by the rapid devastation. What had appeared to them as an intangible conglomeration of large discarded items seemed to have erupted volcano-wise and the laval flow of flotsam and jetsam had quite obliterated any tenuous resemblance to a dwelling.

'Get on with it, damn you! You lazy good-for-nothings,' he screamed. They half-heartedly began to lug apart the various components of the homestead.

Mary hadn't moved. She stood erect, her hand resting on her broom as a Guardsman's might on his gun. Any ludicrous impression was quite counteracted by the aura of reserved dignity that surrounded her.

Green glowered angrily and opened his mouth to shout at her to shift, but something in the condemning sternness of her gaze made him think better of it. He glanced towards the men instead.

'Anything worth taking?' he demanded.

'The 'en 'ouse might have been but the end's broke now.'

'How about the waggon?'

'It ain't got no wheels.'

'That will do then. Come on!' He untied his horse, mounted and rode away.

The three men picked their way out of the debris, trying to avoid treading on anything fragile.

'Good day ter you, Ma'am,' they said deferentially. 'Sorry, Ma'am,' touching their hats.

Mary smiled and nodded and then turned to look at the remains of her home. She sighed and bent down to pick up a dainty china cup. It had never had a saucer but it was delicately hand-painted with red strawberries and green hulms hanging from a trellis-work of lustre leaves and coiling tendrils, and it was quite unharmed! This fact alone was sufficient to reassure her. She put it gently down by the trunk of the birch tree and began to sort the nearest edge of the laval flow. She began to sing, slowly at first and then with gathering momentum:

> A bunch of may I have brought you,
> And at your door it stands.
> La-la; la-la; la---la.
> It is but a sprout but it's well put about,
> La-la; la-la; la---la.

She swept the broken pieces of wood suitable for burning into one heap, the things broken beyond repair into another but, amazingly, the heap at the foot of the birch tree grew faster than either of the other two. By the time Harry came home Mary, at any rate, could calmly assess the damage as 'nothing we can't mend after a fashion by tomorrow!'

'And you was all alone!' he marvelled.

'Yeah. Didn't matter. A few men like that don't frighten me and I wanted to do some clearing up anyway.'

'It's going to be the best clear-up you've done for many a year, gal,' laughed Harry, hugging her affectionately.

CHAPTER 60

Gossip

Sarah visited the Nursalls after they had put their home together again. It really didn't look much different, except that one side of the coach was badly mutilated.

'We could do with a larger one. I'll keep me eyes and ears open,' said Harry philosophically. 'When I have time to do a proper job, you'll never know Farmer Green ever visited us.'

'But how about evidence for the Sessions?' asked Sarah.

'Well, I've the word of the neighbours and I shall try to get them fellers that came with Green. You see, *they* didn't actually do no damage at all. They just watched him and then moved the coach a bit.'

'Where did they come from?'

'Woburn Union work'ouse. I know their names and I've told the Chief Constable what I am suing Green for damages.'

'Will he help you?'

'Aye. He's got to. It's got to be heard within a certain number of days what the Act of Parliament states and he's got to serve it on the magistrates and I'll bring witnesses.'

Sarah smiled gleefully. 'If you need a solicitor I can send a message to Mr Place,' she said.

'Nay, I reckon I'll manage meself.'

'When are the Sessions? We must all be there. This should be very good.'

'I'll let you know, gal. We'll declare a special holiday. Our good ol' Farmer Green will have to be there to defend hisself.'

'I wonder if he'll lay the blame on the Select Vestry and Devereux?'

'I doubt he will. He wouldn't be a member no more if he did, and he gets good pickings in the way of cheap labour and stuff from being on the Vestry.'

The round table group at The Bell were particularly jubilant.

'An' ol' Harry Nursall be suing Farmer Green for damages in the 'Igh Court!' gloated John.

'They'll never let him!'

'Well, Jerry, it do sound too good to be true but it all looks legal enough,' said George Dunne.

'How about costs?'

'They may lay them on Green's plate, but if they don't he can pay them from the compensation,' suggested Dicken.

'What they'll do is make the costs equal or outstrip the compensation if I know anything 'bout it,' said Phillip Wooding.

'Maybe, but it's a brave try and we'll do what we can for ol' Harry, won't we. He's allus put his hand in his pocket when we've asked him to,' said George.

'If it's possible, trust Harry ter get it done. He got us all these affidavits. I never understood quite how, but he had a friend what helped him arrange it and it's him what's looking after them now.'

'And you don't know who this friend be?'

'Neow, no idea, excepting that he seems to have summat to do with Dr Crisp.'

'Your Sarah'd know. She's living there, ain't she?' said Dicken tactlessly.

'Living with Dr Crisp?' cried John, reddening.

'Well, neow, John. Not *with*, like. She's lodging in rooms there,' corrected Dicken.

'She ain't told me.'

'Your Tom knows because I helped him shift some

boarding from there the other evening,' said Jerry. 'I was just walking up Woburn Lane and he and Miss Ruddock and that ol' Mrs Jones were loading it into a pony trap and I stopped to help. Mrs Jones lives there too and she and Miss Ruddock look after the house for Dr Crisp, they said.'

'I see,' said John darkly, with downcast eyes. 'Mrs Jones lives there too, does she?' He stood up and walked over to fetch his hat off the peg.

'Are you going, Johnny?'

'Yeah. You'll do well enough without me and my connections,' he said, opening the door.

'That's your fault, Dicken. You ought ter think before you opens yer mouth!'

'How was I to know he didn't know? There ain't nothing to be ashamed of anyway, is there?' he asked, scanning his companions' faces.

'Neow, of course not,' said Jerry stoutly. 'I've a deal of respect for Miss Ruddock. If anyone's heard different I'd say it was idle gossip.'

'You'd best say that to John.'

'What, now?'

'No, leave it till tomorrow when he's sobered down,' said George.

It might have been better if George had sent Jerry after John, although John would probably have been in no mood to listen. He strode up Woburn Lane, reflecting darkly on Sarah and her fancy shop, her clothes, her church pew and now this imputation of harlotry, so that by the time he swung into the drive of the villa and hammered on the door, he could hardly contain himself.

Mrs Jones, with her usual presence of mind, wedged the back of a chair beneath a panel frame so that the door would only open a crack.

'Who is it?' she demanded shrilly.

'John Ruddock. I've come to see me daughter.'

'She ain't expectin' you.'

'Oh dear! Is she h'entertaining then?' he asked sarcastically.

'Neow, but I ain't letting you in till I've asked.'

'Oh you ain't, ain't you, you . . . you old crab?'

Mrs Jones pushed the door shut and went to fetch Sarah.

'He's in his cups, Miss,' she warned.

'Oh dear. I'll have to let him in. I'll take him to the kitchen.

'Well, Father? Aren't you going to sit down?'

'I'd rather not in a place like this.'

'What's wrong with the place?'

'It ain't the place so much as the people. When I thinks how I've tried to bring you up decent, to show you what's right and just. I didn't stand in your way when you wanted to leave home. I told you what I thought but I didn't stop you, and then you come back aping the gentry, setting up that fancy shop full of gew-gaws and ribbons what no respectable woman would want. You throw my principles in my face by going to church and *renting* a pew to show off yer finery, and I've borne up to all that, but not this final insult, Sarah. I can't stand by and see you a common . . .'

'Father, you are drunk, but let's get it over and done with. What am I – a common . . .?'

'Surely you don't want me to spell out what you are?'

John was breathing heavily and quivering from head to foot with emotion. His blood-shot eyes stared through his straight black hair as he leant across the table.

'Yes I do. It will make it easier for me to defend myself,' said Sarah coldly.

'How can you defend yourself? Perhaps because they are only gentlemen who are brought up to know no better, eh? Honest working men would know what was right and not let you forget it. Is that your defence, eh?'

'Father, you have been listening to idle gossip. You have no evidence of what you accuse me of. I have a written contract with Dr Crisp to look after this house in his absence. It suits him and it suits me and it is none of your business. Do you really enjoy torturing youself?

'If you come to see me when you are sober, I will tell you exactly how much I care about your principles. You had better go home now,' she gasped finally, holding back her tears.

'Yes, off you go, John Ruddock,' cried Mrs Jones, entering on cue, 'and I just hope you feels as ashamed of yourself as you should, tomorrer morning. You aren't fit to be the father of a nice young lady like that.' Mrs Jones bundled him out, slammed the door and returned to comfort Sarah who was sitting at the kitchen table with her head in her hands.

'Don't you take no notice of him, dearie. He's drunk. They always feel bad about what they says next day.'

'I know that, Mrs Jones, and I shouldn't care if it wasn't all true,' sobbed Sarah.

'"True", "not true", what does he know, eh?'

'Not very much.'

'No, 'course he don't, dearie. Men can't understand, but we do. We knows what a woman has to do if she wants a bit of h'independence.'

Sarah looked up at the old lady and smiled wanly. Mrs Jones saw her upstairs with an understanding hand on her shoulders.

'No, they shout and carry on and think they're putting the world right, but they don't know! They don't change nothing,' she muttered, with cold comfort.

CHAPTER 61

Harry Goes to Court

Sarah and Vaughan were strolling in the garden of the villa on a beautiful evening in early April. The sun had sunk but the luminous duck-egg blue sky reflected enough light for the clumps of daffodils to hover like pale lanterns beneath the be-blossomed apple trees. Their fingers were lightly linked and they were deep in thought. Eventually Vaughan broke the silence:

'It is so peaceful here with you, Sarah. How I wish we could wander on and on in a ceaseless twilight.' Sarah only smiled.

'You're very quiet tonight, my love.'

'Yes. I have a lot of things on my mind.'

'And none of them me, eh?'

'Ah, Fran. You are always there. I have to get used to that.'

'What a nuisance!' She nodded and kissed his fingertips.

'Please tell me one of them.'

'Harry Nursall is claiming damages from Farmer Green for knocking his home down. It comes up before a special session on Wednesday.'

'Yes, I have to go, but why are you so interested?'

'My business speculations, of course, but why are you going?'

'The Select Vestry thought it prudent to have an observer there. Devereux is very worried that Green will incriminate him so he doesn't want to go himself. He thinks I am a disinterested party.'

'How wrong he is.'

'Yes, I feel quite sorry for the wretched man. I have caught him regarding me in a strange way once or twice

363

lately. I wonder whether Theresa's foolish fancy that I have cuckolded him has reached his ears.' Sarah laughed gleefully.

'Well, I think it is you who should feel guilty if that is the case, young lady,' reprimanded Vaughan.

'Oh no, I am quite unscrupulous in such things, and of all the misused parties Devereux and his wife are the last I shall pity.'

'My, how fierce! I am constantly aware that I am only allowed to know a tiny bit of what is in your mind. Do you know, I have a foolish fancy that you have another quite separate identity that I know nothing about.'

'And if you discover it's true and my other life is wicked and disloyal to you, what shall you do?'

'Disloyal to me? I wonder how? I am sure it can be in no way that matters so I shall . . . just love you. I have little choice in the matter anyway.' He paused beneath an apple tree and lifted her up so that a low branch caught in her hair. He studied the pointed face gazing down at him with bunches of snowy blossom peeping through the unruly brown curls.

'Oh Sarah. My beautiful child bride. I owe you so much that I can never repay.'

A few minutes later Sarah said:

'I should like to go to the court, Fran. Mrs Lyle says she will look after the shop.'

'Well, you can drive over in your trap easily enough.' Sarah was silent for a moment.

'Dobs seems to be lame again.'

'Whatever do you do with that wretched animal? The farrier has been twice this month. He was perfectly sound when I took him out last week.'

'I . . . I do use him rather a lot.'

'You don't canter him on the roads, do you? You should always trot, Sarah. I think you must be too impatient. He cannot be expected to go at the speed of a carriage and pair.'

'I think I really need a larger, stronger animal.'

'Oh, nonsense! He is exactly the right size for the trap and yourself. You couldn't manage a thick-necked beast. I shall ride over to the court, of course. It would not do for me to take you in my chaise anyway.'

'No,' agreed Sarah sadly.

In the end Sarah walked to the court. She arrived just before the session began and she carefully avoided catching her father's eye. He was sitting among his comrades from The Bell and looked ebullient and happy. It was, after all, a landmark in their struggle to challenge the people who held the power over their lives and forever forced them down into humiliating poverty. They were happy because, whatever the outcome, they had thrown down the gauntlet and their unlikely champion, Harry, would certainly not fail through lack of support. Most of the people who lived on the Heath were there, and Sarah now caught sight of her mother pushing Willy before her and dragging a distraught-looking Mary Nursall after her. John rose to help them in and Jerry and Dicken stood up to let them sit down. Mary's battered bonnet was totally askew and she clutched desperately at her shawl as she struggled through the press of people. When they reached their seats Eliza tried to adjust her bonnet and to pat her clothes into place as if she was a child.

Francis Vaughan was in a raised area partitioned off at one side of the court to protect a small group of gentry from the press of the illiterate poor. He looked as handsomely self-sufficient as ever, chatting gaily to a well-dressed lady at his side.

'Oh, Mr Vaughan, do look at that hilarious little scene over there. Doesn't it remind you of the entry of the peasant players in *A Midsummer Night's Dream*?'

'The old woman certainly looks somewhat *distrait*, not to mention *déshabillé*. She would have looked more in place standing in the middle of a field with outstretched arms. In fact, I should never have given her a second glance there!' he replied.

'Oh, you *are* unkind!'

'Ha! These affairs do have a certain value as diversions, what?' guffawed a red-faced Squire who hunted with Vaughan.

'It makes one respect the Rector and Doctor who have to earn their livings among them, eh?' said another of Vaughan's male friends.

'Well, I am sure they get some satisfaction from helping the poor things,' simpered the lady, flirting her eyes at Vaughan.

Sarah watched them bitterly through her lowered eyelashes. She did not need to hear their words. The direction of their looks and the expressions on their faces told her all. Her first feeling had been one of relief that she was not a member of the ridiculed group but she immediately despised herself for it. Mrs Nursall and her mother had lived through more privations in one day than those people would meet in a lifetime. What right had they to be amused by the appearance of an elderly woman who had watched her precious home destroyed with a courage and dignity they could never begin to contemplate? Sarah wished she had had the courage to be sitting with her family and friends.

The Clerk to the Court called out.

'Silence in Court. Silence! Please be upstanding for His Grace,' and with much creaking and rustling and murmuring everyone stood up while the elderly Duke entered and took his place. The murmuring of excited conversation grew louder.

'Silence, please!' called the Clerk. 'Would the defendant please to stand up. Are you Frederick Green, farmer of Aspley Guise?'

'Aye,' snorted Green.

'Will you be represented or present your own defence?'

'Represented by Mr Day, there.'

The Clerk continued briskly. 'The charge, Your Grace, is that on the afternoon of the 15th of March of this year, Frederick Green did damage the dwelling of Henry Nursall of Aspley Guise by breaking it with a pick axe. Do you plead guilty or not guilty?'

Mr Day stated that his client pleaded guilty but had mitigating circumstances. The Duke conveyed to the Clerk that he would like to hear them.

'This man, Henry Nursall, did not live in a proper dwelling but in some disused vehicles which were situated on Parish common land. My client, Mr Green, was in possession of an order of eviction and had warned Henry Nursall a week before, so he was acting within his rights.'

The Clerk consulted the Duke again.

'On whose authority was the order of eviction issued?'

Vaughan sat up attentively.

'On my own,' said Day. 'I am the acting solicitor for the parish in such matters.'

'May we see the order of eviction, please, Mr Day.' Day handed it to a junior Clerk who handed it to the Court Clerk who gave it to the Duke.

'We shall now deal with the case for the prosecution.'

Harry was prodded to stand up.

'Are you Henry Nursall?'

'Aye.' The Clerk repeated the charge and asked Harry if he intended to be represented.

'Neow.'

'It is my duty to inform you, Mr Nursall, that your interests are better served if you are represented by a member of the legal profession, and the case may be adjourned for you to make appropriate arrangements.'

'I ain't got money to pay no-one and I think what my case has got to be heard within twenty-eight days of the h'event occurring.' Murmurs of support sounded round the room.

The Clerk consulted the Duke, who nodded.

'We shall then proceed. Do you wish to call any witnesses for the prosecution, Mr Nursall? If not I shall ask Mr Day if there are any questions he would like to ask you.'

Day stood up.

'Aye,' said Harry firmly.

'What?' asked the Clerk.

'I wish ter call witnesses.'

'You are not allowed to call your wife, Mr Nursall.'

'I ain't planning ter. First of all I want to h'establish that the dwelling place what Farmer Green destroyed were a very convenient and comfortable home what me and me wife Mary have lived in for nigh on twenty years.'

'You need a witness to corroborate that,' sighed the Clerk.

'Oh, you ain't taking me word for it?' asked Harry in a hurt voice.

'I am afraid not,' said the Clerk patiently.

Harry glanced round the Court.

'If she don't mind then, I should like ter call Sarah Ruddock as me witness.'

A look of horror passed across Sarah's face.

'Leave to speak, Your Grace?' said Day. The Duke inclined his head.

'The young lady is not obliged to give evidence. I am sure she would rather not,' he smiled ingratiatingly towards Sarah who sprang to her feet.

'Of course I shall be a witness,' said Sarah loudly.

A rustle and murmur of interest passed through the Court.

'Come round here, please, Ma'am,' said two junior Clerks, making a way through for Sarah. When she gained the witness box only the top of her hat was visible.

'We can't see the witness,' complained Day. The Clerks scurried round and produced a large legal tome which they wrapped in a gown for protection and stood Sarah on so that her face was just visible above the box, and she was sworn in.

'Will you tell them about our home, Sarah, please,' said Harry.

'Er . . . Yes,' she said giving him an exasperated glance and desperately trying to decide where to begin.

'It was certainly an unusual home but Mr Nursall is a very competent builder and joiner and he could have made a very good ordinary one if he could have afforded the materials when he first moved on to the Heath. As it was, they had to make do with discarded odds and ends and then they became so fond of this home that they didn't want to change it. I was very fond of it, too. Ever since I was a child I have spent many rough winter evenings with the Nursalls and have always been very cosy and comfortable.'

'Thank you, Miss Ruddock. Do you wish to ask the witness any questions, Mr Day?'

'No,' he said sullenly.

'Have you any more witnesses to call, Mr Nursall?' The Clerk's tone was rather more respectful.

'Aye, I shall call Mr Giles to h'ascertain that the dwelling in question was destroyed,' said Harry confidently. He was beginning to enjoy himself now.

Jasper Giles, the most articulate of the three men from the workhouse, was assisted to the witness box and sworn in.

Green jumped to his feet.

'This is one of my men!'

'Please address yourself to His Grace,' cautioned the Clerk.

'May I have leave to speak, Your Grace?' asked Day. 'Henry Nursall cannot call a witness for the defence.'

After consultation with the Duke the Clerk said:

'His Grace suggests that Mr Nursall examines the witness first and then you do, Mr Day.'

Harry cleared his throat and spoke out in his best legal manner.

'Mr Giles, would you be so good as to tell His Grace what happened when Farmer Green grabbed the pick axe off yer and set about our home.'

'Well, Yer Grace . . .' The sudden realization that he was talking to a Duke left Giles speechless.

'Yes. Get on with it,' encouraged Harry.

'Well . . . Yer Grace . . . it sort of h'exploded.'

The Duke's brows furrowed in bewilderment.

'Did he break down the end of the 'en 'ouse (that was our kitchen, Yer Grace)?'

'Yeah.'

'Did he smash open the coach (that was our bedroom, Yer Grace)?'

'Yeah . . . and . . . and the roof fell in and all the stuff that was tucked about the place fell out so that it looked as if it had sort of . . . h'exploded.'

'That's all, thank you, Mr Giles,' said Harry, and Day rose.

'Would you say, Mr Giles, that the devastation was rather more apparent than real?'

Giles looked at him blankly.

'Make the question plainer,' said the Duke speaking for the first time.

'I asked you,' sighed Day, 'whether the "explosion" you speak of was more because the . . . er . . . abode was very untidy inside than that Mr Green had damaged it very much?'

'Oh he damaged it dreadful. It were remarkable how much damage he'd done so fast, but he were very angry with the lady.'

'Was the lady Mr Nursall's wife?'

'Yes, sir.'

'Was she obstructing Mr Green and using bad language, then?'

Harry shouted out: 'He ain't allowed to ask questions like that.'

'Please address yourself to His Grace, Mr Nursall.'

'Will you rephrase that question, Mr Day?' asked the Duke.

'Was Mrs Nursall resisting Mr Green's efforts to carry out the eviction?'

'I understood yer better the first time,' said Giles crossly. 'Neow. She were wonderful brave. She just stood quiet, after she had said he couldn't evict her because she weren't going.'

The comrades and one or two others cheered and Mary turned very pink.

Having got nicely into the swing of the legal protocol, Harry was going to make the most of his opportunity and he proceeded to call the other two men who were too timid to add substantially to the case, but wasted a lot of the Court's time and Mr Day's patience. Harry finished up by calling John Ruddock to testify to the devastation as he had seen it on his return from work that evening.

Eventually, the Clerk to the Court said wearily that if there were no other witnesses to be called, His Grace would sum up and pass judgement. He visibly wilted as Harry jumped to his feet yet again.

'Please, Yer Grace. I should like you to look at this affidavit, all properly witnessed, stating what I have lived on Aspley Heath in four and a half acres of land for nineteen years two months and regard it as mine except for those parts what I have sold or bartered.'

The document was handed to the Duke, who put on his spectacles to give it a thorough examination.

'Mr Day, may I ask you whether your client, Mr

Green, inquired into the existence of this affidavit before he applied for the eviction order?'

'Yes, well, someone did on his behalf,' stammered Day.

'And what did Mr Nursall say?'

'He said he hadn't got one.'

'Your Grace, please,' said Harry, 'the *person* asked me whether I had it in my home and I very honestly (as I would be bound to be talking to *such* a person) said "no I ain't", because I hadn't, see?'

'Humph,' said His Grace, peering over his glasses at Harry distrustfully.

'Well, this has been the most reprehensible affair. After living all that time in his . . . er . . . abode on the Heath, Mr Nursall should not have been disturbed, particularly when it turns out that he, in point of fact, has freehold right to this piece of land. Mr Green should have ascertained that for himself. I grant Mr Henry Nursall fifteen pounds in damages to be paid by Mr Frederick Green, which should enable him to build a proper dwelling house. The Court costs of twenty pounds should be divided equally between the plaintiff and the defendant. They shall pay ten pounds each.'

The Duke smiled around benignly at the Court, which erupted into a disgruntled surge of voices.

'Silence in Court!' roared the Clerk. 'All to be upstanding for His Grace.'

The Duke gathered up his papers and sailed out, and Harry gathered his friends and supporters round, all congratulating him.

'I wonder how much of his abbey His Grace could build with five pounds, eh?' said Harry sardonically.

'Well, it ain't the money, is it? You've beaten them, Harry. You've got all our affidavits made right!' cried John exultantly.

Harry made his way over to Sarah who was talking to Mary and Eliza.

'Sorry about that, gal, but you did do it splendid.'

'I was very pleased to help you, Mr Nursall,' said Sarah. And she was. She savagely repressed the bereft crying of her soul: 'Fran!'

Outside, Fran was chatting to his group among their carriages and horses.

'Must say his first witness was a demned attractive little thing – what, Vaughan?' asked the Squire.

'Er, yes.'

'Come, man. The tales that are afoot about you, you can't fool us with such coolness,' chaffed the other man.

'Very attractive,' conceded Vaughan. 'But would you marry her?'

'Marry her? Lord, no! That wouldn't be the thing at all. So unnecessary too,' he said slyly, winking at Vaughan.

CHAPTER 62

Sarah Changes Her Terms with Three Men

Late on the evening of the Sessions, Sarah was sitting listlessly by her fire at the villa with some unfinished sketches on the table beside her. She was still wondering, as she had been for many hours, how Fran had reacted to her dénouement. Her mind was firmly made up on her course of action but she could not decide whether she was relieved or disappointed that he had not come. All evening, each tiny sound downstairs had made her sit up in nervous anticipation. Now, when she had decided he definitely would not come, she heard the sound of a knock and Mrs Jones opening the front door. She heard his tread on the stairs and braced herself for the confrontation as she rose to open the door.

He looked pale and grave.

'Well, all has been revealed then, Miss Ruddock!' he said with a bitter smile.

'Yes!' said Sarah defiantly.

'Could you not have told me?'

'It was difficult, because I needed your help to get the affidavits done.'

'Ah yes, you wanted a foot in both camps.'

'Partly, yes, but it has been on the tip of my tongue to tell you many times. I believe what really held me back was that it made the gulf between us so impossibly wide and I suppose I have been trying to persuade myself that it was not so great. It is, of course! I realized that today when I saw you among your friends at the assizes. You see, I had never seen you among your own sort except for your family and Dr Crisp.'

Vaughan hung his head, unable to meet her eyes.

'Yes,' continued Sarah angrily. 'Did you realize that the untidy elderly lady you were laughing at was Mrs Nursall, whom Mr Giles spoke about in his evidence?'

Vaughan shook his head miserably and Sarah resumed.

'No, I had no need to hear your voices to know the sort of things you were saying. I am afraid I have been very weak-willed, which is not at all like me. I suppose my head must have been turned by the attention of so eminent a man with so much experience of charming women, although I have been offered the protection of a lord and that did not sway me. Of course, you offered me nothing that I could not return and I suppose that had the effect of closing the gulf between us.

'But it is not too late. We must cease seeing each other. I have known this for so long and failed to act upon it.'

'Is that *all* you have to say to me, Sarah?' he burst out, stepping towards her.

'No! Come no closer please, Mr Vaughan. That is absolutely all. When we have to meet in the future, I beg you will address me as if this ill-considered friendship had never taken place.'

He gazed at her abjectly, without a trace of his usual buoyancy and it took an enormous effort for her to maintain the uncompromising severity in her voice.

'Please go now!'

Sarah's lonely depression was relieved the next evening by an unexpected visit from her father.

Mrs Jones showed him up to her room this time.

'Well, this be very grand,' he said distrustfully, as he gazed around at Sarah's sitting-room, so large by his standards and with its new floor cloth and velvet curtains and comfortable armchairs.

'Yes Father, but surely you haven't come to reprimand me for that again?'

'No, no, Sarah, 'course I ain't. Quite different. I've come to say I'se sorry for what I said before.'

Sarah smiled.

'Sit down, Father,' she cried. 'Yes, sit down there, silly, that's what chairs are for!'

Nevertheless, he only rested uncomfortably on the edge of the seat.

'Me breeches are probably muddy,' he explained.

He looked down awkwardly at his hat.

'Come on, Father! Please tell me what you've come to say.'

He smiled up shyly at her through his fallen dark hair, so differently from the other evening.

'I'se come ter say ter me brave little daughter that her bad ol' father has bin too hard, often, and in particular last time. I was sorry when I remembered what I said just afterwards and I'm a lot more sorry now I know that nothing – well, almost nothing – of it were true.'

Sarah knelt down and embraced him, too full of emotion to speak.

'I was really proud of you at them Sessions yesterday,

and when Harry told me you were the friend what had arranged getting them affidavits and who'd bin looking after them for us, I felt so ashamed of meself.'

'Oh, Father! Thank you for coming, you don't know how happy it's made me,' sobbed Sarah. 'It isn't that I believed you really meant it all, because I've lived with you long enough to know the way your tongue runs away with you when you get angry. I ought to, because mine does the same. But . . . but . . . I do hate you thinking badly of me, especially now.'

'Why especially now?' he asked, ruffling her hair affectionately.

'Oh just that I was feeling very low.'

'That's bad. You must cheer up for Tom's wedding.'

'Yes, I *must*,' said Sarah with determination.

'He's done well, ain't he?'

'I hope you aren't suggesting that *he*'s got something the easy way, Father?'

'Oh no, Sarah! Don't let us start arguing. I don't think I were, anyway. No, he's a hard-working lad. I think ol' Tennant will have no regrets about him for a son-in-law. I just sometimes wish he'd see further than the end of his nose and help us fight, but then he'll have no need to, now. He'll be on *their* side, I suppose.'

'Yes. But perhaps if he can build the pit up so that he has his own business, he'll take more care of the needs of the men he employs. He ought to, after what he's seen.'

'Yeah, I must keep him up to that.'

'Don't expect too much of him, Father. He doesn't think about things like we do. Harry Nursall's done more for the people in this parish than the Charter ever will, I fear.'

'Don't say that, Sarah. It's in our hands,' said John angrily.

'Oh yes, if you disregard the gentry, the legal profession, *and* all the others, and Parliament. Apart from *them*, it is entirely in our hands,' cried Sarah sarcastically.

'I ain't here to argue with you, gal, and I ain't going to but, like George Dunne says, if you ain't got faith that it's possible, then there ain't no point in starting.'

'No, that's true enough. Don't you listen to my bitterness, Father.'

They had been so absorbed in their discussion that they hadn't heard Mrs Jones open the door to another visitor, so Sarah couldn't understand the look of urgent anxiety on her face when she appeared at Sarah's door.

'Come out here a minute, Ma'am! There's that young gentleman from the Academy, Mr Griffiths they call him,' she hissed.

'Oh, that's good. Do ask him to step up, Mrs Jones,' said Sarah, quite forgetting her tear-stained face and dishevelled hair.

Dafydd Griffiths came into the room timidly and looked at John in embarrassment.

'I'm sorry. I really don't wish to intrude. Please allow me to call another time, Miss Lacelle.'

'No, please, Mr Griffiths. I am sure you have met my father already?'

'Your father!' Sarah laughed at his amazement.

'Oh dear! I am always surprising you with my relatives in the most inconsiderate fashion. Yes! My real name is Ruddock, Sarah Ruddock. Lacelle is only my . . . er . . . my professional name,' finished Sarah grandly.

A transformation from acute awkwardness to happy enthusiasm took place in Dafydd's face and manner that was almost as spectacular as upon his introduction to Tom.

'I *am* pleased to meet you again, Mr Griffiths,' declared John, shaking his hand warmly.

'It is indeed delighted I am to meet you in this new aspect, sir,' beamed Dafydd.

'We were just discussing the prospect of success for the Movement,' said Sarah. His face clouded.

'Oh it is bad, that it is. So much effort and so much suffering, but they will present the petition again, will they not, Mr Ruddock?'

'Aye, that we will, comrade, and it will be an even bigger petition next time. It will be bound to win through.'

After this, Sarah could not complain of being lonely since Dafydd Griffiths began to call most evenings and stayed longer and longer. He was sometimes joined later on by the nucleus of the comrades who looked in for a few minutes when they left The Bell. Sarah often had to pack them off, begging some time to draw out her dress designs.

She kept repeating to herself the list of Dafydd's very reasonable qualifications as a suitor, just as she used to repeat Fran's disqualifications. He was young enough. His background was similar to her own. He was intelligent, sensitive and kind. He was well educated and ambitious, perhaps not so ambitious as herself but, since a double helping of that asset might overburden a partnership, it didn't matter. He had a respectable job which could not only be expected to support him but should launch him into the lower echelons of professional society. He was acceptable to her family. Why then did she persistently divert his honest efforts to propose marriage to her?

CHAPTER 63

Earth is Struck and the Wedding Prepared

Harry, John and Tom stood by the remains of Dr Crisp's summer house at the pit edge.

'Aye. That will serve well,' said Harry, 'only you'll need more of the heavier timber for tying it in.'

'How do you mean, Harry?' asked John.

'Well, make a frame out of two inch by three inch timber just the size of the shaft and nail it to the boards every five feet or so to stop them caving in. Don't you worry, Johnny. I'll do that for you as you need it. And Tom! Don't you go digging any more down there. You get that boarding up right now, see. We ain't snatched you back from them grisly jaws to have you buried on Tidbury two months later,' finished Harry sternly.

'No, Mr Nursall. I'll start doing them boards now.'

'And I'll go and get some timber for the ties.'

'Do you know where there is some?' asked John.

'Aye, enough to get you down a few more feet and then we'll have to think.'

'Thank you, Mr Nursall.'

The shaft was soon made safe and Tom dug on down, handing up sack after sack of sand to John who stood on a ladder within reach of the top. Just as the shaft became so deep that John had hardly the strength to climb up with the sacks, Harry appeared with a winch and tackle whose origin he seemed loath to discuss, and John began operating a pulley system from three stout tree trunks that Harry and he erected over the top of the shaft. By some mysterious genius, Harry managed to get a supply of timber for shoring up the sides, and they went on down.

Late one Saturday afternoon Tom gave a muffled

shout and began scrambling up the rickety hand-made ladder. John rushed to the shaft top, stricken with terror, but Tom continued to rise until his broad shoulders were just clear of the top.

He gazed up at his father speechless with some emotion which was hard to read, because as well as his curly hair being full of sand, his eyebrows and eyelashes were encrusted with it and dark sand adhered to the moist skin beneath his eyes and at the corners of his mouth and every bit of him was stained yellow. It seemed an age that John had to scan his son's features fearfully before Tom's blue eyes opened wide and his white teeth gleamed through his sandy lips.

'Father, look! Earth!' He held out a fistful of pale creamy substance which broke cleanly to reveal a very fine waxy texture.

'How much?'

'Can't say. Quite a bit. I knew as soon as I felt me spade drive into it. What shall us do?'

'Get Harry.'

'Let's get half a sackful up to show him.'

'Right. Down you go, lad. Take care!'

'Well done!' cried Harry, as excited as Tom and John.

'We'd best start working along the seam now?' queried Tom.

'Aye. It might be sensible to go a bit deeper so you've got the earth all round yer tunnel. Won't cave in so bad as the sand, eh?'

'Yeah. That's what we did at Jenkins's mine.'

'But,' said Harry, 'let's keep this quiet. You ain't got an affidavit on this bit of land yet. Now's the moment that folks sit up and start getting interested.'

'Not tell *anybody*?' cried John.

'Best not.'

'Not even me comrades at The Bell?'

'No, John. I shouldn't if I was you. George Dunne is

a steady fellow but I don't know how good the rest is at keeping their mouths shut.'

'Jerry's a sound lad.'

'Yes, but he's young. Least said, better kept, and it's Tom's fortune we're guarding.'

'You ain't told *him* not ter talk,' grinned John.

'No, but that is one thing you can depend on with our Tom, ain't it?' Harry clapped him on the shoulder affectionately, but Tom's sandy brows furrowed.

'What's bothering you, lad?' asked Harry.

'I should like to tell Rosie and her mam and father.'

'Well, tell 'em not to let it go no further.'

'Oh, they won't,' smiled Tom happily.

He told Rosie that night as they lay in the hay loft.

'Oh, Tom, love!'

'Ain't you pleased?'

'Y--eah,' she replied uncertainly. 'But it do make you so yeller. You're yeller all over, Tom.'

'Does that matter to you, Rosie?'

'Well, not really. I don't think I should like you *black* so well. I'm glad you ain't found coal in yer pit.'

'There ain't any here,' scoffed Tom. 'Rosie?'

'Yeah.'

'You can't see me now?'

'Not to see what colour you are.'

'And you ain't seen me all over, anyways.'

'Neow . . . not quite,' she giggled. 'Not while you've been yeller, anyways.'

'Rosie!' cried Tom, scandalized.

'Well, I had ter help Mam when you was really ill. You was a-muck with sweat. Anyways what does it matter. We'll be wed next month.'

'I'se looking forward to that, Rosie.'

'Oh, Tom love, so am I. It seems so long.'

'I'se ever so fond of you, Rosie.'

* * *

The preparations for Tom and Rosie's wedding had begun as soon as the day was fixed. At the farm, fifty gallons of beer was set to brew and the ingredients ordered for forty plum puddings. Sarah wrote a letter to Mrs Tennant saying that she would be very pleased to make Rosie's wedding dress and arrange for the making of a suit for Tom if the stuffs were chosen and bought. Rosie and her mother promptly called at the salon and were soon charmed by the variety of material which Sarah showed them, and by her creative pencil.

'What you must consider, Miss Tennant,' said Sarah formally and firmly, 'is that the weight of the stuff you choose is suited to the design you have in mind. For example, if you have this heavy satin that you like and try gathering it into that band above your elbow, do you see what will happen? You will end up with shoulders as broad as Tom's which will never do with your height!' Rosie pouted.

'I am sure Miss Ruddock is right, dear. I should be guided by her. Have this light brocade,' advised her mother. Rosie walked home with a sour little twist on her lips. Sarah had decided upon both the stuff and the design in the end, but Rosie relented on her next visit for a fitting.

'Oh, you look like a dream, Rosie!' cried Sarah, forgetting her professional formality. 'Just imagine Tom's silly old face when he turns and sees you walking up the aisle towards him!'

'He's that nervous already, I don't think he's going to notice if I'm wearing a sack!' said Rosie prosaically.

'Is it going to be a large wedding, Mrs Tennant?'

'Quite large, yes.'

'And who will be there?' asked Sarah, her eyes gleaming with professional interest. 'Will Farmer Hawkins and his family? I understand that *his* eldest daughter is betrothed!'

'Well yes, and the Squire and his lady shall be invited, and Farmers Miller and Green I suppose.'

Sarah looked up sharply.

'Oh dear. Do you have to invite Farmer Green? Tom's father won't be comfortable.'

'Well, how can we invite some neighbours and not others? After all, it ain't Tom's father's wedding, is it?' asked Nell warmly. Sarah shook her head miserably. She visualized her father coerced along by her mother and herself and obliged to behave for the ceremony and then running amok after a couple of tankards of beer and laying the foundation for a generation of family feuding.

'Mam, do you have to? Tom can't abide Farmer Green either and he'll never open his mouth at all if there's the Squire and Vicar,' pleaded Rosie.

'You won't ask Rector Devereux, will you?' cried Sarah in alarm.

'No, no need to do that and the Squire probably won't come, but if we're going to have a proper wedding we've got to have guests, ain't we. Tom won't open his mouth anyway,' said Nell.

'Ain't he got to make a speech?' asked Rosie tremulously.

The three looked at each other in consternation.

As the day drew nearer, even Rosie began to wonder why they were required to prove themselves for marriage by such a social ordeal.

'I'se getting ever so nervous,' confided Tom. 'What about the church and all that?'

'I'll be there, silly,' said Rosie.

'I'se just thought of summat,' cried Tom in alarm. 'I don't think me father will go to church!'

'Well, he's got to, ain't he.'

'P'raps we could do it in a Chapel?'

'Neow, don't be daft, Tom! I want ter be married proper.' Tom shook his head abjectly.

'Whatever is wrong with that Tom of yours, Rosie?' cried Nell Tennant in exasperation. 'He's stopped eating proper again. He'll be all skin and bones by the wedding. Your father and I turn ourselves inside out to keep you two happy and we can't win whatever we do!'

Mr McKay was sewing Tom's suit but Tom refused to go to him to be fitted for it, so Sarah had him kneeling on the floor in her shop while she bustled round him with a mouthful of pins.

'Do it again, Tom,' she ordered, taking them out for a moment.

'And . . . and I want ter say . . .' He looked at her miserably and she nodded vigorously at him.

'. . . er, thank you . . . thank you ter me father and mother . . .'

'. . . in-law,' spluttered Sarah.

'Oh yeah . . . in-law . . . for . . . for . . . for . . .'

Before he left, Sarah stood him in a corner and bullied him until he managed to gabble off in one breath,

'I want ter say thank you very much to me father-in-law, Mr Tennant, for letting me marry Rosie and giving us this good wedding and thank you to everyone what has come . . .' after which he nearly collapsed in tears.

Mrs Tennant was most anxious about the weather. The main bridal party and the honoured guests were to eat at the huge oak table in the kitchen, but there was no room there for the rest so tables were spread outside in the adjacent rick yard for the children, maids and farm hands, just as for the 'harvest home' dinner.

How Tom resisted regaining his appetite was a marvel because the old timbered farm house was full of the smell of the joints from five sides of bacon boiling, innumerable sirloins of beef roasting and, on the Friday, a kitchen full of newly baked bread. Daughters and maids from the surrounding farm houses were drafted in to help and the place was in a shrill pandemonium of feminine activity.

Rosie escaped for a moment to search for Tom and eventually found him crouching behind the last of the hay he was meant to be moving out of the barn to make room for the dancing. He was muttering:

'. . . and ter . . . ter . . . thank them . . . for . . . for . . .'

'Oh Tom, do stop worrying. You'll think of it all on the day or more likely you'll forget, but it don't really matter. Couldn't you try to look forward to it like we used to?'

'Look forward to it!' cried Tom aghast.

'Just think of turning when you're stood at the front and seeing me coming up the aisle towards you in me wedding dress. It is beautiful! Your sister has made it lovely.' Tom carried on shaking his head miserably.

'Tom! Kiss me please. Proper! Not a peck. There, that feels better, don't it?' she said, ruffling his curls lovingly.

CHAPTER 64

The Wedding

As Saturday dawned, Robert Tennant drew the bedroom curtains and threw up the window.

'How is it, Robert? Only tell me if it's good,' murmured Nell sleepily.

'It is . . .' he paused teasingly, 'the most beautiful May morning I have ever set eyes upon.'

'Oh, oh, "Sun before seven, rain before eleven",' wailed Nell.

'No, it will hold.' And the farmer was right.

Tom was sleeping at the cottage on the Heath and soon after half past nine a happy little procession set off down the sandy lane. Tom was the least happy, but even his anxiety and recent loss of weight enhanced the effect of his new dark suit to make him look imposingly tall and mature. Harry Nursall set about making him smile.

'Well, it certainly be a sad day when the young groom has to press an old fellow like me into doing the duties at his wedding. It just bears out what I've bin saying for years: the youngsters ain't ter be trusted any more. You knowed all them young men would lose Rosie's ring for you, didn't yer, Tom? Hey, dang me! Wherever is it?'

Harry began an elaborate charade of turning out his pockets and looking in his hat until Tom's face was a study of anguish.

'Ah, here it be, young fellow-me-lad,' cried Harry, triumphantly holding up his little finger.

'Oh, do stop it, Mr Nursall! I'se worried enough,' begged the laughing Tom.

'Well, *you* stop it, man! It don't matter! We're going ter marry yer today whether the ring's got lost and you've forgot yer speech. We're going ter marry yer and enjoy ourselves come what may!' cried Harry clapping Tom's shoulder.

'That's right, Tom. We are all going ter have a great day!' confirmed his father.

Sarah joined the procession as it passed through Aspley Square. She was so excited that she embraced everyone, starting with Tom.

'Oh, how handsome you look! So mature and distinguished. There are going to be such a lot of envious hearts a-throb today. Even I feel resentful at Rosie Tennant carrying off my big brother.'

It was obvious that Eliza and John shared her pride.

Sarah had been very busy. She had designed and supervised the making of a dress and bonnet each for her mother, Tize and Mary Nursall. New dresses were a rare luxury and they were still standing and moving awkwardly in great self-consciousness. Sarah had taken particular trouble with Mary's dress. She saw this as a real challenge for her craft, since Rosie's plump fair beauty would look well in any wedding dress, but it was much more difficult to capture and enhance Mary's unworldly, elderly charm. Furthermore, the chosen dress had to stay in place on her spare, agile body. Sarah held Mary affectionately at arm's length to gauge her success. The high-waisted style suited the white muslin sprigged with forget-me-nots very well and, after she had tucked the odd stray grey lock firmly under the flower-trimmed bonnet, she was well satisfied. She wished Francis Vaughan could have seen Mary looking so demure.

'Don't you think our bride, Rosie, is going to have some hard competition, gal?' said Harry gallantly.

'She is, Mr Nursall, and if I was you I should not stray too far from this lovely wife of yours.'

'Oh, Sarah, get along with your nonsense,' giggled Mary, 'but it *is* a beautiful dress, dearie. I ain't never had a pretty dress like this, have I, Harry? I allus picks forget-me-nots. They're one of me favourite flowers, although I shouldn't say that because I like them all, all the daintier ones, that is . . .' Mary murmured on dreamily to herself as Sarah's attention moved to her mother and Tize.

The little church of Segenhoe, out in the fields, was surrounded by horses and chaises and people. Tom's panic nearly got the better of him. He was marched in firmly with his father's hand on one arm and Harry's on his shoulder as if he was in the hands of a press gang. From that moment, his and Rosie's day passed in a confused dream from which they found it difficult to pick out any one clear impression when they went over it later on, but there were a few.

Tom *did* turn to look over his shoulder as he stood with Harry as the service began. He could hardly believe that the beautiful apparition amongst the pale flounces and frills advancing up the aisle could possibly be his

Rosie. It was, and he managed to say 'I will' when Harry pummelled him for a second time, and the ring was safely transferred from Harry's little finger to Rosie's left third. As soon as Rosie put back her veil, Tom clung to her for dear life and as they left the church at the end of the service they scuttled to their pony trap through showers of flower petals.

Quite an army of maids and farm hands waited for them outside the door of the farm house, which was thrown wide open to invite the procession in. The old studded door and soft brick must have opened its welcoming sanctuary to many other young married couples, the last being Robert and Nell of course. Tom and Rosie only gained the low-ceilinged hall through yet another cascade of flower petals and happy laughter.

The house was full of excited dogs and children who dashed between the legs of helpers and guests. Rosie crouched in the hall, surrounded by the billowing folds of her skirt and received the slavering congratulations of her retriever and his friends, with Tom smiling down at her.

'Oh, Rosie! Mind your dress,' scolded her mother.

At last, everyone who could expect to be, was seated and Harry quelled the talking and laughing for a moment.

'My friends, I know we are all here today to see Rosie and Tom settled happily.' Cheers and table banging ensued. 'And just so that Tom can start enjoying his happiness all the sooner, I should like you to listen to a few words he has ter say. It won't keep you from this splendid feast for more than a moment because I'll warrant he's forgot most of it and there ain't no man what can blame him, seeing his bride, Rosie, looking as lovely as what she does.'

Cheers and calls of 'Tom, come on Tom!' and 'Silence for the groom,' greeted this address.

Tom, blushing deeply, was pushed to his feet. He

opened his mouth and allowed his eyes to travel up and down the long table, which was a mistake, because he began to close it again.

Sarah's voice prompted him.

'I should like . . . Come on, Tom!'

'I should like . . .'

'Yeah! *What* would you like, Tom?' shouted a man's voice and was greeted by guffaws of rough laughter which needled Tom into shocked eloquence.

'. . . ter thank . . . Mr Tennant an' . . . an' . . . Mrs Tennant . . . for Rosie . . . an' . . . an' . . . all of this,' he ended triumphantly.

'Well said, Tom! Well done, man!' sounded through the cheers and clapping, and Tom did begin to enjoy his wedding.

Robert Tennant pledged the couple's health and the sliced sirloins and hams began to disappear apace. Children carrying jugs of beer appropriate to their size were kept busy refilling tankards and even the bowls of mustard and pickle had to be constantly replenished. Most of the forty plum puddings were eaten and a trio of fiddler and pipers moved among the tables playing. After a couple of hours for the guests to rest and the tables to be cleared and carried to the barn, more players arrived and Rosie and Tom led off the long line of couples in the first dance. Dancing, eating and drinking continued long into the crisp darkness of the May night, and after Rosie and Tom had seen the last group of guests on their way, they stood for a little while among the few remaining ricks in the rick yard gazing at the stars and crescent moon, which seemed brighter, clearer and more full of exciting promises than they ever had.

'I'm that glad you lost your job at the mine, Tom.'

'Yeah. I'm even glad nobody'd pay me enough until I got here.'

'Do you think you've bin paid enough now, Tom?'

'Y-e-a-h!'

CHAPTER 65

The Speculators

Sarah had more or less succeeded in numbing the aching loneliness in her heart by immersing herself in the bustle of making wedding dresses. She was carried along by the excitement of the day and, to all outward appearances, seemed happy enough, but she could not completely suppress the little worm of bitterness which began to gnaw deeper when the wedding was over. The sheer simplicity of Tom and Rosie's love and future taunted her. Tom no longer had any worries about his earnings and his life beckoned him on to carry out steadily the seasonal, thought-quelling labour of sowing, haymaking and harvesting. Rosie would be happily employed in the farmhouse kitchen and busy with her brood of healthy well-fed youngsters. There would be bound to be the odd tragedy of a toddler struck down by childhood ailments, but most would survive, robust and strong, to carry on the future generations of sowers, haymakers and harvesters. Sarah told herself that such a life would not suit her; how bored she would become without a challenge to her intellect and ambition, but she could not quite convince herself that she really relished feeling her way along the precarious tight-rope of survival. Did she want to consider the merits of each decision for her future in terms of how much self-esteem and happiness should be bartered for how much comfort and income? When she used to ask herself how such a life would end, some rosy phantom of happy marriage would hover unconvincingly in front of her, but just recently she had come to know the end of her present road with reasonable certainty. It was before her, every day, in the inescapable form of Mrs Jones; the hardworking, unscrupulous, opportunist old woman. Sarah could so clearly see how, as her youthful charms began to fail, Mrs Jones had had to be ever more aggressively alert to ensure her survival. Even the touching loyalty which the old lady showed towards Sarah now, confirmed her own recognition of Sarah's destiny.

'What do you think of Dr Crisp, Mrs Jones?' asked Sarah quite irrelevantly in the kitchen one night.

The shoe-button eyes examined Sarah's face keenly and took a shrewd sounding of her thoughts.

'He's a hard man, Miss. He'd treat yer bad if you let him. I expect you could manage him, though.'

There was no deluding Mrs Jones.

'Supposing he asked me to marry him and I accepted, do you think I should enjoy it?'

'Enjoy?' exclaimed the old lady, non-plussed. It was clearly an aspect of marriage that had not struck her. Sarah smiled.

'Well, I should have more control. I could entertain friends and invite interesting people to stay.'

The old lady did not answer. She seemed to be searching back through her memory. Eventually she said:

'I suppose I did like being wed for a little while, but it weren't long. Babies kept coming and there weren't enough food ter feed them and not enough wood ter keep them warm and then they got sick. Jimmy weren't a bad man and he was very big and strong, like your brother Tom, Miss. But all men are the same. They get in their cups and start hitting yer and yer need the money what they spend on beer for the food.'

'How long had you been married when he died?' asked Sarah gently.

'Oh, be about eight years. I'd had five little ones and buried three.'

Yes, Sarah could not be surprised that 'enjoyment'

391

was not a thing that Mrs Jones readily associated with marriage.

Soon after this conversation, Dr Crisp spent two weeks at the villa and Sarah made an exploratory effort to be particularly attentive. He rode out with Vaughan most days and seemed disgruntled that his friend would not drop in so readily as before to spend the evening chatting with him and Sarah. He eventually issued Vaughan with a formal invitation to dinner.

Sarah and Dr Crisp were discussing the menu for the meal.

'Should you not invite Mrs Vaughan as well?' asked Sarah.

'Oh, heaven forbid! Such a vacuous woman. No, I am sure there is no need. Anyway, I wish to discuss business with Fran.'

'Have you had any responses to your articles?'

'Oh yes. A great many. I must read you some.' He walked over to his desk and took out a folder.

'Now this is a letter from Sir Joseph Briggs. He has a consumptive wife and would like to move here. Can I put him in touch with a land agent? And there are letters in the same vein from Lady Dartford and a Mr Josiah Higginbotham and a Mr Samuel Brown. There is a great deal of money to be made from this land, Miss Lacelle.'

'Perhaps you should see if you can buy some.'

'Yes, certainly. Do you, by any chance, know a man who would sell to me?'

'I shall enquire. How much would you be willing to pay for it?'

'It is very poor soil. It can't be worth much an acre,' said Crisp cautiously. 'I should also like to buy some at the bottom of the hill, on the way to Wavendon.'

'Oh well, that is good wheat and pasture land. You would have to buy that off farmers and they know what the land is worth.'

'Yes, that is a pity, but I should get the Heath land cheap.'

'Not if I can manage otherwise,' said Sarah to herself. But aloud she said,

'Why do you want the low-lying land, Dr Crisp?'

'Oh, just a speculation of mine,' he said evasively.

Sarah intended to furnish a particularly good meal to celebrate her first appearance as the hostess at Dr Crisp's table, and she spent quite a lot of time helping the cook in the kitchen. Crisp was liberal with his wine cellar and the two men were soon talking freely about Crisp's financial speculations.

'I am sure Sarah will prove a useful go-between for you to buy land on the Heath, Mat,' said Vaughan, with just a hint of bitterness, Sarah thought.

'Yes, she has already found someone interested in selling. He is calling tomorrow.'

'Dr Crisp is also wanting to buy some low-lying ground towards Wavendon,' said Sarah.

'Oh really! Are you thinking of joining our farming fraternity?' asked Vaughan.

'No, not at all. Farming seems a poor way of getting a return on capital. I should never consider it.'

'What shall you do with this land, then?'

'I plan to sell it to a Railway Board!'

'A Railway Board!'

'Yes. They are beginning to form all over the country. There will soon be a network of railways radiating out from London with strategic cross-connections of which the Oxford to Cambridge line will be one of the more important.'

'Oxford to Cambridge through Aspley Guise, eh?' said Vaughan thoughtfully.

'Well, it clearly cannot run in these hills but it will come as close to Woburn as it can and run through Bedford.'

'The important thing is to work out precisely where

and then buy up narrow strips of the land before the word gets round.'

'Exactly the reason I have brought this map with me, my dear Fran. All we now need is a ruler. Railways must be as straight as the geography will allow.'

'And when we have our railway, recolonization of the Heath should gather momentum!'

'Exactly.'

'You look positively radiant with interest, Sarah!' said Vaughan. 'Do you foresee dresses and rolls of stuff travelling by rail?'

'Hardly,' Sarah simpered, but what she did foresee were sacks and sacks of fuller's earth.

CHAPTER 66

Proposals and Transactions

The man who had the land to sell was Lunnon but Harry Nursall came along in order to see that they got the highest price that Crisp could be induced to pay. As might be imagined, Dr Crisp had a hard time side-stepping and sparring with Harry, whom he initially took for an idiot and, in the end, Lunnon was delighted to hand over his three-quarters of an acre for thirty-five pounds, which was approaching two years' wages for him.

Sarah visited the Heath to talk over plans for the future with her parents and Mary and Harry were invited to the Ruddocks' cottage.

'How would you feel about us selling out, Harry, 'cause our bit is right beside yours?' asked John.

'Oh, it won't bother us, will it, Mary?'

'Will they build big houses on it?' asked Mary anxiously.

'Only one, I should think, and they're bound to build it near the lane. It won't disturb your birds much, love,' said Harry.

'What about our beautiful cottage?' asked Eliza.

'I'll build you a better one,' said John.

'But where? I shouldn't like to go back to the village now.'

'Well, with forty pounds in our pocket, we can live almost anywhere you choose, Liza.'

'I wonder if you could buy a bit of land at the bottom of the hill on the way to Wavendon,' said Sarah.

'Well, Jo Kemp was saying he wanted rid of his tile pit and kiln. He's getting too old for the job.'

'Really? You ought to try to get that, Father. He's got a little brick cottage there, hasn't he?' cried Sarah excitedly.

'T'aint very big but I could build another room or two on, I suppose.'

'Why there, gal?' asked Harry eyeing her keenly.

'Dr Crisp says there's a railway being built between Oxford and Bedford and Cambridge and the line he drew on his map would have gone just about through Mr Kemp's tile pit.'

'Well there you are, John and Liza. So long as you don't mind tossing to and fro like ships in a storm, Sarah's got you all lined up to make another fortune,' said Harry, cynically.

'Yes, but if they just sold a narrow strip beside the pit to the Railway Board, they'd still have enough left, and the house, and think how handy it would be for sending away tiles and fuller's earth by train!'

'Yes, if this railway's really going to be built, it could be the making of us,' cried John enthusiastically.

'Aye. They're building big stations in London and a lot of rail is already down. I fear it will happen,' sighed Harry.

'Well, don't you want it to, Mr Nursall?'

'Oh, I don't hold with this so-called progress. We've just got them turnpikes right so that coaches can dash hither and thither far too fast and now, hey-presto, railways! An' what will happen to the coaches and horses and inns, eh? Finished! No more need for the fast roads, neither.'

'They'll still run the coaches surely, Harry? People won't want to ride in them trains. They'll be good for heavy stuff and mail, perhaps, but I can't see people taking to all that smoke and steam and clattering along iron rails. Just think of the clamour. You wouldn't be able to hear yourself speak!' said John.

'Want to have a wager with me, John? Might be yer chance to make a third fortune, man,' said Harry. 'No, if I'm right, Mary, we'll have so many useless coaches on the Heath you'll be able to live in a regular palace of them.'

'It would be strange without coaches on the turnpike,' said Mary wonderingly.

Sarah remembered the deafening clatter in the yard of the Angel on her first visit to London and wondered whether a train could be any worse, but it was nearly four years before she had a chance to find out, and quite a lot of changes took place in the fortunes of the Ruddocks during that time.

John and Eliza's first grandchild was born in the November of the year that Tom and Rosie married. Considering how early the birth was, he was a remarkably robust baby, weighing nearly eight pounds. His two grandmothers, particularly Eliza, became dedicated slaves to Thomas from his first lusty cry. He was succeeded in close succession by Mary Rose and Robert, who was named ostensibly after his grandfather but soon became known as Bobby and filled an empty place in John and Eliza's hearts. Aunt Sarah took little more than a polite interest in her nephews and niece although she did enjoy using remnants to make elaborate little Sunday dresses for Mary Rose.

John and Eliza sold their piece of the Heath to Dr Crisp for the enormous sum of forty-eight pounds. Sarah played her part in cajoling the last eight pounds from her master, and it nearly cost her dear.

'Why you should persuade me to pay so high a price to Ruddock just because he's your father, I cannot imagine, Sarah!'

'Blood is thicker than water, they say.'

'Yes, but it's your blood and my money,' he replied peevishly. 'Which does bring me on to the subject of the household expenses. There may be a certain amount of inflation nationally but it is certainly not running at as high a level as my household accounts are.'

Sarah gazed at him plaintively, her head on one side.

'Are you satisfied with the way I run the house? Remember you are here much more now and we often entertain. Remember Lord and Lady Hethrington congratulated you last week on the excellence of your cook. Remember that you do not have a particularly good cook and certainly not an expensive one. It is I, Dr Crisp, who manage all this for you.'

'Yes, well . . . You do manage exceedingly well, Sarah.'

He paused, as if turning something over in his mind and Sarah's heart began to pound. She had a strong premonition that he was about to make the offer which she was bound to accept; the change in status which would lift her clear of the destiny of Mrs Jones.

'Sarah, my dear. I have been considering asking you something for some length of time and I really think that this is the moment. Would you honour me with your hand in marriage?'

Sarah's voice did not respond in the way it should have done. All on its own she heard it ask quietly:

'Why exactly this moment, Dr Crisp?'

'Well . . . er . . . er . . . it seemed a good one.'

Her erring voice attempted to continue by saying something in the vein of,

'I suppose wives may be expected to keep houses more cheaply than housekeepers?' Sarah managed to subdue it and reach a compromise.

'It is a very generous offer, Dr Crisp. I do hope you will not be offended if I do not reply immediately. It is such a big decision, I should like to think about it and reassure myself that I am worthy of such an honour.'

He was clearly taken aback that the honour had not been seized upon without delay, but he managed to smile coolly.

'No, quite so. It is, of course, an hon . . . a proposition that you should consider most seriously.'

Sarah spent several wretched days considering it during which time Francis Vaughan visited them for an hour one Sunday morning and they sat in the garden drinking coffee together. Sarah wondered whether he had been told about Crisp's proposal, but he gave no sign that he had. He sat relaxed and debonair, bantering away amicably, making them smile at a dozen amusing turns of phrase. Sarah watched his straight profile and fair side burns glinting golden in the sun as he turned his head, the creases in his cheeks as he smiled and the way his thick wavy hair curled behind his ears and over his collar. Crisp only contributed the odd sour comment and he had no physical favours, but the most oppressive thing about him was his calculating caution and total lack of joy. Sarah sighed hopelessly.

CHAPTER 67

An Agreeable Business Alliance

Vaughan was sitting again, with a glass in his hand, in Crisp's study one evening the following week.

'I have decided to return to London tomorrow,' said Crisp morosely.

'Oh, so soon?' asked Vaughan in surprise.

'Yes. I have suffered a slight repulse and shall retire to lick my wounds.'

'Oh, did you not succeed on the deal with Mills?'

'No, that is all arranged.' He paused and then decided to confide in Vaughan.

'To be perfectly honest, Fran, I have proposed to a woman for the first time in my life and been rejected, or at least asked to give her more time.'

Vaughan frowned and leant forward in his chair.

'A woman! May I ask who?'

'Why Sarah, of course,' snapped Crisp, rising irritably and going to his desk.

'She repulsed you, you say?'

'No, that's too strong a word. She asked me to repeat the offer in a few months, if I would be so kind. It is hard to know how to treat women when they behave so capriciously.'

'Yes,' mused Vaughan, smiling gently. He wondered what plan Sarah had which made her reject Crisp's offer. He had to confess to a quite unjustifiable sense of satisfaction, but he did not allow himself to harbour any illusions about her motive and he quite thought he had stumbled across it the following week.

He called unexpectedly at the villa in response to a letter from Crisp asking him to forward some documents.

'Miss Lacelle has a visitor, sir,' said Mrs Jones as she let him in.

'Oh, that does not matter. I just want some documents from Dr Crisp's desk. He wants them sent to him in London.'

Vaughan's eyes rested on a pair of red leather gloves lying on the hall table and, on his return, he picked them up. They were of an unusually large size and the palms were well worn, having protected their owner from some very heavy manual work, but they were undoubtedly made from the leather he had given Sarah two years or more before. As he returned them to the table, Sarah's door opened and she came out followed by the fair young giant himself. Vaughan quickly identified him as the inarticulate youth he had watched digging on the Heath.

'Oh, Mr Vaughan. I was not expecting you!' cried Sarah gaily. 'Let me introduce you to Tom.'

They shook hands, Tom mumbled something and blushed and smiled.

'Well, do you visit Miss Ruddock often?' asked Vaughan provocatively.

'Neow. Not much,' said Tom, shaking his head.

Vaughan looked questioningly at Sarah, determined to get to the bottom of their relationship, but she only smiled mischievously.

'Tell Mr Vaughan what we have been talking about, Tom. He might be able to help us,' she said.

Tom shrugged and smiled shyly.

'It were about the pit,' he said.

'The pit?'

'Yeah. Fuller's earth pit on Tidbury.'

'Oh yes. I remember seeing you starting that.'

'Yeah. They're trying to turn us off now.'

'They?'

'Farmer Green and Rector Devereux and the Vestry.'

400

'We need an affidavit or something to show them,' said Sarah.

'I don't see how I can help,' said Vaughan.

'Suppose Tom sold you the land and we got Mr Place to draw up deeds of some sort?'

'Why should I want a fuller's earth mine?'

'There's a lot of earth there. If I had more time ter dig or you paid a fellow . . .' said Tom earnestly.

'There's the railway coming to transport it,' said Sarah.

'Yes, but how do you two benefit?' asked Vaughan, puzzled.

'Just that we want to keep an interest in it and we badly need some money to buy a good strong horse and cart and shovels and sacks. You know how it ruins poor little Dobs's legs!' Sarah looked up slyly at Vaughan.

'Oh, I see now. That is what's been sending the poor pony lame every other week!' said Vaughan indignantly.

'I'se sorry, sir,' said Tom. 'I didn't want to use him but we hadn't got anything else and Sarah said you wouldn't mind.'

'You see, it's a family business. My father and Tom could have one share and you the other. It would be a very good investment for you because all the hard work is done and they've found a thick seam.'

'Yeah. And me and my father will do most of the work but he do need another fellow to help when I ain't there.'

'Your father?' queried Vaughan. Sarah began to laugh, well aware of Vaughan's mistaken deduction.

'Tom is my giant!' she teased, patting his arm proudly. 'My giant brother!'

'Brother!' exclaimed Vaughan in amazement.

'Oh, Sarah!' reprimanded Tom crossly. He failed to see the joke and thought it very rude of her.

Vaughan was laughing now.

'Forgive your sister. She is just a mischievous little monkey,' he rallied Tom.

'But how would it look in the Select Vestry Committee when Devereux and Green began complaining about "paupers misappropriating parish land" (forgive me, Mr Ruddock, I am just quoting their arrogant way of speech), and I say "Well, actually, *I* own it"?'

'How much do you care about how it looks in the Select Vestry meeting?' asked Sarah sulkily.

'Well, not much, I suppose. I very often don't approve of their decisions. In fact, I usually find myself carrying one end of the banner of non-conformity with poor old Hall, these days. I could resign my position.'

'Oh, don't do that!' cried Sarah in alarm.

'I see. I am a valuable spy in that camp, am I?'

Sarah smiled non-committally.

'And how much money are you asking for this bit of parish land? I know I shan't get a bargain.'

'But you will get a very valuable investment, Mr Vaughan,' Sarah assured him.

'How much?' They both turned their eyes questioningly to Tom, but he was recuperating from his unusually large contribution to the discussion so far.

'Does fifty pounds sound reasonable?' asked Sarah.

'No!'

'Well, forty-five?' she hazarded with a beguiling smile.

'How much land are we talking about?'

'There be one and a half acres inside our bank,' said Tom promptly.

'I shall offter you thirty pounds for the land and a repayable loan of twenty pounds to buy the equipment, if . . .' he put out a restraining hand towards Sarah who seemed about to embrace him in delight.

'. . . if Mr Place can draw up a convincing deed of transfer which safeguards me a half share in future profits after the twenty pounds is recouped.'

'There, Tom! You and Father will be very happy with that arrangement, won't you?'

'Ye-ah. P'raps we'd better tell him.'

'I think you had,' smiled Vaughan.

'In the meantime, perhaps you would ask Dr Crisp to make arrangements for the agreement since I am sure my father will accept your kind offer.'

'Of course, Madam. It shall be done promptly since I have to write to him tonight anyway.'

Vaughan bowed and Sarah inclined her head imperiously while Tom looked from one to the other, quite bemused. He stepped towards the door and Vaughan picked up the gloves and handed them to him.

'You'll be needing these, Mr Ruddock, to dig up all our fuller's earth.'

'Ye-ah,' smiled Tom. 'Thank you.'

'There, you see,' said Sarah, closing the door behind him, 'even your piece of red leather will prove a good investment.'

'Do you really think that I am as mercenary as you?'

'No, Fran. But you have no need to be. That is the really inescapable difference between us. Anyway, I have not been acting in a sensibly mercenary way lately,' she sighed.

Vaughan gazed at her a moment, his eyes deeply troubled.

'I must be going, too. Goodbye, Sarah.'

CHAPTER 68

Heart over Head

Within a year from making the deal with Vaughan, John Ruddock, who had long ago given up the thought of ever being his own master, independent of the farmers

403

and the roundsman system, was employing five men. Two helped him at the fuller's earth mine and three carried on the production of the coarse tiles and drainage pipes. Not only did they all receive a fair wage but they had a small share in the future profits of the businesses. Two large houses had been built on the Heath and three more were under construction, so there was a demand for the products of the tile works without having to cart them further than the Heath. Between them, John, Tom and Vaughan owned two heavy draught-horses, a dray and a cart so the tiles and pipes travelled up to the Heath and the fuller's earth came back down. Some earth was sent to London and Northamptonshire but most of it went into stock at the tile works waiting for the railway to open, when it could be despatched to the fullers of Gloucestershire and Yorkshire. John and Eliza had got a good price for the strip of land they sold to the Railway Board and had cleared their debt to Vaughan. They could hardly believe in their good fortune. John was for starting a whole multitude of new businesses to run as workers' co-operatives. The round table at The Bell was full of magnificent ideas each evening but the members of the family co-operative shook their heads firmly, mentioning the inadvisability of running before one could walk, and insisted that any spare funds should be invested in the two businesses they already had. These were by no means the only flourishing ones between the Heath and the new railway line. Each family who had sold their squatters' rights to land on the Heath, had set up as bakers, butchers and even candle-stick makers and their futures were assured at the new property owners settled in. Vaughan, Crisp and several other gentry of a speculative frame, had purchased land for a new church and were forming a fund to build it, since it was generally held in such circles that 'church building is an advantageous speculation when sites for new villa residences are available nearby'.

'And of course,' mentioned Harry Nursall cynically, 'it be all for the good of their 'ealth that these weak-chested folk are being h'enticed on to the Heath.'

The only unsatisfactory thing about the neighbourhood, in this respect, was its name. The hamlet with two small inns which had grown up around the turnpike was called Hog-Sty-End!

Such is the perversity of some humans that, as the future began to look so rosy for her family, the more dissatisfied Sarah became with her own life. The salon was doing a steady trade but it had found its level and could not be expected to expand any more. There was no room to do so anyway. The girls were already cramped and by the time Sarah had paid them and the punishing rent that Cox was exacting, there was little enough left. She could certainly not maintain the standard of luxury she enjoyed without Dr Crisp, and he was pressing for her decision.

As she repeatedly told herself, she had no option. Dafydd Griffiths was still waiting patiently but he could not afford her and, more to the point, she didn't want to jeopardize his happiness as she knew she would if she accepted him. At least she felt no loyalty beyond a business one to Crisp. She would grant him his due, enjoy his wealth and make sure she was not imposed upon. She wondered how many children she was expected to bear. Perhaps she would be unable to have any; that would be a happy release. She would make sure it would be no more than two anyway, and nannies and governesses were readily available. Yes, she could cope with two children. But . . . but . . . she wished there was someone she could speak to.

'Mrs Jones! Shall I marry Dr Crisp?'

The old lady stopped polishing a candlestick and looked out of the window, thoughtfully.

'Yeah, I think you'd better. Be best in the long run.

He's a rich man and allus will be,' she said, resuming her polishing.

That was exactly what Sarah knew, of course, but it didn't satisfy her.

'You'd best put the other one out of yer mind, Miss,' added Mrs Jones suddenly.

'What? Mr Griffiths?' asked Sarah, quite taken aback.

'Neow, t'other one.'

'Not Mr Vaughan?'

'Yeah. He's no good to yer. Too old; married man; no staying in him; brought up too soft.'

Sarah smiled unhappily.

'He's been brought up the same as Dr Crisp,' she said. Mrs Jones shrugged.

'Maybe, but *he*'s a real gentleman. Crisp ain't.'

Sarah knew what she meant, but Crisp wouldn't have done. He was due back at the villa the following day and he had given Sarah a firm ultimatum that he must have her answer then. Desperate to escape, Sarah put on her hat and coat and walked down the lane to the shop. There was nothing to be done that could not be left until tomorrow, but she began moving lengths of cloth and tidying up here and there, just to ease her mind. After a time, she heard a tap on the door. It was a timid one and her heart sank as she braced herself to admit Dafydd and face yet another complication to her decision but, to her surprise, Francis Vaughan was standing on the step.

'Oh!' exclaimed Sarah.

'Yes, I was prowling about unhappily and saw the candle burning. May I step in for a moment? What are you doing working so late and alone. You are alone, aren't you, Sarah?'

'Yes, I am trying to bully myself into a firm frame of mind to ride to the scaffold tomorrow.'

'That sounds dreadful. What, pray, is happening tomorrow?'

'Dr Crisp is to have the final answer to a question he put to me a long time ago.'

'And shall he be satisfied?'

'Oh yes! I have known all along what the answer must be, but I lacked the courage to say.'

'It is your life, Sarah, and I know you usually manage it with superb calculation and courage, not to mention hard work, but happiness is a very precious commodity.'

'Luxury! Happiness is a luxury.'

Vaughan sighed.

'Oh, how hard-hearted you are, Sarah.'

'No. My heart is as soft as anyone's, Fran,' she cried wildly, 'at least it is at the moment. A few years of life with Dr Crisp will probably cure it of that weakness.'

'Don't torment me, Sarah. I know the decision you made three years ago was the right one, but please don't torment me any more. Just do what you have to.'

Vaughan had only stepped just inside the door and he turned, pale faced, wrenched it open and fled, pushing it to sharply behind him. Sarah ran upstairs and threw herself on the couch, sobbing convulsively.

Crisp arrived the following afternoon and found Sarah in one of her prettiest dresses, but subdued and grave. Even he noticed that she lacked her usual sparkle. She had arranged a particularly dainty but satisfying dinner which they ate together, drinking a particularly fine wine, and the moment that Sarah's destiny would be decided, drew closer and closer.

Crisp rose briskly and extinguished the candles on the table, leaving only a candelabra on the sideboard alight.

'Ah, romantic dimness,' thought Sarah.

'Well, Sarah, I trust I have now given you ample time to overcome your . . . er . . . maidenly shyness,' his tone was sarcastic, 'and I now require the answer to my proposal. Will you do me the honour of becoming my wife?'

There was a pause and a stifling suspense grew, making it more and more difficult for Sarah to break the silence. She gazed into his protuberant cold eyes and could think of nothing . . . except . . . fish! Yes, the huge dead codfish she had seen lying on a blood-smeared slab in Billingsgate market. Why should such a recollection come to her now? She closed her eyes, feeling that something must shatter. She wasn't sure whether it would be the crystal chandelier above her or something inside her chest, but shatter it must.

'Well, Sarah?' His voice sounded a long way away.

'Er . . . er . . . yes, please,' she muttered inadequately.

'You *will* marry me?' Sarah nodded miserably. Nothing had shattered. She felt so utterly empty, she supposed there was nothing left that could ever shatter again.

Crisp rose clumsily from his half-kneeling position and folded her in his arms. Her shoulder became caught under the arm of his jacket so that even that simple act became awkward. He pressed his whiskery moist lips to hers . . . 'codfish . . . codfish' whispered her soul. He fumbled with the fastenings at the side of her bodice and ripped them apart to insert his hand, groping about her back, her side, feeling for and eventually engaging her breast. She didn't feel like the fish herself, she didn't feel so elusively slippery. She felt more helpless, like a piece of meat which the coarse, bloodied hand of the butcher was shaping into a joint, pushing into shape, lacing up with string, another loop and another knot, until he reached for his sharp knife and . . .

Crisp was suddenly thrust away from her. It happened exactly as it had with Frank Cox. She could not believe it was she who had done it. He tripped and reeled heavily across the room, knocking over first a dining chair and then a jardinière which broke, scattering water and flowers and, as he sank down against the sideboard, she took a wine glass off the table and flung it at him and then another one and a plate . . . She was remembering the men pulling up her fruit trees on the wind-ravaged night of the eviction; the guttering of the candle reminded her of the flames from her burning home, leaping to flare across her adversaries as she, the tiny demoniacal fury, hit at their legs and threw handfuls of turf and sand. Ah, she was winning again. Crisp struggled awkwardly to his feet, holding one arm up to shield his head from the missiles and, with a gutteral snarl, he stumbled from the room as Mrs Jones pushed past him to get in.

'Mercy me! Whatever has 'appened?'

Sarah stood quite still, her breath coming in short gasps.

'What's he done to you, Missy?' screamed Mrs Jones.

'N . . . nothing; I must go, now, quickly.'

'I'll come. Wait, Miss. Yer hat and coat. You can't go out like that. Yer dress is all undone. Wait!'

Sarah was running down Woburn Lane with Mrs Jones, her arms full of hats and coats, toddling after her crying: 'Wait for me, Miss.'

There was a man walking up the lane towards them. He broke into a run as he saw her but she didn't attempt to avoid him. She was absolutely certain who it was, as if she had known he would come. She fell sobbing into his outspread arms and he clasped her tightly to him.

'Whatever has happened, Mrs Jones?' asked Vaughan.

'Terrible. It's bad,' gasped the old lady. 'I think Dr Crisp has been beating 'er.'

'Why, darling? Why, Sarah?'

She shook her head.

'It's me that's been beating him.'

'You've made an awful mess,' said Mrs Jones reproachfully, 'and you'd best put yer 'at an' coat on before you catch cold.'

Sarah allowed them to dress her and Mrs Jones put her own hat and coat on.

'Where shall we go now?' asked Vaughan. Sarah laid her head against his chest, absolutely passive. She did not care about anything so long as he kept his arms about her.

'The shop?' suggested Mrs Jones.

'Yes, and then I shall get out my chaise and we shall go to Dunstable.'

'Dunstable?' queried Mrs Jones.

'Yes, to the Sugar Loaf. It's a very good inn. Sarah and I have been there before.'

'I ain't leaving her!' declared Mrs Jones.

'No, I should think not, and neither am I.'

'What about yer wife?'

'I have just told her I *am* leaving her.'

'You ain't wasted time thinking, have yer?'

'Well, to be honest, yes! I told her the same thing three years ago,' said Vaughan defensively.

Sarah suddenly came to life.

'Three years ago! You never told *me*!'

'I most certainly tried to. You refused to let me speak and sent me away with a flea in my ear, never to return.'

'Oh, Fran! Fran, my darling.' Sarah was trying to laugh but tears were streaming down her face.

CHAPTER 69

Postscript

The Classical Academy was sold and the proceeds divided between Theresa and Vaughan. Dafydd Griffiths remained teaching there and soon became a senior master. He never quite recovered from his infatuation with Sarah, but he was reconciled by marrying her sister,

Tize, which pleased John who could never quite accept Francis Vaughan as an adequate son-in-law. Tom became so indispensable at the farm that he relinquished most of his share in the fuller's earth mine but he was gratified to see the way it expanded as soon as the railway line was opened. Mary and Harry Nursall added several beautiful coaches to their accommodation, but little else changed in their life. Mary communed happily with her family of birds, flowers and the Ruddock grandchildren and Harry kept a benevolent eye on everyone and everything so that his wisdom was as much sought after as ever. Eliza and John found their middle age so full of happy successes that they never ceased to marvel at their good fortune. The Chartist cause seemed a lost one in terms of hard achievement, but as Sarah, John, Dafydd and the round table group at The Bell, frequently commented, the seeds the Movement had sown were still growing and the social inequalities were so widely acknowledged that, little by little, they were sure to be mended.

Sarah opened her own shop at Hog-Sty-End with plenty of room to cope with the steady increase in business from the Heath. She was highly respected as the financial manager and general policy maker for all the family enterprises, but the one person who never obeyed her instructions implicitly was Francis Vaughan. His insubordination was committed so gracefully and the affection between them was so great, that Sarah tolerated it even when they were married. They designed and built a beautiful house on a steep ridge overlooking Tidbury Hill and the wide plain beyond, and there they lived happily, with Mrs Jones, not so very far away from the site of the Ruddocks' old cottage on the Heath.

Teresa Crane

A Fragile Peace

It was a lovely summer's day – perfect for a garden party. Everything seemed at peace for the Jordan family. But by the time the party was over, the Jordans' tranquil, ordered existence had been shattered.

The year was 1936.

Molly

Molly is a fabulous saga set in London's East End at the turn of the century. It is about the struggles of Molly O'Dowd, a young Irish girl, who comes to London penniless and in search of a job, and who ends up running several companies. It is about the men in her life, about the family she raises. It is a marvellous picture of working-class life at that time, teeming with wonderful characters, and alive with the changes imposed by both industry and impending war.

The Rose Stone

When Josef Rosenburg, fleeing the Jewish pogroms of Imperial Russia, reached Amsterdam, he owned nothing but the clothes he stood up in. By the time he reached London, he had the price of prosperity in his pocket – a prosperity that had been bought at an appalling cost.

FONTANA PAPERBACKS

Distant Choices
Brenda Jagger

In a world of mill barons and railway kings, two sisters Oriel and Kate share the same uncaring father. But whereas Kate is legitimate, Oriel is not.

Oriel learns from an ambitions mother to be cool, to calm the fire in her heart. Kate, with emotions untamed and no mother at all, yearns to break free from her loveless life.

Drawn together by fate as well as by birth, the two sisters are friends. And then Squire Francis Ashington, poet and explorer, comes back to live in Gore Valley . . .

Also available
A Song Twice Over
A Winter's Child
Days of Grace

FONTANA PAPERBACKS

The Golden Cup
Belva Plain

At nineteen, Hennie De Rivera's dreams have no place for the suitable marriage her parents plan for her. Instead her thoughts are all of the young radical scientist Daniel Roth and their plans to change the world. But their stormy, passionate marriage will bring them into conflict not only with the establishment world of Hennie's prosperous family but all too often with each other . . .

From the riches and rags of turn of the century New York to the squalor and the slaughter of the First World War trenches, *Golden Cup* is another compelling novel by the

'Queen of family saga writers'
New York Times

FONTANA PAPERBACKS

Fontana Paperbacks Fiction

Fontana is a leading paperback publisher of both non-fiction, popular and academic, and fiction. Below are some recent fiction titles.

- ☐ FIRST LADY Erin Pizzey £3.95
- ☐ A WOMAN INVOLVED John Gordon Davis £3.95
- ☐ COLD NEW DAWN Ian St James £3.95
- ☐ A CLASS APART Susan Lewis £3.95
- ☐ WEEP NO MORE, MY LADY Mary Higgins Clark £2.95
- ☐ COP OUT R.W. Jones £2.95
- ☐ WOLF'S HEAD J.K. Mayo £2.95
- ☐ GARDEN OF SHADOWS Virginia Andrews £3.50
- ☐ WINGS OF THE WIND Ronald Hardy £3.50
- ☐ SWEET SONGBIRD Teresa Crane £3.95
- ☐ EMMERDALE FARM BOOK 23 James Ferguson £2.95
- ☐ ARMADA Charles Gidley £3.95

You can buy Fontana paperbacks at your local bookshop or newsagent. Or you can order them from Fontana Paperbacks, Cash Sales Department, Box 29, Douglas, Isle of Man. Please send a cheque, postal or money order (not currency) worth the purchase price plus 22p per book for postage (maximum postage required is £3.00 for orders within the UK).

NAME (Block letters) _____

ADDRESS _____

_____

_____

While every effort is made to keep prices low, it is sometimes necessary to increase them at short notice. Fontana Paperbacks reserve the right to show new retail prices on covers which may differ from these previously advertised in the text or elsewhere.